BUT THE WICKED SHALL PERISH

CATORI SARMIENTO

RUNNING WILD

This novel is dedicated to my husband, my daughter, and my grandparents.

A special acknowledgement goes to Rivka Begun, who gave me valuable feedback on the story. I want to also thank Rabbi Mendel Adelman at chabad.org for patiently answering my many questions about the intricacies of Jewish practices.

This novel was inspired by the years I lived in Italy and by the many times I visited the Campo di Ghetto Nuovo.

האדון ממית ונותן חיים.
.. .הוא משליך לעולם התחתון; הוא קם שוב
אבל רשעים יאבדו
בחושך.

The lord puts to death and gives life.
He casts down to the nether world; he rises up again. . .
But the wicked shall perish in the darkness.

1 Samuel 2:6,9

CHAPTER ONE

Those first memories were of murky soil, the kind that lay moist on the banks of the lagoon, the kind I could still taste between my teeth. The warm evening sun glimmered through spear-leaved olive trees. The echoes of proverbs and songs sailed on the sea breeze that lifted wisps of hair across my forehead and naked chest. I emerged on the other side with only the curtain to cover me. My bare feet on a stone street were cold and wet from the presence of flood waters around the soles of my feet. My stomach clenched from hunger and thirst. The discomfort was a sign that I was alive once more.

I clutched the veil against my skin. In my other hand I held a candle with a burning flame. Burning but not consuming. When I looked at my fingers, they were stained with blood. And on my tongue was a bitter iron taste. I stood on slick cobble stones, naked, barefoot, clutching the curtain and a candle with a fierce flame that burned nothing. When I touched the flame, it felt like a wisp of warm air against my fingertips.

Remember, remember, I willed.

Nothing but the darkness and the earthen grave appeared,

and the strong hands that held me. As I walked, thoughts came to me, reminding me of what may have been my life. Muddled images passed, voices, a multitude of voices. I heard Hebrew prayers, and mixed among them were whispers in Latin. I saw a woman lying on the floor and a shadow in a veiled mirror. There were candles lit on a silver menorah. There was a mother holding a newborn and singing from *Shir HaShirim*, the "Song of Songs." I listened to the final lines as if they were echoes in the dark:

"My beloved is mine, and I am his, that feedeth among the lilies.
Until the day breathes, and the shadows flee away, turn, my beloved, and be thou like a gazelle or a young hart upon the mountains of spices."

The words caused tears to flow from my eyes. I wiped them. The little I could remember was of love and sadness. The longer I wandered, the more details came to me. Not enough to have full knowledge, but enough to begin to piece together what my life had been.

I remembered a dense and vibrant grass wherein a lion had been rent apart, its flesh and skin torn in pieces, its blood staining the grass crimson, and its innards spilled upon the ground. When I looked upon its face, its eyes were bright and open, its mouth agape as if frozen in a silent scream, in the moments before life escapes and a soul cries out for salvation. I heard a piercing buzzing coming from within the carcass and saw a hive built within the flayed ribs where honeybees swirled around. One buzzed near my face and then came to rest upon the lion's eye. I watched as honey oozed from it, a golden nectar permeating through its orifice.

I saw a goat slaughtered in the street and gathered its blood in a silver bowl to hold it above an undying flame. The heat of the flame boiled the blood, turning it to crimson ash, and this ash I spread across my face to consume the essence of the soul.

I came to a mirror enshrouded in lace, and in the glass was my reflection.

In the small moments of consciousness, I heard a familiar prayer. Spoken prayers ushered unto me a divine knowledge that emerged from the ancient words captured in the Holy Torah. I heard a thousand pages turning as the flapping wings of a flock of doves.

I remembered hands. They were strong, unremarkable, and covered with dirt, hands that wrought their way around my neck. All memories were a haze. One emerged, then disappeared, like a fish in the canal obscured in the murky water until it drew up for air to show its face only to submerge once more, a symptom of my fractured soul. They melded, making me unsure of which were mine, but they held one truth clear throughout the obscurity: I had been murdered.

I stopped walking and stood against a wall. I had died, and I was alive once more. Doubt came at first, that such a thing was impossible. And yet, miracles happened through HaShem, when he sought to dispense them. I had been murdered, but I had been brought back. For what purpose? I could not think.

I was becoming slowly aware of the moving bodies around me, though it seemed they did not touch me. They were blurry spots of color in my vision, bodies without faces, a suggestion of humanity without the details. I had to focus to find the small indications of individuality. There were men in trim suits or in white shirts and slacks and ladies dressed in the *la garçonne* style with elongated frocks that shaped them into straight lines and few recognizable curves. I wandered, unsure of where exactly I was, but at each sloshing step through the flood water, I became more lucid. The pungent smell of the canal waters and the sights of gondolas and shallow boats sweeping over the surface of the dusty beryl waters gifted me with a recollection. I was in Venessia, as the locals called it. To tourists it was Venice. I always knew it as Venezia. *La Serenissima.* The city where I spent my childhood and youth until they were taken from me.

While not completely destitute, it had lost the grandeur that it once had. The cathedral did not shine as brightly in the morning sun, the canals seemed darker than before, the people sparse, the streets and alleys quieter, all excitement gone with the change.

Money was made in trade. The Venezian ports remained a causeway between the East and West. Their government may have changed, but the merchants remained essential.

I knew where I was, but how long had I been dead? If too much time had passed, my murderer would no doubt be gone. I searched for an indication of the day and of the year. The presence of the water around my feet meant that it was late in the year. Though late in the day, I looked to where the *tabacci* shop may have a daily newspaper on its racks. When I arrived at the narrow building, the windows were shuttered, and the door closed. However, in the nearby trash there were crumpled papers, one of which seemed to be a newspaper which was spotted with grease. I reached in and pulled it out. It was a page from *Il Popolo d'Italia, The People of Italy,* a newspaper which espoused the benefits of the military and of Italian Nationalism. The rhetoric did not matter to me. What I needed was the date, and I found it under the title, under the name "Benito Mussolini." It was 1922. One year after my death. One year since my eyes had been closed.

I kept staring at the page, all the while thinking about who I had been and where I could go. Where I lived in youth was in the Cannaregio in the Campo di Ghetto Nuovo, the Jewish *ghetto*. I considered going there, to see my family, to see if they were still there, to hear what they knew of my murder. The thought of seeing my mother, my sister, my father, my entire family, made me want to turn my feet to the alley which would take me to their house. No. I could not go there. I could not bring my poor self to their door. Not yet.

A soft memory reminded me of Christian charity. When I was at school, my friends and teachers had mentioned it often enough, they being Roman Catholic and prone to eschewing the benefits of their religion. There were religious houses which allowed the impoverished. Entering a church, being in a sanctuary was *Avodah Zarah*, strange worship, and it was forbidden for a Jewish person. Even so, I needed help, and I knew that they could give it.

There, I could gather my thoughts and decide my next course of action. Grudgingly, I stepped through the mighty wooden doors of a church. At first, the vacuous expanse was threatening, but I stepped in regardless. There was a silence, an unmediated silence that disturbed me, but in the emptiness, I listened to whispered prayers in foreign tongues—pleading and begging for divine help.

I stepped through the passage and into the stone expanse of the church where the only sound was the soft tap of feet against the marble floor and the gentle pops of the white candles. The stack of white candles, generic wax candles, stood in contrast to those that were partly melted and dripping down the bronze handles. The newly melted wax stained the aged wax that stuck to the handles, a reminder of the thousand other contrived souls who prayed before him. I looked up at the placid white face of Christ who stared into the distance, seemingly at nothing, and then turned to the altar where a statue of

5

the Virgin Mary gazed down compassionately with a smile on her face.

I could not feel that her loving smile was for me, or that the flickering candle flames would carry their desperate prayers to the heavens. Whispers came from the prayers of those who had no other place to turn to. The altar, the gilded framework surrounding every inch of the building, sparkled against the lighted candles, and there was a thick smell of incense in the air.

As I walked forward, bathed in the glow of chandelier candlelight, a man in brown robes came to me.

"Are you well?" he asked, looking at me and my scant clothing.

I opened my mouth to speak and could think of no word to say but uttered, *"Bahir."*

He looked at me, appraising my poor condition.

"Come," he said, "we will help you."

Instead of responding, I nodded my head.

"Do you have family here?"

I nodded. "I—I have family in the Campo di Ghetto Nuovo."

As soon as I said it, I wished I had not. The man's eyebrows knitted together, a slight change of expression to show that I had revealed myself as a Jew.

"Ah," he said knowingly.

After that, we spoke no more. He led me behind a door and through a hallway to another room. This one was full of noise and bodies. The man called out a name, and a woman arrived. She looked at me with a blank, tired expression.

"We have enough Romani that are here."

The woman scrutinized me.

"Will you work?"

I nodded.

"Come in," she said.

The room was crowded. Beds full of mothers, children, men, all with the same desperate face. A brother and sister played, running from one end of the room to the other, the sister speeding ahead, laughing when she beat him to the end, and the boy shouting at her, trying to catch up. Some sleeping bodies—had their faces obstructed by blankets.

I held the candle close to me, hiding it under my veil.

The mother pulled the curtain from my shoulder. I shirked away from her touch. Then, I heard the mother stand up to speak to the others surrounding me. I turned away again. Seeing faces, feeling sensations was too much. I had been dead and was alive again. I had been given a chance for vengeance. I closed my eyes to piece together the moments before passing from the land where I was a wandering soul to becoming flesh. What I wanted most was to know my family; knowing them would lead me to know myself.

Thinking of them led me to memories of my death. I had been murdered. Whatever my life had been before was taken from me, taken from my family, and I descended into a chasm of despair. My death, my murder, the memory of it seeped into every synapse, scorching my thoughts so that one remained. I suspected two who might have caused my death. My brother was one possibility. His strict religious compliance was often at odds with my rebelliousness–or, it could have been my young lover with whom I shared kisses–and more than kisses.

But were any of them capable of such a murder? I railed at myself to remember the face that looked down on me as I died. In the quiet moments of the day, I dwelled on it. I would find whoever killed me, and if he were roaming amongst the innocent, then I would bring justice upon his head.

Exhaustion took me. I closed my eyes and slept against the hard floor.

CHAPTER TWO

I woke, still holding the candle in my dry and dirty hands. My stomach groaned and another, stranger vestige pulled at me from within. The sensory memory of that bitter iron emerged. Thinking of it made me salivate. I sat up.

At the end of my feet was a neatly folded pile of clothes. I felt them at first, unsure that they were real. The coarseness of the rough wool skirt fed my fingers. I took the clothes and walked down the hall to the shared toilet. There was a line. I considered huddling in a corner, but decided against it, not wanting to risk dropping the candle.

At my turn, I entered, closing the door, flipping the hook lock. A sour smell of urine and feces and sickness hovered in the air. I wrinkled my nose at the smell and removed the curtain, folded it, and set it on the sink. I squatted over the hole to relieve myself and then stepped to the cleaner portion of the floor and put on the borrowed clothing. The materials were an assemblage of styles. The brown wool, full-length skirt, with a checkered pattern was worn at the hem. It buttoned high at the waist, but being a size too large, fell under my navel. The blouse was a clean white with hand embroidered roses at the collar and the cuffs, and a length of bone buttons up the front. I was able to tuck the short blouse into my loose skirt waist. When a knock came to the door, calling for me to hurry, I pulled on the borrowed stockings and shoes. The shoes were perhaps a half size too large with worn soles and scuffed tips but comfortable. The final item was a short black coat. Unlike the other items, the coat looked and felt new. Though a simple design, when I put it on, it was warm and slightly long in the sleeves so that I could fold the cuffs.

They were clothes that others could do without, that they would not miss, but for which I was grateful.

I folded the veil into a small square and stuffed it in one pocket while I hid the candle in another. As I placed my hands in the pocket, I felt a sharp object. When I removed it, I saw that it was an old hat pin. The slender silver stick marked with age spots glimmered in the dim light. On the tip was a red coral cameo of a woman whose gaze turned downward as if wistful. Wavy locks of hair cascaded around her cherub-like face. I turned it around in my fingers, and on the silver setting on the back of the cameo was a small inscription that read "Bona Dea." Perhaps that was the name of the previous owner.

I tucked the hair pin back in my pocket and brushed the candle, but the flame did not burn my skin.

I wished I could remember what the mother looked like so I could thank her. It was the first kindness since my rebirth that I would try not to forget.

When I returned to the room, I saw the matron who first greeted my arrival.

"I see you're dressed. Eat your meal and then find me."

The thin soup and bread were not nearly enough.

"There is a woman who cares for bastards and motherless

babies. As is, she needs a helpmeet to care for her overcrowded home. Do you have experience with children?"

"I have six brothers and sisters," I said before I realized that that was no longer true.

"Good. This will be much the same. You will do as she asks and will be paid a monthly sum. If you can't, I suppose you'll end up back from where you came," the matron said. She withdrew a letter from her pocket and shoved it into my hands. "Go to this address and give her this letter."

I was uneasy, restless, expecting a bad turn at any moment. Like a canal cat, I was distrustful of an altruistic hand offering food. I could recognize her kindness, the generosity that was offered to me, but I could not feel it.

I left with my candle, the veil, and a note with an address to a house near the Campo San Polo. I followed the alleys, stopping when I became lost. I passed a begging Romani who huddled near the street holding out a hand, and I wished I had something to give. I had walked these streets before, and yet at times, they became strange and did not take me where I thought I was going. More than once I asked a passer-by for directions. One was a tourist who spoke none of my language, who smiled and shrugged and went on their way, and another was a uniformed man, part of the Arma dei Carabinieri, one of the city's elite police force, who looked briefly at the address and told me the exact road to follow. I walked to the Rialto, the white bridge where merchants peddled, and beggars pilfered. There was always singing from one merchant or another. A tune would begin with one merchant, and it would fade only for another to take up a song. I listened to the bustle as I continued along.

Then a smell stopped me as I passed the shop. A stream of blood flowed from the butcher's door, across the stones, and into the canal. The scent of it disarmed me at once. The muscles in my chest tightened, and an ache that prickled across my skin endeavored to persuade me to consume the substance. I dipped my fingers in the blood. As I did, I saw the ritual: the sacrifice, the gathered blood, the spreading of bloodied ash.

I knelt to the ground, almost pressing my face to the threads of blood that followed the gaps in the cobblestones. The blood ritual appeared before my eyes. It told me to slaughter a creature to take its blood and absorb it into my own. With their blood, I could live for a few days more. I pressed a fingertip to the surface and lifted the red-tipped finger just in front of my nose. This blood would feed my craving, ease my befuddled mind, and yet. . .I turned to the apex of the bloody streams to find that they emerged from beneath a gap under an unmarked door.

Much as I wanted to take the freely flowing offering, I could not risk it without knowing the animal which was being butchered or if it had been slaughtered properly. I stood up slowly, though my head became dizzy as I did. I took a step back and steadied myself against the outer wall of the butcher shop. I closed my eyes and inhaled, trying to calm my aching muscles as I wiped the blood on my skirt. I salivated at the smell of the iron in the blood and could envision myself kneeling over it, spreading it on my face, and relaxing as I became whole. A small voice told me to resist. This was not the time. Not here.

I exhaled slowly and held my breath. With my eyes open, I pushed my hand to force myself away from the scene. I walked the streets and slowed down when I could hold my breath no longer. When I recovered my breathing, I was inundated with the comforting smells that were worthy of the city's nickname *"La Serenissima"*; the aroma of sweet breads, sea air, and briny, putrid canals.

I removed the paper from my pocket and checked the

address, then replaced it. The house would be a far walk. As if in protest, my stomach grumbled. I had not thought where I would find food. I would have to rummage for it in the trash or else steal when eyes were averted.

Where is there the most food? I wondered.

The best place to find an abundance of food was wherever there were tourists, and most tourists passed through San Marco's Basilica where there always seemed to be travelers and tradesmen. I traveled along. The tourists and locals sauntered as one mass with each person pushing through the number of bodies to get to the other side. Intermingled with the noise of the crowds were pockets of silence, silence in the areas where no tourist would think to go or knew to go. Each area was a secret labyrinth.

When I looked at a wall, I realized that it was not as solid as I had thought, but rather a corner doorway that led into a wholly unexplored crevice. Every turn led into a new world within the city. I felt that even if I spent a lifetime searching through the endless passages, I would never perceive everything that the city had to offer. It wrought upon me a kind of cynicism that nothing was permanent, even in a place so small. As I looked at the homes and corresponding crossways, it all began to flow together so that one was indistinguishable from the other. I made my way under an arch where a cleanly dressed man played a dulcimer. An Alsatian dog sat loyally beside him and a glass jar filled with a few *lire* coins. I thought briefly of pilfering the coins but pushed the thought away. I could not help but find my vision drawn to the man while others kept walking, unaware of my existence. The music was serene. He looked up at me briefly, his sharp chestnut eyes wide with sincerity. He gave a slight nod and then turned back down to his instrument.

I walked on, down the corridor steeped in shadows, until a light before me opened to the *centro*.

I looked around quickly and grabbed the half-eaten tarte and dashed away into the crowd to the far end and under the arch. I turned the corner and kept walking. With sparser crowds in this more residential area, I stopped a moment to eat the tarte. I began with the uneaten side and consumed it until I reached the portions with small bites. This piece I tossed on the ground, leaving it to the alley cats and mice. With the few morsels in my belly, I felt a little more human.

Continuing through the alleys, looking up now and again to the stone plaques naming the streets, I found the name which matched what was written on the paper. The alley led to another *centro* where a group of older children chased each other around a water well. I circled the center, passing each plaster-faced house, until I found the one with the matching address. It was a house the color of an egg yolk. A sign above read "Orfanotrofio dei Bambini Pii."

The Orphanage of the Pious Children, I thought. I wondered how true that was, hearing the crying coming from within.

There were cracks in the plaster, some torn to reveal brick underneath. Above the door was a single window with open shutters, the glass partially opened so that I could hear the sounds of babies coming from within.

I knocked on the wooden door. When no answer came, I knocked again. I raised my hand a third time but stopped when I heard the click of an unlatched lock. On the other side was a woman whose black nun's habit shifted, tickling the cheek of the small boy she held in her arms.

"I was sent here by–" I started, but then stopped when I forgot who sent me. Instead, I held out the letter to the woman holding the toddler. The young boy grabbed the letter. She pinched his hand and took the letter back, leaving him whimpering. The woman read it quickly and then put it in her pocket. She looked me over from head to fingertips, tightened her lips together, and then relaxed.

"You will work?" she asked.

I nodded.

"You can take care of children?"

"Yes, I–"

"Good. We all go to Mass on Sundays. Of course, you will be here to take care of the babies, but there will be some days when I will need you to go," the woman said. She peered at me from under half-open eyelids, tilting her head downwards. "Will that be a problem?"

Her tone and expression indicated her thoughts clearly. That if I did not go with them, then it would be a problem. What choice did I have? To be homeless or to accept the situation I found myself in? I would be like the *B'nai Anusim*, those Jews who came before me who were compelled to attend Catholic rituals.

"No," I said.

I tried to curtail the resentment in my voice. If the woman detected it or not, she did not show it.

"You'll have one day off a week. Do you prefer a day?"

"Saturday," I said abruptly. Saturday was Shabbat.

The nun scratched her nose.

"You'll be here from eight o'clock until six o'clock every day, except for Sundays, to help with the children, help me cook, and tidy the house. I pay weekly. You can take a room upstairs with Irina," she stated.

I thought of the candle and of my need for blood and of my need for privacy. I also thought of the night I spent on the street. I had an immense desire to avoid that experience again. Maria-Elena was being generous, and I was grateful for it. It would be a comfort to know that I had a warm bed. I could decide the details of how I would hide my condition from the household.

"*Grazie,*" I said.

"*Bene.* You can thank me by being dutiful. Come in," she said. "I'm Maria-Elena. Ah, what was your name?"

I stepped in. At the question of my name, I was unsure if I should use my true name or a false one.

"Aviva," I said, using my deceased grandmother's name.

"Lovely," she said. "Is that Italian? I haven't heard it before."

"Hebrew," I answered.

Maria-Elena nodded once in understanding.

"Here's the house," she said. She closed the door behind us and placed the child on the floor. He toddled off eagerly. "That little one is Giorgio, and here. . ." she said as she walked through the narrow hall to a drawing room where there were two cribs and three babies in each, "are the babies."

The drawing room was sparse, with little in it but cribs, toys, and a shelf piled with dry cloths, some of them spotted with yellow stains. There was another nun in the room who was busy changing a diaper on one of the babies. She was a stout woman who greeted me briefly with a curt smile so that I noticed her crooked front teeth and a stye on her left eye. When she finished changing the baby, she grabbed a toy and left it in front of the baby who attempted to crawl towards it. The woman passed by, holding the soiled cloth diaper in one hand, disappeared down the hall, and then reappeared.

"You must be the extra set of hands," she said in a deeper voice than I expected.

I nodded.

"I am Maria-Giulia. It will be a blessing to have someone

else to help. Just tending to the twins needs five hands," she said and then laughed.

I looked at the set of twins that were awake and both sitting up, and in the other crib, a sleeping child that looked a little younger than Giorgio. Giorgio walked over to the sleeping child and reached through the bars.

"Ah, Giorgio, leave her," Maria-Giulia said and pulled him gently aside.

He cried when she did, and Maria-Elena came to the room and picked him up, then passed by me to the bottom of a set of stairs in the hall, and soon she called out, "Irina!"

Footsteps tapped on the marble steps.

"Yes?" came an irritated voice.

"Take Giorgio so I can show this one around."

Just then, a head peeked out from behind the wall. A young girl of perhaps thirteen peered at me with wide eyes the shades of a brown pear and a head of short black hair that hung just at her chin. She smiled at me and opened her mouth to speak until Maria-Elena said, "Here," and held out the young boy to her. Irina took him in her hands and went upstairs. With the two indisposed, the woman came back to me as I was perusing the room.

The nun showed me each baby, pointing at each one briskly and saying their names. She said them so quickly that I did not hear them. I was fixated on how many of them there were in that small space. In my childhood, there was always a baby or two in the house, but there were also my older brothers and sisters besides. I felt pity for the children here, to have neither parents nor siblings to help them.

"What sort of house is this?" I asked.

She turned her eyes towards me and raised her eyebrows as if to read the meaning behind my words.

"Do you mean to ask why there are so many children?"

"Yes."

"Bastards, most of them," she said. "Mothers leave them at churches or hospitals. Some go to families who want them; others come to me. There are always too many babies and not enough families who want them." She took a deep breath. "So, you can work until six and then I will see you tomorrow." She pointed to two babies who shared a crib. "Those two are Umberto and Ursula. Soon the twins will need to be tended, and when Beni wakes, he will need milk."

"I will go to Mass," Maria-Giulia called and went to the hallway.

One of the babies cried. Maria-Elena looked at me expectantly, but I was distracted watching Giorgio tug at the rosary on her waist.

"Oh," I uttered and turned to the crib.

The next hours were hurried and mindless. I tended to the babies and made their milk from powder to feed them. At times I played, though more often hovered around them to ensure they did not hurt themselves. When Maria-Elena began to cook, I helped as best I could with my split attention on her and the children. At one point, the girl, Irina, came down the stairs to greet me briefly only to leave out the front door, announcing that she would be outside.

Once evening came, I fed the babies and ate as much as I could sneak from the kitchen. Then, I cleaned, which was not an easy task with the young ones about. When I was thoroughly exhausted and eager to sleep, Maria-Elena said to me, "Have some rest." She then handed me a roll of bread. "You will need it for when one of them wakes in the night. I won't take tardiness. Upstairs, there is a room at the end of the hallway. There is an empty bed that you may use."

After leaving, I devoured the bread and ached for rest. I walked up the steps with tired legs and found the door at the end of the hallway. I passed Irina, who came out of what I assumed was the toilet, and she only glanced at me. When I opened the door, I found two beds within and a crib at the end of one of them. One bed was unmade, with a blanket and a quilt crumpled as if the occupant flung the covers off as soon as waking. There were magazine and newspaper clippings tacked or taped to the wall, most of them pictures of other places: Paris, Cairo, New York. All the places where a young girl would want to go if she had the freedom and the money. There were also drawings, some of them obviously done by children and some others drawn by a more practiced hand. By the bed was a short pile of schoolbooks, a notebook, and a few pencils left loose on the floor.

There was one narrow window that divided the room. Irina's bed was on one side and mine on the other. It was clear which bed was mine by the sparseness that surrounded it. It was a simple bed with one quilt and a pillow. There were pictures on the wall, but not as many, and all done by children, as if they had run out of space elsewhere.

In the night, a baby's cry woke me. I looked to see that the previously empty crib was occupied with one of the children, so I patted the baby, hoping that it would go back to sleep, but all it did was crave my touch and reach out its hands to me. I picked it up to settle it back to sleep. Each time I tried to place it back in the crib, it would wake, feeling the distance between us. I lost count of how many times I had put it down and picked it up before it finally slept. Some of the other babies woke, and I tended to them, half-asleep. I had done the same with my own siblings. I suddenly had the memory of being woken by a colicky baby when I was a girl and listening to my father as he patted its back until it calmed.

I woke with the sunrise feeling weaker than before because I was hungry, but the fatigue that came to me was altogether different. At once I knew what it must be, and when I looked at the candle, I saw that the flame had dimmed. I would need blood soon.

All were asleep. Irina was in her bed, lying on her stomach with the blankets covering her haphazardly. I slid the candle into my pocket and bent my legs to stand. Each muscle in my body pleaded with dull aches that made movement slow. When I stood, my head throbbed. I ignored it and snuck outside. I had to concentrate so that I would not splash into the putrid canal nearby. With my feet on the stones, I walked to an empty alley where I squatted against the wall to relieve myself before continuing on. Discarded bread and cheese were what I could rummage from open bins in the alley. I was not alone in my search for breakfast as I was joined by scrawny cats and another poor, homeless young man who kept scratching the rashes on his skin and face.

"I've not seen you before," he said. When he spoke, I noticed that half of his front tooth was chipped, causing a slight whistle when he spoke.

I shook my head.

"Lost work?"

"No," I said. When I spoke, my breath smelled sour. "I just found work but am waiting for my pay."

"Good. Listen to me," he said, tipping his head so that a few hairs slid over his brow. "Keep it, no matter how bad you think it is. Any bad job is better than this."

He turned back to the trash and pulled out a wadded napkin. When he opened it, he scrunched his nose and tossed it back in. One of the cats happily snatched it with one paw and ate the contents.

"Hm," he said, rifling through the trash. He stopped a moment, said "Ah!" and pulled out a green-hued wine bottle.

He shook it to hear the spirits slosh inside. Then, he opened the bottle and drank.

"This is perfect," he said, cradling the bottle. Then, he walked away, leaving me and the alley cats to ourselves.

When I returned to the house, Maria-Elena was up and asked where I was.

"I just needed some fresh air," I explained.

Maria-Elena chuckled.

"It's all the milk and soiled cloth. I've been around it so long I can't smell it anymore, but I guess it would be a shock to you."

She told me to wash myself in her bathroom. I knew I smelled and was thankful for the opportunity to wash. When I left the bathroom, I found Irina standing on the other side. She was startled when she saw me.

"Ah," she began. "I thought you might like this." She raised her arms, presenting me with a yellow dress decorated with tiny red flowers. "It's mine," she added nervously, "but I don't care for yellow, and your clothes seem. . ." She looked at my state of dress and shrugged.

I chuckled at her honesty. It was true how I must have looked to others in my medley of clashing clothes. The dress was not a color I preferred, nor the style that I may have chosen, but I accepted it. Though, I wondered why she felt compelled to give it to me. Was it generosity, or was she trying to make my appearance acceptable?

"Thank you," I said.

"You can wear it now," she said eagerly. "And put one of Maria's aprons on so it won't spoil. She then left me and went to her room, shuffling around inside as if she were a dog searching for a mouse. I looked closer at the dress. It was a more modern style compared to what I was wearing, though it showed signs of slight use where a thread was unraveling at the end of the long sleeve. I hesitated to change. I had the candle stowed in the deep pocket of my skirt where it was safely hidden. In the yellow dress, the outline of the candle would easily be seen.

Irina returned with a seashell pink cloche hat. From behind her, a small gray piebald cat appeared.

"You won't change?" she asked.

"I wouldn't want the babies to spit up on such a lovely dress," I said as an excuse.

"Just use an apron," she said. "And here," she said, holding out the hat and a small glass bottle of perfume.

I managed a little smile, a quivered upturn of the corners of my mouth.

"Of course," I conceded.

Maria-Elena then called for me, and I welcomed the intrusion. The babies were crying, each for a different reason, and I needed to tend to them.

"Excuse me," I said.

Irina frowned.

"I'll change after," I offered, which seemed to lighten her demeanor.

I took the dress and hat with me downstairs and placed them in the hallway.

"What's that?" Maria-Elena asked when she saw me.

I explained what Irina had done and Maria-Elena grimaced but said nothing in response. Soon, Irina came downstairs in her school clothes and slipped on her shoes in the hallway. She had books in her hand, but she dropped one. The sound of the book falling on the floor startled one of the babies and cry. Irina picked up her book, said a quick farewell, and left out the front door.

For the remainder of the day, I followed the instructions that Maria-Elena gave to me. At times Irina would emerge to help take care of Giorgio or to do chores. It seemed that there was no time to be idle in that house between preparing food, milk, changing clothes, washing and pinning soiled cloth diapers, and all the little tasks that came with tending children. Even sitting for a moment gave no comfort as it was spent feeding milk to the babies or entertaining them in some way.

By the evening, I was exhausted. It became clear that I needed blood. More than once I dozed off while feeding milk to the babies, and I feared that if Maria-Elena saw that, she would rescind her employment. I could put it off no longer. I had to find some animal to consume. There were plenty of cats to choose from whom I doubted anyone would miss. I pushed away the idea because I did not want to kill cats. But what other animal was in abundance in the floating city? I turned my mind towards fish. A fisherman would not miss one that slipped from its net.

At this time of day, how many fishermen were there? I walked to the nearest dock. Finding nothing, I went to the Rialto where I knew there to be fishmongers. Hopefully, one would have a live fish I could pilfer. When I arrived, the merchants were vacating their market stands, so I slunk behind one which sold fish and found that in the waters by the street there were several floating fish. No doubt these were unsold. I bent to look at them. As long as there was still fresh enough blood, I believed I would be sustained. I picked the liveliest one, one that was still gasping for breath, and held it in my hands. Soon, there was another beggar near me who did the same as I, though this poor man grabbed as many fish as he could carry and departed without a word, leaving the rottenest ones behind.

I needed a place to take the blood without so many eyes about me. I walked until I found an alley that stopped at a broken boat landing. The alley was narrow enough for one person, and with the landing broken, I doubted anyone would arrive to see me. I worked quickly. Even if it was forbidden to consume blood, I felt there was only a correct way to do so through the *shechita,* the proper way of slaughtering an animal. I had *neshamah.* I had the breath of HaShem raise me to life. I was not an animal to run another down and clamp my teeth around their neck, to whip and sever their jugular without consideration.

Since I was not a *shochet,* I did not know the specific ways to ensure that the animal was slaughtered correctly. All I could do was my best approximation. There was a knife on the counter next to a chipped porcelain bowl that held two apples with brown spots. I discarded the apples and took the bowl in hand. Then, I placed the fish's head over the basin. Its eyes stared at me, and I could see my small reflection in them. The fish barely attempted to breathe. Its mouth made slow movements in a last attempt to avoid suffocation.

Do it, I urged.

I sliced its throat and let the blood drip into the basin until it slowed. Then, I placed the knife and the dead fish on the counter. With one hand holding the bowl steady, I held it over the candle flame. I waited, prayed, and watched impatiently for the blood to coagulate and become ruddy ash. How did the candle flame cause this reaction? The flame interacted with nothing else, burned nothing else, but when it touched blood, it caused the substance to change. I chuckled. Why should I look for reason in the divine? It simply was. Just as I could be raised from the dead, so too could a flame be impermeable.

With the concoction prepared, I grabbed the bowl quickly, burned my fingers in the process, and placed it on the ground so rapidly that it sounded as if I had broken the base.

Inhaling, I discovered that the scent of the burnt blood calmed me. I swiped sore fingertips across the ash and spread them across my forehead and my cheeks. At my second breath, a serenity cascaded over my body, easing every ache in my muscles and relieving all pain. My mind refreshed, eradicating the confusion that had been there since I was reborn.

Rejuvenated, I removed the candle from my pocket. The flame burned vigorously. Then, I placed it on the floor next to the bed and sat on the thin mattress and looked down at it.

A soul flame, I thought. *Nephesh.*

Consuming the blood, the essence of a living being, renewed my life. The fire showed me the spirit of my soul. I wanted to keep it close, always.

If one could see it and touch it, could they snuff out the flame and eradicate me from this world?

Placing the candle in my pocket, I felt lace. I still had the veil that covered me when I re-emerged into the world, so I took it from where I stowed it in my pocket and held it in my hands. I ran my fingers over the lacework, feeling every hole and ridge as if to scry its secrets. There were brown blots of dried blood on the bottom corner that must have come from the events of my return.

I remembered little from those feverish moments between the mirror and my rebirth. The veil was my connection to *sheol,* to the land of the dead. That must have been where I came from, an afterlife where all the dead remain until their judgment, a place where the dead could return to the living. I closed my eyes to force the memory to return. I saw the carcass of a lion being swarmed by bees, the beckoning call of an ethereal voice, and the words of the sacred texts. In the moments before rebirth, I absorbed the words that I had once been apathetic to. The light of the Torah, the strokes of each Hebrew letter, appeared to me with new understanding. Perhaps I had to die to understand them.

What did those holy words say of murder?

לא תרצח

You shall not murder.

HaShem made exceptions, I considered.

It was only a sin if it was *retzach,* a murder that was not justified. In the *Parshat Shemot,* or Exodus, Moshe Rabbenau had killed an Egyptian. The Egyptian killed another Hebrew, and so Moshe sought justice. I was told I should not kill, and yet, how often is that forgiven by HaShem? The Torah sets some explanations, but it was all dependent on HaShem. Some were acceptable and others not.

Killing the sinful is itself no sin, I thought. Even so, there were doubts that crept into my conclusion.

I wanted to find my murderer. I had work, I was earning money, I had a semblance of a home, and I was sustained. Without the worry of destitution, I could focus on discovering who had killed me. I would begin with my death and let the breadcrumbs show me the way.

CHAPTER THREE

After a week of tending to the babies and consuming the blood of small animals, I used my leisure time on Saturday to visit a sparse island across the lagoon. Brick stone walls enclosed the *Beit Chaim*, the Jewish cemetery at Lido. Within the walls was a garden of stones and ancient trees whose dense leaves covered the expanse in shadows and pockets of sunlight. Roosted there in the brambles was a raven, black as soot with a sharp face. Motionless, only its obsidian eyes dart here and there. It sits, talons gripped atop a branch, aged. Light broke through in yellows and whites, illuminating the black feathers in a glossy sheen.

Gravestones, both weathered and new, erected beneath the shade of trees, ancient and skewed by softened soil and rolling earth. Tombstones etched with Hebrew epitaphs, simple and sublime. Among them were two sarcophagi with triangular cases, and on the flat planes were the Hebrew letterings that embalmed their life in words. All the stones amongst each other, lush grass and moss grew between the weathered cracks, kept in community even in death.

I passed these exalted stones where the lamenting prayers of *"El Maleh Rahamim"* were sung by faceless voices. They could have been mourners, settled under the branches, hidden amongst the stones. They could have been the stones themselves, for it seemed to me that they were singing, if stones could sing. Whether human voices or stones, I ensured that I averted my eyes. I was not there for the living.

Elaborate and plain stones marked those that belonged to the deceased in my family. The dates varied until the year that terrible sickness *L'influenza Spagnola* spread throughout the city, claiming several members of my family, including one of my young siblings, barely six months old, and my grandmother, *Safta* Aviva. I thought about her. She was the only grandparent I had met in my life; the others passed away years before my birth. She was the mother of my father. I remembered her laugh, a bubbly trill that would make me laugh along with her, and how patient she had been with me. I looked for her grave. Most were the same, small and with a curved top, while a few stood out, such as those of my grandparents, and of Aviva, whose name I took to hide that which was given to me by my mother. My throat swelled, and my lips tightened. I turned away from the stones to settle on the swaying tree branches. I closed my eyelids for reprieve and waited until the gentle breeze and chirping birds calmed me. When I refreshed my vision, I saw the shadow of a man standing before an ancient grave, one so worn that it was merely a weathered stone overtaken by moss. The figure stood there silently. As I stared, I could nearly decipher his features that were hidden under the wide brim of a sleek beaver-skinned top hat and the high collar of his jacket.

His head turned, and I shifted my gaze so that he would not catch my prying eyes. When I peeked from my peripherals, he was gone. I breathed again and looked at my family's graves.

There, among them was my name.

צפורה

Tziporah. I whispered it to the air. Rather than the Mourner's *Kaddish,* I uttered my own prayer. I had nothing to offer that gravestone except my words which rested as a stone of vengeance.

My heart was beating rapidly. A memory overtook me then. On a warm spring night, I lay with a young man underneath a hazy sky. Overcome with happiness, I began to sing softly, having no thought or care as to the *Kol Isha,* the singing voice of a woman that was forbidden for men to hear. Still, I sang to the sky and to him and to celebrate my own joy.

A te, o cara, amora talora. . . It is no sin, I thought.

I left to take the *vaporetto* across the lagoon from Lido to San Marco *pieta.* As I stood at the stern, I contemplated how I would find the man who murdered me. It would not be easy. I considered first that the man must be someone I knew. I had thought that my brother might be capable. He was shrewd, conservative, and with his past career in the Italian Army, he would know how to kill. I wondered if a priest would have the gall to attack a young girl just for a little mischief. I was not the only child who would run into the church on a dare to snuff out the prayer candles. I thought then of my sweetheart. I still could not recall his face with clarity, but his voice was clear, as were the memories of his touches. How often did love turn bitter? In a passionate fury, could he have been the one to wrap his hands around my throat?

I needed more information. I tensed my shoulders at the thought of knowing who could give it to me. I was not prepared to see them so soon. There would have to be another way to gather knowledge about my death that let me avoid my family. I wanted to see them; I yearned for them, and still I was not ready to see them. I did not know if they would receive me, a stranger, into their home, and if they did, I was not sure if I was ready for the memories that would come to me when my feet passed through their door. One day would come when I would have to meet them again. For the time being, I would focus on other ways to find my murderer.

I thought about my gravestone, about the body buried there, and how it came to pass.

Once a body is found, what happens next? I wondered.

I considered what I would do if I found a dead body on the street.

They call the polizia.

As soon as the *vaporetto* docked, I walked a straight line through San Marco's Square, unsettling a dozen pigeons who were resting on the ground, to the *polizia* headquarters. Never having to bring myself there before, I had to stop to ask the way from a patient old woman who was watering her potted blue-bells in front of the door of her house.

I followed the woman's directions until I came to a building on the other side of a short bridge squished between a *chiesa* and a cafe. The office was a small affair. Were it not for the official seal on the door, it was easily missed.

It took two hands to pull the door open. The brief outside light tore a seam through the dim interior lit by phosphorus oil lamps. It startled the officer sitting behind a wooden front desk with a marble top. So accustomed to the low light, he squinted at me.

"*Si.* What is it, *signora?*" The officer behind the desk asked at once in a clear Venezian accent. He was an older man, though his full black beard and mustache made his age difficult to determine.

I stepped in, letting the door slam closed behind me in one deep boom. I approached the man sitting at the desk.

"*Signore* de'Angelo," he said, introducing himself.

"*Grazie, signore.* I am a cousin of the Curiel family," I began.

"Ah, 'The Drowned Jewess,'" he started. "A rotten death. Who would do that to a woman? We fish out at least one man every month or so, usually run afoul of debtors, or fell in the canal because he was drunk. But never a woman, least of all a Jew. Strange case. Rumor is that at her funeral, a woman disappeared. Not just any woman, Zampieri's daughter–you know?"

I shook my head.

"He's a rich man, Zampieri. He owns maybe a quarter of the trade ports here. Such a shame. She was just newly married soon to–"

A young officer walked in from the far hallway to a door, opening it, and overhearing, warned, "Careful what you say. Your mouth is why you're stuck at that desk."

"It's no more than what you hear down at the bar," he retorted, dismissively.

The young officer murmured to himself. As he entered the room, I saw that inside, there were cabinets with labels, one of which read "case reports." An idea formed. If I could find the one on my case, the information could lead me closer to my murderer.

"Don't mind him," the older man said. "He's still young and idealistic." He scratched his chin beneath his beard and let out a single "Hah!"

The young man came back suddenly, approached de'Angelo, and said, "I need the key."

De'Angelo chuckled. He reached into his front pocket and removed a small silver key with a tag on the end. He gave this to the young man who took it and walked briskly to the file room. If I could get that key. . .

"What was her name?" I asked.

"Eh?"

"The rich man's daughter."

"Oh, Faustina Zampieri. Did you say you were family. . . friend?"

I considered before answering, "Distant family, yes. I came to visit her grave."

He nodded.

"It was suicide," he said bluntly. "Threw herself in the canal, and the current took her. Drowned bodies are never pretty," he said with a sickened look. "Bloated, filthy, stinking things. Would barely know who she was if she wasn't wearing the *tichel*." He motioned at the top of his head.

"You know what it is called?" I said with a tone of surprise.

He seemed insulted at the prior assumption of his ignorance.

"*Si, signora.* True, it's not within the common jurisdiction," he said, checking the clock on the wall, and then taking an elegantly designed snuff box from his breast pocket to take the bitter contents in two rapid inhales. He then replaced it securely. "You don't spend as long as I have in this place and not know everyone's particularities. If she didn't have that, we'd never guess to check the *ghetto*."

"It wasn't murder?" I ventured, sharply gauging his reaction. He could very well be one of the murderers. It would be easy to murder unpunished if one of them were within the police force. I scrutinized his hands to venture if I recognized them. Despite his pugnacious exterior, his hands were quite feminine in shape. They were lean, his fingers long, nails trimmed straight across in a blunt line. There was a fresh gash on the knucklebone of his index finger, stitched closed and scabbed over. The knucklebones were nearly flat, without a hint of roundness.

"No, no," he said, his demeanor dismissive to my inquiry,

hand waving the thought away as if it were a mosquito in his ear. "Nothing on her that showed foul play."

"A clever murderer could make it seem like a suicide," I said.

He furrowed his brows at my comment and then shifted his gaze to the right before settling back on me and scoffing with a wry half-smirk. The young man returned with a file in hand and gave the key back to the officer. De'Angelo took it, and I watched with rapt attention as he placed it back in his pocket.

"The criminals here aren't that clever," he said factually.

Though I wanted to prod, his tone suggested the finality of his opinion, so I kept further questions to myself.

He glanced at the clock again. This time I followed his sights as the hands neared six. He said, "I must be going. It was a pleasure speaking with you."

Before I could utter a word to stop him, he had stood and walked to the back hallway, leaving me to myself. I sat there for a moment, still in the chair before an empty desk. I needed to know what he knew, so I looked to the office door that held case documents and knew what I had to do. I called out to the young man who sat at a desk behind the counter and asked if there was a bathroom. He pointed me in the direction of the hallway. There was a single bathroom, and as I suspected, there was a window as well. I unlatched it and pressed it open just enough so that a fingernail under the frame could pull it loose.

I left the headquarters and followed de'Angelo down the street to a bar. He held the key that could open the door to the information I needed. Though I did not like the idea of stealing, it seemed like a small infraction. I needed to know more about the murder, and I had no other way of discovering it, so I waited for what I felt was long enough. When I opened the door, I saw that he was already three glasses into the evening. He seemed drunk enough, so I approached his table.

"You look familiar," he said slovenly.

"Do I?"

"The Jewess," he said.

"What?"

"The Drowned Jewess," he said more clearly. "You were her sister?"

I stared at him, unsure now if he was truly drunk.

"Cousin," I answered.

"Ah." He sucked in air through his teeth, placing his glass on the table. "Such an interesting case. And what brings you to this bar, on this day, when *I* happen to be here?"

He knows, I thought. *Somehow, he knows.*

"You're not the first. Come, sit, drink," he said. I obeyed. "Bereaved come in all the time wanting answers. They come to us, they go to God, or they go to wine. I prefer the latter, myself," he added with a smirk. "Why does one person kill another? Do you know how many murders I've seen?"

Unsure if it was a trick or not, I decided to answer truthfully.

"No."

"I've been *polizia* for fifteen years," he said, "and in Venezia there is a murder every week. These days more than ever." He reached in his pocket and pulled out a hashish cigarette. He lit it and began to smoke. The plume was thick, heavy, and slowly dissipated. "Fifty-eight murders I've seen," he said. "And of those, seven have had the murderer tried and imprisoned. Seven!"

He held out the cigarette to me, offering.

"Perhaps a new one," he said, giving me one from his pocket. I thought of refusing but considered that earning his trust might be beneficial.

I took it, let him light it, and held it to my lips. As the man took a long draw on the cigarette, I glanced at the bartender who passed, and de'Angelo stopped him with a touch on his forearm. The bartender was a man whose age was hidden under a trim black beard, which had a gap at the chin where there was a pink scar and a groomed mustache with a few stubborn hairs sticking out. At the touch on his arm, his eyebrows shot up, causing his forehead to wrinkle. A group of two men and one woman were farther down, calling to the bartender. He saw them, but did not yet respond.

"A bit of *grappa* this time," he said, then turned to me. "And one for the *signora*."

Not wanting to drink the foul alcohol, I put up a hand to refuse.

"No," I said.

De'Angelo leaned back, resting his arm on the bar. The cigarette burned, leaving ash to fall on the counter.

"Who comes into a bar and refuses alcohol?"

I feigned a smile. "A lady who doesn't sip a sailor's drink."

He laughed.

I looked at the bartender, who also was smiling, and then back at de'Angelo.

"Are you paying?" I asked.

"But, of course, I am a gentleman."

There was one drink I always wanted to try.

"Absinthe," I said.

The bartender went to tend to the rowdy group and returned with a small bottle filled with green liquid, a clear glass, a strainer spoon, and a rock of sugar.

"You've had this before?" the bartender asked.

I shook my head and then ceased when a memory appeared of a drink in my hand with the green substance inside as I giggled along with a friend or two. I drew on the cigarette, inhaling deeper than I intended. Upon my exhale, my muscles relaxed, and my head filled with a euphoric numbness. I stamped out the end of the cigarette into the coaster.

"I once saw a man drink a whole bottle like this," he said and tapped the top of the bottle with his middle finger. "He poisoned himself, went to walk home, and fell off the Rialto."

"Such as drunks are wont to do. What is Venezia but a city on the water?" I said.

He placed the strainer across the rim and put the sugar in the center. The bartender poured the liquid and stopped just as immediately as he had started, leaving it a few centimeters full. As I watched, I felt the effects of the hashish fade, and my senses returned.

De'Angelo puffed on the cigarette. "Drunks fall all the time. Good riddance to them."

"Ah." The bartender raised a finger in thought. "Those are customers of mine. One dead drunk means less for me." He let his hand fall to the counter. "What harm are they? What harm are *you*? Aren't you a drunk, too?"

The man laughed. I shared a chuckle. Perhaps he would find himself at the bottom of the canal after a drink too many.

"*Salute!*" De'Angelo lifted his glass and drank the remaining grappa.

The bartender struck a match and placed it over the surface of the sugar. No sooner than the ignited match touched the air around the rock that a small blue flame appeared on the top, dancing to and from. I winced and watched as the sugar melted through the strainer and onto the surface of the absinthe. The subtle aroma of the burning sugar reminded me of a dim room and veiled mirrors.

The bartender placed an ice cube on top, extinguishing the flame. When he did, the door opened, and there were sounds of laughter and ruffling skirts. The bartender removed the items that were needed for the preparation and met the newcomers at the bar. One man, at first, tried to drink and dribbled the alcohol over his collar, staining it with drops of burgundy.

As I watched them, I envied their abandon.

De'Angelo followed my line of sight.

"I'm glad I'm not working tonight," he said. "There's sure to be some mischief."

I turned away and took the glass in my hand. Lifting it to my lips, I sipped it. There was a wonderful affinity of sweet and bitter.

I should be careful, I thought. *Remember why I am here.*

We sat together, both silent, though the bar became raucous, and soon there was singing at one table. De'Angelo tipped his head to appraise me. I met his eyes. I feared that if I looked away, he would consider me suspicious.

"I don't doubt there will be some dead tonight," he said. "A knife in the belly or a fight that went too far." He shook his head. "Men are full of untampered passion."

I was drawn to his clear chagrin.

"I'm sorry it has to be that way," I said.

"Ah," he said, drinking again, and then pointing a lazy finger at me. "How did your Jewess lady die?"

I wondered if he was drunk or mocking me.

"They said she drowned," I answered.

"Drowned, yes. That's what they all say when a body is found in the canal. Have you seen a drowned body?"

I shook my head.

"Terrible thing," he said, filling his glass and drinking again. "By the time one of us finds it, the body is all swollen, no color; you can hardly tell it was even a person. By then, there's barely a sign of murder. What can we do?"

"It seems it would be easy for a murderer to get away with it."

De'Angelo raised his eyebrows and nodded.

"We *polizia* can only stretch our hands so far, you see." He held his hand out vertically, his arm bent at the elbow, keeping his wrist at the level of his chin, and fanned out his fingers. "And so, the Mafia comes to fill in the gaps." He brought his other hand to thread the fingers on both hands together. "But even then, you see..." He wiggled his fingers. "There are gaps." He released his hands, lifted them in a dismissive gesture. "So, what are we to do if there is a murder and no one to bring to justice?"

I eyed him carefully and waited for his answer. Would he tell me that it was impossible or that one should be a vigilante, or perhaps that it should be left to HaShem? In the end, he said nothing; each time he blinked it seemed like he might fall asleep.

I stared at the green substance, tapping the back of my tongue against the inside of my mouth where the bitterness seemed to remain, trying to loosen it. I swallowed, relieving the sensation for a moment. I inhaled, straightened my back, and adjusted my dress and the vial I stored in its pocket, then looked at the man who, by now, appeared drowsy. His eyelids drooped, and his cigarette faded as he pressed the lit end against the counter.

De'Angelo spotted my still full glass.

"No good?" he asked.

"It must be an acquired taste," I said.

"Oh, then let *me* acquire it," he said.

I brought my hand to the glass and passed it to him. He drank in one dose, and when the glass left his lips, he gagged, nearly dropping the glass. I reached out to take it and place it on the counter, along with steadying this man who was about to fall from his chair. I took the chance to slip my hand to the top hem of his trouser pocket and feel for the key. It was there. I could not grasp it as he sat, without being conspicuous. After helping him, I backed away.

"*Grazie,*" he said and slouched on the chair.

I should have let him fall, I thought, tapping my finger against the counter.

"I always wondered what it must be like to be a Jew," he said suddenly as his words began to slur.

"I would hope it's not much different than it is to be a gentile," I said.

He tilted his head slightly, as if to nod.

"Though," I added. "I hear it's more painful for the men."

At first there was silence, and then the man chuckled.

"No doubt. I cannot imagine such commitment to faith."

"Nor I."

I was distracted by an argument at one of the tables. One man pushed another, resulting in the instigator getting punched in the face. There was a pause, and then both men laughed together and drank some more.

De'Angelo's cigarette had faded. He lifted it to his mouth, tried to inhale, then seeing the dampened end, shrugged his shoulders and attempted to slip it into his breast pocket, missed, and then with careful observation, dropped it. He looked back at me, narrowing his eyes.

"I forgot what I was going to say to you," he said.

The man rubbed his left eye and cheek. "I think I am too drunk tonight."

De'Angelo searched his pockets and finally removed some *lire* and left it on the counter, not bothering to count it, and stood. When he walked, he was sluggish. I took a cursory glance at the bartender and then at the others. All were occupied with the trappings of their own interests, so I let the man walk out and then rose to leave.

A shout from the bartender stopped me, so I turned. He held the *lire* in hand.

"It's short," he said.

I should ignore him, but also did not want the undue risk that came with withdrawing attention the bartender following me if I didn't pay. Impatiently, I returned to the bar and settled the tab.

"*Signore* de'Angelo always finds someone to settle his bill," he said.

I exhaled, Although I was upset at being used to support the man's alcoholism, I did what I needed to do so that I could leave as quickly as possible in pursuit of the man him, I left in pursuit.

Outside the pub, I searched the area. There were so many places he could have gone. Then I heard the unmistakable sound of a man retching and followed it.

"It must have been the absinthe," the man murmured.

He sat against the wall with his shoes in the puddle of sickness that he had made just moments before. His eyes lapsed from drooping to opening, as if he were trying to remain conscious.

I knelt before him and slipped my hand in his pocket, unafraid of his reaction. The man's protest came in the form of an indistinguishable murmuring from his sour breath.

I found the key and took it from his pocket, unfortunately feeling his flaccid manhood against my fingers.

"Oi," called a voice.

I snapped my head to the voice coming from a Carabinieri.

"What are you doing?"

I stowed the key in my pocket and steadied my nerves.

"Helping this man. We were drinking together just there. I am afraid he had too much."

De'Angelo looked at me suspiciously, then down at his colleague and cursed when he recognized his face.

"Sir," the man shouted at the unconscious de'Angelo. When no answer came, he shook him.

"Ask the bartender if you don't believe me," I said.

The man looked to the bar and then to de'Angelo.

"*Signore* de'Angelo," he murmured. "When will you learn?"

The man turned to me.

"You go along. I'll take care of this old one."

I departed from them as quickly as I could and went home to wait until late evening when the sun barely hovered over the horizon. I changed my clothing to the ensemble I received at the church.

Dressing as a beggar was the best way to become invisible. Except for the most compassionate, everyone ignored such a pitiable figure. Night was the obvious time for burglars, thieves, and murderers. Dark things crept when the pious were sleeping. The only men on the streets were the desperate and the drunk, and who would trust them?

I stowed the stolen key in my pocket and kept my hand there to ensure it remained. I had the key to the inner office but not to the front door, so I would need to sneak in. Once I arrived at the headquarters, I found the door shut and locked. I jiggled the handle. It did not move. I looked around the front to find any windows, but there were none. I tapped my finger against the key in my pocket and turned to the nearest alley to search for a back entrance to the building where there was a bathroom window I had unlatched earlier. I passed a shadowy figure who glanced at me briefly before continuing on its way.

I have to do it tonight, I thought. *I need to know.*

I surveyed the building again and saw it. It was not easy to detect in the dim light, but there was a narrow glass window on the first floor that was open just enough so that the edges popped out. I could climb through it.

I looked around to ensure that no one was watching and gripped the edge of the window. I pulled it open and slunk inside.

With my feet on the floor, I waited, listened, to ensure that I was alone. Hearing nothing but my own heartbeat in my ear, I tiptoed farther inside, following the dark hallways to where I needed to go. Once at the door, I removed the key and unlocked it. Then, I smiled at my own success.

Within the room were filing cabinets, all marked with numbers and letters. I started with my former surname, Curiel, and opened the file cabinet gently, rifling through each folder until I found it. I inhaled as I withdrew it, dissociating myself from what I was about to witness.

When I held the file in my hands, I saw there were photographs of the body, notes, and reports. Staring at the photograph of my death, I viewed it mechanically, taking note of the set of the arms, the open eyes, the body bloated with canal water.

The result, written plainly, was "drowned by suicide." There was nothing else. I looked again, wishing all the while that I could take the files with me, but stealing *polizia* files would arouse suspicion. Instead, I had brought a sheet of the discarded newspaper *Il Popolo d'Italia* that I found in a waste bin along with a pencil to write on it. I copied everything I could as quickly as I could and would have to analyze it later. It felt like hours I was there transcribing the statements and reports, what few there were. Before replacing the files, I snatched the photograph of my dead body.

Pointless, I thought as I re-filed the document.

I stood there in the darkened room, defeated. A voice reminded me of a young woman, newly married, who died before a veiled mirror. I tried to remember the name that the old *polizia* officer told me.

I looked up the dates in the index and searched the files for the name Zampieri.

The pictures were mesmerizing. She was a beauty, like del Cossa's portrait of Saint Lucia holding a palm branch in one hand and a pair of eyes in another. Her glance was humble and serene. The woman in the drawing appeared to be sleeping, without a mark of death upon her. It was ailing to witness such a contrast to my own memento mori. My dead body was bloated from the rancid canal, my hair wet and tousled; my eyes were opened, pale.

It is only a body, I thought. *A body long dead. I should not feel anything. I did not need to feel anything.*

And yet, I could not linger on it any longer.

When I was finished, I replaced everything as it was. As I did, there was another file that caught my eye. It would have been easy to ignore it, but for the small handwritten note next to the file name that read, *"scomparsa zingaro."* Disappeared gypsy.

I skimmed the report. Reading it gave me a stronger revulsion, an ascent to anger that neared what I felt towards my own faceless murderer. I was incensed with a blinding hatred towards a man who could beat a child to death without reproach. Even worse was the monetary compensation, as if money could replace a child. I wrote down the man's name and address. I did not know what I would do if I found him, but I knew I must do something.

CHAPTER FOUR

I snuck out of the *polizia* building and returned to my room. I was careful to be quiet, but shortly after I arrived, one of the babies awoke. I settled it back to sleep and then prepared for what I would do. I took with me the hat, which I secured with the Bona Dea pin, and another glass object. I had emptied the perfume bottle Irina gave me and hoped it would serve my needs.

It was not difficult to find the man. I went to his address, and a woman answered, surprised to see me on the other side. She had on her night dress and whispered when she spoke. From within the house, I could hear a child snoring, as she explained her need to remain quiet. When she asked why I needed to know where he was, I fumbled at first, not having thought of a reason and then created the explanation that I worked at an orphanage and was seeking donations.

"I haven't any money," she replied. She shook her head. "My husband has the last of the *lire*. You want charity, you'll have to get it off him."

"And where might he be?" I asked.

"Just down the street at the *osteria*. If you can get the *lire*, bring some back to me. God knows we need charity as much as you do."

Before I could thank her, she shut the door.

I followed the street to the sole pub. When I went in, I saw the man sitting alone. He held a glass in hand that was half-empty. I introduced myself and asked if I could sit with him. He had the kind of smile that was both kind and menacing, as if he were feigning politeness. I recalled the notes I had scribbled about this man. He had beaten a child to death. The child slipped a hand in the man's pocket to steal whatever money or possessions hid there. The man admitted to it, and as punishment from the authorities had received the inconvenient penalty of a small fine and was allowed to continue with his life.

I smiled back at him. Men liked that. They always wanted to feel desired. Give them a smile, and they will follow you anywhere, for better or worse. No small wonder why women would hide their smiles.

"Are you lonely?" he asked.

Taking my smile as an invitation, the man touched my waist with an unskilled hand that revealed a golden ring glimmering on his finger. Seeing the matrimonial band in the dim light caused a wave of heat under my skin. I had no patience for an adulterer and even less for a murderer.

"Are you?" I asked.

He laughed. Cup by cup, he drank, while I smiled, sometimes letting him smell my hair as he tried to steal a kiss. Grappa was potent. Too much and the blood stalled. Alcohol worked easily on men. It worked to inhibit de'Angelo's better judgment, and it worked on this man. I decided that he was drunk enough for his inhibitions to subdue. Was he repentant? I wanted to know.

"You seem familiar," I said.

"Everyone knows me!" he answered.

"Oh, yes, I think I read about you in one of the newspapers," I prompted.

He slapped his hand on the counter.

"That mess," he said with slurred speech. "It ruined me. Fifty *lire*! That's how much I–" He stopped to quell a burp. "I had plans for that money." He shook his head. "I should've gotten an award for getting rid of one of them."

Why were men so drawn to seeking out their own destruction? All I had to do was wait until he began to vomit, and I took him by the hand, leading him to the alley. This action was met by some knowing glances from other men, some envious, others leering, more still laughing at the drunkard's luck. When he removed his trousers, a rosary fell from his pocket. It made me hate him more, this faceless man.

Everyone who sheds the blood of the impious is as acceptable as he who offers a sacrifice, I thought.

He collapsed, spewing vile liquids, splattering the hem of my dress and the tips of my shoes. I was startled then by laughs coming from an indistinguishable person down the alley. The man saw them and shouted.

"Leave them," I said.

They were right to laugh at him. He was a ridiculous and pitiable sight.

"More of them," he mumbled.

Before I could reach out to stop him, he rushed after the laughter. He was unrepentant in his murder of an innocent, and he was going to do it again. I knew that I should not want his death. My faith had taught me not to seek out murder, that I should die rather than commit that cardinal sin. One life was not preferable to another. And yet, this man was a *rodef*, a pursuer, a murderer of the innocent.

I looked around, checking that I remained alone, sure that I noticed a shadow in the corner of my eye hovering near the alley wall but finding none. I wobbled as I watched his life drain, feeling my soul ache for his blood. I pulled the pin from where it secured my cloche hat, kneeled, and in one sharp action, thrust the metal pin into the pulsing vein on the softest part of his neck.

He cursed as he jerked a hand to the wound. He tried to rise and, unable, swung a fist at me. I stepped back to avoid it. He coughed, then tried to swallow. One strike was not enough. I then brought the pin up again, and with my arm bent at the elbow, I stood over him and thrust the sharp end into his neck again. The man gave a hollow gasp. I withdrew the pin with great effort, causing the man to fall forward, lying on the stones, gasping for air. He tried to speak, but his voice emerged as croaks and ill-formed words. I looked around me, ensuring that none saw the dying man, and then focused back on him, and found that I was invigorated by his death.

There was power in it that was incomprehensible. It shattered any reason, clouding coherent thoughts from forming. I could only experience mindlessness, an escape from my own body, and as I disassociated, I saw a shadowy figure for the briefest moment before it disappeared. It was as if I were watching my corporeal body standing over the man, waiting for him to die. Finding that I still held the hat pin, I wiped the length of it on the man's pant leg before sheathing it into its spot above my right temple.

His blood flowed onto the cobblestones. The metallic smell dampened that of the urine-soiled stones. I removed the empty glass perfume bottle from my pocket, placing it at the wound to gather his blood. Any blood I gathered lasted three days. After the third day, whatever soul was left in it faded, and I would have to gather more. Human blood was the most potent, the most invigorating. Animal blood was the easier option, though weak. It kept the candle alight with the dimmest flame while the blood from human souls sent the flame ablaze.

When I agreed to the curse, the voice gave me a few instructions. One of which was a ritual prayer to bind the soul blood. I uttered it upon the death of the animal, then punctured a vein to draw out the blood. This I collected in an opaque jar small enough to fit in my pocket. A drop of blood was then poured over the candle flame, with the remaining residue spread over my temple. At my next breath, I felt the tingling sensation of life.

I left the body where it lay for the moment while I felt my rational mind returning gradually as a cloud dissipated in the dawn. In a moment of lucidity, I dragged the man across the stones to the nearest bridge overlooking the Rio dei Greci. I struggled to haul the heavy body. So, when I heard footsteps, I nearly dropped him.

"Everything alright, there?" came a woman's voice.

I looked up and saw a woman holding hands with a bearded man. They were both dressed in solemn shades, so that it seemed they were two faces floating in the night air. The woman adjusted her hat, and when she did, a lock of auburn hair fell out of place just above her eye, and she tucked it back in.

"Oh," I said, catching my breath. "Oh, just my brother taking too much to drink."

The woman shrugged her shoulders and rolled her eyes to the sky.

"Of course," she said. "What man doesn't on a Saturday night?"

"Is your home far?" the man asked. "I'll help you carry him."

"No," I said louder than I expected and so sought composure to steady my voice. "That is, I would rather not trouble you."

"It's no trouble," the man said, letting go of his lady's hand.

Why were men so kind when it was ill-timed?

The man released his lady's hand and bent to pick up the dead man by his feet. He struggled for a moment as he carried the weight.

"How far did you say it was?" he asked.

I searched for an answer. *Where is the closest place nearby to be rid of them? A place of few people.*

"Not far. We have a bed at San Georgio dei Greci, just over the bridge here," I lied.

"Charity?" the woman asked as she walked alongside.

"Of a kind," I answered. "My unfortunate brother spent rent on drinks and other . . . unsavory endeavors."

"*Maria*," she said.

"Then it's fortunate you're in a house of God. Perhaps that will change his ill countenance."

"Perhaps."

At the bridge, we took the stairs carefully, but the bearded man slipped once. He recovered with a grunt, and they walked once more together, the man breathing loudly first from his nose and then from his mouth, showing his slight overbite, sometimes passing others, one of whom was a tall man who took one glance at the two carrying a body and released an audible laugh.

"Had a good night, that one!" he said as he walked away.

"I would say he's in for a rougher morning," the woman said, laughing to herself.

They followed the white stone path to a white arch with an iron gate. Here, I stopped. The man released the feet and let out an exhale. He slid his hat off with one hand and dabbed his moist forehead with his sleeve. I was eager to be rid of them before they found out that the man who I carried was dead.

"Thank you," I said. "I can continue on my own."

The woman looked at me quizzically.

"Are you sure?" she asked.

"Yes," I insisted, more forcefully than I intended. I adjusted my tone to appear friendly. "I would hate to take advantage of your time."

The man looked at his companion to gauge her opinion.

"It *is* getting late," he said.

The woman seemed as if she were about to challenge him, but then replied, "Well, I trust you can take care of him from here."

Relief calmed my nerves.

"Yes, thank you," I said.

"You'll make sure that he doesn't drink?"

I chuckled at this.

"If every woman could control what a man drank," I said, "I daresay the world would be free of drunkards in a night."

The woman laughed along with me as the bearded man replaced his hat.

"I suppose you're right," he conceded.

The man gave a cursory nod and took the lady's hand again.

I watched them leave and waited until they had turned the corner and disappeared. Unceremoniously, I lifted the body over the stone walls and pushed it into the canal. It fell with a splash, and I waited, watching, as the body sank into the black waters, pushing away spume and bits of discarded food: an orange peel, a sliver of crust, a fish tail.

Fatigue set in. I turned, walked away from the stone walls, and rested against the iron gate so I could listen to the currents below. When I felt a reprieve, I grasped one of the iron bars and pulled myself up. The gate clinked against a lock. When I turned to the sound I saw, looking through the bars at me, a giant stone head affixed above a door arch. The bearded stone face with blank eyes stared at me wearily. His face was marred in darkness, illuminated by the moon and the dim oil lamps lit across the canal.

Urgency overcame my curiosity, and I slipped through the bars and into the empty courtyard. I searched the area, pulled on the doors, all of which were locked. Then I found the door at the bottom of the *campanile* was stuck but not locked. A few strong pulls and the door opened. I walked the steps to the top and sat under the old bell, holding fast to the bottle in my pocket, which was still warm. I wondered when they would find his body or if it would drift out from the canal to the sea. My stomach lurched to think of his bloated face and sickly skin. Or was it guilt that turned my bowels?

I killed a man, I thought. *I killed someone.* And then a small thought whispered, *He deserved it.*

In the safety of the darkness, I took off my shoes, my hat, and my dress, leaving them in a heap on the floor. I removed the full bottle from my dress pocket and took the candle from its hiding place. The sacred candle burned low, yet never consuming. I placed it on the fireplace mantle.

I had never used human blood before, only the meager animals that I caught and slaughtered. The Torah forbade consuming blood. I remembered the words: "And you shall not eat any blood from any of your dwelling places, whether from birds or from animals. Any person who eats any blood shall be cut off from their people."

I was already cut from my people, I recalled grimly. To keep my state of being alive, I must perform the sacrilege of consuming souls, whether animal or man. I uttered the ritual prayer upon the death of the animal, then punctured a vein to draw out the blood. I let the blood drip into an opaque jar small enough to fit in my pocket. A drop of blood was then poured over the candle flame, with the remaining residue spread over my temple.

If there was wrong in it, I thought, *why was I brought back?*

It was not only my life that had been extirpated. Justice would come for the others that died.

It is done.

I held the bottle over the flame until it boiled, then cooled and dried into flecks what I removed. I poured the mixture on my hands and spread it against my cheeks, inhaling the metallic smell as I let my skin absorb the blood. I sat on the floor, breathing deeply, and with each breath, I felt myself strengthen and my heartbeat with renewed vigor. In my recuperation, my eyes closed, and behind them swirled images and memories that were not mine, but of the dead man. In consuming a part of his soul, I found that his memories trickled into my mind, the pieces of them showing how justified his death had been. I killed this man. This nameless man. I watched as his blood seeped from his wound. It would be such a waste, I thought. That blood was no use for him anymore. I took it, and I walked swiftly back to my home.

The blood was warm when I tipped the lip against my finger and spread it across my lips. I had never consumed a human's blood before . . . And yet, when the smell of the bitter iron reached my nose, I felt calm. With the tip of my tongue, I tasted the sinner's blood. The effect was immediate. It was as if I had been jolted awake. It felt so close to the first time when I rose through the mirror and took the girl's soul for my own.

My mind sharpened with acute speed, and I was filled with a force of energy that had been lost to me in all these months. With that burst of energy came memories, detached, strange, but I recognized them. I was as a shorn cloth being mended once more.

I spread the rest of the blood over my face, absorbing its sustenance.

Why did I not try this before? I thought briefly.

With the new blood, a strength of will empowered my resolve.

I am myself, I thought.

Basking in the sensation, I did not hear the footsteps approaching.

As the top of the *campanile* filled with the scent of the flame burning high, I flicked my eyelids open and turned my head to the sound; the door remained closed. Yet, the air had changed. It was warmer, of sweet wax and polished wood.

A shadow of a man appeared from the darkness. I was startled, thinking that it was one of the Carabinieri that had seen the man's death and followed me. If it were, fighting back would do nothing. I did not maim without reason, and killing a man of the law would only draw more of them to me.

I had no weapon but the pin. I grasped it, held it at my side, but did not yet threaten its use.

Then my nerves were assuaged by the voice of the stranger.

"The first time is always the sweetest," he said.

From the shadows, he became corporeal, and I recognized him vaguely. It seemed as if I had seen that same face before amongst stones and ancient trees.

"It's been some time since I've seen that candle flame," he said, walking towards it.

His approach to it made me grip the pin tighter.

"Do not touch it," I warned.

"Why?" he asked with a smile. "Afraid I'll blow it out?"

He leaned in with his lips pursed as if to kiss it. Fearing the extinguishing of the flame, I rushed forward, holding the knife tip to his neck but finding no solid resistance there.

"*Prego*," he said, lifting a finger to pull the collar farther down, exposing more of his flesh.

I expected a pulse, a heartbeat, and yet there was none. Slowly, I rescinded.

"What are you?" I asked.

He smiled, and he moved his hands to his top hat. I saw jagged scars upon his wrists as he removed the hat to reveal a pair of ram's horns at either temple. Staring at the oddity, I was unsure if it was my imagination at work, manifesting a cursed being to entertain my despair.

As I searched his eyes for truth, for a tender moment, some beautiful danger passed between us, reflected in black irises that captured bubbles of light. Those onyx pools spoke to me of ancient sins and sacred rituals borne from the pages of the Vayikra in the Torah and in the apocryphal texts of the book of Hanok. I thought of the texts, of the memories I had of their knowledge. In the Torah, two goats were chosen where one would bear the sins of Humankind and be sacrificed to the desert. In the apocryphal stories that I recalled, he was a demon who corrupted humanity and encouraged them to fall from grace.

I knew his name at once.

"Azazel," I said.

He tipped his head, as if in a nod, then said, "And you? A *dybbuk*, an *ibbur*, or some other sinister *shedim*?"

The demons of mysticism. Both creatures possessed bodies; one was malicious and the other benevolent. Mama told me of those creatures that were not spoken of within the walls of the synagogue. Legends that crept in the night, hid under the bed, waited until their victim slept to grasp them in a time of weakness. I considered the book of Solomon. There was a story of a demon who consumed blood. I envisioned the words and spoke them aloud:

"'And behold, when the Temple of the city of Jerusalem was being built, and the artificers were working thereat, Ornias the demon came among them toward sunset, and he took away half of the pay of the chief-deviser's little boy, as well as half his food. He also continued to suck the thumb of his right hand every day. And the child grew thin, although he was very much loved by the king.'"

When I finished, I stared at him, watching his movements carefully. A demon should know. Was Azazel the same as Solomon's demon? Was I? How much did Azazel know of the ancient texts and the truth of life and death?

"Ah, another demon," he said as he rotated his wrist. "There is truth to the most fragmented story. Ornias consumed blood to live; you consume blood to live. An *ibbur* or a *dybbuk* is a possessed soul; you are a possessed soul. Or perhaps you are one of the *shedim*."

"They look for the weakness in your soul," Mother would say. "And tempt you. We are strong against evil only when our heart is protected by HaShem. We cannot fight it alone."

The creature before me was a demon in name; the man who killed me was a demon in act. I did not trust often, but the way his soft eyes peered into mine calmed me. I was sure that among anyone, I could confide in a demon.

"He called me a whore when he killed me," I admitted.

Azazel laughed.

"Man's ignorance never ceases to amaze me."

The demon walked around my room, inspecting my meager living.

"Not the most comfortable, but I suppose it's better than the street," he said.

I scowled at him as he made himself comfortable, resting

against the inside column and stretching his arms to rest behind his head. I wondered how he could sit upon the stones when he could not touch the candle, and then I noticed that he was floating, pantomiming his relaxation. Finding myself staring, I turned away.

"Is there a reason you're here?" I asked sharply.

"You," he said.

I met his eyes. Black orbs without irises.

"What would a demon want with me?" I asked.

"Now, that is the question, isn't it?" He stood and went to the candle once more, passing his fingers over the flame, though his touch left it unaffected. "I never thought another would accept," he muttered.

"Speak plainly," I said, standing, wiping the coal dust on my legs, though some remained on my fingers, blackening the fingertips.

"And so I will," he said. "I've seen that candle before and knew one who kept it. With it, he could kill the shameful and sinful and live a thousand years. No man could kill him, and he could not die. You went beyond death. You took the deal. You could do the same."

I imagined a *chalaf*, the ceremonial blade held against the throat even as the ram struggled, eyes wide and terrified, knowing what must come next as the blade severed the throat, esophagus, trachea, arteries, and veins in one strong stroke. The head is then let as blood spills upon the cobblestones in exsanguination.

What was so sacred about blood? We used the blood of the lamb to mark our doors, the blood that saved us from death. It was blood that saved me from death now. The Catholics drank the blood of Christ to cleanse their souls. What was it that made blood sacred? I remembered that the soul had five names: *Nefesh, Ruach, Neshamah, Chaya, Yechida*. Only

Humankind was given *neshamah*. The breath of God that brought us to life. As I sat, blood on my face, absorbing what was left of the man's *nefesh*, I wondered if all humans contained these souls or if some were missing. Certainly, every human had a *neshamah*. But could they lack everything else? If animals had all but *neshamah*, could it be the same for Humankind?

"Beyond death," I murmured.

"I do not know the intricacies of the pact," Azazel said. "I know the rules that govern it but not the reasons. One could guess at why or how, but why bother?"

I chuckled then, thinking of all the rabbis and biblical scholars who spent hours and lifetimes doing exactly that.

"Tell that to the rabbis," I said. "All they do is sit and study, sit and study, praying for HaShem to give them insight."

"A waste of life," he said. "If He wanted you to understand Him, wouldn't He have made His desires plain? Why shroud it in mystery and doctrine? Why speak in riddles and parables?"

I did not have an answer. When such questions arose, there would be a rumbling of mutterings and voices, each faithful one explaining their interpretation, their belief, their answer as to "Why?"

Why did I live? Why did I die? Why was I reborn?

"Too much time is wasted wondering, 'why?' What are the truths in life? You are here, now. The purpose, the meaning of it, has been given to you. Why bother wondering about 'how?'"

"Are you here to tempt me?" I asked. "Here to present me with an offer?"

"Perhaps the offer of immortality," he said.

I exhaled sharply through my nose. "I had not thought about life after finding my murderer."

Azazel laughed.

I balked. "My murder is humorous to you?"

He clicked his teeth, shaking his finger. "Not your murder: your murderer."

"It's not—" I started, and then paused, a spark popping into my head. Azazel was a demon. If he could see every sin, then he could also see who it was who killed me.

"Do you . . . know who it is?"

His answer was a nonchalant shrug.

"The sins of men are my burden," he said.

"You know," I said, excitement filling my reprieve. "Tell me."

He stepped towards me. "And who are you to dictate to me?"

I peered at the candle flame. "There is something you want," I said. "Otherwise, you could have snuffed me out already."

He broke into a wry smile that made him appear quite charming.

"Not many take the deal," he said. "And none of them have been like you."

I scoffed at the flattery.

"Oh, if I were a genteel virgin, I might believe you," I said.

He laughed. His smile was disarming.

"You should. I'm too old to waste time on lies."

I turned away from him, hoping he would disappear while another part of me wished him to stay.

"As I am, I cannot touch those beloved of HaShem, no matter how sinful." His voice softened as he neared the candle. "But *you* can."

He stood there a moment, his eyes darkening at the sight of the flame. "I have seen the disgusting things they do while justice remains unserved. There are those who are better when dead. So, there it is. We need each other."

What he said made me think about the earlier events of the

night. I had succeeded in resolving an injustice. How many more could I redeem with the help of a demon? Was I alive to impart this divine will? I wondered how often killing was justified in my faith. HaShem had often commanded others to enact His will. I thought of how Joshua and the army of Israelites had conquered the Canaanites and slaughtered every wicked man, woman, and child. If their acts were sanctified by Him, surely mine were as well. I could do as Azazel asked, for through the demon was the will of HaShem. Could His will for me be *Tikkun Olam*, the mending of the world? All Jews had the obligation to repair the broken world in some way. Who was I to defy such an obligation? Yet, I had one scruple.

"If I do," I considered, "it would only be those who are *rodef*."

He laughed.

"As you like," he said.

"And then you will tell me who killed me?"

I faced him. When I did, I found that he was still by the candle, nearly touching the flame. I opened my mouth to tell him to stop, but then withdrew. Though at first it seemed he was touching the fire, I noticed that his fingers did not disturb the flame.

"I will," he promised.

His eyes brightened. To see him joyful at my acquiescence, and at his relief knowing that I was the only one who could fulfill his desires, imbued me with a satisfying sense of power.

Not only can I exact justice, I thought, *I hold a demon in my pocket.*

I went to him, touching his warm skin, his arms, and then my fingernails along his neck, running them higher to one of the horns on his head, and resting my hand there, a few fingers gently touching the base. His response was a light moan and a hand upon my waist.

"So, I will help you so long as you do the same for me."

"Ah," he said, and pulled me closer, warming my cool skin. "That is of no consequence, once I see the man. For now, let us rid this city of the worst of men."

Azazel pressed a finger to my forehead.

"And you will see their sins with my eyes."

I hesitated, considered for a moment, and nodded once.

"Shall we look to hell together?" he asked.

The space above my brows became warm, and my skin prickled. I wrapped my fingers around the pin and placed it in my hat. With Azazel by my side, I went into the square. Since it was so early in the morning, dark before the sunrise, there were only cats and mice. While I knew that it ought to be dark, my vision was all splendors. When I looked up at the moon, it shone as brightly as a silver sun, and the stars in the sky glimmered as drops of mercury. There was lightness all around me, so when I noticed the skulking cat nearby, all of its colors were as bright as they would be in daylight. She meowed at me, and I saw flashes of her memories. They were of chasing mice, lapping cream, and pouncing on another alley cat.

I strolled through the alleys to where I knew there would be people. There was an *osteria* near the pier which tended to remain open for the tourists. At first, I peeked through the window, and at once was lambasted with images and sensations that were cluttered and impossible to discern. Whatever faces were inside the building were blurred, and all I saw were detestable sins and benign transgressions. I saw abuse, drunken shouting, along with vomiting from overdrinking.

I stepped back.

"What is this?" I asked as I put a hand on my forehead. Azazel had said that he could view human transgressions, and yet, I had not expected the visions to be so raw, so invasive.

"The Demon Eyes let you see every sin," Azazel said.

I quickly became dizzy and leaned against the wall.

"So it seems," I said.

I took deep breaths to calm my heartbeat and clear my mind. It was overwhelming, but the eyes were too prodigious to refuse. I would have to become accustomed to them. I could not run from the sins, so I inhaled deeply and tried to focus as I entered the *osteria*.

I found it difficult to walk correctly and stumbled a bit. I assumed no one would notice if a person were stumbling in a tavern. With all the intrusive thoughts, I was quickly gaining a sharp headache. Azazel spoke, and I heard his voice but could not understand it.

Attempting to focus on one person, I closed my eyes and tried to force the other memories out, turning to one of a woman throwing up and then laughing. I saw the world through her eyes as she rode a train to Venezia with her parents. On the train, she watched as a man stood up to leave when the train pulled into a station. Some money fell from his pocket, and when no one was looking, she pretended to get up to stretch her legs and snatched the money. With that money, she snuck away from the hotel where her parents slept and walked to the *osteria* to buy the wine she was forbidden to drink.

I pulled my attention away from the woman and to another in the room, a man who I thought I might have known. It seemed to me that I recognized him. Somewhere deep in my mind, I had an itching thought that we had a connection. I fixed my sights on him to delve into his memories, but as I did, my headache was so powerful that it seemed that my brain was throbbing against the inside of my skull, blurring my vision and making me see black spots. I became fatigued. I needed blood, so I left the *osteria* and walked sluggishly to my house. I stopped at some points when I was too dizzy to stand up and threw up on the street. When I tried to steady myself, my hands were shaking. I gripped the wall to stumble home. At home, I had some blood still, enough to keep going. I could not waste away on the street.

How had I been drained so quickly? I had absorbed blood the night before. The singular change had been the use of the Demon Eyes. It must drain my soul more than I knew. Everything in my line of sight was bright, an unending brightness that strained my eyes.

I made it back to the *campanile* to spread bloody ash on my face. I kept it on my skin and collapsed on the floor, but I did not sleep as I was in a state of resting wakefulness. Though there was no fire burning, I felt an internal warmth that came when my soul was satiated.

From the confines of the room, I heard Azazel. He made no footsteps on the ground, but I knew he was there by the change in temperature.

"I didn't think it would have that much of an effect," Azazel said.

I groaned.

He ran his fingers through my hair. The sensation rolled throughout my body, causing me to shiver.

"I don't remember it doing that before," he mused. "But then, that one did not have qualms about taking lives."

I opened my eyes to see a blurry image of Azazel. I closed them again.

"Your morals will make this dangerous," he said.

I turned to my side. I did not care to listen to his argument. I had killed already. If I followed him unyieldingly, he would have me kill with abandon.

I cannot touch those beloved of HaShem, I remembered. He could not touch the flame nor anything else made by Humankind or consecrated by HaShem. I wondered if I could touch him. Was I still beloved of Him, to be left uncorrupted by a demon, or was I already damned either by my rebirth or by the absorption of human blood?

Curious, I stepped closer. I held out my hand, reaching my fingertips outward. He turned then, making me hesitate. His black irises reflected none of the light in the room. I stepped closer until my fingertips touched the soft skin at the tip of his collarbone. Azazel inhaled sharply. His eyelids relaxed, and he released a soft moan.

"I wondered. . ." he started.

He touched my hand. He knew exactly what he was doing. That confident, brazen charm exuded through a smile. I hated that there was an inexorable attraction to him. In my rational mind, I knew it was lust. But there was a stronger desire, beyond rationality. I did not care that it might be a sin. I was a sinner already.

I placed my hand on his chest, just above where his heart should be, and felt nothing.

We tumbled together into temptation. A wanton desire pulsed throughout, urging me onward. Lust was euphoric. Surrendering my lust was freedom. There was only pleasure in the dark room lit by a small fire and a bright candle flame. It felt as if a brush dipped in warm cream stroked me from my inner thigh to my chest. My skin prickled. There was music in the movement: Rhythmic breathing, fluttering eyelids, skin pulsing together. His deep exhales and the pleasurable sensations of his satisfaction matched mine.

I became as I was in those moments between life: Thoughtless, present, freedom from the confines of my body. It was the closest I came to understanding HaShem.

As I lay, pleasurable exhaustion overtaking me, there were other memories swirling about. A window overlooked the sea and the lavender sunset. A gondolier was singing, barely heard from behind heavy glass. Nervous excitement showed in my flushed cheeks and quivering lip as he kissed me. His hand brushing my hair away from my neck, pushing the sleeves off of my gown.

I had been worldly enough. I had kissed and been kissed. I let my hair flow freely. I danced in the *centro* when the violinists practiced. I heard whispers of my ill-behavior, but nothing more from anyone besides my orthodox brother who despised all but the most sacrosanct.

Beyond redemption, I was free to indulge in darkness. Who better to share it with than a demon? When I kissed his warm lips, all thoughts emulsified.

"How sweet you taste," I said.

An odd churning of revulsion, excitement, shame, and arousal. Then the cold came to me. My heart rushed. Azazel had distracted me. I dressed quickly, gathering a small flask to place in my pocket, disturbing his luxurious rest.

"And where are you skulking off to?" he asked with a voice so gentle that I stopped.

"Off to sleep in a real bed," I answered.

"Ah." He smirked as he tapped a finger against his chest. "Then I will see you soon."

I did not have the patience to reply. I sped quickly through the night alleys to return to the orphanage and to my bed.

CHAPTER FIVE

I returned to the orphanage without being noticed. Maria-Elena and Irina were still asleep, as were the babies. If Irina had noticed I was gone, she must not have mentioned it. Though I saw that she had been tending to the babies while I was gone: there was an empty bottle. I would have to make it up to her. I was still wearing the clothes from the night before. I decided to change. As I grasped my skirt, I heard a small *clink* and followed the sound to the stolen key that lay on the floor. I checked that I had not woken Irina. I hid it under my mattress, nestling it under the stolen files, and then fell asleep.

That morning brought no *polizia* to the door. I felt better after having what little sleep I could grasp, but my head was still fuzzy from the night before. Through my blurry vision I noticed Azazel sitting in a corner tapping his forefinger on one of his horns. I rubbed my eyes. The Demon Eyes were an asset, but I would have to use them sparingly because of how rapidly it drained my vigor. I also wondered what effect it would have on me to view the unencumbered sins of others. How long would I be able to witness their worst impulses? I suddenly felt pity for Azazel. I had a choice of whether or not to see their sins; he did not. The eyes had given me more insight than I had thought possible. I wondered what else they could bestow.

"Azazel?" I whispered, careful not to wake the sleeping Irina.

He grazed a fingertip down the back of my ear.

"What else can I do with the eyes?"

"Seeing everyone's sins isn't enough?"

"It is enough," I said. "I am not sure how you can bear it."

He laughed. "How touching for you to care." He took a deep breath. "After so long, there are some things that I've become used to. Petty crimes and moral failings are easy enough to ignore. You'll find that most humans make bad decisions in one way or another. It's the larger, more egregious acts that I find frustrating. I can bear it by exiling myself from them."

I reached behind me to take his hand and pulled his arm over my waist. In response, Azazel rested his cheek on my shoulder.

"There is another gift that the eyes can give," he said.

I looked over at him, at his scalp and the horns that protruded from his temples.

"What would that be?"

He lifted his head, turned to me, and smiled impishly.

"Perhaps later," he said.

I felt Azazel dissipate. Annoyed as I was at his departure, I had to let myself rest.

It was before dawn when the baby in the room woke. I settled it back to sleep and took a walk to the streets below before anyone else in the house awoke. Azazel was by my side as I reviewed the newspapers at the *tabacci*. There was no mention of a dead man. No one cared when poor children were dead. That was true of the child that man killed and of myself.

Before arriving at Maria-Elena's, I often strolled through San Marco's Square to pilfer any scraps left on cafe tables so that the pittance I earned from work stretched farther.

Soon, the hot smell of leavened bread filled the atmosphere. It roused my appetite that was barely staved by the stolen breakfast. My mind thought of the *lire* in my pocket, and I tried to rationalize spending it at a cafe. I had to be careful with my money, even as my aching belly tried to convince me to fill it.

The streets were vacant except for the boats drifting across the horizon. I walked to the edge of the step and sat down, letting my feet dangle over the septic water as I nibbled on the ends of a brioche. The gondolas hit the wooden poles, creating a booming sound like a bass drum.

Mist covered the air. It slicked the marble, imbuing it with a marine glow as if the whole of Venezia were underwater. Save for the rare solitary shop cleaner, I was alone in the square with the morning and the pigeons. As the dim light turned into a bright morning, the gondoliers removed the covers from their gondolas from their overnight slumber. The boats increased their number, and the square became busy with the sound of carts and the energized steps of early tourists. Azazel came near me, placing a hand on my back just below my neck. I met his touch and tilted my head to rest on his forearm. It was a pleasant moment, to be with each other in peaceful silence.

As the sun rose higher, I knew I had to leave. I returned to the orphanage. Before entering, I already heard the familiar irritable cry coming from one of the newborns, complaints from Giorgio, and the general noises babies make throughout the day. I felt strange about passing through that door. I killed a man not long ago. He was a sinner deserving of death, and I was the one who had taken his life and soul. To step into a home, a home that was occupied by nuns, and care for the most innocent when I had committed a trespass gave me pause. Still, I did not have the luxury of giving credence to my scruples.

When I knocked, Maria-Giulia answered with Umberto in her arms. The baby whimpered, and she beckoned me inside.

"*Buongiorno*," she said with raised eyebrows and pulled me in with a hand on my shoulder. "And where have you been?"

"I—"

"The twins are in a state today—teething. Irina is refusing to help. Sister Maria-Elena has been waiting for you."

Since it was not a school day, Irina was home, and I noticed that she was usually expected to care for the children. I could not blame her for becoming weary of tending to so many babies. Maria-Giulia nudged me towards the kitchen, and she returned to the drawing room.

I entered the kitchen, a cozy room that can squeeze in three adults if needed. At the moment, it was occupied by a hungry baby toddling in, impatient for the bread baking in the wood stove and Maria-Elena stirring a pot. I picked up the crying baby and bounced him gently in my arms. His cries softened but did not completely cease as he nuzzled my own breast looking for sustenance. I lifted the baby to my shoulder, patting her back until she burped, and placed her in the now vacated crib.

"*Maria*, they're joyful today," Maria-Elena said with a hint of irritability, soon masked by a laugh. "It would have been nice to have some hands to help this morning."

"I am sorry," I offered.

"Don't let it happen again," she warned.

"Or what?" Azazel mused.

I was less confident. I needed Maria-Elena.

"I will not."

"Good."

Maria-Elena took care of Giorgio, stopping periodically to

sing to him or to hold Beni over the floor so he could practice pushing up with his legs. Maria-Giulia was in the washroom cleaning every soiled rag and diaper. After a time, I was able to sit so I could feed the twins. I gathered up the baby gently, shushing it, and singing softly.

"Such hungry babies," Maria-Elena said as she watched me feed each one.

I looked at them.

"It's a pity," I said. "That they have no mother."

"I am as wonderful as any mother. Better to be here than to live in sin," Maria-Elena said.

Irina came down from upstairs and headed to the door.

"Where are you going?" Maria-Elena asked.

"Out," Irina said curtly.

Maria-Elena scoffed.

"Not now, you aren't. There are babies needing milk, and it's far too late to go out."

I heard Irina slip on her shoes. At the sound, Maria-Elena stood and placed Beni back in his crib, causing him to cry and for Giorgio to run after her.

I heard arguments from the hallway. Beni tried to pull himself up in the crib, and when he fell, he was crying, his face was red, his nose was dripping, and he had tears streaming down his cheeks. I went to him, wiped the mess from his face with my sleeve, and picked him up. He nuzzled his face into my shoulder, searching for my breast, as he was still hungry and wanted milk. I shifted him farther up my chest and stroked the back of his head to calm him.

Between Beni's crying and the other babies fussing, I could barely hear what Maria-Elena and Irina were yelling about. I did, however, notice the strong slam of the front door. A few moments later, Maria-Elena returned.

"Oh," she said while rubbing the back of her neck. "It's been quite the day."

"Is Irina . . .?"

Maria-Elena waved her hand. "She is a young girl wanting to be a woman." Maria-Elena sat on the chair with her legs spread and stretched her neck until I heard an audible crack. Giorgio rushed up to her and climbed up to her knees.

I went to the kitchen to boil water for the milk powder and tried to calm the baby as he became impatient for sustenance. I prepared the bottle, and when it was ready, I held it as the boy sucked it down, his eyes drooping. He would stop periodically, falling into a daze, and I would tickle his underarm to wake him so he would suck some more.

"I suppose she just wants to have fun, like the other girls," I said, thinking of how often I enjoyed spending time with other girls and boys my age.

"Such fun makes . . ." She pointed at the baby in my arms.

That was certainly true. How often did a boy and girl play together in innocence only to have it evolve into a lustful curiosity? I felt my cheeks become warm and turned from the matron in the hopes that she did not see.

"She is too naive," Maria-Elena said. "She wants friends, wants to be liked, that she'll do anything for someone else."

I thought about that and looked at my yellow dress, feeling a twinge of guilt that I had judged Irina for giving it to me.

"Sometimes she doesn't know that I do things for her own good. Still," she sighed, "there is not much time left for her to be a girl."

Maria-Elena stepped in briefly to announce that she was going out and would be back by evening. I did not like being alone with all the children for too long, but before I could say anything she was gone. Irina returned with a paper box filled with fancy paper, string, and gathered sticks. Once she saw me, she smiled.

"You're wearing the dress," she said.

I asked her what was in the box, and she explained that it was a mobile, meant to be hung from the ceiling.

"We'll fold the paper into little birds," she said, "and hang it up for the babies. I saw one in the shop and thought we could make it together."

Irina's face was bright with anticipation. Though I wanted to refuse, I could not deny the girl's enthusiasm. In between putting the baby down to sleep and preparing lunch, I would briefly help to fold one or two birds, after careful instruction from Irina. A curious hand made its way to the tabletop, fingers reaching for a piece of paper. Just at the lip of the table I could see the unmistakable curly brown hair belonging to Giorgio. He put too much weight on his hands and tipped the table. Irina caught it, but not before several sheets of paper and loose string fell, along with Giorgio. He let out a sharp cry, which took my attention from the boiling pot for a moment so I could tend to the boy before could cry, waking the sleeping baby. Irina scolded him while bending over to pick up the fallen pieces. Some of the pieces of paper were crumpled, so she flattened them out on the table.

I picked up Giorgio. To settle him down, I began to hum the melody to *"Durme, Durme."* It was the Sephardic lullaby my mother sang to me. It was the song I used to use to help my baby brother calm down until his cries became whimpers and then ceased. I wiped his eyes, and he sprung up to his unsure legs to walk off in search of more mischief. He found it in chasing the cat from one end of the room to the other, trying to grab its tail.

Irina sat at the table, folding the paper into birds and then using a threaded needle to pierce the centerfold. She asked me for help, but with the pot boiling and lunch needing to be made, I had to refuse.

"But I wanted to do this with you," she whined.

"I'm sorry," I said. "Someone has to cook. Besides, I stop doing my job and Maria-Elena kicks me to the street."

"She wouldn't do that."

"She would. We work for our keep. Without work, we get nothing."

"What about the church? They give charity."

I stifled a laugh at that. Too fresh, the memory came of being refused shelter from every church except for one.

"The church will do as they will," I said.

I cut the vegetables. The knife blade was dull. It took some force to cut through the zucchini. I followed by wiping the blade with the dishcloth and continued to slice tomatoes. Once the sharp end of the knife pierced the thin skin, the pungent fragrance of sweet spring grass emerged to awaken my senses. The juice moistened my fingers when I picked up each slice and dropped it in the steaming water.

"You do not want to become a beggar on these streets," I said.

I moved the knife and wiped the counter. Taking the flour and eggs, I made a simple dough. I rolled it thin and sliced it into narrow strips and also dropped them in the pot. Giorgio came to my legs, tugging on my skirt and whining.

"It is coming," I said to placate him.

I looked down at the little boy.

"Are you hungry?" I asked.

Giorgio did not answer. Instead, he pulled at my skirt and arched his back and tossed his head in protest. I cut a piece of zucchini and gave it to him. Too caught up in his own emotion, he did not see it, and I had to tap his head a few times and hold it in front of his eyes before he paid attention. When he saw it, his cries stopped, and he took it enthusiastically, gnawing on the skin. Holding Giorgio in my left arm, balancing him on my hip, I wiped the counter clean of flour.

"Take care of Giorgio, will you?" I asked Irina, who grudgingly obliged.

With one hand, I moved the pot and replaced it with another, filling it with the water from the still. The still was almost empty, and I would have to go out and fill it soon.

I took the container of instant milk and a clean bottle. I turned to see Irina still sitting, focused on her craft, and I groaned. As the water boiled, I turned to the prepared lunch. Using the strainer, I poured out the contents. A great plume of steam rose from the sink when I did. The baby began to cry, and soon Giorgio had returned to pull at my skirt again. I took a bowl and a spoon and scooped a serving for him. This I placed on the table, scooting away the folded paper birds. Irina huffed when I did, but I had no time to pay attention to her. I then prepared the milk for the baby. A moment of quiet ensued. Everyone was focused on eating, and Irina on finishing her project.

I could only tend to one at a time. The others would have to cry until I could help them. I did not like that. If it were my own baby left crying, I do not think I could let it weep for long. The thought led me to how they came to the orphanage and how Maria-Elena had called them bastards.

How could a mother give away a child?

There were two windows facing the stone street which were often kept closed. The window facing the canal let in the light and with it the rank air. Though pungent, it was better to let in a breeze through the house that often had the odd mixture of smells that accompanied babies: sourness, defecation, and milk. The baby in my arms was peaceful for a pristine moment. As I held the bottle for him as he drank, I had never noticed his deep hazelnut eyes before, and in the reflection on his iris, I saw a face. I looked up to see Azazel in the center of the room, squatting near the twins' crib, staring at Ursula.

"Funny little things," he said.

I glanced at him. I could not speak freely within the house. Though I was sure none but I could see Azazel, if Irina or Maria-Giulia saw me speaking to the empty air, they would consider me of unsound mind. I smiled a little at that thought. Of course, I was of unsound mind. How could I not be?

"Curious that God should make these humans so innocent when they are born," he mused. I shook my head at his brazen use of His name. He then stood and walked over to me, leaning over to look at Beni.

"Innocence depends on belief," I murmured.

"Not for me," he said, tapping at his cheek under his right eye. It was easy for him to take a confident stance on morality when his Demon Eyes could show every sin.

He stood, straightening his back.

"The pious call these children bastards, but there is no truth to that. I see no sin in these or any newborn children."

"When does sin begin?" I whispered.

Azazel shrugged.

"Did you need me?" Irina asked.

She came into the room, holding the finished mobile, almost walking into Azazel.

"I heard talking."

"Just soothing Beni," I said.

The mobile in her hand was jiggling, some of the birds with several folds where she had made a mistake and corrected it. I had been upset that she had been too focused on making paper birds and not on helping me, but seeing the finished product and having her offer to help softened my emotions. I had been her age once. I had acted similarly when my own mother needed my help.

"That turned out nicely," I said.

Irina beamed. She held it up so that the birds balanced out. Azazel stepped away from Irina's closeness.

"I'll put it over Beni's crib," she said. "He likes birds."

Irina left the room and returned with a tack. As she did, the front door opened, and Maria-Elena stepped inside.

"I hope all is well," Maria-Elena said.

Irina ignored her. She balanced on the empty crib to attach the mobile to the ceiling. The cat was lurking around me, pawing at the milk bottle. I asked Irina to tend to her cat. She made a clicking noise with her tongue against her teeth to call the cat to her. The cat perked her head, turned her body upwards, and stretched towards Irina. I was overcome with the need to know the cat's name, so I asked.

"Baci," Irina answered.

His name meant *"kisses"* in Italian.

A knock came to the door, and Maria-Elena answered it. Whatever the conversation was between the two, I could not hear, for the babies were stirring. Soon after the door closed, Maria-Elena came into the room.

"You will come with me," she said. "Irina, you will have to help Maria-Giulia tend to the babies."

Irina groaned.

"None of that," Maria-Elena said to her. She turned to me. "Put him down. We have to go now."

I was reluctant to move, knowing that once I did, Beni would be disturbed and would cry. Still, I followed her directions, and once I moved, he began to whimper, which turned into a scream when I placed him in his crib. I met Irina's eyes briefly, and they looked at me, pleadingly. I shrugged. There was not much I could do but go with Maria-Elena. She dipped by the washroom to tell Maria-Giulia that we would be going, then ran up to her room, rustled about, and returned with a basket in her hand covered with a handkerchief. I followed her out the door, and as we walked farther from the orphanage, I began to worry about where she would be taking me. Had she found out that I killed a man? I feared she was taking me to the *polizia*. I thought of running but decided against it. The man's death had not been reported. No one had seen what I did, save for Azazel.

"Where are we going?" I asked, finally.

Maria-Elena's shoulders tensed.

"To a brothel," she said. "A . . . woman there needs help."

I did not hide my surprise.

"What would we need to do there? Surely any help she needs she could find . . ."

Where could a brothel woman find help? Likely nowhere.

I changed the subject. "Will Irina and Maria-Giulia be alright with all the babies?"

"She will be fine. I have left them with the babies before. Irina is not perfect, but neither is she negligent. I will make it up to her."

At the mention of the other nun, I mused aloud, "Why bring me when Maria-Giulia or even Irina could be more helpful?"

Maria-Elena chuckled.

"Irina might be approaching womanhood, but she is not prepared to see what we will see in this house, and Sister Maria-Giulia's unfailing dignity would not let her set a foot near a place like that."

"And how do you know I do not share the same opinion?" I teased.

"I could think of no one else to help me. I took a chance on faith."

The destination was much like the others in the narrow alley. I recognized it. Why did I recognize it? I had a memory of walking by the alley and my father's voice. The alley was the same as the one my father had shown me years before in order to know which alleys to avoid and which to traverse. The place which he and other more pious young men avoided. I remembered it for another reason. I felt myself against the wall, welcoming curious hands on my warm breast.

"Here," Maria-Elena said, her voice breaking me out of my reverie.

She stopped in front of a two-story house with a white plaster facade and a few windows that were firmly shuttered. We went to an alley, and Maria-Elena knocked at the narrow door. The one mark of uniqueness separating this house from the others was an ornamental door knocker sculpted in the form of a crab whose two pincers held the heavy ring above the plate. Maria-Elena struck it twice, and after a short wait, the door opened, revealing an older woman clad in a well-worn dress, while the front was covered by a stained white apron. Relief spread over her aged face as she welcomed us immediately, and once we stepped in, shut the door behind us.

"Come," the woman said.

We entered a hallway, and the woman began walking.

"Things were going well," the old woman started, her voice slightly quavering. "We thought the baby would come easily, but then it seemed to stop."

Maria-Elena queried the woman on various important details while I was entranced with the trappings of the place.

"When was the onset of labor?" Maria-Elena asked. "How long are the contractions?"

The questions and answers bounced back and forth between them as I followed the women through the dim hall. Though the doors were closed as we passed, I could hear the muffled groans and moans of pleasure seeping through the walls of the next-door rooms and where our shoe soles tapped against the tile floor like ripples on a lake, signaling our presence.

The older woman stopped at the door, which could not muffle the deep groans indicative of unmistakable labor bellowing from within. The moaning was louder now, tumbling down the hall.

"We will get you whatever you need," the old woman said. "Do what you can."

The woman walked away.

Maria-Elena took a deep inhale and looked at me.

"Prepare yourself," she said as she opened the door.

CHAPTER SIX

I closed my eyes to the smell. The thick pungency of a laboring body filled the stale air, reminding me of the immediate smell that came from a butchered goat, like the final cut against the throat as blood spilled, mingling with the musk of the animal's hair and skin.

The woman was naked, and there was blood on the floor, on her thighs. I saw the limbs first: arms held tightly by the two other women, hands grasping, a naked body squatting on the floor. Long hair fell over her face and stuck to her back from sweat. She grunted and breathed, and when the contractions passed, she sighed and relaxed.

"How long has she been this way?" Maria-Elena asked.

"Since this morning."

Maria-Elena put her head near the floor, under the woman's legs, and looked in. She pushed her fingers gently inside. Maria-Elena stood back up.

"The baby's head is there. Is she pushing properly?"

"How can she not be?"

"Get her on the bed," she said. "Get the sheet from the bag and put it down."

I did as I was told. As I removed the thick canvas sheet from the bag, I noticed several tools at the bottom, one of which included a sharp blade that nearly sliced my finger. With mild protestations, the women moved the laboring mother to the bed. I helped steady her by holding the back of her head. She lay down, her hair falling so that I could see her face. Her eyes were squeezed shut, wet where there had been tears of exhaustion seeping out the sides. Her lips were chapped, tinged blue, and her skin hot to the touch. The back of her neck was slick with sweat. At her throat was a necklace. A thin golden chain hung long, drawn down by the golden pendant that stuck against her chest. I tried to look, but the chain had twisted, pushing the icon towards her skin. One of the women left without a word, and the other stayed. She was tall. Even when hunched over, she was taller than I was. Her head of sleek black hair was kept from her face by a green headscarf, with a few wisps peeking out from underneath.

"What is your name?" Maria-Elena asked the black-haired woman.

"Crina," she answered with a slight accent.

"Get a bucket of water, blankets, and rags if you have them," Maria-Elena said.

Both women complied. Their shoes tapped against the marble tile floor as they walked past closed doors and plaster walls to a small room where a scrawny woman sat at a round table filled with lengths of sheep intestines. In her hand she held a small portion and fiddled about with a needle and thread. The woman perked up when she saw us enter.

"How is she?"

"Same," Crina said as she went to a cupboard and grabbed sheets. The woman stopped her sewing to make the sign of the cross and then returned to her task as Crina handed a disheveled pile of sheets to me.

"You take those back, and I'll fetch the water."

Crina left, causing me to find my own way back to the room. I turned back through the door and walked speedily past the closed doors where I could hear the unmistakable sounds of bodies in the midst of pleasure.

Whatever Maria-Elena did made the woman yowl in agony and just as quickly fall into silence. Her body slacked, and I checked that she was breathing. Her lips moved, attempting to form words, and nothing came. Her eyebrows furrowed, and her mouth pulled in a certain direction that made her look befuddled. I looked at the woman's chest, at her shallow breathing, at the chain, and the pendant that now faced upwards, showing the engraved image of a half-naked man against a tree with arrows piercing his body.

"The baby is alive," I whispered in her ear. "A boy . . . with black hair and bright eyes."

The woman opened her eyelids slightly, just enough for me to see the color of her honey brown eyes. She closed them again. Her pallor was paler than before, her heartbeat slowing. Crina had been holding the woman's hand tightly, and she began to murmur prayers to her in a language that I did not recognize.

I turned to where the baby cried and found Maria-Elena severing the umbilical cord and tying the stub. She then wiped the birthing blood from him with a damp cloth, and I turned back to the mother.

Certainly, men have seen death. How many wars have been fought; how many thousands of men die at the hands of one another, bloodied, and cleaved? This was a different sort of death, the uncontrollable kind. In war, I supposed, there was some essence of control: a man, a weapon, and his will could determine if his eyes would open to a new morning.

This woman was dying of childbirth. Her body was pale; her lips were dry. There were dark circles under her eyes, and her long hair stuck like tendrils to her neck and shoulders. It took me a moment to realize that the woman was alive, though barely. Her breathing was shallow, labored, as if it would disappear with the ticking of the clock. It was almost unnecessary for Maria-Elena to be there. One glance at the woman and death was obvious. Maria-Elena was calm, her voice steadily kind as she told the husband of the inevitable outcome, leaving me alone with the dying mother and the now sleeping newborn. The room smelled of sickness, of the closeness of death. The baby made a strong whimper, causing an immediate reaction from the mother whose eyes flicked open. She glanced at the baby and then at me. She licked her lips, a gesture that seemed to consume a great amount of her remaining strength, and whispered, "Bring him here."

I did not want to touch the child at first. He was small, and I was afraid that the act of picking him up would break his frail body. Yet, I could not deny the poor woman of the right. The baby's whimpers had become stronger cries. His face reddened with the screaming, eyes squinted shut, mouth wide and pink. His arms flailed, searching for a body to hold. I reached my hands in, scooping him up in my arms, all the time worried that I might drop him. Gingerly, I brought the newborn to his mother, laying him on her chest. The mother gave the smallest smile as she slowly brought her arms up to cradle him. His cries softened, though his head nuzzled her chest, searching for her breast.

There was nothing to be done for the woman. It was obvious even to my inexperience. All that was left would be to make her comfortable.

"You are dying," I said. In her closed eyes and pallid face, I saw myself. How I must have looked as I died and what I would have wanted someone to say to me in those last moments. "We will take care of your baby."

She gave a slight nod, a dip of her chin and then back up, and smiled.

Maria-Elena placed the crying child at the woman's chest and laid the woman's hand on it. Crina settled her hand on the dying woman's and remained by her side in silence.

So compelling was her death that I could not look away. The deaths I had thus far witnessed were ones of struggle, of refusal, even as the inevitable came. Crina's was different. In her eyes there was the desire to live, but there was also calm. The woman raised her bloody hand to my cheek. At once, the familiar euphoria infused into my mind. My skin prickled as if a sudden frigid wind gust blew through the room. There were memories that slipped through my mind, even as I tried to focus on them. The incoherency of them made it impossible for me to understand. I could only feel the emotions behind them. A great well opened in my stomach as I began to feel the unmistakable joy that came with reaping a virtuous soul. My heartbeat strengthened. My skin warmed. Clouds dissipated from my mind. I felt wetness against my cheeks and hand and realized that I was crying.

A hand patted my shoulder, and I turned to see Maria-Elena.

"It's never easy to watch a mother die," she said.

Maria-Elena wiped the still moist hair from the woman's face. "Let her be at peace."

"She did not deserve it," I said.

Crina took the baby in her hands and wrapped the blanket more tightly around him. She unclasped the necklace from the dead woman's neck and tucked it into the folds of the blanket.

"He is so beautiful," she said.

"Was a name chosen?" Maria-Elena asked.

Crina shook her head once.

"She hadn't thought ..." She looked at the dead woman. "Her name was Antonia."

"He'll be in good company with three other boys in the house," Maria-Elena said with a sigh.

Crina nodded once, her eyes glazed as if her mind was elsewhere, and another was controlling her voice.

"Take care of him," she said. "Until I can come for him. It's what she would want."

Crina left suddenly, and when she returned, she gave some *lire* to Maria-Elena. "This is all I have for now." She motioned out. "You can leave so we can take care of her."

They followed their instruction. I, intrigued at the house of pleasure and how close I came to being in one were it not for Maria-Elena, ventured slowly through the hall. My skin responded to the lustful noises by warming. I stopped at one door and peered through the keyhole where I could barely discern body parts, as it seemed there was a fleshy creature with six arms and six legs. Maria-Elena hissed at me, and I quickly followed back out the alley door and into the street. Upon feeling the cool night air, the baby began to cry.

"We'll have to get home and feed him straight away. You'll have to stay all through the night, I'm afraid."

I looked at the boy, wrapped snugly, held close to Maria-Elena's chest. I placed a pinky finger in his mouth. As he suckled, he calmed.

"Crina said she would come get him," I said.

Maria-Elena scoffed.

"All the women say that. They promise to come back for the baby. One year passes, then two, and soon enough the child is grown without ever seeing who birthed them."

"She seemed sure."

"Of course, she is . . . now. But the longer they wait, the more it all seems like a dream. They wonder if it really happened at all. Or they become distracted by the world and find they have no interest in the baby. It is better for everyone, really. How can a woman like that take care of a baby?" Maria-Elena stopped for a moment and scratched her calf beneath her skirt, then started walking again. "No. Better to have the baby with me. At least he will have a future."

I wanted to disagree, but I knew that I also depended on her for money and couldn't risk upsetting her and ending up on the streets again, so I held my tongue.

"Pious old *signora*, isn't she?" asked the voice of Azazel. "She thinks herself a saint, I expect, saving all the little children from their poor, sinful mothers."

We left, walking together without saying much. The baby began to fuss.

"He'll need milk as soon as we get back," Maria-Elena said.

She held the baby closer to her body.

Once we entered the home, the babies were all asleep. I had never been in the house during the night, so the quietness felt eerie.

"Good. Irina and Sister Maria-Giulia must have gotten them to sleep," Maria-Elena said. "You go prepare the milk, and I will get some clothes for this boy. Bring it up when you are done."

I obeyed and went to the kitchen, expecting to see Maria-Giulia, but the place was empty. Although it seemed that Irina was able to put the babies to bed, the mess she left in the kitchen took me some time to tidy. Then, I boiled the water and prepared a bottle. I took it upstairs to the only room with a light on and peered inside. I had never been in her room before and was curious now to see how she kept it. From where I stood, there was a simple wooden bed covered by a pink and white patchwork quilt. Maria-Elena stood in front of it, bent over to dress the baby. The rest of the room was mostly bare except for a dresser on one side, which had drawers opened slightly as if overstuffed with clothes. There were pictures on the wall of children's drawings, some with years and names on the bottom of children who no longer lived here. Adjacent to her bed was a cross and under it a small desk with a Bible set atop it. Under the desk, slightly obscured by the wooden chair, was a metal safe.

I knocked gently on the door frame.

"Come in," she said.

"I did not see Maria-Giulia," I said.

"Oh, she has probably gone home or to daily Mass."

I continued to survey the room, propelled by curiosity. A light came from a bedside lamp. The lamp itself had a bronze stand in the modern art deco style. The shade was of yellow glass at the top and blue at the base, and decorated around the entirety of the shade were bronze reliefs that depicted a city scene in the topmost area covered in yellow, and an ocean scene below in the blue glass.

"That is Marrakesh," she said while picking up the baby. As she did, her back popped, and she let out a relieved sigh. "I lived there before the Zaian War forced me out." She cradled the baby, who was now dressed in a white cotton sleeping gown with a knitted turquoise cap covering his soft head. "I bought that lamp some years ago to remind me of happier times."

"What war?" I asked.

"Oh, a skirmish between the French and the Moroccans." She blinked hard, squeezing her eyes shut and then opening them again. "I try not to think about what I cannot change. War came, and I had to leave. I came here, and with the help of the church, started an orphanage. I do my best, but there are always more children who need warm beds. In the past it was the Ospedale della Pieta that would take most orphans, even train them in the arts."

"But not anymore," I said.

"Times change," Maria-Elena said.

"You have some nice things," I said. My eyes were drawn again to the safe. "What's in there?" I asked, gesturing to the object.

"Gifts for when the children are old enough to leave," she explained and then added, "You can go."

I was reluctant to return to my lonely room. It could have been the fresh memories or the energy that the dead woman imbued into my blood that made me want to stay with the newborn.

"No, thank you," I said. "I would rather help with the baby."

Relief relaxed Maria-Elena's face.

"*Bene,*" she said. "I could use some sleep."

I had the bottle in one hand but held out my arms to offer to hold the boy. She passed him to me gently. I wobbled when I sat, as her mattress was softer than I expected, but soon, I was upright and had the baby nestled in my arm, coaxing him to drink from the bottle with my other hand. He turned from it and cried. I tried again. With the other babies, it had been easier. They were accustomed to the bottle and took it eagerly.

"Rub the nipple on his lips first. Let him smell it."

I took the tip of the nipple and rubbed it gently over his lips. His mouth searched for it, and I placed it farther in so he could latch on. He began to suckle.

"When he is done, see if he will sleep." She pointed to a basket on the floor at the foot of her bed which had a single white sheet covering the base. "And do not wake me until the sun comes up."

She went to her dresser and changed in front of me, taking off her habit and wimple. I was surprised to see a head of bright copper hair, cut short. Without her spiritual coverings, she appeared more human, more corporeal. The baby cried a little, so I turned my eyes down, focusing on the baby instead, who would drink the milk and pause periodically. The poor boy. He should be with his mother, drinking from her breast and feeling her skin next to his. How cruel life was to take her from him. He had so little to remember her by. Just then, I considered how the dead mother could be part of him. Her name had been Antonia.

"Perhaps we should name him Antonio," I said.

"As good a name as any," Maria-Elena said dismissively.

I felt the bed dip and turned to see Maria-Elena pulling the quilt up to cover herself. She laid her head on the pillow and then turned over to her side. Soon, her breathing was calm and deep.

I looked back to Antonio, who had fallen asleep, and I checked the amount of milk remaining in the bottle. It seemed a waste to have him drink so little. I decided that some was better than nothing as I brought him closer to my body. I tried to remember the last time I had held a baby so small. It would have had to have been one of my siblings, but when they were so new and fragile, it was my mother who held them. Often, out of necessity, for it seemed the new babies were always at her breast, drinking milk. When they were not, it was either my father or one of my older siblings who held the newest baby. How comforting to know how many hands there were to hold up a new baby. I longed for Antonio to have that same comfort, that same support, from a family who loved him and could care for him no matter whose hands held his. All he had now were mine, and I was not sure they were enough.

I tended to the baby until the sun rose, never letting him

out of my arms, and when I woke Maria-Elena, I was reluctant to pass the child to her. Still, I knew I must. She took him dutifully and told me to go rest.

I was tired, but before doing as I was told, I decided to go to a bakery to purchase the old bread that did not sell. The man who owned it often gave me an extra brioche or tarte with my order. Despite my initial refusals, he would give them to me or sneak them into the paper bag.

As he placed my choice of bread into a bag, I noticed his features for the first time. I hardly paid attention before; he was just another face. Seeing him after all that had happened, I decided that I wanted to remember what he looked like. He was older, having few wrinkles and smooth skin. He had a charcoal black beard with a few white hairs that was cleanly and closely trimmed and a mustache that grew into it. In the center just above his left eyebrow was a brown mole that made one eyebrow appear larger than the other.

"What is your name?" I asked him when he gave me the bag, and I gave him the *lire*.

"Daniele," he answered. "And yours?"

I did not answer him at first, unsure of which name I should speak.

"No matter, *signorina*," he said.

He gave me my order.

"Every night after nine I leave the unsold outside the back door for the street cats," he said, gesturing a hand behind him. "If you ever find yourself with a hungry belly."

His kindness silenced me. All I could do was tighten my lips and nod to him. I took my food and left.

It was still early. Early enough to read my notes about my murder and about the death of the girl, Faustina. Azazel was in my room, sitting by the windowsill. I removed the newspaper from under the mattress and read the notes once, twice, over and over to memorize what I had written, hoping some new insight would emerge from the hastily written words. It was all factual. Dates and times, clothing, skin color, hair color. There had been no autopsy of my body; my family would have never agreed to a desecration of the sacred body, so the cause of death was a supposed drowning. Faustina's, conversely, had been ruled as a failure of the heart. Neither body had any clear indications of violence. I had been strangled, but a body swollen with canal water would not show the bruises or lacerations from such a murder.

I had decided to take the photographs. They were crude and offered little insight from what I could see, but in a better state of mind I might discern something from them. I put the notes away and stared at Azazel. He had an infinite knowledge of sinners. He could tell me who it was as soon as he saw the man, and I tensed. I wanted to know who it was and thought of walking the street until serendipity intervened.

"How much wandering would it take to find my murderer?" I asked.

I walked over to the window where Azazel sat and opened the shutters. Outside, the sun was setting, and a haze settled over the rooftops. Azazel turned to look out.

"A lifetime or more than a lifetime."

I exhaled. I would not wait that long. I needed to know more about my murder. The *polizia* had been of little help. Though I had avoided it, I would have to return to my parents. They would know the most about my death, and I hoped they would tell me all I needed. Would they speak to me, a stranger, about the death of their child? Even if they would not, I had to try. I hoped they would.

CHAPTER SEVEN

I subsisted on the blood of fish, but with the evening turning into night, and the promise of a day of rest, I could indulge Azazel in removing a sinner from the streets. I wore the hat Irina had given me and secured it with the Bona Dea pin. My candle I hid in the front of my dress, cradled against my heart and the fabric of my brassier.

The air was warm with spring as the bells from the tower marked the dusk hour, and I walked along the street in silence. Azazel stopped to look at the small *chiesa* we passed, raised his eyebrows, and kept walking.

"You'd think they had enough churches," he murmured.

As we walked in seemingly no clear direction and without a purpose, I became slightly irritated at his nonchalance.

"Is there a point to this?"

"I can't take a walk?"

"You never do a thing without reason."

He lifted a finger.

"Quite right." he said and stopped at a canal. There was a set of four slanting steps, the center worn down from wear, and at the bottom platform, a boat sat tied to a post. He raised a foot and mimed as if it were sitting on the edge of a boat. The oars sat inside, resting on the single wooden seat with a flat embroidered pillow with a center worn down and the inner stuffing shifted to either side.

"Taking me for a romantic evening tour?" I teased.

"Hm," he mused, moving his foot from its place and setting it on the ground. "We shall see how the night goes."

I smiled a little at his response and placed a hand on my waist. "And where are we going?"

"To the Isola di San Michele," he answered.

I furrowed my eyebrows.

"That place is just churches and cemeteries," I dismissed.

"Not *just*," he said.

Whatever reason he had for going there suddenly intrigued me. It would take me from my endless poring over the notes of "The Drowned Jewess," but perhaps it would give me new insights as well. In any case, I was not tired and could resume my dedication when we returned.

I nodded and stepped gently into the boat, balancing my weight so I would not fall into the canal. I then untied the rope and pulled it into the boat so that it lay in a pile next to my foot. I then took the oars and settled them into the rests and began rowing carefully. Though I had lived in the floating city all my life, I had not had much personal experience with boats. What little I knew came from short excursions with friends or relatives. It was enough to make me confident that I could travel in a straight line. The island was close enough to the shore that I did not fear becoming lost in the lagoon.

Azazel reclined, stretching out his legs so that his feet rested on a sliver of empty seat next to me. As I followed the length of his legs and up his body to his face, I noticed he held a smug grin.

"You could help," I said.

He held out his hand. When I drew the oar handle towards her to give to him, I found that it passed through his fingers.

"Convenient," I said.

"If I could touch anything but you, I would solve my own problems." He leaned on the side, placing his hand into the water. "What I wouldn't give to wrap my hands around these sinners."

"Is that where we are going?"

"In a sense. There were rumors I heard of a man, and I want to see if they're true."

"It is a waste of time to idle on gossip."

"Is it? The little problems Humankind makes can be quite entertaining. Just this morning, your rather noisy neighbors were arguing over who ate the last of the jam. Being that they were both drunk the night before, neither of them could remember and so took to inspecting their fingers to see any remnants. How pointless. Even more so considering it was the cat that had done it."

I laughed, which broke my stride and made me readjust the oars.

As I rowed, I slowed at points to rest. Though the island was close, traveling to it under my own power made it seem farther than I expected. The sun had nearly disappeared, and in the indigo sky a few white stars glimmered in the distance. At times I turned my head to ensure that we were traveling straight. The island seemed like a strip of burned brick in the moonlight. The parapets, tower, and domes of the *chiesa* merely highlighted the insinuations of space. As I pulled us into the open dock where there were already two boats of similar build, it was a relief to replace the oars and tie the boat down.

A few minutes after we stepped onto the ground, my stomach grumbled, though I tried to ignore it.

"You will eat soon enough," Azazel said.

"Hm," I wondered.

I assessed the surroundings of the quiet cemetery. There were stones and trees and silence. The small differences were in the presence of the crosses that marked the entrance and many of the gravestones. As I walked, I noticed that there was a cordoned section of graves belonging to those of a different Christian denomination. The Greci and Protestant graves seemed long abandoned and in varying states of decay. Statues of angels marked some spaces. At one point along the shrubs and flowers, there was a headstone with a carving of a woman. She stood with a shroud covering her head, draped over her shoulders, and falling to her bare feet. The folds of the cloth had spots of moss and lichen. The dark spots of age grew over the left side of her face from her eyebrow to her chin where a hand rested. Her eyes were nearly closed, and her head tilted towards the inscribed name as if pensive. I stared at her for longer than I intended. How could a stone face protect the dead? Was it the dead she was protecting, or was her face there only to calm the bereaved?

Every cemetery, every place where the living respected their dead seemed the same, no matter the type of stone or what words were written on them. Those who lived on endeavored to remember the generations which came before, no matter their faith. That gave me some comfort.

My sights turned to Azazel who was walking down a white stone pathway. In the moonlight, the stones glowed so that the demon that walked atop them seemed illuminated. He was like a wraith passing by the stones, and I was compelled to follow.

Turning the corner, I saw a man next to a freshly dug grave. He jumped down, and soon I heard the unmistakable noises of singular pleasure. What he did next made me turn away, though Azazel kept watch.

"Hm," he murmured, "I guess the gossip was wrong. They said he was eating the bodies, not—"

I held my hands over my ears to muffle the egregious sounds coming from the man and began walking back to the boat.

I was already sitting in the boat, ready to take up the oars when Azazel stopped me.

"Where are you going?"

"Away from here," I said, and I began rowing, doing so slowly as my arms were sore.

"The man is despicable. Why not take his blood?"

I rested. What the man was doing was grotesque and was worthy of loathing. Defiling the body after death deserved a punishment, that was true, though I reasoned that it was not worth death.

"Despicable, yes. But who is he harming to please himself?"

Nivul Hamet, the prohibition on desecrating a body, pertained to those who followed the Jewish faith. There were prohibitions about corpses and what should or should not be done to them. How similar was this to the Catholic ideas of a dead body? What punishment would be incurred for such defilement? I could not justify killing a man for a crime that harmed no one, no matter how disgusting his acts were.

"The dead body has no soul." I took a deep breath and picked up the oars. "You brought me here for nothing."

"Take his life, his soul, and bury him with all the other corpses here. He is a man alone. None would see you."

I glared at him.

"*I* would."

Azazel groaned and looked up to the ink-blue sky.

"I bring you here with a free sacrifice and you refuse."

"I refuse to kill him," I said.

Another thought came to me. I put the oars down. Maybe I did not have to kill him. I could wound him and take his soul. I did not know if that was possible. Did they have to die for me to reap their souls? Curiosity made me consider the alternative.

"Perhaps I do not have to," I said.

I picked up one oar and walked to where the man continued his arduous lasciviousness. Azazel walked beside me, smiling. As I came closer to the man, I softened my steps, though it hardly seemed to matter. The man was so focused, his eyes squeezed shut, that I doubt he would have noticed me if I were standing in front of him. I raised the oar, despite my tender muscles, and in one swift plunge, knocked him over the head with enough force to incapacitate him, leaving the corpse to fall to the ground. To ensure the man would not wake, I bludgeoned his head a few times. His face was bruised, purple, red, as if his skin were bloated fish scales. I placed the oar on the ground and removed the hairpin. With it, I pricked the inside of his left wrist and pressed the vein there to fill the bottle. When it was full, I let his wrist fall before replacing the pin in my hat and looking over to the dead body of the woman. The clothes she had been buried in were disheveled, and there was an odd stench coming from her. I replaced her skirts. The man still lay on the ground with his pants below his knees, and I hoped he would be found that way, in all his shame.

"It would be simple to rid him from the world now," Azazel mused. "Here, sleeping, you could push that pin in his neck and let him bleed out. His life is no loss to this world."

I stared at the unconscious man. It would be simple to kill him as he was. Simple, but not moral. I had what I needed from him.

I turned to Azazel. He was looking down on the man, all

the while staring with a wrinkled nose and a frown, his judgment clear.

With the blood in one hand and the oar in the other, I returned to the boat. There, I used the candle flame to burn the blood to ash. Once prepared, I continued the ritual until I felt the effects of the blood. It flowed in me muted, its effects dampened, satiating my need for the moment but leaving me unfulfilled. I could not help but compare this blood to that I took from the child's murderer from earlier. I saw no memories with this rapist's blood, though my mind seemed more alert, while with the murderer, I absorbed some of his, and my own were somewhat restored. The soul absorbed through the blood of those I killed was potent; the ones taken from those still living was weaker. Still, it was stronger than taking the blood from an animal. My body energized enough that the soreness from earlier had dissipated. My stomach grumbled and cramped. I began rowing for shore, and Azazel followed wordlessly.

Once I returned the borrowed boat, I headed straight toward Daniele's bakery. A few cats strutted around the back, with one lounging on the stones. As promised, there were old loaves and rolls of bread in a paper bag set next to the *cestino*. Seeing them was a relief. I had seen such selfishness and despicableness at the cemetery that a sign of compassion was a welcome reprieve. I took the entire bag.

The next morning, I awoke without a fog clouding my thoughts. I was hungry. The events of the night before had reminded me that while I had cleared my body of the effects of a dimming flame, I had not satiated my hunger. It was quite the opposite. I found that I had an appetite that could not be quelled by the stale bread that I hoarded on my counter. When I stood, I looked at the soiled and sweaty clothes that I wore from the day before. I relieved myself in the chamber pot and tossed the remains out the window. As I did so, I heard the sounds of the children who were already awake. Maria-Elena had begun putting Beni to sleep in the crib by my bed. He was up, fussing, and chewing on the bars of his crib. I picked him up and took him downstairs where the others were already bustling. Upon seeing me, Maria-Elena took Beni and shooed me away, knowing what day it was.

It was a comfort to hear it at times as it reminded me of when I was a child living at home. However, this day was one of my personal days off, and I was eager to have time on my own where no one expected anything of me, so I removed my dress and changed into the only other set of clothes I had. I would have to launder the dress later. Then, I walked to San Marco's and found a cafe that was open on a Sunday.

Those around me stood at the bar and sat at the small tables in a conundrum of loud conversation. It was a medley of dishware striking together, the loud sound of steam from the espresso machine, and the fumbling of money into the cash register. It was enough to make my head slurry over while my belly ached for the taste of a buttered brioche. With all the *lire* in my pocket, I bought four different sweet breads and a cup of macchiato. Finding a sliver of open space at a standing table, I ate, savoring each ravenous bite. The bread was soft, fresh, its aroma rising into my nose, and I took bite after bite, not caring when flakes tumbled over my chin or stuck to the sides of my lips. After eating two of the brioches, I drank the dark *caffè*, surprised at the strength of the caffeine that emerged from such a small cup. My parents had never allowed me to drink coffee. They would say it was for adults and that I had no need of it until I was older. At times, my sister Miriam would make a cup of powdered coffee for my father or mother in the mornings and let me sneak a sip. It was a secret, sneaking moment of adulthood. I felt that way standing at the table, drinking the macchiato in a cafe full of foreign men and women on a Sunday.

After my stomach was full, I returned to my room to wash my dress. I tried to ignore the babies that reached out for me because I wanted time for myself, but a baby's cry was compelling.

Once I was free of the babies for a few moments, I focused on cleaning my dress. Without soap in the washroom, I made do with the water and rang out the dress, bringing it back upstairs damp, and hanging it over the window shutter to dry in the morning sun. I then turned to my bed with its single mattress and old pillow. I had been using the veil as a blanket, and in my sleep, had disheveled it. Taking two corners, I lifted the veil into the air, allowing it to float down and settle on the mattress; then I spread out the wrinkles. There were still marks of dried blood that stained the white lace. I stared at them, considering that I could clean them off, but I concluded that I did not have the will to do it. The rust-colored spots were the tactile reminders of my rebirth. I wanted to keep them.

I would go to see my family today, knock on their door if I had to, and find out what they knew. I was not sure if it was the caffeine from the macchiato or nervousness which made my heart flutter.

At moments, I would look up and see Azazel pacing around the room silently, still upset that I had let the man from the cemetery live. I ignored him and read and re-read my notes. How long did it take for a body to decompose to a state where it was filled with gas? My mind wandered to the first man I killed. I had placed his body in the canal, and it was found soon after. It had not yet suffered the same effects that my own dead body had. That meant that my body had either been floating in the canal for days without notice, or that it had already begun decomposing before it was placed in the water. It was unlikely that a body would go unnoticed in the busy canals of Venezia for long, so whoever killed me must have kept my body until they could no longer hide it.

As I looked at the photograph of my death, my *memento mori*, my stomach roiled. I turned away to gather my senses, but I had to know, so I inhaled and did my best to harden my heart against the image.

It was a wet body on a stone street. The eyes were open in surprise. The mouth was closed in silence. The entirety of the body had swelled so that many of my distinguishing features had smoothed into an unrecognizable corpse. It could have easily been some other unfortunate girl whose body had been thrown in the canal. I focused on the photograph, retracing the lines around the body, the disheveled dress, the uncovered hair that stuck to the skin, the mucous that oozed out nostrils, the pallid neck. It was then I noticed a bauble pinned to the dress. It was a brooch, a jeweled mosaic pattern with two lovebirds side by side in the center of a black background and a crescent moon above them.

I felt a hand place the brooch in mine and then the sensation of a kiss on my cheek. Who was the lover that gifted it to me? A man so close in my affections would know about my death. My family would know. I may have considered myself stealthy in my youth, but my mother's keen eye would know to whom her daughter was besotted. I needed to see her, to see my family.

I hid the photograph under the old mattress. As soon as the dress had dried, I put it on and left the abandoned house, leaving the candle, my hat, and Bona Dea pin. I walked through the alleys and over the bridges which would take me to the ghetto, passing the familiar *farmacia* where I had gone often enough to get medicine when someone in my family was ill.

When *l'influenza* came, I remember going inside with my

mother to plead for something, anything, that would ease the illness, and the kind *farmacisti* would sell my mother some pills. I stopped to look through the window, at the locked door closed due to the late hour and the dark interior, though I did take a step closer to the window and to press my hand on the glass. My fingertips were as hot as if I had pressed them against a boiling teapot. My throat tightened, and I swallowed to ease my discomfort before removing my hand from the heat of the glass. I looked down at my fingers, expecting them to be red and swollen. My skin was just as it was before. I touched the glass again and this time felt a cool surface undisturbed by my presence. I looked up at the glass once more. It was as if I had seen a shadow of a bird pass across the windowpane only to disappear when I looked closer.

CHAPTER EIGHT

I t was strange to be amongst the walls where I so often spent my youth. The center was busy with families and guests gathering around the synagogue, ready to enter. I scanned the covered heads for my family but did not see them. Perhaps they were already inside.

Stepping forward into the crowd, I waited my turn next to a woman holding her child's hand and a book under her left arm. She tapped me on the shoulder, and I turned.

"Is this your first time?" she asked with a smile.

"I–" I was going to tell her that I was a Jew, that I had often been to prayer, but stopped. *Was* I still a Jew? I had not considered it since my rebirth. I felt that I still was, that some part of me was. My soul belonged to HaShem before, and though I was broken, that faithful piece of me, that part that lived through the *Gilgul Ha'Nehshamot*, the transmigration of souls, remained.

"It–it is the first in a long while," I answered.

She nodded once and absentmindedly rubbed her lips together. I then recognized her and the child as my neighbors.

Her name was Gia Peixoto. Before my death, she would come over to the house during the day to take tea or coffee with my mother while we children played. She and her husband gifted us with pencils on Chanukah. A welcome gift, for in a house of students and curious children, it seemed we were always wanting pencils.

"It is never too late," she said.

For my house will be called a house of prayer for all people, came a voice either from my memory or from a stranger's soul.

I looked up, squinting against the sky, at the unassuming facade of the building where Azazel perched himself on the outcropping over the entrance, letting one leg dangle over the heads of the faithful. I watched his expression change from humor to dismay as the crowd filtered inside.

"*B'ezrat HaShem,*" I said.

Gia took the book from her arm and held it out to me. It was a *Tanakh,* the three sacred writings of Judaism, bound in leather and embossed with gilded Hebrew letters.

I shook my head to refuse the gift.

"Take it," she pressed.

"I–thank you, but no."

She took my hand and placed the book in my open palm.

"One day," she said, "there will be as many Jews as there are stars in the sky."

I did not know what to say to her. I hoped it would come to pass. With the persecution that beguiled our people, I could not be sure what our ends entailed. I was reluctant to share my doubts, fearing that they would depress her faith. Instead, I followed her as I entered the synagogue and took a seat beside her where all the women sat behind a wooden barrier. All was silent and dim. Light shone through a ceiling window above the *amud* and through open transoms. Hanging from the center ceilings were chandeliers each glowing with a dozen candle flames. Crimson curtains covered the side windows. Carved spiral columns framed the *amud*.

The rabbi removed the centuries-old Torah contained within a gilded *tik*. It was a cylindrical object half the size of the rabbi himself, with golden filigree at either end and golden embroidery that connected the superficial red and white cloth. He opened the *tik* and began.

In the celestial songs the rabbi recited, I receded into the comfort of the ancient words, the same songs that kindled my childhood memory. When I was a girl, I remember sitting with the women. I was careful with my surreptitious glances towards the men, who among them I spied my brothers and father. They prayed, eyes closed, as mine ought to have been. Their shoulders were covered with the white and blue *tallit*. I turned back, head bowed, hoping my prayers were heard, willing them to fruition. I would dance to the tunes the street players sang. I would run amongst my friends, playing games and teasing the boys. I took off my *tichel* to cool my head on summer days, uncaring of who saw me. My elder brother Aaron would see it and hit me with a stick, telling me to obey; my sister would flick my ear when I misbehaved, or my mother would send me to bed without supper, but my pride was stronger than their admonishment. I would let my hair flow freely, feeling the air through it as I ran through the market chasing cats.

I would go to synagogue to pray, say prayers before Shabbat, at Passover, but they had been no more than words and stories to my young mind. My passion was in life, not faith. No matter how Mother tried to have me heed the words in the Torah, how she made me read the passages to her or to my brothers after supper, I had considered it a chore at the time. I was thankful for her determination now that I could see the works of HaShem for myself. There were other things she taught me. She had been studious, often reading to us or going to the library to learn new philosophies or listening to Father repeat what the men debated together. It was from her that I learned of the Zohar, the sacred texts of the *Kabbalah*, and the mysticism and tradition that my mother had been taught as a girl, as a Spanish Jew, before her family moved to the floating city.

Unlike in my girlhood, I now sat in the synagogue and prayed. I prayed for insight. I prayed for revenge. Though I was alone in prayer, I felt I was still a voice amongst the generations that preceded me. I wanted to hear the voice of HaShem, to know he was there to guide me. When I opened my eyes, there was Azazel sitting atop the chandelier and whistling. I wondered how he could exist in the holy space. Behind me were footsteps, and I turned abruptly to see a woman, tall, thin, her head covered by a *tichel* and whose face I recognized at once.

Mama.

I wanted to run to her and hold her in an embrace and never let go. Then I saw my sister enter shortly after, and I was rendered speechless.

"You look like," the woman started, then stopped. She looked again, and smiled. "Oh, my eyes are not what they used to be."

I bit my tongue to stifle the tears that threatened to pour from my eyes. My sister's face was a contortion of confusion as she tried to decipher who I was and, no doubt, why I looked so familiar.

"You must be new here," she said.

"Yes," I said.

"Where have you come from?"

I tried to think of a convincing lie, so I told her I was traveling, that I came to visit my deceased cousin.

"Have you no family here?"

I shook my head.

"You'll spend Shabbat with us," she offered. "You seem to need a place to stay. So few guests come to the house anymore."

My parents were kind. I expected an invitation. Though I was nervous that I would see them again, I believed it would give me the chance to find my murderer if he was among my family. It would be heartwarming to speak to my father, to hear his deep, loving, voice, and to see Mother and the rest of her siblings in that cramped, crowded house. It was also terrifying. What would I remember? What had I forgotten? How painful would it be to see them all again, knowing that I had been taken from them? I tried to push those thoughts away, even as they persisted.

"*Toda raba,*" I said.

I could still hear Azazel whistling behind me as I followed my mother and sister out of the synagogue and to a familiar house.

It was just as I remembered. At the right side of the front door mantle was the *mezuzah*. I reached out to touch the cool, polished surface and brought my fingertips to my lips. The simple reverence reminded me of the thousands of times I had made the same gesture, sometimes hurriedly, sometimes thoughtfully.

Inhaling the smell forced my eyelids to close. A rush of memories flitted by, each one without clear context or rhyme.

"Are you well?" my mother asked.

It took her hand on my arm to startle me into awareness.

"Oh," I said. "Just a little tired."

"Here," she said and pulled me gently.

I fixated on the black coats and hats that were hung on the plaster wall. One half consisted of a tall bookcase filled, with some empty spaces, with hardcover bindings, some of them tomes with Hebrew titles, others thin Italian books either for study or entertainment.

The house was filled with the noise of a family. My siblings bickered and played. I heard the sound of my father's voice joining in with them. I smiled. Their banter, even just the sound of their voices filled me with a tender happiness that I had not realized had been lost.

"Tavi," mother called.

A few heavy footsteps on the floor, and I was face to face with my father. Though not incredibly tall, it was his presence which made him seem larger than he was. He was a lean man who had a slightly rounded stomach that came with age. His face was clean-shaven but for a thick black mustache speckled with white hairs. In his arms was a brown and black spotted puppy who tended to lick the underside of his chin.

"A guest!" he said once he saw me. "How wonderful."

Father placed the puppy on the floor. It sniffed around my feet, and Father chuckled.

"This is Romeo," he said. "As you can see, he is infatuated with young ladies."

I bent down to scratch the back of his ear. He was a cute puppy and lent his affection easily. It was not often that we had pets in our home, though once Mother had kept a finch in a wooden cage outside her window, and we had once taken care of an alley cat for years until one of us let it out one morning, and we never saw it again. Whether it had died or merely found another family to care for it, I never knew.

Father went through the pleasantries of asking where I was from and what my name was. When I answered, his eyes widened.

"Aviva?" he asked. "The same as my mother, *aleha ha-shalom.*"

"I am sorry to impose–" I began.

"Impose? What? You are invited. Stay, stay," Father said. His eyes brightened. "I will have to show you my pocket watches! Have you ever seen a Nuremberg Egg?"

"You may have to show me later," I said.

He clapped his hands together and smiled. I shared my father's excitement, knowing how proud he was of his collectable clock. The Nuremberg Egg was a precursor to the pocket watch that he kept in a locked wooden case under his bed. Though a replica, his was a golden cylinder with a clock face at the top. It had taken him years to find one. The day he came home with it, each of my brothers and sisters had a turn to hold it while my father explained the history and intricacies of the device. My mother was as eager as I was to examine it, and as she waited, conversed with Father about how it functioned. My father delighted in sharing anything related to his knowledge of clock making.

"Have you washed?" he asked me, pulling me from my memory.

I shook my head. He pointed me to the washroom, though I knew where it was, and excused myself to clean up. I placed the copy of the *Tanakh* I had been holding on the table in the hallway, reminding myself to take it with me when I left. Once in the tiny washroom, I had to hurry as two of my younger siblings, a boy and a girl, were waiting for me to finish. As I washed my hands and face, I glanced at them from my peripherals, trying to remember their names. I could not. When I finished, I dried off and then asked their names. The youngest spoke first, "Moshe!" he said. Next came my sister, who said "Leonora."

Moshe pushed past me to the sink where he enthusiastically turned on the faucet and splashed in the water while Leonora tried to calm him. As I left the washroom, I heard their back-and-forth struggle of Leonora turning off the faucet and

Moshe turning it back on. Seeing them together, hearing their chatter, reminded me of what I had lost. It was too much at that moment.

I focused on the mundane to calm myself. As a rule, my mother made sure that there was always money for books. These were kept in one room, resulting in two walls occupied by bookcases. One bookcase was dedicated to holy literature while the others contained a more colorful variety. I scanned the bindings of the books and found one of my old favorites, *I Promessi Sposi* sitting next to another titled, *Dio Nella Libertà*. I picked up one, flipped through it, and did so with the other, letting the smell of the pages fill my senses. When I put them back on the shelf, I drew my forefinger across the letters on the binding, all the while wishing that I could experience the happiness I once had for the words inside those pages.

I looked away. In the room there was also a reading chair and a roughly worn olive green sofa. Covering the stone tiles was a faded Persian carpet. The intricate patterns in the center were a blur of what they once were and the border a burnished orange, all of its delicate weaving worn from treading feet and years of children playing. There, on the wall, was the grand-mother clock, ticking quietly.

Placed centrally among the pastoral paintings on the walls, in a gilded frame, was a portrait of Napoleon Bonaparte. My father brought it home from the market days after the gates of the ghetto were torn down and hung it in the center of the drawing room. There came soon after an argument between him and my eldest brother, the latter of whom opposed such veneration on the grounds that it was the worship of an idol and blasphemous, not to mention that it was also the French who looted the city and sacked the churches. My father would laugh at his orthodoxy and said that if it were such a sin to honor the man who bestowed them such freedoms, the rabbi could come to their home and take the picture down himself.

The *Serenissima Republica* that had lasted a thousand years was razed as easily as a scythe cutting through wheat. What was left were the skeletal remains of a once grand city; the gilded sheen that had seemed to envelop it faded. Palaces, grand halls, abandoned and home to stray cats and beggars, all because of one man. Next to the portrait of Napoleon was of another bearded man I did not recognize at first. I touched the frame and then remembered. Mother had purchased the picture while we shopped together for a new pair of shoes for Miriam's birthday. The man was Luigi Luzzatti, the first Venezian Jew who served as Prime Minister of Italy.

A streak of orange light passed over the portrait. I turned to the glass window that let in the evening light where the simple blue cloth curtains were tied into knots. I looked out the window that overlooked the Rio della Misericordia. When I was a child, I would stand by the glass and wave at the boats that happened to pass. My grandmother would have been with me. If it was someone she knew passing, she would crack the window and shout a greeting. When *l'influenza* came, that window was often the only way we saw anyone from outside the ghetto. The sickness spread so quickly and was so contagious that we rarely risked contact with anyone outside our family. We would draw pictures or write messages and affix them to that window. I blew hot air on it to create a plume of condensation and drew a heart in the center.

"How sentimental," said Azazel.

I ignored him.

My attention was drawn to the other side of the room. The long table was set with six chairs and two stools so close together that the edges touched. My mother and sisters went to and from the kitchen while Little Moshe, the youngest brother, slipped his hand under the cloth that covered a dish and tore bits from the *challah* when no one was looking. My older siblings, busy with the bustle before sundown, took no notice. I offered to help with the food and was given a plate of cooked and filled fish that I set on the table. I stepped carefully so as to avoid tripping over the puppy who romped around the table.

Once the setting was finished, we all stood as we waited for Mother to light the candles for her *mitzvah*. I passed my eyes over each member of the family. Some names came to me easily: the eldest brother Aaron, his wife Bilhah, their oldest girl next to her, and in her arms, a baby. Aaron had been in Trieste when the Italian Army liberated the city. Had been there before in a battle that he would mention but never speak of. It had been three years ago. While he was gone, I remember Bilhah often spending the nights and days with us, though she and Isaac had their own house not far from ours. She was gone from it so often that she and Mama decided to rent it out for the time that Aaron was gone.

There were the other boys, two of them to include my brother Aaron and Moshe. Of the girls, I knew my sisters Miriam, Fiona, and Leonora. There were more, two older girls in the family who had since been married and so spent Shabbat at their husband's house, and then the three who died as babies, one scarcely older than a week. Mother lit the candles, passed her hands over the flames, and covered her face. The baby in Bilhah's arms let out a soft coo.

"*Barukh atah Adonai, Eloheinu, melekh ha'olam asher kidis-hanu b'mitz'votav v'tzivanu l'had'lik neir shel Shabbat. Amein.*"

The cloths were removed, revealing the two loaves of bread and the tiny bites therein, giving the appearance that a mouse had been nibbling on the crust. I could not hold in my amusement and smiled widely.

"You have quite the family," I said.

Father laughed. Aaron scolded Moshe, though the child ignored him.

"We have a knack for it," Mother said with a grin.

Father took a knife to scratch certain sections on the bread. He then replaced the knife on the table and took both loaves in his hands. He closed his eyes and recited the *bracha* for the *challah* and ended with *"Min ha'isa."* Father opened his eyes, tore a piece for himself, and then passed the loaves to my mother. When she took her piece, she dipped it three times into the dish of salt on the table, a Kabbalistic custom only she adhered to. The *challah* was passed carefully to each person. Miriam then passed the *challah* to me. I took my piece and passed the bread along. Once everyone had their *challah* and ate it, the remaining portion of bread was kept in the center of the table. Father then began to take his helping of food from the dishes on the table and passed those in the same order as he did with the *challah*.

"And how is your family?" Father asked me, finally.

I shook my head gently. I knew them to be too kind to press further.

"Is this all of your kin?" I asked, prying gently.

"Most of them," Miriam answered. "My older sisters are married and Tziporah—"

My heart leapt at the sound of the name. My dead name. Miriam was interrupted with a loud hush from my mother. I stared, caught in those lifeless eyes. How I wanted to embrace Mother and say, "I'm here," and in her warm arms remain. A mother's arms were love and safety, and all the incomprehensible soft emotions that a wordless child felt while sheltered within.

Moshe took a piece of meat from Fiona's plate. When she noticed, she screamed.

"Moshe, give it back. If you want more, you ask."

As they spoke, Azazel walked behind them. If he could see their sins, he could tell me what Aaron or any of my family knew about my death. I had suspected that my brother may have been responsible for my death, but I had also thought it could be a lover, the one who had been closest to me, who shared their body with mine. I was unsure who it was who dug my grave, who suffocated me, who stood over my struggling body as the dirt packed tightly in my throat. If only I could remember more from that day. Only the shock and pain and the few fragmented memories remained. Yet, I could hardly ask them so many questions about it around the Shabbat table. I ate, all the while listening to them speak and thinking about how I would talk to my sister. I wanted to curse at Azazel for refusing to speak to me when I needed him the most.

"Will you stay in the city for long?" Mother asked.

I nodded. "I found some work for the time being."

"Oh? Where?"

"At an orphanage, helping to take care of the babies and children there."

"How nice," Bilhah said.

"Why would you want to be around babies all day?" Leonara asked.

Mother scowled at her, and in response Leonara bit the inside of her cheek.

Because it was the only place that would take me, I wanted to say.

"You must be compassionate," Father said. "It can't be easy to have such work."

"Such is the way for all mothers," Mother said.

Father raised one finger into the air and nodded his head in agreement to acknowledge that he had taken his wife's point to mind. It was a comfort to sit around a Shabbat table and pretend that my life was normal.

"What orphanage is it?" Miriam asked.

I told her.

"Catholic?!" Leonara asked. "How can you stand to be around them?"

"I do not mind it much," I answered.

"*I* would," she said. "The ones at school always bother me about going to Mass."

"I suppose they're trying to be helpful," Bilhah added.

The baby fussed, and Bilhah positioned it on her shoulder and patted it gently on its back.

"I don't think so," Leonara mumbled.

"Do they have you attend Mass?" Aaron asked.

I took a deep breath. Aaron had always been overly concerned with faith and with following the rules of faith. I decided not to answer. My silence seemed to cause him to pry.

"You should avoid it no matter the cause," he said. "It is all idol worship, the way they prop up their saints and saviors." He looked at me in that same way he did when he would give me strict advice that he expected me to follow. "Remember what Moshe ben Maimon wrote: 'we deal with them as we would pagans.'"

Azazel laughed. I found Aaron's world of absolutes infuriating. Had I followed Aaron's beliefs, I would have starved not long after I was reborn.

"I cannot agree," I said. "HaShem works His will through all manner of people and in all manner of ways." I straightened my back. "I doubt I am any less Jewish by walking into a church on a Sunday."

My brother's eyebrows furrowed. Bilhah flicked her eyes over to him to watch his response. As soon as my brother opened his mouth to speak, Father interrupted.

"Aaron, speak to the rabbi about such things and leave our guest be," Father said, looking at me.

Mother sighed. "My son likes to discuss the holy books. I suppose it's my fault, being the scholar of the family."

"Ha!" Father exhaled. "You would be the scholar of Jerusalem."

Mother twitched her lips in what looked like a bashful smile. She then composed her expression into one of concern and gestured towards her husband.

"Eat," she said, "before Moshe takes it from you."

At her command, we all obeyed and ate with few interruptions.

When finished, I insisted upon washing my own plate and walked into the drawing room again. There, I saw a mirror and my grim reflection in it. I was pulled towards it, as I had not remembered the mirror here when I was a girl. Perhaps it was always there, and I never had the occasion to find it significant. In the glass, there were aged black speckles. In the glass was my obstructed face and behind me, in the shadows, were horns covered with buzzing honeybees and eyes as eclipsed suns.

In my first steps beyond the mirror, I was as warm as summer.

Near my feet was a body, face down. Copper brown hair flayed around her face and shoulders, obscuring her features. I looked at the body and knew what I had done. My memory blanked, and the body was gone, absorbed into my own, leaving in its place a candle burning with a vibrant flame and blood upon my fingertips.

As I looked at myself in the mirror, I saw my features were entirely new, those of my soul and the copper-haired woman transmogrified into a new body that I didn't recognize. If that memory were true, then I had killed to be born again. In passing through the mirror, another soul had to be sacrificed.

The woman who had died. Faustina. The documents and newspapers flashed before my eyes. The young lady who had unluckily attended a funeral, and died.

I could not process the revelation, not in my family's house. I quelled the emotions that threatened to rise. Whoever I became did not matter. What mattered was fulfilling justice. Miriam was my closest sister. I had to speak with her alone, but I did not have to wait long, for she soon joined me.

"They are so happy to have a guest," Miriam said. "Very few come to us anymore. They think we are cursed."

"Because your sister died?"

"That, and more." She hesitated and looked away from me.

The loneliness that shrouded her face made me want to reach out to her. I wanted her to trust me. She was the sister who I confided in when I could not speak with my mother or father. She was the one who kept my secrets.

"I know what it is," I said, "to lose someone you are so close to."

"I cannot talk about it with them," Miriam said. "Whenever I try, well . . ." She gestured towards the dinner table. "It is like I am the only one who wants to know what happened."

Being with my sister filled me with ease. I could tell her about everything. If I could trust anyone, it would be my sister. Still, I could not be sure. I might tell her, but would she believe me? What would the truth cost her? I decided that I could tell her some of the truth.

"You are not the only one," I said. "My cousin was found dead, and I was never sure how she died. I came here to see her grave, to try to remember her." I looked over at the mirror. "Before she died, I was not so devout. I did not follow the faith as well as I should have, perhaps. When I saw her body . . ." I distanced myself from the words, unable to finish, unwilling to recount my death aloud. Then, I turned to my sister's face.

"Sometimes I think ..." I paused to exhale. "I think not knowing is worse than the truth."

Miriam met my eyes and nodded.

"For my sister, it is not just her life, but her soul. At least if I knew how she . . . If I knew what happened, I would know where the sin lies. I am sure she was murdered, of course, but there is always doubt."

Miriam pressed her lips together.

"Do you believe me?" she asked, her voice breaking.

"I do."

I startled at a sudden grab of my hand. Moshe interrupted our conversation to hide behind me. When I looked down at him, I saw a face looking up at me, spotted with crumbs and sauce.

"Moshe!" Leonora called as she entered the drawing room.

"Come along," she said, trying to pull him from me. "You have to wash."

I took him into my arms and wiped the crumbs away from his face with my thumb. He pulled his face away and, to get him to turn back, I tickled his neck. He giggled, and I laughed with him all while trying to clean his face.

"Thank you," Leonora said. "I can take him."

Though Moshe whined, I handed him to my young sister, and she took him out of the room. When I turned back to Miriam, her expression had changed. Her eyebrows were furrowed, and her lips were slightly parted as if she were deciphering my face and found an answer lacking. A moment later, she relaxed.

"Would you mind if I showed you something?" she asked.

I was pleased that she could trust me. I wanted to know more about the admirer she mentioned.

"Prego," I said, letting the Italian word that meant "after you" roll over my tongue.

CHAPTER NINE

S he led me upstairs, past the bedroom doors, most propped open since so many children were coming and going through the house. At the end was a door, which had led to my room. As she took me inside, I paused, holding a hand against the inside of the frame, before going in.

It was the window that intrigued me. I saw myself sneaking out of it at night, climbing down the outside wall by steadying myself on the window outcropping and using the drainpipe as a ladder. I would return hours later to find Miriam still asleep in her bed across the room that we shared. The beds were still there, though the reminders of my life in that room had gone, no doubt tucked away somewhere alongside the old baby clothes of my dead siblings.

"We used to share this room," Miriam said. She sat on one of the beds, which had a quilt that my grandmother had made when Fiona was born. It was a periwinkle color that used corded quilting patterns of flowers and vines. Grandmother Aviva had tried to teach me how to quilt in that style and laughed at my impatience. I paced around the room, glancing at the plaster walls to which I had once tacked a magazine cover with a photograph of Carmen Boni, which quickly earned my father's displeasure.

"I complained about it for so long. Now that I finally have my own room, I miss sharing one." She sniffed, and I saw that she was crying, so I sat down next to her. I did not know what to say to calm her, nor could I summon speech in the face of her sadness. All I could do was hold her hand. She wrapped her fingers around mine and placed another hand over it as if she were going to fall and gripped me to keep steady. We sat there together until she took a heavy breath as her crying subsided and removed her hand from mine to wipe her cheeks.

"Since it happened, I wanted to talk about it. I want to know how she died, but my parents tell me to leave it. Mother told me it was right to be sad, to mourn, but that we had our answer." Miriam shook her head and turned to me so that I could see her red-rimmed eyes. "I tried to forget about it being a murder. I thought I could convince myself once that she did it to herself. I cannot believe that."

She looked away and exhaled.

"Every night I think about her, about her soul. I have dreams where we are together, and she is calling my name, and when I wake up, I can see her standing by the window." Miriam let go of my hand and stood up. She took a few steps away from me and crossed her arms over her chest.

"Mother likes to tell stories, mostly about golems and giants. But there were other stories, too. Have you heard of an *ibbur*?"

I glanced at her. Azazel had asked whether I was a *dybbuk* or an *ibbur* when he first came to me. How could Miriam know what I might be? I thought back to when she and mother saw me in the synagogue. Mother seemed like she had recognized me. Had Miriam as well?

"Is that a demon?" I asked, feigning ignorance to see what she would tell me.

"Not quite," she said. "Mother said it was like *gilgul neshamot*, but instead it was a rebirth of a soul into another body so that the soul can carry out a *mitzvah*."

Miriam stared at the floor, her face concentrating on solving a puzzle in her mind. If she could guess what I was, even if her idea of me was clouded by the stories Mother told, I hoped that she would trust me even if I could not tell her exactly who I had become.

"Until so many in our family died, *Safta* Aviva, baby Levi, Tziporah . . . I always thought those were like fairy tales."

Mother would come into our room to scurry us into bed. One of my favorite tales was of Shaul HaMelech and the witch and how she fooled him into summoning a spirit. It was a story that should have scared me when I was younger, but which I found exciting. I had not believed in such things as *shedim* or *mazikin*, demonic spirits which roamed among us. Since being reborn, since meeting Azazel, I could hardly deny their existence.

"All those old stories have some truth to them," I said.

"Truth," Miriam whispered, more to herself than to me.

She walked away from me to the window. Her cheeks were like a ripe persimmon in the glow of a sunset. Miriam closed her eyes. Behind her came Azazel who watched her movements carefully as if to avoid her touch and bent to stare at her face. I watched him curiously, wondering what he might be doing. As soon as Miriam began to speak, I forgot about Azazel.

"You said that your name is Aviva. The same as my grand-mother. I was always able to tell her everything," Miriam said and smiled a little. "And Tziporah . . . She always thought I was asleep. Every few nights she went out this window to meet him. She thought she was so cunning, never getting caught. It was because I protected her. More than once, Mother would walk down the hallway because Moshe woke up at night, and I would make sure the window was closed, or I'd arrange her pillows to look like she was sleeping. I thought I was helping her." Miriam fidgeted with her sleeve. "She showed me a brooch once."

"A brooch?" I asked. At the mention of the object, I envisioned the design of two birds in the night sky captured in resin and surrounded by a silver frame.

"A gift. She was so happy. She said she was sure of his love. I wanted her to be happy. I did not think I should have taken that from her. If I told Mother or Father about what she was doing, I was afraid that they would keep Tziporah away from him." Miriam shook her head. "Then one day, a little after Yom Kippur, she snuck out and never came back." She took a deep breath. "Maybe I should have told them, then she would still be here."

Miriam had protected me, and I had known nothing about it. How many times had she ensured that I could rush to my lover when I could have been caught at any moment? I stood up.

"No," I said. I stepped closer to her and placed a hand on her shoulder. "You have no fault. The guilt is with her murderer and him alone."

Miriam knew who it was that I loved. The admirer. The lover that I had fragmented memories of.

"What was the young man's name?" I asked, unsure if I was ready to hear it.

"Ephraim Sarfati," she said.

I let my hand fall from her shoulder. In the shadowy spaces

of my mind, where I had tried and failed to reconstruct his face, a clarity emerged. I saw his face. His youthful, beautiful face. I recalled at once the way he would set his chestnut eyes on me, and he would smile with full happiness. I wanted to cry out. It could not be him. I tried to keep my composure, to ensure that I gave no hint to Miriam how I felt.

"When she died, he did not come to the *shiva*. He had gone as soon as she did until her *yahrzeit*. And who should he bring with him, but his wife?"

I squeezed my eyes shut. "He married?"

That knowledge may as well have been worse than the murder, that our love could be so easily replaced. The man was a memory of a love I once had. That love, that possession of love, aroused envy. Mother had often counseled me against such thinking when I was young, that envy was the root of all conflict, that it was worse than wrath. All I could feel now was envy.

"A gentile girl," Miriam explained. "She was kind and pretty. I did not want to talk to her. How could Ephraim, who loved Tziporah, marry another so soon? And not just marry, but convert? It is a blessing that his parents did not live to see that."

"He brought her here, and then she was dead. Dead, in our house. How could a young girl fall down dead with no explanation?"

I swallowed.

"So, that has left us as we are. Ephraim ran off somewhere."

"Do you know where?"

She shook her head.

"No one does. Such a shame. I have some choice words for him if I ever see him again."

I gathered my thoughts. Ephraim had been my lover. A lover who soon after married a different girl.

"Do you think *he* could have done something to . . ." Unable to utter my name, I said, "your sister."

Miriam considered.

"I cannot know for certain. If I could find out who it was . . ."

"What about the *polizia*?"

Miriam scoffed.

"What about them? What help can they be? They ruled it a suicide and wiped their hands of it. Who cares about a Jewess found dead in a canal?"

"If you could do something about it," I inquired, "what would you do?"

My sister drew her lips downward, forming lines around her chin that were not present before, making her appear much older than her years. Her eyes became glossy as if they would overflow with tears.

"It is not right for me to say, but ..." She held her hands together, tightening her fingers. "Retribution," she said. "Let the one who killed her suffer the same."

We stayed there together until my mother broke the silence, calling Miriam downstairs, telling her of the lateness of the hour. Miriam wiped her eyes and cheeks again. She then cleared her throat and stepped away. Before leaving the room, she stopped as if she forgot a possession and was trying to remember where it was, then came back to me and gave me an abrupt hug. She took my hand in hers, gently, as if in suggestion.

"Please come again," she said.

Miriam and I went downstairs. Mother was sitting in the drawing room. Father sat. The puppy, Romeo, remained attentive while his tail wagged as slowly as a metronome. Father stroked the puppy's brow, and then prepared his pipe for smoking. Aaron played with his daughter, picking her up and swinging her gently back and forth as she laughed, and while he did, I saw his own smile and laughter at her enjoyment. Hearing the commotion, my younger brother went out with them, begging for his own turn.

Bilhah looked out at them while nursing the baby. Her eyes were closed, her face tired from fatigue. Mother walked past her as she tidied up the table and tucked a few misplaced hairs that had fallen from her headscarf and then stroked her forehead gently. It was as if I could feel her touch on my own head, for how often had Mama done the same to me when I was a child? Mother returned with a plate of sliced *challah* spread with a thin layer of jam. She offered one to me.

"N–," I started at first, but then, remembering how proud Mama was of her Marmellata di Corbezzoli, how she saved to buy berries from the market and boil them, then preserve them in her miniscule glass jars, to be used only on special days or for special guests, I said, "Yes, thank you."

I took the slice gingerly. She took one for herself and placed the plate next to Bilhah. Soon after, the younger children were herded to their rooms by Miriam and Mother, and the sitting area became quiet. Bilhah dozed on the chair, her baby sleeping in her arms. There was a spare knit blanket on the couch that I picked up and draped over the sleeping mother.

I looked at the baby who appeared to be no older than three months. A tuft of black fuzz topped his scalp. His eyelids flickered as he slept. I could not decide which parent he looked like. He smelled of milk and warm skin.

Upon smelling the tobacco coming from my father's pipe, seeing the family, my full stomach, the continuing memories that came to me were those that I could scarcely comprehend. Experiencing each vision of my stolen life brought fatigue. It became increasingly difficult to keep my eyes open.

"Do you need to rest?" Miriam asked.

"Oh," I said, shaking the sleep from my eyes. My heartbeat sped. Much as I wanted to stay in the warmth of the home, I was on my second day, and if I spent the night and woke up on the third day, I wondered where I could find the blood I needed. "It might be best if I leave."

"You ought not leave after evening," Aaron said.

I almost laughed at his concern.

"It is safe enough," I said.

"For a young woman, it is better not to be alone," he answered.

I softened at his tone.

Father stood, startling Romeo to hop out of the way.

"A walk is just the thing," he said.

"I would not want to bother you," I said as I tried to refuse. I did not want anyone in my family to see where I lived. I did not want to see the pity in their eyes to learn how low I had fallen.

"No bother at all," he said. "I am sure Romeo would like a walk." Father looked down at the puppy and smiled.

"It is a little far," I said, attempting to dissuade him, even knowing how stubborn he could be once he settled his mind.

"I will take you halfway," he answered.

Father walked to the door, and Mother and Miriam came also. At the table, I picked up the *Tanakh* I had left there.

"You should never travel alone without the words to keep you company," Mother said approvingly.

Father bent down to affix the collar and leash to Romeo. When he straightened, his spine popped, and he stretched his back.

"Are you well?" I asked.

"Ah," he said. "You see, we carried all the stones for the pyramids, and that's why we all have back pains."

I laughed.

Before leaving, I thanked Mother and Miriam, and I hoped I would see them again.

Outside, the sun had already set. Azazel stood some distance away, pacing around the synagogue. Father continued to smoke his pipe as we walked, stopping at times when Romeo lifted his leg to relieve himself, sniffed at a stone, or followed a scent left by a cat. Father asked how far we should walk. I took some time to answer to be sure that we would stop near enough to the house so that father would feel content in his assistance and yet far enough away so that he would not see where I lived.

"The Rialto," I told him.

Father let out a grumble. I turned to him.

"I forgot to show you my Nuremberg Egg," he said and inhaled sharply through his half-closed lips that held the pipe. He glanced over at me and smiled. "So, you will have to visit us again."

"I suppose so," I said. "Your wife was kind enough to invite me."

"You were kind to accept." Father puffed on his pipe. "I will take you down this path, here," he said.

I smiled. I knew the route and the stories that he would tell. I had been on that same walk many times, usually forced to do so, and I would often complain or daydream as he spoke. Even though I knew what he would say and where he would take me, the thought of just being with him and hearing his voice again appealed to me.

"Have you been to Venezia before?" he asked.

"A few times," I said.

An orange cat slunk along a wall, and Romeo pulled on the leash to chase it. Father picked up the puppy to calm him as we turned to a corner where I had been some time before with Maria-Elena. On this late night, there were the night ladies standing outside. One of them was Crina in a scarlet dress. Her hair was left down, kept up at one side with a bejeweled flower hair pin. She wore lipstick as red as fresh coral, and on her cheeks were hints of pink blush. Crina had a young man speaking with her. They flirted and touched and kissed. She must have seen us, for in a moment, she removed her embrace from the young man's and turned to wave at me.

The young man was persistent, so Crina turned from me and took the young man inside. Seeing her again made me think of Antonio and how much he needed a mother.

"Ah, here," Father said, pointing toward Crina. "You see the ladies?" I knew the story my father would tell next, for he had told it to me before.

"My first time in Venezia, just when I moved here, my friends and I would walk just down by this street after work. As we walked on a Friday evening, we would see the wanton ladies call to us from the windows, just there." He pointed to the second floor. "Oh, how persistent they were!" he said, lifting a finger and raising his eyebrows. "But we never went in."

We shared a laugh and walked together some more until I insisted that I walk the rest of the way alone. At first, he would not let me go until I told him in honesty that my home was shameful to me, and I did not want him to see it. He nodded once in understanding and left me to myself. As I watched him depart from me, I thought of myself as I was when I was small and how I would call out to him to wait and let me catch up. When did I let myself grow so far apart that I no longer called out for him?

A cat's yowl caught my attention. The lanky animal strode across a high wall and then jumped down, so I walked up to it and held out my hand. "There, there," I said, beckoning it closer. It took a cautious step towards me.

"Careful," called a voice.

I noticed the shoes first. They were polished leather that looked like they had never touched dirt. When I looked up, I saw a man standing in front of me. Judging by his tailored gray suit and silver watch, he must have been a man of means. When he stepped closer, the cat scampered away.

"Those cats have wicked teeth," he said. He then pushed his left sleeve above his wrist to show me two crescent-shaped white scars on the inside of his wrist bone. They looked like they were from an animal, but not a cat. As I glanced from the scar to his face, he smiled, but his eyes were joyless. My attention lingered on him until I felt Azazel's finger stroke the back of my neck.

"What a pity," I said.

"Yes, it stung for weeks."

"I meant for the cat." I smirked. "Men are an acquired taste."

The man scowled at first but then chuckled, and I tensed at his laugh.

"Good evening," I said quickly. "I have work to do."

I walked away, but he followed. "Work at this hour?"

"Yes," I said. I took a different alley that led back the way I came. I considered that the sight of an unscrupulous business might scare him off.

"Oh," the man said knowingly. "I see. I can't say I ever noticed you before."

"What?"

He gestured toward the brothel and then shrugged. "It's embarrassing to admit, but I'm not a stranger there. Not for the reason you may be thinking, though."

"I do not care what you may be thinking."

"Such terrible manners!"

"I help the poor women here when they have, shall we say, ailments. My name is Agostino Vianello. I'm a *farmacisti*." He gave a perfunctory smile. "So, you see, I know all the ladies here, except you."

"I do not need help," I said.

He raised his eyebrows and nodded once. This time, he did not follow me when I walked away.

CHAPTER TEN

I was fixated on what my sister had told me and on the face in the mirror and on the intrusive voice. That voice was like a honeybee caught in a jar: soft at first and then at other times a buzzing that was jostling to escape. I needed to be someplace quiet to think, and I needed Azazel to talk to me.

When I returned to the house, to my room, Maria-Elena welcomed me by immediately asking for my help. I told her I would wash first and went upstairs to place the *Tanakh* the woman gave me on the end of the bed. Seeing the old bread on my table, I was thankful to have my mother's cooking settled comfortably in my stomach.

Once I washed, I went back downstairs to tend to the babies until it was time to go to bed.

When it was finally time to go to sleep, I went to my room where Irina was already asleep on her bed while Giorgio snuggled with her. I sat on my bed to think. Ephraim was the name that tapped against my brain. I knew I had a lover. I could still feel my body next to his. That love and how it had been taken from me was one of my first memories once I came from the other side. That memory of love turned to envy and anger. He had married. He had loved me and married barely a year after my death. He did not wait for *yahrzeit*. He had found someone quickly and committed to her. That commitment was suspicious. What kind of man marries so soon after the death of his sweetheart? Not only did he marry, but he also converted. And he married the daughter of a wealthy, connected, tradesman. Had not Ephraim desired a path in trade? A cause and motive formulated, melding together to present a story of my murder. A young man had it in his mind to become a tradesman. How best to do that than to marry the daughter of one of the elites who owned a trade company? The only hindrance to that goal was his religion and his lover, and he rid himself of both.

Ephraim would have been able to do it easily. We had often met in clandestine corners in the darkest hours of the night or early mornings. It would have been a trifling matter to silence me in that darkness and dispose of the body in a canal. I sat back at the realization. Had he killed me so he could marry another? But why kill me? There was an opaque memory and whispers that slipped through the mist.

The desire for him overwhelmed my rationale. My skin flushed hot, and there was an immense need.

Lust, I thought. *The unyielding presence of lust.*

I braced against the stone wall. There were countless alleys in the city. It was simple to find one out of the way, dark, and private, even on the busiest afternoons. It was also part of the thrill, knowing that we had to be quick, careful; it was the lusty game of youth. A game that unhindered gallivants play. In that narrow causeway, we were two bodies stealing a moment's warmth. I could still smell the hint of canal in the air, the damp moisture from the morning mist still collected on the stone walls, San Marco's *campanile* bell sounding overhead, ushering in the morning.

A sin. Not between a wife and her husband. Or intended husband. I could never agree with that dogmatic teaching.

"We are all human," I remembered saying to him. "He made us this way. How can HaShem punish souls for using the bodies He gave us?"

There was no life without *neshamah*. I tried to piece together the memories that were as if I were peering into a milky pool. I saw some as pieces of visions or as feelings, sensations. I offered to place his hand on my belly. There was a being within there, a child and yet not, for a child could not be alive without the first breath, the virgin breath once they passed from the womb into the world. What rollicked in my womb was the hope of life. I felt at once disquiet and dread.

Ephraim had been romantic, kind. That was my child as much as his. We could marry, raise it, and be happy together. I had not known what I wanted in life. Perhaps this was what HaShem was giving us. Instead, had Ephraim wanted me to disappear? Had I become a nuisance, an inconvenience?

Guilt consumed me. I passed through all my foolish actions. Had I been truthful with my parents, would I still be alive? If I trusted them as I trusted Ephraim . . . My excuse then was that I wanted someone for myself, something secret and that belonged only to us. I wanted our love to be our own. I did not want to share it with my family, with the others in the ghetto, not yet. I had wanted to wait until we were sure. Until we agreed to marry. I wanted to be sure that it was more than young love and lust. How foolish I was to wait.

My anger diffused into sorrow, as if another soul had control of my emotions, stifling the rational rage I felt towards my murderer. I began to cry, rubbing my palms against my eyes to stem the tears. When my head became dizzy, I lay on my side, and traced the lace patterns with my fingers, following the lines and swirls in the memories of lace as if they would lead me to a path of understanding. Hopelessness grasped my mind, shackling me into ineptitude. I could recall sharply the singular vision I had of confronting my murderer and ushering him to death. How satisfying it would be to watch him die, as he had done to me. I would confront him, show my face. I would see him and kill him and watch him die. Perhaps he would whine as he did, or call out for HaShem, or his mother, or perhaps say nothing at all. I only wanted to see him in those last moments of life and know that it was me who had done it, that it was HaShem doing it through my hand. That fervor had since gone. Then, I thought of remaining bedridden until the inevitable; that the candle would dim, snuff out, and I would go with it. What use was there in fighting when it seemed impossible to succeed?

"I am so tired," I said to the dark and to the shadows hiding there. "Why can't it stop? I don't want to do this anymore. I want to go back to how it was. I remember being happy, and I used to find happiness in the smallest things. Now those same things leave me empty." I pressed my lips together, biting them, and squeezed my eyelids shut. "I wish I could feel like that again."

I hoped that tears would give me some catharsis and willed them to pass, but I could only think of kissing Ephraim and how we held each other in the night. I had loved and was loved. I wanted to stay in that world no matter how the darkness enveloped me.

"I hate to see your sadness," said Azazel.

I glared at him. "You decided to speak to me again?"

"I have become bored with my own thoughts. Refusing to kill that one man was an annoyance. I am sure your conscience will allow for the next one."

The next one, I thought, mulling over the words and their implications. I pushed them aside.

"I cannot think about that today," I said.

Not long ago he was surveying my family, assessing their minds and their sins.

"And what did you see while you were walking around that house?" I snapped.

Azazel shrugged. His indifference made me punch the mattress beneath me. At the sound, he glanced at me.

"You should find comfort that the culmination of their sins was of the mediocre kind."

He looked down at me, his expression kind, soft, as if he would listen to anything I would say.

"You have eternity ahead of you; there is no need for tears."

I took my hands from my face and wiped my nose. Despite my annoyance with him, how he pushed me to murder, I found his voice a comfort. A demon, such as he, knew me, more than my family, more than Ephraim. I could confess every thought to him.

"I know who killed me," I said.

"Mazel tov."

I exhaled sharply, trying to expel my emotions from my lips.

"I thought you would be elated."

"I hoped it would not be someone I loved," I said.

"Hm," he mused. "Is that not the way? Love and hatred flow in the same river of passion."

I did not care for his continued indifference.

"Some consideration would be appreciated," I said.

When I looked up at him, he was pointing at himself with his eyebrows raised.

"Me? Perhaps you have me confused with someone else."

I scoffed.

"Perhaps I confused you with someone who cared about me," I retorted.

"And so, I do."

"Then prove it," I said. "I know who killed me: Ephraim Sarfati. You told me that if you knew the man, you could see his sins."

Azazel raised a finger.

"If I *see* the man. I have to be near enough to him to observe his thoughts."

"Why is it so hard to find one man?" I asked.

"If a man does not want to be found, he will ensure it."

Ephraim. I tried to materialize his features in my mind. I had an idea of his voice. He had a youthful, optimistic tone, unmarred by hardship. When he laughed, he did so with a full smile. I focused on remembering the outline of his face, the color of his hair, the set of his eyes and nose. All I could imagine was a suggestion of how he might appear, as if his face were a hazy daguerreotype. With these were my own fragmented memories of the events before my death. The newspaper report of my discovered body, even the *polizia* report that I also transcribed. I began writing down what I remembered from the conversation with my family. It jostled some memories loose. I could not think clearly. The rapist's blood was enough to subsist upon but not to excel. I would have to push through the clouded memories. I did not have the stomach to kill men tonight.

"I have to find him," I said.

Why should he kill just so he could marry? I wondered how expensive a lace veil was, and who could afford it? The gentile was no simple woman. What had the *polizia* said about the Case of the Drowned Jewess? A woman disappeared. A wealthy man's daughter. Ephraim could have been desperate to marry her and would have done whatever it took to ensure that the marriage was bound. Money. It was always money that drove men to make the worst choices. Ephraim married a young woman, and when he came to my *yahrzeit* soon found her dead. When I glanced at the mirror in my childhood home, I saw a woman dead on the floor and found my life restored.

I glanced around the room for Azazel.

"I have been thinking about the souls I take," I told him. "There was a . . . woman."

Azazel looked at me with eyebrows raised and eyes open. He stretched his legs out behind him and slid down until he was prostrate on the mattress.

"To be born, there must be blood."

A grim realization settled into my stomach, turning my body still. When I was naked on the streets with only a veil to cover me, there had been blood on my fingers. I looked at the veil spread out upon the bed where Azazel lay, where the dried spots of blood remained.

It is the mitzvah of Hawwah. She who ate the fruit of knowledge, I thought. *For me to come through the mirror, it was destined that another must die.*

It was through destruction that life was created. Destruction of the mother to give birth to a child. Destruction of the earth to make it anew. I thought of fire. How often a fire would raze a forest and, in that ash, new life flourished. We seemed to be relegated to this destruction, we humans. The world was at once beautiful and wicked. How is it that the same earth exists in purity and darkness? There is beauty in wickedness and wickedness in beauty.

For me to be reborn, I had to destroy. Without that soul's destruction, I could never have returned. Without destroying the souls of the sinful, I could not continue to live. Was it the undying curse of Eden? That original sin that flows through the blood of Humankind? Was it our curse to destroy each other?

"Did I kill someone to come back?" I asked, even though I knew the answer.

I collapsed on the bed, knowing what that must have meant. To come through the mirror, to be born again, I had to have killed. I had taken a life, likely an innocent life, one who was loved as I had been, and I had taken it from the world.

Taking the veil into my hands, I gripped it and then threw it across the room, disturbing the Torah that sat on the bed. I buried my head in my hands and felt tears welling in my eyes, blurring my vision. That sorrow came from both souls, mine and the one I stole. I thought of the young prostitute who birthed the child Antonio. The birthing blood that spilled from within, the child that emerged, covered in pungent fluids and blood, who cried with life as the mother weakened to death. The blood which gave the child life.

The other side. Beyond the smell of moist soil was a sheen of petrichor. The lull of canal waters against brick where it was damp and green and all about were mangrove trees. A ruined dock jutted out into murky water. Cretaceous fauna shaded the solemn sun. Water droplets rolled down the center of the leaves, pooling, dripping off the pointed edges.

Promise, the voice came. Not mine, someone else's, a whisper emerging from the thick air.

Empyrean trees. Eons of growth as veins rising from beneath the moist soil. Rough arms emerged, sprouting. Leaves that rose so high I could not see them but for the dark mass overhead. In the desert, there was the eviscerated lion and the hive therein. When I looked at my corporeal arms, honeybees crawled, flew, and landed.

A glass pool, overgrown with lichen and age, cracks worn into the silver pane, blackened in places that marked it as ancient. In the cracks there was a figure dressed in white lace. The late sun shone on her golden head, creating a soft halo. If this were the path to heaven, then surely, I must take it. It drew it in, away from the heavy air of the marsh where my senses dampened to deafness. The figure was like an angelic statue that I had seen overlooking the cathedral spires. Its kind expression beckoned me closer, closer. Before, I had been told better, that the angels of the gentiles were false saints, visions of a fantasy that placated the harsh truth of creation. That only humans could help themselves appease HaShem. The guidance of angels was no truer than the tales of witches who roamed the alleys and causeways, cursing minor offenses. And yet, there I saw one, on the other side of the glass. What else could it be?

And then I pressed my fingers to the warm glass.

A thousand shards sliced through flesh, veins, muscles, eviscerating my body. I screamed and heard no sound as my bones shattered, pulverized into ash, and then remolded, becoming a combination of the sensation of an early dawn frost with the heat of new embers, forging a life from the broken masses. In that creation came memories, recognizable and foreign, culminating into shared consciousness. It was my final death and my new life.

When I was dead, my soul existed in a forest, a voice, and in another, was flesh once more. I felt a voice whose words I could not remember. The voice that was an empyrean boom. There was a pact in it. Blood for blood. To return to that world, I would have to agree. Who was that voice? I had assumed it was HaShem who beckoned me out of the plane of existence. The truth was more sinister.

"Was it you who brought me back?" I asked. I then laughed at the absurdity of my initial assumption. "Are you *Nachash*? The cunning serpent?"

Azazel lifted his upper body, resting his weight on his elbows, and placed his hands on my bare feet as if in conferral of ordination. He faced me, but I turned away from his obsidian eyes.

"I am as I seem," he said.

And who am I? Meeting my family once more showed me who I had been, who I could have grown to be. Tziporah. That girl was dead, and I had stolen another life to enact retribution. A life which was barely beginning, which had such happiness in store. An innocent life which I took. Was I an *ibbur*, as Miriam supposed, or something else? Did it matter? Whoever I became was an amalgamation of those stolen lives. A new soul, a fractured soul, beholden to my *mitzvah*. HaShem created the light and the dark. All came from Him; all were servants of Him, even the demons. I recalled a verse that passed my lips.

"'The lord puts to death and gives life. He casts down to the netherworld; he rises up again. But the wicked shall perish in the darkness.'" I met Azazel's gaze. "Is that not me? Is that the purpose I have been given?"

I thought about the vision of the lion and the honeybees. When I looked into Azazel's black eyes, I saw my own miniscule reflection shrouded in shadows.

"And if you had known that before you passed through the mirror, would you have refused the offer?"

I parted my lips to refuse his implication, and I glanced at the Torah on the end of my bed. With the knowledge that I had to kill to live, that I had to reap an innocent soul, all for the chance to find and rid the world of my murderer, would I have made the same choice? I wanted to say that I would have refused. It would have been the moral answer, but it was not the truth. I had wanted to live again. More than that, I wanted the one who killed me to suffer. I had survived *l'influenza* when so many others had died. There was so much more for me to experience in my life and that had been taken from me. Now I was reborn into a body not wholly mine, one of many *shedim,* who could live only by taking the life of others. It was against *Pikuach Nefesh*, that life was holy; only HaShem could give it or take it away. Still, HaShem had given me life once more to fulfill His will. So often there were stories of Him using humans as a vessel for His will. I believed it was the same for me. How could it not be?

I closed my eyes and shook my head slowly to one side and then the other.

"I live for justice. That is all," I said. It was the nearest to the truth of why I kept living. Had my murderer kept me alive, Faustina would have also been spared. His violence cost the lives of two women. Two souls that could have lived full, exceptional lives had been stolen. She and I had been innocent enough of the wrongs that often befell women. What right did he have to remove us from the world?

I was a *shefikhut damim*, a shedder of blood. There were three exceptional sins for which self-sacrifice was obligatory: idolatry, forbidden sexual immorality, and murder. To right all the wrongs that were done to me and that I have done, the thought occurred to me that I, too, deserved death.

"At the end of all this, I should die," I said, more to myself than to him.

Azazel narrowed his eyelids.

"Should you? Not quite a Jewish thought, is that?"

I shot him a spiteful glance, but then softened. He was right. It was against *Halakhic* law. My death would not correct the deaths of others. There was no penitence in allowing myself to die. The wrongs that I had done were not made right by another death. For me to continue living, I was required to kill. Be it animal or man, I had to kill.

I could not reconcile the two conflicts: that I should not die, but that to live, I must also kill.

Who is to say that your blood is redder than his, that your life is worth more than the one he wants you to kill?

I was tired of the pestering.

"You care only for yourself," I said. "Is that why you came to me?"

"In part. You are the only one who can touch me, who can see me. Who else will you speak to about your plight? We can stay together, like this, always."

I thought about how I would die at the end of all this. Should I wait until I fade away? I thought of going to the cemetery where my memorial stone stood and lay there under the trees until I fell asleep. Perhaps I would dive back into the river and drown. I could end it quickly by opening my veins to the air.

"For what? You would waste such a power given to you? As long as that candle flame burns, you live."

Immortality.

"At the cost of murdering."

"Then choose the ones who deserve it. There are absurdly enough of them." Azazel's mouth opened into a wide grin. "What do I care if a sinner is dead?" He laughed. "I rather prefer it. It would give me peace to see them all gone. Then I can walk the Earth and witness only beauty." He shifted his weight and sat up. To my surprise, he embraced me gently, with a hand about my waist and one at my back.

I resisted. I had not wanted to kill. Still, I had done it before. I considered how HaShem enacted His own justice and how he used man to fulfill His will. There were some, it seemed, who deserved death, and I could give it to them. I would have to find Ephraim. The closest to him was dead, but another still remained: Faustina's father. If he was as rich as I supposed, it should be easy enough to find where he caroused and learn what I could from him. Until then, I could try to find Ephraim the only way I knew how.

"Azazel," I said. "Give me your eyes."

He looked up at me and grinned.

Azazel furrowed his eyebrows and tilted his head downwards, and I steeled myself. The muscles in my shoulders tensed as a dull irritation began itching at my spine. I shirked, but then paused at the sensation of his residual touch, and an impulse teased my mind. I was at once distracted by his body and my reaction to it. An intensity that I had not felt before with a man.

"Azazel," I said, and I walked to him and felt his skin with my fingertips. I kissed him. As I felt my heart flutter, my skin warm, I pulled away slightly, and looked up into his black eyes.

He let out a pleasurable exhale, and he threaded his fingers through my hair.

"Now look out the window at the first one you see."

I stepped to the window, and once I set my eyes on a woman, I was overcome with borrowed memories. I witnessed the woman stealing coins from the pocket of a market shopper and spending them on wine, then that same woman pushing a child so she could be first to pray at Saint Joan's dais, then the woman in church praying, then the woman pushing a Romani out of her way. I turned from the window.

"What did you see?"

"A hypocrite."

"Is that all?"

"Does it show all of their sins?"

Azazel groaned. "There's some nuance. Most of what I see are memories. They can be actual sins or what the person *believes* are sins." He stepped up to the windowsill, his feet teetering over the open frame, and in one step, fell from the window. I went to the open window and looked down to see him in the dark alley below, sauntering away at a slow pace, his path intruded by a stray cat. He stopped and looked up.

"Are you coming?" he called. "I have more to show you."

I stood a moment, staring at him. Though my body was

tired, my mind was restless with the possibilities of what the Demon Eyes could show me. Pulling on the only jacket I had, I placed a glass bottle in the pocket along with a few *lire*. Then, I settled my hat on my head and kept it in place with the Bona Dea pin.

"Where are you going?"

I froze when I heard the voice. It was Irina, mumbling from where she lay on the bed. She had her head turned towards me and was watching me with half-open eyelids. Had she heard me talking?

"You woke me up," she complained groggily.

"I am sorry."

"It's all your talking. You talk too much when you sleep. Some odd language."

Hebrew. She heard my conversations with Azazel. I would have to be more careful.

"I will be quieter from now on," I said.

Irina's answer was a grumble, and she turned her head back and nestled with Giorgio. I took a deep breath.

Once outside, I noticed that the air had an odd smell that I attributed to the murky canals. When I looked overhead, the moon was a shining bolt of mercury in a honey sky. The stars were spots of brilliant white. The city was so vibrant with color that it seemed different altogether. When seeing it from my exhausted, human eyes, I noticed the murkiness, the darkness. With the eyes of a demon, all was bright and beautiful.

I furrowed my eyebrows. Seeing the city so vivacious and serene was akin to how I viewed it as a girl. I was distracted by the flowers that grew from window pots; their violet petals glowed as if light shone from within each fiber.

However pleased I was at seeing such beauty that had been hidden from me, I reminded myself to focus on my purpose. I would see what the Demon Eyes could show me about my murderer. Ephraim's parents were dead, I recalled. The other lead I had was Faustina's father. I tried to remember her last name that I had written down. Zampieri. If he was as wealthy and influential as I was led to believe, he should be easy to find.

Faustina, I thought, concentrating on the woman whose life I took.

Although the sky was bright, I knew it was late. Most gossip happened at the *osterias,* and I thought I could find some of what I needed there, so I went to one near San Marco's. A quaint pub, it stood before an inlet where gondolas were kept in lines, crowded together until the morning. Azazel kept close to me, watching me carefully. As I came to the door of the pub, I peeked in through one of the windows to see a few people inside. What I saw made me back away. It was not their faces that caused my shock, but the intensity of the images that flooded my mind. Each of their sins or misgivings bombarded me. Depravity, abuse, and even their immoral thoughts disarmed my previous demeanor. I walked away. The farther I walked, the more the images dissipated. Once they were mere whisperings, I stopped and leaned against a wall to exhale.

I put my head down to avoid eye contact with anyone passing. A brush at my shoulder sent me to a schoolhouse where the teacher beat a boy with a thin rod. I kept moving. Where would he be? A wealthy man would be where all the rich and influential men dwelled. I walked the alley, through the corridors where I looked up to ensure I was following the way, and I passed a young girl and saw her hiding a broken pocket watch under her bed, a fishmonger selling a questionable catch to a poor man, a tourist stealing a mink fur scarf from the empty chair, a man stabbing a Prussian soldier, the terror on his face, the crimson blood that flowed from his gut.

"Not quite what you were expecting?" Azazel asked.

I turned to him. He leaned against the wall with his elbow and rested his hand on the side of his head.

"Now perhaps you understand my plight," he said. "Their sins, their crimes, swarm me no matter where I go. Any beauty I witness is interrupted by their bestial proclivities."

Whatever ideas I had about finding out more about Ephraim were stilted. I could do no more on this night. My mind buzzed, my thoughts jumbled. I needed to leave.

"Where are you going?" Azazel asked as I walked back to the house.

"I cannot think," I said.

As I continued, I was stopped by another intrusive thought.

A baby was screaming, and then I saw it with blue lips, dead in a pool of water. I tried to shake it away, and when I looked, I saw a woman in a window. Was the thought I had hers? The nearest door to the house was closed, so I went down the alley behind to the back door and though it, too, was locked, the latch was so worn and flimsy that I was able to push my way in.

I found her in the midst of cruelty: a woman with the body of a newborn in her hands, plunged into a water basin. I shouted, and the woman turned, surprised, but unaffected.

"Get off," I said.

I expected the woman to show some response to my presence beyond a mundane glance. Instead, the woman did as I said and took her hands from the child. Why was she so obedient? Did the Demon Eyes have an influence on others that I was unaware of?

I came upon her at once, striking the pin through her neck.

"You don't understand . . ." she started, but I killed her before she could finish. I let her fall upon the floor, struggling for breath until the sounds of her thrashing gradually subdued.

I went to the basin to retrieve the child. I saw the limbs extended over the edge, pink and new.

Please, I thought.

My heart beat faster. I wanted the baby to live.

When I pulled the head out from the water, the body was already lifeless. The most terrible sight was that of the dead child. I took it in my arms and embraced the body, though clammy and slack. It almost felt to me like the wheat husk-filled dolls I played with as a girl. As the water dried from its head, I could still smell the unmistakable sour-sweetness of milk. I rose, looked about the room to find a basket settled on the one bed in the room. Inside it was a quilted blanket and a linen cover, so I put the baby there and wrapped the blanket gently around its shoulders.

The baby seemed scarcely different from the China dolls that graced the toy shop windows in the richer parts of the Piazza di San Marco. I placed my hands on the baby's soft head and whispered the *Kel Maleh Rechamim,* the prayer for the soul of the departed. When I finished, I took my hands from the child and turned to leave.

It was then that I noticed the familiarity of the room. It was much like my own. An apartment meant for one, shared by what was a small family. There was one center room and then two wardrobes on either side of the bed. There was one shuttered window and the stream of daylight that cut through the gap in the shutter. Set on the adjacent wall was a wash vanity with the missing basin. There were two tables. On one table, there was a delicate porcelain bowl decorated with entwining ivy. It held ripe pomegranates. The other desk held a stack of books. I went to it, skimming the embossed titles. On the table were a pencil and an open book, and on the inside cover was a message, written in slanted and erratic writing:

I'm sorry. I'm sorry. I can't do it anymore. I'm nothing. I can't take care of anything. It's too much. I'm tired. I've never been so tired. All I want is to sleep and all he does is cry and scream. He nurses but spits it all up. He doesn't want me. I wished you would be here more to help. I am not myself anymore. I used to be someone. I remember being someone. Now nobody wants me. Not you. Not the baby. We're both going somewhere better.

I stared at the words. I had seen the discarded babies from mothers who didn't want them or couldn't take care of them. A deep melancholy must overtake these women. A melancholic and inescapable loneliness. How long had she been here, alone? Where had her husband been? If she had one. Why did no one care that she was falling so quickly into despair? I moved her hand to close the book, but let it linger in the air, deciding it was best to leave it. Someone would find her and read it. She was dead already, relieved of her suffering. The baby was gone.

I left. That was a woman whose blood I did not want to consume. I did not want her soul absorbed into mine, but I kept the door open so that the bodies would be found and buried, not left to rot. As I walked, the Demon Eyes faded. The world was no longer as bright and scenic, but the intrusive and despicable thoughts disappeared. I felt weak, as if all the blood had been drained from my veins.

What had happened was too much for one night, so I exited the house and entered the alley to walk home along the Fondamenta Ognisanti. On the canal was a small rowboat passing, and inside was a man rowing past. In the second seat was a crate of blood oranges. I caught the scent of them as he passed. The pungent citrus cleared my head. I stood there for a moment to savor the smell, allowing it to overtake the senselessness that had been saturating within my skull. My body began to wobble from the after-effects of shock and fatigue, and so I sat with my legs hanging over the canal waters.

When I placed my fingers on the cool head of the pin, I noticed that the face in the portrait seemed to look away from me, to some undetermined horizon.

"I am never sure," I said. "There are always doubts."

Azazel's hands were on my shoulders. At his touch, I was calm.

"Doubts are for humans," he said.

I chuckled.

"And I am not human?" I said.

"Precisely," he said as he slid one hand down my arm gently. "So why concern yourself with them?"

"Because I would like to think I still have a conscience."

After all I had done, those doubts remained. The other soul whispered to me, placating me with unease.

"After killing the mother, I was not sure if my killing had done any good. The baby is still dead." I tapped my finger against the pin. "Why had she allowed me to kill her so easily?"

"The Demon Eyes have more than one use," Azazel said.

I considered how willing the woman had been to my commands.

"I can make people do as I want."

"Not precisely, no. They make you more persuasive. Think about Eve and *Nachash*. He did not force her to go against her will but allowed her to accept it. You will find that you could do the same."

"Killing her gave her peace. She had wanted to die and to join her child in a better place free of suffering."

"And you gave her that peace."

"Yes," I murmured. Speaking my mind assuaged my doubts.

CHAPTER ELEVEN

I woke early in the day with a headache. The events from the night before had left me exhausted. Since it was my one day off a week, I was keen to lie slovenly in bed. Still, I could not. I needed blood. The candle flame was dimming. I also needed to find Faustina Zampieri's father. There was so much I had to do, and I felt time was slipping from me. I was not thinking properly on the night I had the Demon Eyes. They were enrapturing. When I sat up, my head continued to throb as if my brain were pressing against the inside of my skull, trying to escape. The crying and whining babies did not make it any better. My vision was blurry with brightly colored specks that appeared wherever I looked. Before I could do anything else, I needed blood. I still wore the yellow dress. Though I smelled musky, I was presentable enough to go outside, so I left the orphanage, paying half-attention to all that occurred. Maria-Giulia would talk about her days, and all I heard were muffled murmurings amidst the cries and laughs of babies.

It was an overcast day, which made the light easier on my eyes. In my search for an animal, I admonished myself for not taking the woman's blood from the night before, but I did not want her soul to taint mine. With the way I was feeling, though, my moral scruples seemed a weakness, and I should have taken what was offered to me. I would have to try to ease the headache by using animal blood. I settled with purchasing a small live fish from the Rialto market and going to the *campanile* at the abandoned church. After absorbing the blood, I felt more at ease.

The *polizia* officer had told me about the murder before. Perhaps he could tell me more. As soon as I finished for the day, I went to the office headquarters just as they were opening after siesta. There were already a few people in front of me, so when the door was unlocked, they went in quickly, and I went with them. Once inside, I scanned the room and found no sight of the officer, so I went to the front as I was impatient. The woman inquiring at the desk scolded me. I ignored her and asked the man where I could find the other officer. He asked me to specify, and I realized that I could not recall his name at first. I closed my eyes to think and said, "De'Angelo."

"Oh, I know him," he said. "He's infamous nowadays."

If he knew him so well, perhaps he had the power to help me more than I knew. Perhaps I had misjudged his persona, and he was more respected than I thought. The front desk clerk's sudden laughter told me otherwise.

"That drunkard lost a key and his job," he said. I felt my face fall. The key. The key that I stole from him to search the files. "I'm surprised he lasted as long as he had. Mistake after mistake for him. Ah, for old *polizia* like him they like to wait for them to retire. The key was a reason to get rid of him."

The young man looked at me. "I hear he's a bum now, living somewhere around the Accademia." He waved a hand dismissively. "You might find him there if you get out of here."

All this misery over a key. Why get rid of someone over a missing key, of all things? It seemed trifling.

I thanked the man and left. When I was outside, I kicked the ground with my heel.

Why is it that all the men I need to find disappear?

"Like chasing ghosts," I mumbled.

I could not waste my time complaining. I walked over bridges and stolled by afternoon tourists to the Gallerie dell'Accademia. Then, I walked down the Rio Terra Foscarini, atop the cobble stones, glancing at the portions of the exterior walls of the Accademia where the pastel plaster peeled to reveal the red brick underneath. Poplar treetops peeked over walls from within a walled courtyard, and shrubs spilled over the brick walls or window banisters.

There were small shops designed to attract tourists with postcards and souvenirs, and other small cafes with chairs and wide umbrellas set outside the entrance. At one of the tables by a canal there were three tourists drinking and laughing together. One of them, an older woman, took pictures of her friends and the surrounding scene with a portable camera. Just next to the cafe was a sign for a hotel. I searched around the area, then decided to turn around and try another street, which is when I found a narrow alley down the Calle Larga Pisani, which had few people.

There were homes here, some of them with windows boarded or barred. Overhead were streetlights, one of which had a sparrow resting, calling out to the sky before flying away. On another, I saw Azazel balancing on the iron bar and then jumping to the roof of the opposite building. When I looked back to the alley, I saw a man. A beggar man with a beard and a recognizable face. It was the *polizia* officer, de'Angelo. My heartbeat pumped frantically, and I inhaled slowly to attempt to calm it.

He had a hat upon the ground and asked for money from people who passed. Some stopped to toss a *lira* coin; others ignored him and continued on their journey. I approached him and relinquished one of my lesser value coins.

"Don't I know you?" the man asked.

"Yes, yes. I do. We drank together."

"Oh, yes. Wild night that was. Don't remember much from it. I must have had one too many."

"It happens to the best of us." I looked at him, at his state. "But what happened to you?"

He waved a hand in the air.

"Ah, a bit of bad luck. I lost a key. A key! And for that, they throw me in the alley. Fifteen years and I get the boot for losing a bit of metal. I thought if I were ever to be pushed out it would be for something serious."

"Have you no one to care for you?"

He opened his arms wide, as if to gesture at the obvious.

"If I did, would I be here? I have no parents and no wife. A pure bachelor, am I."

"Will the church not help you?" I asked.

In answer, he lowered his chin and lifted his eyebrows.

"They helped me for a day and a night. Men, I'm afraid, are not given much space when there are children and mothers who need it. The *exceptionally* cheerful nun told me that men were often the bearers of alcoholism and violence, and it was better for the women and babies to have no men about." He groaned and stood for a moment. "I can't fault their observations."

The man then walked a few paces, faced the wall, and pulled open the front of his trousers. I turned my head away but heard the unmistakable sound and sour smell of his urine spilling against the stone wall.

"Apologies, *signora*, but without the public toilet I must do it here. I hope I don't offend," he laughed.

"It would take more than piss to offend me," I said. "I just cannot stand the smell."

He laughed as I heard him re-clasp his trousers.

"Could I ask you to buy me a drink?"

I preferred to avoid any more pubs.

"I hope you mean *caffè*."

"Ah, I was thinking of something stronger."

I glowered at the man who wore what seemed to be his only set of clothes: a wool suit and leather shoes that he had clearly been sleeping in gave him an unwashed smell. He had the smell of the alley and canal on him as well. His face had the hair growth of a month of being left unshaved. Guilt made me want to help him. Guilt, and the hopes that the offer of a drink would make him more pliable to my needs.

"I'll take you to a cafe," I reiterated.

He nodded in acquiescence.

"The Caffé Florian." he said, to which my response was a grimace. The place was expensive. "If I'm only going to have that, it'll have to be the best."

I did not care to spend so much of my money on a cup of coffee. Still, I needed his help, so I agreed. He smiled and took his hat from the ground, making sure to pluck the coins from within and shove them in his pocket.

He walked ahead of me with the same pomp and assurance as he had when I first met him.

The cafe was sparsely populated with people sitting outside. I stepped onto the diamond mosaic walkway, waiting behind two ladies who were trying their best to speak Italian, which was clearly not their first language. They were polite when they spoke to the attendant, a pleasant looking middle-aged man who wore a crisp black suit and white shirt complete with a black tie. One of the ladies had what appeared to be an Italian language dictionary and referenced it when she became flustered; then she would giggle and try to use a different word. A waft of air came from within. The aroma of sweet bread, frosting, fresh coffee, rolled over the air and made me salivate. The ladies were ushered in and given a table.

The attendant looked at de'Angelo.

"I'm sorry," he said, "but there is a dress code here."

"Dress code. Ha!" de'Angelo said. "Do you not recognize me?"

"Should I?"

"De'Angelo, *polizia*."

"As was," the attendant said.

I stifled a smile.

"And where were the *polizia* six months ago when our register was robbed?"

De'Angelo's face fell.

"*Se tu volessi*," I said. "We could sit somewhere in a corner."

The attendant softened at my suggestion.

"Very well, but he has to behave."

The attendant turned to show us in, and a waiter emerged to guide us to our table. The cafe's opulence was disheartening. It meant that whatever price I was about to pay for the meal would be exponentially expensive. And yet, at seeing the richness, excitement overcame me. The finely dressed ladies sipped from gold accented cups, then sliced a fruit crostata with a gilded knife and dessert fork. I imagined myself sitting amongst them, sharing in the luxuriance that I was hardly afforded. We followed the waiter to *la sala cinese*, the Oriental room, and to a curved corner under a Pascutti painting of a man and a woman embracing. Their table was a cool white marble, just large enough to hold two servings of a small meal. I looked up to see the gold embellished mosaic ceiling. The candle lights danced in their reflection, and I could almost see myself in the flames.

The waiter read us the list of the day's menu in a heightened Venezian accent that made me suspicious of its authenticity. De'Angelo ordered a macchiato and, "The sweetest cake you have," while I kept to a lavender tea and pastry.

In the seat across from us sat a single man in a fine suit. Before him on the table was a porcelain cup painted with the images of peacocks, accented with gold and silver. It sat on a saucer where he rested his forefinger as if in preparation of slipping it through the curved handle. He glanced over at me, green eyes upturned from behind the daily newspaper. He smiled. It was an expression of sincerity as I noted no malice or expectations behind it. It was not the kind of smile I had seen cavalier men use with their salacious eyes to wordlessly express the expectation of reciprocation. This stranger, on the other hand, showed a most simple display of courtesy. I smiled back at him. As he lifted his cup to drink and returned his gaze to the newspaper, I realized that de'Angelo had been speaking to me, and I removed my focus from the green-eyed man. Hearing him speak made me wish I were sitting with someone else, or even alone, but I had to find out what he knew.

"—now, finding the best clay for making a vase all depends on where you get it from. The clay from Napoli, for example, has bits of ash, which can give a different sort of look."

"You make vases?" I asked, not hiding my surprise.

"Haven't you been listening? Ah, young peoples' minds always wander. Yes, when I had money and a home."

If he had not been a drunk, he would not have been so easy to fool, I thought. Still, I felt some guilt over the destitution he found himself in. I tried to dismiss it. What did it matter if he lost his job? It was for the better. One less to worry about. And a drunk as well. And yet, he had tried to help me as much as he could. Without him, and his drunkenness, I would not have gotten as far as I had. In some ways, I was indebted to him. Surely a small meal was worth that, and I could be rid of him.

"Now what do I do? I'm just like the Romani begging for coins and scraps. A few more days and I'll be rummaging through the bins, too."

"Any man could find work at the docks," I said, repeating a memory that I was not sure was mine.

"I'm not one for fishing," he said, haphazardly cutting through the cake with a fork and placing it in his open mouth. He swallowed, resting his wrist on the corner of the table, the fork pointing upwards, and with his other hand, sipped from his cup. "It's a poor man's job."

"And how many coins do you have in your pocket?"

De'Angelo laughed.

"True. But once you've got the stench of fish on you, it never washes off." He grimaced. "I had the unfortunate luck of having an uncle who was a fishmonger. Whenever he visited, all I could smell was fish. It stuck to him no matter how often he bathed. And now there's my nephew all grown up, spending his better days elbow-deep in fish guts. No. I won't do that."

I tightened my lips. When I had been destitute, I had thanked any opportunity that came to me that would lift me from my street life. I thought of the prostitutes that peddled their skins.

"There are worse things than fish," I said. "You should know, being *polizia*."

"Not for a man." He gathered another piece of cake onto his fork and ate.

"Surely one such as yourself has a friend or two who owes

you a favor," I suggested. *Polizia* had influence, a necessity of their position. I was surprised that he had none.

At the suggestion, he shrugged.

"I thought *polizia* had friends everywhere," I said.

At that he looked sidelong at me.

"Not friends in the kind way. Friends who give you a favor for leniency, and when you need something, they're nowhere to be found."

"Maybe no one liked you."

"Aren't you a charm today? No. I was not well-liked. If I were, I'd still be in that office," he sighed. "I was the old bastard that they needed an excuse to get rid of."

"I'm sure that's not true," I said flatly as I brought my teacup to my lips.

"You don't know them. It's changed. Yes, there was always scum and back dealings; that was the way things were, but now, there's no honor in it. No matter what, *polizia* stayed together. Not now," he scoffed. "A missing key." He finished his cake in two quick successions of bites. "The things I know about them could get them all under a scandal."

I looked around when he said it and noticed a lady turning in my direction, one with distinct freckles on her cheeks and bright blonde hair gathered up into a twisted bun.

"Maybe you should keep your voice down," I said. "This is a nice place."

De'Angelo rolled his eyes.

"I don't care who hears me. What's the worst they can do?"

I put my cup down.

"Kill you?" I asked.

De'Angelo laughed.

"From where I am, that's an improvement."

Maybe I should have killed him, I mused.

"What do you know that would cause a scandal?" I asked.

"Do you have a cigarette?"

I drew back.

"Never."

De'Angelo turned to the blonde lady and asked her, to which she smiled and took one from the velvet green handbag that sat beneath her seat. She even helped light it for him. The man sat back upright, and he took the cigarette out of his mouth so he could finish his macchiato.

"I know enough about who pays who."

I parted my lips to ask, but stopped, and instead placed the edge of the cup to my mouth to drink. I wanted to make sure our conversation was hidden where there were sober listeners.

De'Angelo leaned back to look at me. He tipped his chin up and raised his eyebrows.

"Well?"

"What?"

"You want to know more about that Drowned Jewess," he said. "Few people are kind without wanting something in return."

I gripped my teacup.

"Yes," I admitted. "I thought you could help me."

"And what do you want to know?"

He pursed his lips.

"Where to find Faustina Zampieri's father."

De'Angelo laughed.

"Now that's not what I expected you to say." He drank from his cup and pestered the waiter for a refill.

"Why do you need me for that? Anyone on the street can tell you where he lives."

"Where he *lives*, maybe, but I need to *speak* with him. Do you think he would stop to speak with a stranger like me?"

"If you were wealthy, he might."

The waiter returned with a new cup of macchiato and

removed the dirty one. De'Angelo rested his hands on his thighs.

"There are things I know," he said. "You have money."

I set my eyes on him and felt the weight of Azazel's hands on my shoulders. *You cannot serve God and Mammon,* I thought as I watched the Catholic devotees deposit their coins and the eagerness to which the priests gathered them. I saw it in the gilded statues and trappings within the basilica. All the riches and the corruption from it made me bitter. How guilty was I of the same? I was using money to enact Heaven's will. In their own twisted way, they too were passing coins to better spread their holy word. We were like magpies enamored with a shiny object, jealous to keep it for ourselves. What little money I did have, I saved as much as I could. I had to pay rent. I had to eat. What more could I give?

"I have just a little money," I said.

"You have more than I," he said, gesturing at his clothes. "And I have no more friends to ask."

I considered that. What little I could spare could help me all the more.

"Go to your nephew, the fishmonger, and try to live honestly."

He laughed from his belly.

"If he would take me," he said, waving his hand in the air as if shooing away a fly. I felt for him. I knew what it was to be alone.

"Ah," he said, and flapped his fingers towards his palm. He wanted money.

"I have paid for your meal."

"That was courtesy; this is business."

I sighed. This jaunt into the cafe was already expensive. If I spent more, I would have nothing to eat but rummaged bread for the next month. I also did not want to miss an opportunity. I took a *lira* from my pocket and gave it to him. It was not much, but it made him grin. He took it immediately and concealed it in his vest pocket.

"Ludovico Zampieri is one of the many wealthy men who still have a raucous Carnevale party after Lent."

"Why? Where?" I asked.

He raised his eyebrows. "Any more *lire* in that pocket?"

I grimaced. I needed to keep at least some money.

"Well, then when you have more to spare, come and find me. Unless," he started, "I don't suppose you have a bed to spare?"

I eyed him sharply.

"No."

"Then we will talk another time," he said. "You can find me in the same place, and I will tell you what I know."

I thanked him and I left the cafe. I wanted to know more of what de'Angelo could tell me, but I would not be paid until the next month. If I could steal, where would I do it?

When I entered the simple home where I lived, I closed the door behind me and took note of its poverty. The minimalism gave me pause. I needed very little to survive. Since I woke to my rebirth, I fixated on my singular goal, considering any comfort as unnecessary. Seeing my decrepit bed, colorless, little more than a shadow under the window, I noticed my small table had a bag filled with old bread as sustenance. I walked to the table and saw two flies that sat on the crust of the topmost bread roll that I left on the table. The flies buzzed away when I waved my hand over the top. Seeing the bread made me queasy, so I took it in hand, and when I opened the window, released it to the alley below.

I kept the window open and gazed out, allowing my mind a moment to think.

All the wealthy celebrated Carnevale. Father had told me

that it used to be a festival throughout the city until Francis II forbade it. Only in the past few decades did some people partake in festivities, usually the richer Venezians, and some citizens, who wanted the freedom of anonymity and debauchery. Carnevale was after Lent. If that was where I could find Zampieri, I would have a few months to prepare.

CHAPTER TWELVE

At the request of Maria-Elena, I rushed out to the market to buy something more delicious than old bread. The air became colder, much too cold to be able to wear the short jacket I had. I would have to purchase or find a winter jacket soon. I bought brioches and headed back, holding the bag close to me so that the warmth from the freshly baked goods shielded me from the cold.

An orange cat walked towards me, hugging the wall, curling its tail as it touched the stones. When Azazel knelt to pet it, it raised its head to meet his hand and purred as he stroked its chin.

"Do cats sin?" I asked.

"They have souls, don't they?"

I recalled the animals whose souls I had consumed, the visions I had of their lives at times nonsensical, observatory, and vibrant. Azazel flicked his eyes at me, condescension spread across his face.

"Don't mistake your morality as superior."

The cat, growing bored with Azazel, passed around him

and continued, stopping once to spray its scent on a wall corner.

"I do not," I said.

When I returned to the orphanage, Maria-Elena was dressed, and held a satchel in her hand. Irina was in her school clothes as she played hide-and-seek with Giorgio.

"Ah, you're here. Come, Irina will watch the children today until Maria-Giulia arrives. We have a job."

Maria-Elena held Beni and passed the child to Irina, who took him but grimaced in the process.

"I'll never get to school on time," she mumbled.

"Such complaints!" Maria-Elena said. "Maria-Giulia will be here shortly."

I followed Maria-Elena inside.

"Oh, such a girl," Maria-Elena said. "She should be happy to have a roof and food, as you well know."

"She is still young," I offered. "She doesn't know how cruel the world can be."

"Too true," Maria-Elena said. "Even as a baby, she paid no attention to the dangers around her. She would walk into the brazier if I weren't there to stop her, or jump into the canal to better admire the waves. She has no caution, so I must do it for her." Maria-Elena sighed.

When I looked at the woman, I saw the same expression that my own mother would make when speaking about her children.

"How did she come to be in your care?" I asked.

"Ah." Maria-Elena crossed her arms in front of her chest. "Her mother came to me directly, which they sometimes do." She turned the corner, stepping on a puddle, splashing droplets against the column. "She had five children already. Came to me with a one-year-old still reaching for the milk at her breast. She had tried taking some purgative tea, but the baby kept growing.

Never a more desperate woman. They were already in poverty. Her husband was a fisherman, and she took on washing work at her house and still, it was barely enough for them. It is always the mother that makes these hard choices. It would be better for all women for men to keep their trousers buttoned."

I chuckled.

Maria-Elena touched my shoulder. "I think that is the first I've heard you laugh," she said. "It doesn't sound at all like I imagined. It suits you." Maria-Elena folded her arms again, sighing. "Thinking about Irina makes me so sensitive. And so, I agreed to take the baby, and I promised I would give her the best life I could manage."

"Her mother is still alive?"

"Yes, though do not tell Irina. It's better she does not know her."

I was unconvinced but would not say so to my benefactor.

"Ah, I should compensate her for helping so much," she murmured. "She always wants to go out . . . you could take her out for some fun," she said. "–tasteful fun," she added. "Are you busy on Sunday? I can pay you some extra *lire*."

The promise of additional money piqued my interest. It meant I could convince de'Angelo to tell me more about Ludovico Zampieri. I pushed the thought away to focus on my conversation with Maria-Elena.

"I can chaperone her," I said.

"Bene," she said. "I will tell her when we get back. Ah, here," Maria-Elena said, and hurried on.

I followed her to The Ospedale Civile, the public hospital. I had been there a few times before in my youth. Once, when I had sprained my arm from trying to climb up the side of our house to reach a bird's nest, and then a few times when Mother was having sensitivities to her pregnancy or when Grandmother and baby Levi were ill with *L'influeza Spagnola*. The hospital was a grand white marble stone building that seemed to me to look like a church. So many buildings were constructed to appear as churches that it was difficult to separate which was a building meant for worship and which was meant to heal. Perhaps it was all the same. A hospital was a place of healing, and as I understood it, so was a church. One sought to heal the body and the other the soul.

We went inside to the front counter. Maria-Elena gave her name and was told where to go. We walked together, quietly, shoe soles tapping against the orange and white diamond tiles. I remembered walking on the same tiles here, running back and forth around the columns, or hopping up the steps in the corridors as we waited to hear news about grandmother or the baby. Neither Father nor Mother wanted me there at the time. The *influenza* was spreading rapidly, and they feared that I would catch it if I went outside the house and the ghetto, even when I wore the cloth mask. Being so young, I did not share the same fear as they did, and I wanted to hear it with my own ears whether Grandmother and baby Levi were dead or alive. I also needed to know my mother was still well. With the baby so young, the mother had to be in the room with him, and it was very possible that she could become sick. The unease that I felt at the time returned as I walked with Maria-Elena.

Remembering my grandmother's death, my brother's death, made me solemn. We were barely able to mourn. There was no *shiva* except within our own family. The *taharah* was done at the synagogue, closed from anyone except us from attending. We wailed, we tore our clothing, we mourned within our family, but not as a community. We were alone in our sorrow. It was not unlike the next year that we bereaved properly when the threat of the contagion subsided.

"Is something on your mind?" Maria-Elena asked.

"The last time I was here was because of *l'influenza*," I shared.

"Mm. Many died then. I lost three of my babies and the woman who used to help. Terrible."

"Four people?" I asked. I had been upset by two in my family dying. To have lost four people was unimaginable. It helped me understand how protective she was of Irina and of the other children.

"Yes. Pietro was six and was excited to go to Scuola dell'Infanzia, Helene was four and just started trying to write her name, Nicola was about seven months old, and she babbled so much." Maria-Elena shook her head. "And then Ursula . . ."

"A different Ursula?" I asked, thinking about one of the twins.

"Yes. I named the baby after her."

We turned a corner and went down a flight of stairs.

"She had been with us for . . . I think eight years. She was in her temporary profession of becoming a nun. Part of her duty to the community was to help those who needed it the most. My orphanage is part of the church, so I often had nuns come and help when they were so inclined. But Ursula had a passion for helping children. She was a joy, such a joy."

Maria-Elena came to a green door and knocked on it. The door opened, and a nun was on the other side. She was distinguishable by a prominent mole in the middle of her cheek. When she saw Maria-Elena, she hugged her. The nun then looked at me and smiled. She led us to a room in which there was a baby sleeping in a sparse crib.

"Thank you for coming. By His grace, we had this one come in the night in the *ruota dei trovatelli*. The blood was still on her."

I thought of my mother and my many siblings, all of them welcomed, as far as I knew. My mother treated every pregnancy, every new child as an excitement, as a hope. I thought of the visions of pregnancy that I had, either of my own or of the other soul. I thought of the dead Antonia.

Inside the room were several cribs, some empty, but one or two which had sleeping babies in them.

"These ones are going to be taken in by another orphanage in *Treviso*. But, this baby, I thought, might do better with you."

In one of the cribs was the newborn wrapped in knitted wool and head covered with a white cap, though a few ruddy curls stuck out from underneath.

"I will try to help, but we already have another newborn at the orphanage and Irina—"

"Irina is still with you? Is she not old enough to begin work?"

"She is still young," Maria-Elena answered.

I touched the baby's cheek with a gentle finger, overcome with maternal sentiment. Maria-Elena picked her up. The baby wriggled a little, opened her eyes to look up, and then closed them again. The baby cooed.

"Why would she abandon you?" Maria-Elena murmured.

"Some women find that they cannot care for their children," I said.

"When you are a mother, there is no choice," she answered.

I might have said my thoughts aloud were it not for the faces on Maria-Elena and the nun. Pious, judgmental faces, aimed at the invisible image of the mother who abandoned the copper-haired child. Those were the expressions of people who had settled their minds; no contrary suggestion would sway them.

Maria-Elena brushed a coil of hair from the baby's forehead, and as she did, I saw her press her lips together as if abstaining from a smile.

"I do not know if I could take her," Maria-Elena said.

"Are you sure?"

Maria-Elena straightened her back and handed the baby to the other nun. The baby cried while reaching her arms up to grasp onto Maria-Elena's sleeve. The nun held the baby close and patted her chest gently in an effort to calm the crying child.

"With six children in the house, four of them still on milk, and so few to help, I do not think it is possible."

"You will get the stipend for her as well."

"And what about the help? How many sisters are left now, after *l'influenza*? Are there any sisters or acolytes who will devote themselves to such children?"

"God willing."

"Amen," Maria-Elena said.

The two said no more to each other and we left. She walked quickly, and I had to speed up my pace.

"There is another stop," Maria-Elena said. "Giorgio has been coughing at night."

We walked together to a *farmacia* somewhat near the ghetto. I did not want to go in. This could be the same shop where Agostino Vianello worked. I barely knew the man who I had met by the brothel, so I could not trust what he may say to Maria-Elena. Before the door was a great black dog that lifted its head as I approached. Although its size was intimidating, its eyes were wide and welcoming. I held out a hand and let him sniff it. He licked it with a thick, wet tongue, leaving my fingers covered with saliva, and I smiled.

Maria-Elena opened the door, and I followed her in.

Once my feet settled against the marble tiles, I realized that I had been here before. I saw myself speaking to a man, asking him for a remedy, and then leaving. The emotions that came from the memory overwhelmed me, and I excused myself. Staying outside next to the dog, I breathed, trying to make sense of the intensity that inundated my mind.

"Strange place," Azazel said.

I shook my head. As I stared up to the sky, in my peripherals I saw Azazel turn his head to look through the window.

"Hm," he mumbled.

The door opened.

"No need to worry," Agostino said.

I glanced at him briefly. He walked closer toward me so that he could touch my hand, but I pulled away. He sighed and then held up a thin vial, removing the top. I could smell the ammonia.

"You looked like you might faint," he said. "I thought some of this would help."

He closed the top and handed the vial to me, and I took it.

"Something stronger would have been better," Azazel murmured.

"I said nothing about that day," Agostino said in a whisper.

"Thank you," I said, feeling a pang of guilt that I had mistrusted him at first.

The man nodded.

"Are you alright?" Maria-Elena asked.

I pushed the thoughts away.

"Just tired," I said.

"How can someone so young be tired?" she asked. "Come along."

Agostino waved goodbye as I followed Maria-Elena. At the beginning of the street leading to the orphanage, Maria-Elena stopped.

"I have other things to do," she said, patting her satchel. "Paperwork for Antonio. I will be back late. The civil services move quicker for affairs of the church, but they are still ruled by their stomachs. I may be stuck there until after siesta."

I returned to the orphanage to clean. I had to pretend it was normal, my life. I cleaned the house from the messes that all children make when they are young and helped feed the small babies when the nurse maid was too busy with the ones she had at her breasts. I found that being busy was the easiest way to rid my mind of troubles. Seeing the babies smile when they had their fill of milk made me as happy as they were, but it was a fleeting happiness.

I am sorry for the world you were born into, I thought. *It is a world of suffering and sorrow.*

Despite my dark thoughts, the baby cooed and smiled. I think I must have been like him once. I remember it being so. I saw the joy, the lightness, the beauty in everything. If the streets and alleys were flooded, I would build a paper boat to float upon the surface and chase it to where it led me. I found adventure in the mundane and inconvenient. So vivid was the memory that even though it seemed impossible that I had been that girl, I could not deny her existence.

I was too tired to find another soul, much as I craved it. At home, I was restless, and I felt the beginnings of a headache at my temples, but I could not sleep. I could not think. Making a fire helped me focus on something other than myself, if for a moment.

I sat on the floor and set about making a fire. With the embers burning, I placed more coal upon the flames and closed the shutters to trap the heat. I sat before it, letting the heat permeate the surface, but it felt it went no deeper than that. I took a blanket and wrapped it around my head and body. What caused me to cry then, I was not sure. Was it the drowned baby, was it everything, or something else? What I knew was that I felt a great fatigue, and I wanted this to end. To find who killed me and rid him from the world. I wanted to sleep and disappear. And even as I felt this, there was also the stronger impulse to continue. How could I keep going like this? I did not want to kill other people except the one man. And yet, I was compelled to. Why was I brought back? I kept returning to this thought. Why was I given that choice? Azazel proposed that it was HaShem. How could it not be? It is through HaShem that all things exist. It must be. Still, I grappled with one question: "Why?" Was it the other soul in me that filled me with doubt? That soul which was shielded from such suffering.

I would have to trust in HaShem even when I could not trust myself.

That dead child re-emerged. I saw its body floating in the water basin.

Was it better for the child to die than to be raised without love? The erratic writing from the mother, so like mine, made me wonder if I would have done the same. In my darkest moments, would I release the child from a life of suffering? Would I kill a child? I wanted to say that I would not and yet, I have killed men. I had crossed the threshold of death. I had killed a man. Is it much of a stretch to turn from killing a man to killing a child? I hoped not.

I thought of Abraham who set his son upon a stone intent to sacrifice him to HaShem.

"What happens to the souls?" I asked the air, knowing that Azazel was with me.

"I can't tell you any more than you already know. You were there, in the everlasting forest and the desert between. By ridding these horrors from the streets, at least we'll make the good live better lives while they're here. And I can find some peace hereabouts without seeing the worst of desires intrude upon my thoughts."

"It may yet be an impossible task. Where one is gone, another is born to grow into some twisted sinner."

"True. Man never ceases wickedness. Still, we can dullen it, if only for a time. But only think how it would be to be immortal and be a judge among these people."

I groaned.

"That again," I said. "Do you intend to nag me into compliance?"

I took out the papers and notes I had on my death. I brought them to the table and spread them out, including one of the more important, the brief transcriptions of the dead Faustina's files.

With these were my own fragmented memories of the events before my death, the newspaper report of my discovered body, even the police report that I also transcribed.

Even if I find him. What if he isn't here?

"That is too somber a task," I said.

I sat in the quiet and waited, listening inside my mind, reaching towards whatever soul inhabited there. There was silence. In that silence was an inkling and nothing more. My fingertips ignited that familiar poison that bubbled to the surface of my skin. It infused every part of me so that I was unable to silence my mind of the images running through the back of my eyes and the intense strain of my heart trying to escape my breast.

I whispered Ephraim's name as I felt myself rise and become relieved of the pressure inside me. I saw her face before me with her long hair strewn about her shoulders. It disappeared when my muscles relaxed, and I felt the heat leave me for the briefest moment. In that moment, I experienced a silent liberation. The downfall came quickly when I felt the aching return to my body, returning to the cycle that was so impossible for me to stop.

The silence, the momentary calm, washed over me. In those moments, the world ceased to exist. It was like a living death, and the only freedom that I would feel, trapped inside this toxic body. I endured the recognizable throbbing that spanned my entire body, aching for release. The only recompense was the deafening silence in the resolution; the briefest minutes of calm.

Everything around me was sullied by the pulsating cravings in my blood, as if my bones would erupt from my skin. I let out a deep exhale, allowing the numbness to take over my body for the fleeting moments that it would bring. When it passed and returned with the everlasting throbbing, I curled into a ball on the bed and bit the palm of my hand until it stung and became white between my teeth. My eyes watered with the stinging pinch of my teeth boring into my skin. A wave of heat cauterized my gaping sores.

CHAPTER THIRTEEN

I woke that Sunday to find Irina already up and dressed in an outfit I had not seen her wear before and what I assumed could be her dress reserved for Mass. It was the nicest dress she owned: a periwinkle dress with softened lace on the sleeves and collar, worn down from use. Other than the lace, the dress was plain. When she wore it, she took on a vibrancy that did not occur in her everyday dress and apron that was often covered in spots of baby spit-up or food particles or coal soot. She had only one pair of boots, and she wore those. She had nothing to adorn her hair, but it was washed and brushed finely, gathered up into a simple coif. Standing in the frame, Irina looked like a girl on the cusp of womanhood, eager to jump from the step headlong into the life of a woman. She had curled her hair and had a rose-colored hat settled on her head, complete with a cameo pin.

"You're up!" she said to me and hopped a little from unrestrained excitement.

"Is that Aviva?" came Maria-Elena's voice from another room, calling over the whimpers and cries of babies.

"Yes," Irina responded.

Maria-Elena came to the door holding Umberto and feeding him a bottle. She had a white cloth draped over her left shoulder that Umberto pulled down with his foot, which caused Maria-Elena to emit a sharp exhale as she let go of the bottle for a moment to adjust it. Giorgio, as usual, followed her closely. He tugged at her rosary, whining to be picked up.

"Basta!" Maria-Elena said sternly, which made Giorgio scream.

I picked him up to calm him down. The poor boy always wanted more love than any one of us could give him. He gripped me tightly. I felt a wet bit of snot wipe against my skin, and I wiped it off with a grimace.

"Before you go, here," she said. With her free hand, she shoved it into her pocket and withdrew some *lire*. Before she handed it to Irina, she said, "Some for offering and some for fun."

We were about to leave, and yet when I turned to walk out the door, I spied a woman approaching. She was pushing an empty black *passeggino,* a pushchair for a baby, in front of her that bumped along on the cobblestones. I, holding onto Giorgio, stood and took a few paces outside the door to better see who it was. I stared at the woman with the raven black hair, sure that I had seen her before but was unable to place her. In her hurried steps, her hair bounced around her shoulders. She spotted me, waved, and called out, *"Salve!"*

Giorgio perked up and waved back at her. As she came closer, I recognized her immediately. It was Crina. The closer she came, the more I noticed how different she looked. She had dark circles under her eyes, but her lips were pulled into a smile.

"It is you!" she said when she came to the open door and gave me a welcoming kiss on the cheek. She smelled of floral perfume and *caffè*. "I saw you not long ago. If it weren't for the busy night, I would have been able to talk. But, oh, I am here, finally." Crina tapped Giorgio on the nose playfully, and he giggled. She then smiled and peeked through the open door. "Where is the baby?"

Hearing the commotion, Maria-Elena slipped past me and Irina. She handed the empty bottle that Umberto had finished to me and was holding him so that his head rested on her shoulder as she patted his back.

"May I help you?" Maria-Elena asked in a tone layered with confusion.

"You may! I have come for the baby, as I said I would."

Maria-Elena looked at me, puzzled.

"This is Crina," I said. "She has come for Antonio."

At the sound of his name, Crina's face brightened.

"Antonio? Such a beautiful way to remember his mother."

"I do apologize," Maria-Elena said calmly. "I think you have wasted your time coming here."

Crina's smile faded.

"With the baby here at the orphanage, I am his guardian since the passing of his mother, may she rest in peace."

"Oh," she said. She then bit the inside of her cheek as she looked down to her coat pocket and removed a folded slip of paper. She opened it up and handed it to Maria-Elena. In a glimpse, I saw what seemed to be a legal notice, signed and stamped. Giorgio wriggled in my arm, wanting to be let down, so I placed him down on the ground where he toddled around on the stones. There were cries from inside from the babies.

"Irina," Maria-Elena said. "Go take care of them for a moment."

"But—"

"Now."

Irina groaned but complied.

Maria-Elena kept staring at the paper.

"It is a notice of adoption rights, giving custody of the baby born of Antonia Furlan to me, Crina Bogdan."

Maria-Elena held the paper in front of her for some time. She grumbled and gave the paper back to Crina.

"What do you know about caring for a baby?" Maria-Elena said sharply. "He's much better here where he's being properly cared for."

"Listen—"

"Besides, how can a child be raised by a woman of your profession?"

"That is done," Crina said, waving her hand dismissively. "We . . . I worked there to save money for a worker's license, and now I have it. See ..." The woman opened her purse and removed a piece of paper. "I work at a *legatoria*."

"And while you are working, who will care for the baby?"

Crina raised her chin.

"My sister and I will take care of him."

"These children are meant for better things," Maria-Elena said.

"He is mine."

There was a short silence.

"Still," Maria-Elena said. "Can an unmarried woman raise a child?"

I stifled a scoff. Who was Maria-Elena but an unmarried woman raising several orphans?

"Let that be decided by God."

The woman tried to enter, but Maria-Elena did not move. They stood for a moment until Maria-Elena backed away, letting the woman inside. Her face changed. Her blue eyes became honey brown. I wanted to hug her, but I stopped. It was the dead soul who still felt fresh, emotional at the sight of her friend. I let her into the house, apologizing quickly for the smell and the noise.

"He is here," I said.

I guided the woman upstairs as Giorgio followed me, to where Antonio lay sleeping in a crib, the necklace wrapped around the post with the pendant facing outwards. Antonio slept on his stomach, with his drool-covered fist in his mouth. Then, I heard the door shut downstairs.

Crina stretched her hand over the barrier to touch his soft threads of black hair.

"Thank you," she whispered. She sniffed, and I noticed that she had a few tears rolling down her cheeks. As she wiped them, she said, "I did everything I could to get him back to me. *Everything.*"

Crina took the necklace and put it over her head, tucking the pendant into her blouse. She then picked up the boy gingerly, careful not to wake him. He uttered a small complaint and then nuzzled into her shoulder. Crina closed her eyes and smiled.

"It was worth it," she uttered.

A warmth came from deep within my belly. The remains of the mother's soul welled with happiness and relief at witnessing her child in the loving arms of her friend.

"I am glad he will be loved," I said.

"He will be loved and spoiled, all of his days," she said as she smiled.

Crina began walking downstairs, and I followed. Once at the bottom, there was Maria- Elena with a grimace on her face as she watched Crina take Antonio while she held Ursula and fed her with a bottle. Irina was tending to Beni. Maria-Elena watched and said nothing as Crina stepped down the hallway and out the door. I ushered Crina out the door and helped her to place Antonio in the *passeggino.*

Crina hugged me again and told me to visit her at her work, a book binding shop near the Galleria Dell'Accademia. I said that I would, and I watched as she walked away with Antonio, and I returned to the house.

"Why did that woman take Antonio?" Irina asked Maria-Elena. When Maria-Elena was silent, she asked me.

I thought how best I could explain it to her in a delicate way, since Maria-Elena was there. I knew Maria-Elena wanted to shelter Irina from lewdness, so I decided to tell her the simplest truth about it.

"That was his mother," I said.

"That's good news!" she said. "Well, could we go now?"

I looked to Maria-Elena, who nodded.

"Come," Irina said, shutting the door behind her. She thread her arm through mine, and led me down the alley towards San Marco's.

Along the way, I brushed against a man who was relieving himself against a wall. Irina giggled to see the man as we entered the square to the Basilica di San Marco. The outside was lit with candles on tall spires. As we approached the doors, a poor woman in front of me lifted her arms high and tilted her head upwards, murmuring prayers. Across the main facade were columns and lunettes illustrating the story of creation, the fall of Babel, the life and death of Christ. Above the main lunette was a golden Venezian winged lion standing in the background of a blue sky and golden stars. I looked up at the lunette and squinted to decipher the image that beckoned our entrance.

What I knew of their savior was overheard in my brother's musings, from Catholic friends and strangers on the streets. I knew him as a man, compassionate, but still a man. They saw him as a god incarnate, the sovereign of their faith, and the purger of sin.

The man must be Yeshua. Their savior. A beautiful man of long golden hair lit from behind by a burst of sun. His pale chest was bare, covered by a silky azure cloth that covered one shoulder, teasing to fall. One arm rose to the heavens, and the other cradled a wooden cross offered to him by an angel, and by that angel was the bearded, red-robed Saint Marco clutching his own crossed staff. At the savior's feet was his mother with a green veil covering her head and shoulders, her arms crossed before her chest and above her head, five figureheads piercing through the clouds. Another angel stared up in awe while holding his left foot. Surrounding him were billowy ochre clouds and angels at his side descended from heaven, one blowing a trumpet into the ears of the betrayers and the other heralding the faithful.

The congregants walked forward, around the main facade to a nondescript door on the side of the building. I stalled, and others pushed past me. Irina urged me forward, but however much I wanted to avoid entering that space, I knew that I also had a responsibility towards Irina and to Maria-Elena, and I resented that I was forced into this act. It seemed that they wanted to make me like them. I took a grave humor about it. I had seen what comes after death, and none of it resembled what was painted on the façade.

I did not believe in their god. What harm could there be in setting foot within their house?

"Not shy in delving into your spiritual perils?" Azazel asked.

I ignored him.

Irina and I were the last to enter. A plain man in a silken white robe stood by the door. He looked nearby and stopped when he saw me. He welcomed me inside with a wide smile that showed his yellowish teeth, a few of which were missing, particularly one of his upper canines that made the red gum line visible. When I backed away farther, the man approached.

"Come, come," he said, with a gentle tone. "All are welcome."

The man took my hand in his. His skin was calloused and rough, with large, thick fingers that squared at the tips, with the middle fingertip split down the center, exposing the soft flesh underneath. I looked again at the facade, at a lunette with a depiction of the deposition of Christ from the cross. The body was held by his blessed followers, while two veiled women stood aside with heads bowed and hands raised in prayer. The deceased man of pale pallor remained, a wound in his rib, and bleeding punctures on his hands and feet.

I wonder if that is true, I thought.

"Have faith," he said. In such proximity, I could smell the man's sour breath and unwashed hair. Yet despite his unsanitary appearance, I relaxed in his hands, and the sincerity in his tawny eyes. I let him lead me inside.

Irina dipped her finger into the holy water sitting in the basin and made the sign of the cross. I slithered by, hoping not to be seen, though I met the curious eyes of another younger woman who scowled as she took her own turn.

The first thought that came to me when I saw the inside was, "Bright." Candles and reflections of candlelight gilded surfaces and polished marble. Lifting my sights upwards, I found the gilded domes and the angels and saints imposing. I primped my collar and stared stubbornly at their judgment. At the nave was a rood screen held up by marble polychrome columns alternating in reds and greens. At the center was an ornate silver cross with a man hanging in the center, arms splayed and legs together in sacrifice. Standing on either side of him were seven figures all in varying expressions of reverence.

Behind it were vaulted ceilings, canopies, and reliefs, and on every surface were painted illustrations and Latin.

Hanging from the ceiling by a long chain were bulbous incense burners whose smoke spread a haze through the atmosphere.

Across my vision was brilliance that enraptured the senses.

My synagogue was generally plain, with only certain sections and objects given reverence. The basilica was beautiful and blasphemous. Had not Moshe Rabbenau delivered the commandments condemning idolatry? Yet, these worshippers reveled in their golden faith. Part of me felt comfort in the protection of the angels, the smell of incense, the burning candles that stood in rows before paintings of saints. I remembered what my brother Aaron had said about the churches and their faith. By his reasoning, I should not be standing in the church nor tempting almighty wrath by participating in their faith in even the smallest way. I supposed that HaShem would not be bothered by my stepping foot in a church when it was an act of kindness.

Does an act of good wash away an act of sin? I wondered.

I sat on the wooden bench with Irina, and others sat next to us, some kneeling already with a rosary in hand. I had to look twice when I saw Azazel standing next to me. I remembered how he had hung from the chandelier in the synagogue, but I did not have the opportunity to ask him about it then.

"I wondered how you could enter a house of their lord," I whispered.

"Is it? It looks like a house of Man to me."

I looked up again at the ascension of the holy son. Azazel lifted his head.

"Quite pale for a Nazarene," I murmured.

Azazel's laughter echoed and gained no response from the faithful.

"Did you say something?" Irina asked me.

I shook my head.

As the robed men filed into the basilica, the people followed. The beauty of the basilica could not be denied. The architects ensured that they had built a gilded house worthy of the Lord's presence, a monument in reverence to their faith. A thousand eyes watched me from the facade, following me from the ceilings and walls, painted on frescos and chiseled into statues. At once they were compassionate and judgmental; benevolent and malevolent.

I stared at the face of Yeshua, the Christ Pantocrator who sat on a throne within a gilded dome, draped in a blue cloth not unlike the dress Irina wore beside me. His face was long, framed by his golden hair and golden beard, his eyes fixated to the distance, seeing through me. They seemed to have faded irises that showed a marked indifference. The incomprehensible words the priest produced no doubt spoke the passages that praised the man, the Messiah who willingly sacrificed himself to free all from sin.

"Are you the King of Jews?" Azazel asked.

I looked at him quizzically. He grinned.

Azazel explained, "Their book says, 'Now Jesus stood before the governor,' and he questioned him. 'Are you the king of the Jews?' Jesus said, and answered, 'Yes, what you say is true.' And when he was accused by the chief priests and elders, he made no answer.' That always confused me. Herod and the others mocked him, dressed him up as a king. Why should he say nothing?"

When I turned to Azazel, I saw between his horns a fresco of St. Michael slaying a winged serpent, a dragon partially obscured by the demon's horns. I wondered what had been said to that winged serpent before the spear tip pierced its neck. The depiction of the Archangel Michael calmed me in a way that the eyes of Christ did not. I knew of Michael from the *Ketuvim*. His face reflected the gentile's sentimentalities and filled me with unease, much in the same way as did the golden reflections from the dome and walls, and yet I recognized his actions as familiar. At once, the priest's soft Latin became as melodic as Hebrew recitations from the Torah.

Clatterings and the swish of silk on stone drew quiet. A bedazzling man emerged at the wooden pulpit. On his body wore robes of white inlaid with gold embroidery along the collar and center. Atop his head sat a tall white hat, curved at the sides, and a sharp tip at the top. When he spoke, it was in Latin, of which I recognized only a few words here and there.

"It is a homily on the Parable of the Mustard Seed," Irina whispered in explanation as she listened intently to the priest who talked for some time before she continued. "He quotes Matthew, that 'Though it is the smallest of all seeds, when it grows it is the largest of plants and becomes a tree, so that the birds come and perch in its branches.' It's about Christ saying that the seed is like the kingdom of heaven." She paused and did not speak again for some time. When I looked to see why she had grown silent, I saw that her eyebrows were knitted together as she was trying to follow the priest's words. She noticed that I was looking at her and smiled sheepishly. "Some of the Latin I don't know so well."

I shook my head.

"Do not worry," I said.

Throughout Mass, I kneeled when I saw the others do the same. When the time came for me to cross myself, I did not. They rose and sat again, and again and listened as the priest's voice echoed against the gilded walls, and by the time it reached us, it was scarcely louder than a whisper. At the end of Mass, we departed. At the turn around the corner, Irina looked back and then pulled some object from the inside of her sleeve.

She held it before us: a solid silver coin typically meant for the church offering.

"Let's get some *caffè* and sweets," she said.

Surprised at her brazen disregard for the offering, I asked, "Is that for the church?"

"They won't miss a few *lire*. Besides, Mama-Elena donates enough. If I feel like penitence, I'll take the money from Mama's safe and give it to them. She should have hidden the key better than under her lamp."

"Would that not be theft?"

She flicked her eyes up, thinking, and pursed her lips.

"They're the unpaid wages from so many years of my hard work."

Azazel laughed loudly.

"I did not think you were so impulsive," I said.

"I never get the opportunity!"

Irina slipped the coin back up her sleeve.

"Are there any *gelateria* open on a Sunday?" I asked.

"The one by the train station stays open for the tourists. It's not the best, but it'll do."

We walked through the alleys, which were becoming progressively more crowded as other churches let out. Once we found the shop, there was already a line forming, and we waited until we ordered gelato.

"You never take the holy water or make the cross," Irina said after she licked the *gelato*.

"No," I answered.

"It's a shame," she said.

"As you like," I said as I licked the sides of my *gelato,* which was already beginning to melt.

Irina's cheeks grew rosy.

"It is not what I like; it is the truth."

A foreign warmth spread through my heart that I recognized as a kinship with the girl, so fervent for her faith and her truth.

Is it from myself or the other that shares my soul? I wondered.

I kept my silence. Irina had decided the truth for herself, whether it was reality or not. Nothing of what I could say would convince her otherwise, so I turned my attention to my *gelato*, which was steadily dripping down the sides of the cone. I slurped the lukewarm streaks with the tip of my tongue, then rose to the base and twirled the cone with my hand as I licked the excess.

"What do Jews do on this day?"

"Go to the *ghetto*, and you can see it for yourself," I said with a sharper tone than she had meant.

Irina finished her *gelato* and said, "Why not?"

"Sorry?"

"I've never been there—I've never been much of anywhere —and it'd be nice to see where you're from."

I snorted.

"There is not much to see, and Maria-Elena will expect us back at a reasonable hour."

"We will be. If not, she'll give me a smack." Irina began walking, then said, "but it'll be worth it to get away."

I chuckled at her recklessness. She acted so similarly to how I had when I was young that I came to the conclusion that most young people on the cusp of adulthood must behave in the same manner at some point in their lives. I hoped her impulses took her on a better path than mine had.

I chaperoned her to the *ghetto*. Because of the hour, there were not so many people out in the center. They were all likely inside, spending their day of rest with their families. Still, there were a few people walking around. I did not like the way Irina was looking at them, as if they were the statues surrounding San Marco, and she was a tourist appraising their value.

"They dress rather funny," she said to me with a stifled giggle. "And why do the men wear hats like that?"

I opened my mouth to give a reasoned answer, and when I decided that I had none that she would understand, said, "I suppose because it has always been that way."

From within the houses, I heard the *kiddush* muffled against the inner walls: the evening prayers that sanctified the Shabbat.

"I think it is time to go," I said.

We walked back toward the orphanage. While I walked at a brisk pace, Irina dawdled so that I had to stop at times to wait for her to catch up.

"Do you want to marry?" Irina asked abruptly.

I did not answer immediately. I did not turn to move from my place. When the question of marriage emerged, I remembered it framed as a matter of when. When will you marry? When will you find a husband? When will you find a wife? What Irina asked was a novelty of her youth. Whether there was a desire, a choice.

"No," I answered. "I did once, but . . ."

I fiddled with the offset button on my coat. The words of the *Eshet Chayil* rose from the pages of the holy book and into my memory:

"A woman of valor, who can find? She is more precious than corals ..."

I thought of my reckless childhood, my disobedience, and as a young woman how I stubbornly clung to that wistfulness, hoping that my fervent desires would be reciprocated by the man who shared in our lust. There was no sin in bachelorism, but there was an expectation to follow the covenant of being fruitful. Even as a girl, I had not thought of wanting to marry until I met the man I thought could love me. Thinking of the words praising the ideals of wifedom, the necessity of a woman's sacrifice, the pain that came with life and motherhood, perhaps my death had been a state of grace.

I could not define what led me to seeking him out. What was a man capable of who ignored the rights of my body? There had been a life within *me*. It was *ours*. Of course, there had been. We had loved each other, and soon enough, my belly became swollen. Thinking of it, I was presented with the great gulf between us. I was a young mother whose heart softened at the thought of a swelling belly, at a newborn's glistening eyes and my own revulsion at the same image. It was the loss of self that scared me.

"To be a woman requires too much sacrifice," I said. "As a girl, obey your father, your brother, your mother. As a woman, obey your husband; as a mother, obey your children. Either willingly or forcefully, give them your heart, bit by bit, breaking off shards. Your body belongs to another, always another, never yourself. It belongs to HaShem. It belongs to your husband. It belongs to your children. For HaShem, keep chaste, cover your head, cover your skin. Then, for your husband, spread your body in obligation. For your children, to grow, to suck life so it can thrive. Your body is not your own."

Even as I said it, I heard my cynicism.

"At least," I offered, "that is how we are expected to be. Our bodies are our own, to do as we will. To marry, to not marry, to be a mother, to be childless. You should find your own happiness, wherever that may be."

I saw it in my mother, in my sisters, in myself, in *her*, the other soul.

"We must all marry, or so Maria-Elena says," Irina said.

"And yet Maria-Elena is not."

"No," she smiled, showing her teeth, "she isn't. Not to a man, anyway."

"Still, she is older. Perhaps she once was."

"What about you?" I asked.

Irina crossed her arms.

"I don't know, truthfully. I've often wondered about being a woman of faith, to spend a life with Christ." She looked over to the sweets shop where a few children pressed their noses to the glass to better survey the treats within. "Or work in a *gelateria*, sneaking tastes when no one's looking. Somewhere I don't have to hear any more babies."

"Tired of the little ones?"

"Oh, it's not that," she said quickly. "They're darlings. It's just that it would be nice to be around grown-ups for a while and not have a house full of babies. You'd think they'd stop coming, but there always seems to be more."

"It is the way of things."

"I suppose."

She stared over my shoulder as two women walked by; their fanciful clothing and painted faces made them bright against the gray stones.

"They look happy," she said.

I turned to see the women as they strolled by in wide, confident steps, their satin heels clicking against the cobblestones. Their slips swished below their dresses as they walked, giving the sound of curtains sashaying on a rough stone floor.

"They look happy because they must. Gentlemen follow anyone who smiles."

"Gentlemen?" Irina queried as she watched them walk with her eyebrows furrowed.

"*Sonne donne... molto mondana,*" I said.

Irina continued to stare at the women and then said, "Oh,"

when she realized what I meant, that they were women who knew much of the world.

"It shouldn't be like that."

"No, indeed. But the world is not governed by what *should* be," I said.

"Why would they choose to do that?" she asked.

"I do not think there is much choice." I considered Crina. "Surely Maria-Elena has told you where most of the babies come from?"

Irina nodded. "I've never seen those kinds of ladies before. Well, not this close."

"I am sure you have; you just were not aware before, and now you are. Try not to become one of them."

"No. Is it really so bad? All you do is lie on your back all day."

I laughed.

"Yes, and all the while doing it with men you would never look at twice in the daylight, all while never knowing if they have put a baby in your belly or spread their diseases on your skin."

Irina gave a look of disgust at the mention of diseases. The afternoon sky was becoming dimmer as evening approached. I started walking again and Irina kept up.

"Maria didn't tell me about all that."

Rather than criticize my employer's parenting methods, I said nothing.

"Then we should talk about something else," I said. "I saw that you often go to school."

"Oh, yes. I wanted to stop last year, but Maria pushed me to finish my last year. She said that I should take advantage of as much education as I could get before I regret it."

"She is probably right," I said.

"I didn't want to go back," she said. "Not after last year."

"Oh?"

"I tried to run away." Irina said.

I stopped walking, and so did she.

"There was a boy. We grew up together. He was always there with me. When Maria was busy with the babies, whatever happened, we were together. He's my brother. I don't care that we had different mothers." She looked downwards. "We were supposed to stay together . . . and then . . ." Irina pressed her lips together. "One day, he was gone. Maria sent me out to wash, and when I got home, he was gone, sent as an apprentice to a shipbuilder in Genoa. He sends letters, only it's not the same." She inhaled the briny air and scrunched her nose. "It's not the same as knowing he's there."

Tears began to form in her eyes. "I hate her for letting him go," she said.

I nodded, knowing well the heartache from the absence of a close sibling.

"I had a sister," I said. "I can hardly remember a time when she was not there, somewhere in the house or when she was nearby. You come to take for granted that they are always with you until they are gone. Do you think he could come back? Or you go to him?"

"I don't know. Maria won't let me go. She acts like I'm still a little girl. All the other girls my age are finding sweethearts or doing something with their lives, and she keeps me here. Please don't tell."

"I will not."

"I thought of running off to Genoa. Get on a ship and sail there. It must be nicer there in the sun and the beach."

I saw white sand and green hills and sapphire skies.

"I tried, once, just before you came to the house, actually. Packed everything in a blanket, tied it off, and snuck out at night when Maria fell asleep. I got to the train station. It was closed, so I sat on the steps for a while, trying to figure out another way, but I ended up going home. I don't know what I was thinking. I didn't have any money for a ticket."

I reached out my hand to place atop Irina's, not waiting for her to protest. She pulled away at first, but my well-practiced arms were too strong for her to do so for long.

We said nothing for some time as we walked the winding way back to Maria-Elena's house. I sympathized with Irina.

"I wish I had the money to help you," I said.

Irina shook her head briskly. I thought I could help her in another way. Although I preferred a place where I could have privacy, I also wanted her to know that there was a safe place where she could escape to. It felt like I was talking to myself, giving my younger self the security that I had not had.

"If you ever need somewhere to go, I have a place. It's not very much, though."

She brightened.

"Stay with you?" she asked.

I was not prepared for Irina's strong embrace and nearly lost my footing. She kissed me on my cheek. When she released me, I told her where I often secluded myself in the *campanile* at the San Giorgio dei Greci, confident that she would not tell Maria-Elena. Even if she did, I no longer cared if Maria-Elena knew that I stayed in such destitution, not after how much we had seen together. I told Irina where I sequestered and hoped she would never have to come to me.

When we finally arrived at the orphanage, I could hear babies crying from the inside. I took a deep breath and wiped the moisture from my forehead before knocking in successive trills until the door opened.

"*Maria!*" Maria-Elena said. "Where have you been?" She pulled me inside. "I've only got so many hands."

I went to the first crying baby and picked him up. Irina went upstairs immediately.

"What a horrid day," Maria-Elena said. "Not a few hours after you left did Maria-Giulia come to the door to tell me that she could not work here anymore." Maria-Elena wiped the drool from Beni's mouth. "Gone to serve in a convent in Milan. She showed me the letter from the diocese. So, that's that. It's just us until another comes along."

I had no words of comfort to give. With Maria-Giulia gone, the work of taking care of children would be much more diffi-cult. Still, I could not begrudge her for wanting to leave the orphanage. It was work befitting a certain personality, and Maria-Giulia did not seem the type. I stifled a chuckle. Was I the type?

Once I helped put the babies to sleep for the night, Maria-Elena paid me a week's wages. When I left, the evening was chilly, and I did not want to endure the night chill with only my clothes and a thin veil to comfort me. However, all the shops were closed as it was a Sunday. I would have to sleep by the fire to keep myself warm until I could go to the store in the morning.

CHAPTER FOURTEEN

With more *lire* in my pocket and a day off, I set to meet again with de'Angelo. It was a little cold in the morning, and I reminded myself to buy some warmer clothing before the day was out. I wanted to be in a sharper mind, so I bought three live mackerel whose blood I absorbed and whose flesh I cooked and ate. I felt full of stomach and mind as I walked to find de'Angelo where he said he would be by the Gallerie dell'Accademia. Azazel was with me. At times, he followed behind me, periodically breaking away to follow an indiscriminate man or woman and then coming back to my side. No doubt he was following them to view the sins that buzzed around their brains. The thought of witnessing those sins again made me uneasy. Having used his Demon Eyes before, I was wary of seeing the world that way again despite the beauty that existed there.

I was curious to see if I could find the *legatoria* where Crina said she found work, as she told me it was near the Gallerie. I wandered around, looking for it, eventually having to ask a passerby. After querying four people, one elderly man pointed me in the direction of a small shop cramped between an *osteria* and an empty, boarded building. I peeked in through the window first where there were displays of hard-bound books and glossy magazines. I did not see anyone and so opened the door to enter. When I was inside, no one came to greet me. I called out, *"Salve,"* and waited. A door on the side of the cramped room, filled with books and stationery, opened, and out came Crina dressed in a white smock splotched with ink. When she saw me, she exclaimed:

"You have come to see me!" She clapped her hands together. "You must be wondering about Antonio. Not to worry! He is such a good boy, you know. He is with my sister now. She works at night, so she watches him during the day."

I wondered what the implications were that her sister worked night hours.

"I could not be happier," Crina said. "I wasn't sure I would ever be a mother, but now . . ." She patted her cheek. "Well, I am glad to see you. If there is anything I can do for you, you must let me know."

"Just knowing that Antonio is safe is enough," I said.

Before I left, Crina hugged me. A piece of me lightened when I left the shop.

I found de'Angelo in the same place, though this time he sat on the stones, arms crossed, with his hat over his face. He seemed to be sleeping, and rather than waiting until he decided to wake up, I kicked his foot. He jerked awake, causing his hat to fall from his head. When he looked up to see me, he groaned.

"Oh, today is not the best day," he said. *"Domani."*

De'Angelo placed his hat back over his head, and when he did, I grabbed it.

"I have money," I said.

He furrowed his eyebrows in thought and then relaxed

them. He stood up and pressed his hands against his back as he groaned.

"Ah, the streets are not good for this body," he said.

He desired a meal again, and so we went to a *trattoria* that sat along the Rio Del Vin. It was a nice place with only a few others sitting down to eat. We ordered. Though I had little appetite, I took advantage of the convenience and ordered a small meal of wine and antipasti.

"Here," I said and passed him some *lire*.

He took it nonchalantly and tucked it in his pocket. He continued eating while I tapped my foot and waited for him to finish so that he could tell me what I needed to know.

"Well?" I asked.

"Eh, there is time enough for that. Let's enjoy this meal before we get to business."

I sighed.

As de'Angelo complained about the fall of the Republic of Venezia, about Napoleon, about the awfulness of the annexation of Austria, he fixated on Napoleon, that figure whose portrait sat in a venerated position in my parents' house: the painted face of the man in his feathered hat. What I knew most of the man from my father, my mother, my community, was that he had abolished the *ghettos*. Because of him, I could walk outside those walls. I had not known what it was like, then, but I remember my mother, who could not venture to the *farmacia* after curfew to get medicine for her ill brother. Without Napoleon, the man who de'Angelo insulted, I would have remained behind those walls, relegated to isolation within my community.

"Without Napoleon, we Jews would still be in the *ghetto*." I said.

"And so?"

I gripped the handle on my cup.

"Weren't you protected there?" He relaxed in his chair. "No ruffians to make trouble—except your own. *Alora*, can you imagine what would happen to a Jew out on the street at night in those days?" he shook his head. "There was—is—too much hate against them amongst some Italians. It's the death of Christ, you see. Have you been to a Catholic Mass?"

"As infrequently as possible," I said.

"You see, this is the point: Maria, the mother, saw her son murdered. All Italian mothers see her grief, see her statues holding his dead body, and they grieve with her. But grief is not enough, there is anger, too. How can there not be? A pure and righteous man was crucified, not just a man, but a son. And who put Jesus on the cross?"

I knew the story of Yeshua's betrayal, or rather, the story that the Catholics tell from the mixed translation of Latin that Maria-Elena would share. I wondered how they could know the intricacies of their Holy Book if they did not understand the language it was written in. Maria-Elena would say that they trust the Priests to tell them the truth. I would trust the rabbi, too, with truth, but also be knowledgeable of my own. For it was impossible to read Hebrew and come to one conclusion, one truth, one meaning. Perhaps Latin was different.

"All mothers see this horror and then look to their own sons and wonder: Will they come for mine, too? Will I have to hold my dead son in my arms?" He shoved the dainty cake in his mouth, and in two bites, swallowed. It left an opaque film of cream on his upper lip that he wiped with the napkin, which he left crumpled on the tabletop.

I scoffed. "Are they so fragile?"

"What is fragile about fear? This is what keeps us safe: fear. You fear the lion in the darkness, and so you hide and live another day. We fear God's judgment, and so we make ourselves humble and follow His path. And look at me," he said. "I did not fear enough, and now I live on the streets just like the gypsies."

Al-tirah ki imekha ani. Fear not, for I am with you.

"Did HaShem not tell us: Be not afraid?"

He lifted his eyebrows and turned up his lips. "That is your Jewish book."

"That is Isaiah."

His eyebrows raised and he laughed. For some time, we did not speak. In between pecking at my food with a fork, I would glance up from my plate to see Azazel pacing around with his arms folded, tapping his finger against his forearm. I wondered what was bothering him. De'Angelo finished his meal and wiped his mouth.

"*Allora*. What a meal! Now," he said as he placed his food-spotted napkin on the table. "You want to know about Ludovico Zampieri." He sipped his wine. "You'll find him and all his friends and influencers at their Carnevale party the day after Lent at a *palazetto* in the Cannaregio on the Calle Zanardi and the Rio de Santa Caterina."

My heart pounded. I had nothing with which to write down the address, so I repeated it until I could remember. I moved to rise, and de'Angelo grabbed my hand.

"Stay a little," he said. "There is more."

I relaxed.

"I don't count myself stupid enough to ask why you need this information, and neither do I really care. What I care about is getting food in my belly and wine to quench my thirst. For that, I need money."

"I have paid you."

"And you are done with me?" He chuckled and leaned forward closely enough that I could smell the wine on his breath. "Then tell me how you will slink your way into a place such as that, *hm?*"

"I can manage quite well for myself."

"On the streets, I don't doubt." He leaned back and rested his forearms on the table. "But these rich men have more means than you know. You could disappear and nothing would be done about it."

I eyed him carefully. What he spoke of was what had happened to me.

"You speak from experience?" I said.

"I do indeed. So many years as *polizia* here, I have seen a great many things."

I turned away from him. I did not want to be beholden to him for any longer than I had to. He could remain a tramp in the streets for all I cared. Whatever guilt I had felt for causing his situation had dissipated.

"Then if I need you, I will find you in the same place."

There I left him. As I walked, I continually repeated the address so that I would remember.

I had it in my mind to purchase a jacket before I went home so I did not have to worry about the coming winter chill. Disappointingly, every jacket was much too expensive for my pocket. Eventually, I found a second-hand store which was much more affordable. The store owner greeted me from inside with an absent-minded, *"Buona sera,"* as he stood behind the counter sorting through a pile of dated clothing.

I browsed through the clothes and shoes, some of them in good condition and others which had ink stains or small tears. As I kept looking through the old clothes, I found a long jacket the color of a ripe plum between a patchy brown fur coat and a silk robe splashed with green, red, and blue peonies. I took the jacket and appraised it. I touched the wool, searching to ensure that it was free of holes or significant wear, and then felt the mink that surrounded the collar. Though there was a tiny patch of fur missing from the side of the collar, perhaps from a wayward cigarette ember, and some smoothness around the ends of the sleeves where the wool had worn, and a missing button in the middle of the jacket, it was acceptable. I checked the price pinned on the sleeve. If the shop owner would let me haggle, I could afford it and a blanket.

Holding the jacket and a heavy quilt in hand, I went to the counter.

"I'll give it to you for less than that," he said. "So many clothes—look!—if I don't sell more of them soon, I'll have to throw them out. Most of this is from the ones who died in *l'influenza*. The families either burnt it or piled it outside my door. Almost two years have passed and still, I have clothes, clothes, and more clothes and fewer and fewer customers." He took my money. "Not like those tourists are coming into my shop, no. Where do they take their money?"

I was about to answer, but he kept speaking.

"To the tourist shops, of course. They stay near the sights and barely walk beyond San Marco's." He shook his head as he punched the total into the register and the drawer popped open. As I waited, I heard the door open and turned around. There was a small girl wearing an oversized brown coat that looked as if it belonged to an adult but had been hemmed to fit her height. The man at the register made a hissing noise and shouted, *"Via!"* When the girl did not move, the man rushed out from behind the counter and towards the door, causing the girl to sprint away. The man returned, somewhat out of breath, to complete the transaction.

"*Maria*, that *zingara* comes around here begging for money. As if I had any to give!"

The man finally completed my order, and he gave me my change. I thanked him and began to leave, but once I was near the door, he called, "Why not take a pair of gloves from the window, there? They've been sitting there for three years."

I stopped and looked at the gloves that he mentioned. In the window display were a pair of kid gloves as dark as ebony, embossed at the wrist with a pair of swans touching their heads together. I took them and thanked the man. When I wore the jacket and gloves out of the shop and draped the blanket over my arm, it gave me peace of mind to know that I could stave off the chill.

I also became invigorated with the knowledge the *polizia* officer gave to me. Carnevale at a *palazetto* on Calle Zanardi and the Rio de Santa Caterina. I could find Zampieri, and he would tell me where to find Ephraim. Vengeance came closer to my grasp. I whispered the name of my murderer, my lover.

When I closed my eyes, I could see his face more clearly as it faded from the clouded memories. I reached out as if to touch his cheek and inhaled sharply at the sensation of phantom flesh.

"You feel it when I come to you, like the air between my fingers," I whispered to the candle flame when I returned home.

I felt him there, or was it a memory? I felt my hands at his neck, at the heartbeat that pulsed, and I wanted to kiss him and strangle him. How would I kill him? Would I do it in the same way as he had done to me? Would I be swift and strike him with my hairpin? I imagined plunging the Bona Dea pin into his neck and watching as his blood spilled upon the floor.

When I opened my eyes, the air was dark and empty with the only light coming from the orange flickering of the fire and the glow of the candle flame.

CHAPTER FIFTEEN

I t was the first week of December. There was a curious smell in the air. At once it was sweet, like the scent of sugared bread, and then a wisp of wind would ascend through the canal and a sour smell would invade my senses. In the main square, shop fronts had been decorated for Christmas; evergreen laurels were strung in front of windows and wooden stands for the holiday market. In the *ghetto*, my family would begin to sing *"Hanerot Halalu"* to celebrate Chanukah.

There was a silence that enshrouded the streets daily during siesta. The store owners would pull down a metal screen. Streets would fill with the screeching noise of metal screens descending to the ground, locking up the storefront. All the bustling life that was present just minutes before dissipated, and all who were left on the streets were smokers and tourists. The only crowds were those in San Marco and the Rialto.

There were so many passageways, streets, and alleys that the whole of Venezia was like a random labyrinth built without a sense of escape. The homes seemed to be built atop each other with little space between them, large enough for one person to squeeze through.

I kept my hands in my pockets to shield them from the cold air. The streets were wet from melted snow, though some thin veils of the white powder remained on the shop canopies. There were few people on the streets since the city was between holidays. It was a small relief to walk the streets without having to jostle through alleys or shops, though it was emptier without the tourists and the bustle, as if some charm was lost without the motley.

I kept thinking about Carnevale and of meeting Ludovico Zampieri, the man who would lead me to my murderer. To blend in, I would need a mask, and it would have to be an expensive one so that my social status would not be questioned. I avoided the tourist shops, which sold cheaply made and cheaply sold masks to visitors who could not discern authenticity. I had passed masks shops often enough to know where the quality ones were. The other soul showed me a memory of walking through one with Father. He let me choose whichever one I wanted, and I jubilantly went about the store trying each one on until I found the joyful face of Bacco whose head was covered with gold and purple grapes.

The shop I was looking for was near the Palazzo Ducale but hidden down an alleyway so that it was not as well known to anyone who was not looking for it. I passed the palace. In my youth it was a dilapidated building that had been abandoned to disrepair, but now scaffolding covered the façade as a process of renovation. I walked past other shops and other people. A woman walking in front of me wore a set of shoes with spiked heels, and I stared in wonderment that she was able to traverse the cobblestone streets without falling. At length, I found the shop I was looking for, punctuated by a mannequin in a cloak and mask sitting beside the door.

I entered the dimly lit shop to find masks covered on every portion of the store, from the shelves on the wall to masks pinned upon the ceiling rafters and posts. The vacuous eye sockets of the masks stared down from the ceiling boards. There was some life in them, somewhere hidden behind the upturned lips and curved eye sockets.

I remembered the exact shoes I wore the last time I was in a shop like this. They were borrowed leather heels with rose design on the ankles, edges rounded from wear, a notch on the tip from when I tripped over a stone when dancing in the square to a violinist. I had come to the shop with some school-mates to peruse and play until the clerk at the register shooed us out for our rambunctiousness.

My shoes stepped hollow against the wooden floor, muted by the Turkish carpet. The narrow corridor could barely be seen at the back of the shop. So full were the walls that the narrow opening was invisible to me at first. I entered the room, just larger than a confessional. Within it was an aristocratic décor with a domed, vaulted ceiling, all covered with masks of the richest kinds. Three alcoves held mannequins dressed in centuries-old garb, indicative of the Doge's influence.

The circular room was lit by dim sconces high on the wall. Masks of simple colors, others complex, with gemstones, diamonds, others animal faces, all stared at me. I tilted my head to see the most miniscule of movements from a fox mask on the wall. I thought it was my imagination at first. The ruddy mask twitched. I blinked, then approached with my arm extended, fingers parted, splayed outward. Silver lenses shone in the distance of the empty black sockets. I smiled.

It was then that I saw the body, the outline blended in with the other mannequins lined against the walls. It breathed, though it tried its best to be unnoticeable. I searched for the stripe of exposed skin above the edge of the gilded collar and under the mask strap. I held my fingers just above the soft flesh of its sternum. A comfortable warmth exuded from its skin, a heartbeat, strong, pulsing from a tender vein.

There was some life in them, somewhere hidden behind the upturned lips and curved eye sockets. Overwhelmed with the sheer number of eyeless faces staring at me and smiling, I wandered off to the left side of the store that shimmered with crystal masks and stepped toward the back where a small corridor led to the backside of the shop.

I had to shrug my shoulders as I stepped into the room to avoid touching the masks hanging within the doorway. It was an audience of faces. There was one long shelf built into the side, running around the length of the rectangular room. Between these shelves were mirrors that showed the back of the masks so that no one would have to lay a hand on them.

The longer I lingered, the more the eyeless faces shifted, making subtle movements of the kind that are made when one is doing their best to remain still. Inadvertent twitches, blinks, and the shadows of eyes followed me, as if they were a gateway into a world where the masks had a life unto their own. And in the distance, I saw my face in the mirror—my face and not my face. At once I saw the girl I knew with dark eyes and dark hair that I let fly free, and at once, I saw another with similar eyes but brighter locks. Now I was a face unknown, no different from the masks on the walls.

I saw Azazel through the mask in the mirror. The mask's gold plumage fanned out and glimmered in the dim lighting.

I felt Azazel nearby. His laughter whispered in my ear, even as I tried to banish it. Why would he mock me?

"Is there a reason for your laughter?" I asked.

Azazel slunk out from behind a blue and gold Bauta mask.

"I cannot laugh without you being suspicious?"

I eyed him carefully.

He tapped his forehead with his pinky finger. "They cannot hide from me behind a mask."

I touched an emerald plume on one of the silver masks on the shelf.

"I suppose it has more to do with hiding from Humankind. Without repercussions or social judgment, they can fully enjoy themselves. It is not only you who judges, but all of us," I mused, though I was not sure if I could be included in the pool of humanity. I was not sure if I was human. Miriam had mentioned *dybbuks* or perhaps I was like the *shedim*, as Azazel considered when he met me. In my search for justice, had I become the unwitting reflection of that old blood myth that gentiles believed about Jews? Is that what Azazel wanted from me? Was I to become his marionette, forever dancing to his whim? I was no longer human, if ever I was. How much did it matter? And yet, it did matter.

"Are we both demons?"

"We may be."

I thought of *Helel ben Shahar* whom the Christians called Lucifer.

"Christians say all demons come from Lucifer. Yet Lucifer was an angel created by HaShem for a purpose. The rabbi said all comes from Him and Satan appears to give us the choice between good and evil." I called to my memory a story, "The *Tanakh* says, 'I form the light and create darkness; I make peace and I create evil; I the Lord do all these things.' It is Humankind who chooses to make the world sinful. When will those sins be judged? I hoped when I died, I would find the answer, but all I wanted was to live again. If there was no justice in the afterlife, I would have to find it for myself."

"What was it like on the other side?" Azazel asked, his eyes wide.

I closed my eyes for a moment in contemplation.

"A twilight Eden."

I wondered that if I died as I was, would I return, or would I be banished to some unholy afterlife? The thought made me tighten my shoulders. Azazel had said that I could live in immortality so long as the candle flame burned.

"Is that where cursed ones like us go?" he asked.

"I don't know. I have two theories for what happens to the sinful after we die. The Torah tells that *Gehinnom* is where we face our truth, of goodness and ill, to be cleansed of it to return to the divine. The *gentile* Bible tells of an eternal punishment for the sinful."

"Ah, but those are for humans."

"True." I closed my eyes, imagining the sun on my face. "Where, then, did I go? The Catholics talk of purgatory. For us it was *Gehinnom*. Perhaps they were right. Souls must go somewhere, after all." I rubbed my face with my hands. "Do you have a soul?"

Do I? I thought.

"I suppose I must if I am here. What did that old philosopher say?" he mused. *"Cogito, ergo sum."*

I think, therefore I am.

"What of men that have no thoughts at all? Can evil men have souls?" I asked.

"You must know by now."

"The more souls I take, the less clear it becomes. I thought before that everything must have a soul, that it was given to us. When we are born it is neither sinful nor pure; it exists. But as we live, as we make our choices, does that change the sanctity of our being?"

"Why do you ask? You know it does. You have felt it yourself."

He was right. Every soul I took, I saw the good and the bad for no one soul was completely untarnished.

"Those innocent souls I've taken. Where do they go now?"

"I've not seen anything past this earth. But," he chuckled, "perhaps that's why they sacrificed the goat to me. They put their sins onto the animal and in killing it, they are released, and the absolved can once again become pure. Maybe it's the same with you." He laughed deeply. It reverberated off the mirrors and the masks—an inhuman laughter that left my stomach empty. I stared at him until he gradually calmed, breathing intensely until it slowed, and he straightened his back, walked towards me, and put a hand on my cheek. When he looked into my eyes, I could not see my reflection. In those eyes without color, they were like opaque mirrors, staring at me in stubborn existence.

"I have been alive for longer than I can remember," Azazel said. "There are memories . . . some so far away that I can barely touch them. Shadows of memories, of who I might have been. I don't remember now if I was ever a man or if I just came into existence spontaneously by the will of a god. I live as a witness to humanity's sins. I cannot die, however much I've tried, for men never stop sinning. So take my offer," he suggested. "Kill your murderer and stay with me."

My reborn life was hollow, filled with pursuit of justice. My sole reason for life was to fulfill that purpose and that alone. I wondered if there could be another way. To do so would require more murder. What was the difference between justice and murder? There were the laws of humans and the laws of HaShem that decided the line. The laws of humans had done nothing to bring my murderer to alms. Far from it, the law seemed to allow it. Who stood as judge of this world? Perhaps HaShem brought me from death for this purpose, for *gilgul neshamot*, a second life. This, at the cost of taking the souls of beasts and humans. My heartbeat rushed at the antici-pation of absorbing the blood into my skin. Fresh as the moment, I saw the desperate face of the pitiful drunken humans I reaped.

"I do not have the desire to live after *he* is dead," I said. "Even if I wanted to, the more I kill, the more obvious I become to others. What happens if the *polizia* find me? Lock me in the Ponte dei Sospiri? What good will I do there?"

I sighed.

"Every time I kill, I feel some guilt, whether they deserve death or not."

Azazel dismissed my comment with a wave of his hand. "Guilt is for the self-obsessed. These men are but nothings who deserve it. In any case, did you not feel the ecstasy of reaping their blood?"

"Yes," I admitted.

"Then there is no great loss and much to gain. Who cares about some sinners?"

A part of me tightened. I felt Faustina in my mind.

"Christ would care," I said without thinking.

It was not my voice that said it, but *hers*.

Azazel tipped his head. "I suppose he might." He opened his arms. "But is *he* here? Two thousand years and the murderers and rapists, pedophiles, and abusers, are still here. Are they worthy of forgiveness?"

"Everyone is worthy of forgiveness," I said meekly, barely believing it myself.

"You tell me. What does the god of Abraham do to those who have trespassed?"

There were too many instances of how HaShem had turned his favor from humans. The Torah was clear on how He viewed them when he dared climb the tower to heaven and what He did to those who betrayed him. I thought of what the men had done at Sodom and Gomorrah. HaShem had sent his angels to them, and in response, the depraved men were determined to rape them. Soon, the city was destroyed, razed by the angel's wrath and by His hand.

"His justice is fierce," I said.

"Indeed, so."

I saw the lion's carcass and the swarming bees that nestled within it. Witnessing the vision before my rebirth and seeing it now before me made me question it again. What was the meaning of that vision? The Torah was filled with the lives of prophets and visionaries who could easily discern the messages sent by HaShem or angels. I did not have that gift. I had felt what it meant: that He was giving me permission for justice. Why else would I be brought to life? There was no wrong in it.

"When He sends a message," I began, "should we listen, even if it will mean death?"

Azazel eyed me quizzically. He lifted his chin and narrowed his eyelids.

"I think you already know," he said. "Why ask a demon for permission?"

"I am asking for my conscience."

"Then abandon it," he said. "You need no conscience when I am here to show you the truth."

Azazel gestured to a mask that sat on a shelf before a mirror. What stared back at me was a Pierrot mask with a white face and crimson lips, and around the eyes were golden accents and a single golden tear below the right eye. I looked at it and then at Azazel. I took the mask in hand.

To call upon the wealthy meant a change of clothing. If I looked as I normally did, I would be sent away at once, but dressed in finery, I might pass as one of substance. I searched the shop for a costume and found clothing of new, soft material. The dress was so fine I resented having to wear my own borrowed clothes as I passed my fingers over the silver buttons, feeling the grooves of the lion's head on each one. There was comfort in them. They smelled like opportunity. The dress that hung there was one that was bright, cheerful, luxuriant; of red velvet and golden embroidery.

In the end, I spent all my money on the clothing. If I found what I needed, it would be worth it. When I returned home, I draped the dress behind the head of the bed to keep it from forming wrinkles. As I lay down, I reached up to feel the material between my fingers. Azazel's voice picked at my mind, coaxing me to abandon any conscience, any principles. It would be easier. Without a connection to morality, I would be free to indulge in his whims, in my whims. It would be easier, but it would not be right. I may no longer be human. I may be a demon. I wondered if I would be judged by what I was reborn as or by my conscience. If I did what He sent me to do, it would set the world to rights. I would kill my murderer, I would kill those who deserved death, and I would die. My death meant that Azazel would be alone once more. That left me with some sadness. I had grown used to him, and I needed him, and he needed me. I could not love him, but I did have compassion for him. And with him, I felt both powerful and at once powerless.

CHAPTER SIXTEEN

Without an extra set of hands at the orphanage, the days were more difficult. Maria-Elena was gone more and more frequently. At times, Irina would help if she was not busy with school or when she would leave the house to go to the Christmas market and return smelling of wine *brulee*. More often than not, I was alone with the children. Each day seemed to blend together, and I knew I would need a sharp mind when Carnevale came. I hoped I could make it long enough so that I could evade killing until the day before the Carnevale party when I would need blood the most. While there, I would have to use the eyes, and I could not risk fading before I found what I needed.

Irina was always careful to return home before Maria-Elena. She would wash and rinse her mouth so that any evidence of her gallivanting remained unnoticed. I suspected that if Maria-Elena knew I was allowing Irina some freedoms from the orphanage walls I would no longer have an income. The punishment would be severe if she found out, and yet I could not force Irina to remain when I saw how much she wanted to be away from the home she grew up in. My parents tried their best to shelter me, and all I did was rebel.

When I finished with work, I would sometimes stop at a bookshop or peruse the Accademia before I returned home. Knowing that I had a plan in place, that I would find out more about my murderer, gave me a sense of ease. There were still things I needed to do. Upon my return home, I rested for a few hours until it was Azazel who woke me. I felt his hand on my head, stroking my hair and then felt him lie down beside me.

"Where have you been?" I mumbled.

"Out and about," he answered.

I turned over to him and opened my eyes halfway. The fire I had set before I went to sleep was burning to embers and barely illuminated his face.

"Still subsisting on fish?" he asked.

"I suppose you have something else in mind."

"I always do."

"Hm."

I stretched an arm over my head and thought about the last time I had killed someone. How unfulfilling it had been. Should it be fulfilling? At least those who I killed before had deserved it, and their blood sustained me to further my *mitzvah*. I was becoming tired of killing. I had only wanted to kill my murderer, but I would have to continue.

"I always wondered about Moshe Rabbenu," I said.

"What of him?" Azazel asked.

"After a generation wandering in the desert, he finally leads all the tribes to the promised land, and what does HaShem tell him? 'Because you did not believe in me, to uphold me as holy in the eyes of the people of Israel, therefore you shall not bring this assembly into the land that I have given them.' All that had happened ..." I paused in surprise that I recalled so much of the holy words. "His mother sends him down the river, which guides him to the pharaoh's daughter. There he lives, grows, and becomes as powerful as a pharaoh. Then, after finding that he is born of the chosen himself, wanders the desert, and is found. What does HaShem tell him? To return to Egypt and free the slaves. And he does it, not because he wants to. It is a *mitzvah*. He *must*. Through him, HaShem, creates the wondrous miracles that soften the pharaoh. He leads the slaves out into the desert, transcribes the Torah, the commandments. And what great transgression stops HaShem from letting his prophet into the holy land? Because he hit a rock twice."

I pushed my hair out of my face.

"The rabbi, or my father, or my mother, would say it was disobedience. HaShem told him to speak to the rock, and instead he hit it."

"I suppose that's God," Azazel said. I scowled at him, at his insistence to speak the name of HaShem without reverence.

"Is that how it went? I've heard differently."

"Do the gentiles tell it differently?"

"Not only gentiles. I've sat in synagogues to hear the rabbi explain it differently. What was the sin at the Waters of Meribah? Was it that he struck the stone instead of speaking to it? Was it that he chastised the complaining Israelites? Was it that he simply did not trust HaShem?" I tightened my lips and crossed my arms. "No wonder the rabbis argue. Getting it wrong will incur His punishment."

"How will anyone know what's right?"

"Are my murders blessed?" I questioned, more to myself than to the demon.

"How can they not be?"

Each day in December, there seemed to be more decorations and music. I did not celebrate Christmas generally. At times, my school friends would give me gifts, and Faustina shared a memory of an elaborate celebration at her *palazzo*.

I had no menorah but felt compelled to celebrate the holiday in a small way. I bought seven candles, and when I returned home, I placed them on my windowsill, keeping them in place by burning one of the candles and pouring the wax on the sill and pressing the base of the candles in place. I said a prayer and kept one candle lit. Over the next week, I lit each candle. The flames seemed so small against the bright lights from the Christmas market. The longer the candles burned, the smaller they became until the lights from Christmas drowned them out.

In the days that followed, there was joviality and cheer amongst those I passed in the street and in Irina. But all I could feel was apprehension. My thoughts focused on what would come, and I itched for the year to end and for my cause to come to fruition. Each day I would touch the Pierrot mask or feel the scarlet dress and wish for time to hasten. In the night or early mornings, I would practice with the Demon Eyes. Each time Azazel pressed a finger to my forehead, he seemed as eager as I to observe the sins and memories of Humankind. He guided me to those he deemed unforgivable. And when I saw them in the act of sin, my impulse for justice was often overwhelmed. Inundated with unrepentant thoughts, I would find my pin in my hand and a dead body soon beneath me. Then I would view the blazing candle flame and feel as if I were a whole being capable of happiness. Inevitably, when the effects of the blood faded, doubt and regret would resume.

"Why must I be this way?" I asked Azazel a few days after the new year.

We were walking in the Piazza di San Marco as the Demon Eyes emblazoned my vision in brightness. I could scan the people and allow their memories to exist but not focus on them. At times, a particular memory or sin would be impossible to ignore, and I would have to wait for the eyes to fade or remove myself from the presence. I still had not been able to remedy the physical ailments that came from using the eyes. After using them for a time, I would need immediate sustenance and so began to carry a vial of ash on my person should the need arise.

"That is not a question I have an answer for. Every being must discover that for themselves. Take me: why must I be this way? Do you have an answer?"

I glanced at him.

"Every great thinker has a different answer," I said. "The easiest answer is that it all comes from HaShem. You and I are as we are because of Him."

"Easy answer, but not necessarily correct."

"No answer ever is, I suppose."

In the center was a pyre and atop that pyre an effigy of *La Befana*, a witch made from wood and rags.

I smiled when I saw it.

"I used to enjoy this little spectacle," I said. "It was one of the days where we could toy with fire and burn all the broken and useless things we had in the house. Once I had broken one of Miriam's combs by mistake, and I hid it away until I was able to throw it in the fire."

"So little changes," Azazel said. "Once it was a goat that absolved and now a woman."

"I suppose so," I said.

I felt the early light headedness that came from having the Demon Eyes for too long. Soon, I would have a headache. I could not control how long they affected me, but I could lessen their influence by removing myself from people. When I was alone, there would be no one to see and no risk of harm from the Demon Eyes. I walked away from the pyre. With the fire came change. Soon, it will be the new year. Carnevale could not come soon enough.

CHAPTER SEVENTEEN

When I had last spoken with de'Angelo, I had some doubts about how I would enter the party, but I decided that I could sneak in. A *palazzetto* would have servants and waiters. A small bribe to a footman at the back door would be enough and if not, I would view his sins and dispose of him if I needed. It was the night before Carnevale, and I could not sleep. It was raining outside, causing the canals to flood into the streets.

I had filled the vial I kept with ash made from the blood of one I reaped. I kept this close to my body, hidden inside my brassier. I dressed and ensured that I had the Bona Dea pin with me hidden in my bodice. When I glanced at the candle in the fireplace, I felt confident in its dancing flame.

I went to the *palazzetto* where the evening Masquerade would begin. The orange sun descended into the sea around the square, illuminating the sky in an ethereal glow. The streets were a flood of paper faces as I looked down onto the streets below where pastel costumes stood out from the charcoal clothing around them. It was the Zampieri house. I was stunned by its magnificence. I had expected the house to be luxurious but seeing it with my own eyes left me with a tinge of envy and anger. Red lanterns brightened the alabaster walls outside of the palace. Women wore pastel dresses that puffed out like chrysanthemums. Every part of their body was covered, protected from the outside world. They became the persona of the mask that hid their faces. Only their eyes revealed their intentions to the outside world; any truth that remained was hidden.

I entered with the others as they walked in. Those who passed gave me no second glance, and I seemed to disappear into the watercolor background as just another costume.

Inside it was a palace of walking masks. There was an unmistakable musk of bodies, wine, hot food, fresh bread, the canal water. The opulence within matched what I had seen inside the Basilica de San Marco. Every surface was touched with gold and silver. The marble floor reflected the glittering gilt, as if I were standing on a pool of stars.

A woman danced before me in a blue velvet half-mask embellished with golden glittered spirals. Her lips parted in an eternal exhale, sucking in air to fuel her lungs. Her ball gown flowed around her white heels, and her ebony curls flowed down her back like a black waterfall. The woman reminded me of how I used to be. I had the sudden urge to tell her how lovely she looked. My disguise allowed me to propel forward and grasp her soft hand. She gave an upturned smile that slid across her cheeks.

"Madame, you surprise me!" she said, somewhat breathlessly.

"You dance so well, I had to tell you."

She giggled.

"I do think that there must be a, um, zest, you know, for the world. I tell you, I've been to India, to Turkey, to Russia, and they are so poor, you know, but they have this want for everything good. Then there are some people, and they have everything, they can have everything, like you see here, but are still unhappy. Why?"

I shrugged.

"You see? These people, we all know why we are sad, why we are angry, but you don't even know why. You must find out, and then you can fix it. You see, I've seen a very poor woman who earned her money by picking up the–the shit of others with her bare hands. Even she found oy in life. Joy! And she was picking up shit with her hands!"

She paused for a reaction from me; when I gave none, she continued.

"You know, if even she can find something in life to love, then surely everyone can. You must, um, open your eyes to beauty around you. You are here, in a most beautiful city, and you can only be sad. This is ridiculous."

"You don't understand."

"No? What is it I don't understand?"

"You haven't been around death."

She opened her mouth wide.

"And how do you know this? You think I have not been around suffering. Why do you think so?"

"Someone who's lived through it can't be so . . . carefree."

She laughed.

"But of course, they can. *I* can. It is all up to you, you know, how you want to be."

She let go of my hand and turned away to continue her dance. She was joyful unto herself and kept dancing until at once she stopped and sat upon an empty chair. In a moment or two she had started a conversation with a person in a full-face mask, which greatly resembled a yellow finch. Soon, the woman laughed and touched the person's hand.

"So lively," Azazel noted. "What fun they'll no doubt have."

"No doubt," I said.

I looked away from them. In the great room, all wore masks. In the jolly crowd were others walking through, uninterested in taking part in the joviality, still more unmasked were smiling. Among the Venezians were those in masks, black and colored, feathered and bejeweled, while others were animals, or else dressed as dramatic characters. A plainly dressed man stood before a camera to take a picture of a figure in a porcelain mask. One was all in blue, white, and gold from head to toe, with the only hint of humanity in the eyes peeking through the mask. The figure wore an elaborate gown in the guise of the French aristocracy. Atop its head was a high blonde wig decorated with silver and gold butterflies that glimmered in the light. Around its neck was a red velvet band. I looked closer at the painted face, one that mocked me with a jubilant smile and rose blushed cheeks. The feminine smile was like death mocking me.

I wandered, trying to find the man I was looking for, Ludovico Zampieri. All the while I listened to conversations, dismayed at the wealth of all I saw. The jewels in the women's ears were worth more than my father made in a year. One mature woman struck me as interesting. She stood with a glass of clear liquid in one hand and a red Spanish fan in the other with which she was waving, wafting back and forth, wafting the peacock feather stuck atop her head, fitted between the tight coif of burgundy hair. She wore a conglomeration of clothing styles, both a mixture of masculine and feminine. On her upper half she wore a man's shirt, buttoned high to her collar, with velvet buttons embossed with lion heads. Around her neck was a long silver chain weighed by a silver cylinder that plunged between her breasts. It was clear that she wore neither bodice nor corset beneath her shirt. Her waist was cinched with a thick leather belt, and her ruby skirt was long, decorated with extravagant gold and silver embroidery that glistened in the light. As I looked, I saw that on her skirts were depictions of the Roman gods and goddesses that danced about the folds.

She looked at me.

"Well, don't just stare like some ruddy pigeon," she said, making me jolt where I stood. "Come on over, maybe you'll be of interest." She beckoned me with a turn of her hand. I could not help but follow.

"Bianca is my name, though those about here will call me Donna Bianca. The men here often call me a libertine, as if I had anything to do with the proclivities of de Sade. To the prudish I am a libertine and to the libertines I am a prude."

Donna Bianca had a young man who stood next to her, and she would turn her head and speak to him from time to time. The young man was not much older than I was, with trim black hair and a black mustache combed into clean curves that extended just beyond the edge of his lips. He seemed to me to be quite sure of himself, given the way in which he stood erect with his broad shoulders tipped back so his chest stood out and his chin held just slightly upwards so that he could peruse the array of partygoers.

When she turned to me, I noticed the slight wrinkles and hints of loose skin that denoted her age.

"Oh, another wistful sprite, I imagine. Before I waste my time, tell me: are you a girl with no more a thought in her head than what the fashionable color is for June, or do you have some substance about you?"

"I care neither for fashion nor color."

Bianca laughed. She then made a gesture towards my clothing. "I see."

"*Brava*. At least then I might find you interesting. Now, Cristofano and I were just discussing the topic of sodomy—"

I did nothing to hide my surprise.

"Does the word itself offend you?" she asked. "No need! We are all of us mature enough to speak of these things."

"Perhaps the word excited her?" Cristofano queried and took his attention from his indifferent appraisal of the others to me. He tilted his head downward and looked at me in such a way that reminded me of Azazel. At first, I turned away for a moment at his disarming gaze. Except I was drawn to meet his and then the Donna's.

"Merely surprised to hear it spoken aloud amongst the 'polite.' You see, I've only heard such language come from the lips of urchins."

The Donna laughed again, followed by a chuckle from Cristofano.

"To wit," she said. "For we are all urchins and should not pretend otherwise."

"I think I like this woman," Azazel said.

"Now, surely, amongst these Papist brethren they call that act a sin—a most horrid sin."

"Well, that is hardly surprising, for they all find sexuality sinful."

"Yes, but in this instance that act causes them the most prudishness. Why is that, *signora*?" she asked me. She placed her hand on Cristofano's shoulder and used her forefinger to gently caress the back of his ear. In response, he closed his eyes for a moment, and when he opened them, he took a slow inhale.

"It must be that they fear His judgment. If the priests permit these acts, they fear that the righteous would be destroyed along with the sinful, for His wrath in the Papal Bible is indiscriminate."

"She has a mind, this one!" Donna Bianca exclaimed, turning to the young man. She raised her glass and drank, finishing the liquid. She then turned to kiss Cristofano on the cheek.

"I see you staring at Cristofano," she said. "Who can help it? Look at all the pretty little birds flicking their attention at him. See that one, there, in the garish chartreuse dress?"

I looked to see the young woman Bianca mentioned. The dress was a lavish satin bustle dress embossed with flower patterns with a neckline that dipped, so when she breathed, her breasts pushed against the bust line where there was a prominent gemstones brooch surrounded by silver and gold butterflies. The young woman was striking in the black velvet circular mask that covered her face.

"She has rarely taken her sights from this young cuck since we arrived. I wonder if she will bolster the courage to come talk to him or wait there, apprehensively, for him to wander over and feign attention. Interesting, too, the mask she wears. Do you know it?"

I shook my head.

"It is the Moretta. The 'Silent Servant.' To wear it, there is a button affixed to the inside that the girl must hold with her lips. She cannot speak while she wears it. There must be something alluring in a speechless, faceless woman, for look at the men who pass."

I watched for a short time, seeing as the men in the room peered at her from where they stood or others who leered from the safety of their masks.

"How curious. What does she wait for, do you suppose?" Bianca asked.

There was a memory from the other soul of etiquette lessons, of how to behave around others, about how to act around young men, the proper ways of conduct for a lady.

"She seems to be of a proper upbringing. Young ladies are told certain ways to act, and to do otherwise would place them as a pariah. Consider that she is young. If she, alone, were to approach young Cristofano here and a woman such as yourself," Bianca nodded, "how would the others here react? How would that reflect on herself or on her family? She has much to risk."

"It is an antiquated supposition," Cristofano said.

"For you, perhaps, a young man who risks little by association." As I said it, I wished I had adjusted my tone, for it sounded meaner than I meant.

"She could be right," Donna said. "Because I am a widow I can do as I like with little scrutiny, but before, in my search for marriage, I often found that many men want virgins for wives and whores for fun. If that young girl misjudges you—and I guarantee she has—what gossip will they spread of her?"

He scoffed. "We are in Venezia! Who cares where a lady spreads her legs?"

"It depends on the lady," I said. "And for whom she is spreading her legs."

Bianca laughed. Cristofano's expression remained the same, but he tapped a finger against his glass.

"Ah, but you are still young, too," Bianca said to him. "And thank God for it! You see, these old men sit on their gold and silver, and the young take it out into the world. Like my husband, a stubborn man who took little chance in new endeavors, though he had the money three times over to avoid risk. He'd rather keep it, collect it, leave it there and for what? So he can have the most of it. It's strange, isn't it? What do these old men lack that they must make up for by hoarding money? Money is power. Only the most insecure men desire power. The most secure will give it willingly." She smirked and looked sidelong at her partner. "Is that not true, Cristofano?"

The young man nodded once and had a clear smile on his face.

"Power is what we all want," Bianca said. "It takes us as close as we can to the level of God. When you are in the throes of passion, at the apex of desire, tell me, do you not see the eyes of God?"

I felt my skin warm. I could hear my own voice in my memory blaspheming the name as I felt my body respond. I thought of the bawdy house where we delivered the baby, where I wandered and gazed through the keyholes to see bodies and voices calling out to the almighty.

"Why else do you scream out His name when that climax is reached?"

"Why indeed?" Azazel purred in my ear.

I adjusted my posture.

"I have never thought much about that," I admitted.

She leaned forward and stroked her finger on the hem of my sleeve as if to appraise my garment.

"If you are not a woman of means, how did you come here?"

"I have means enough."

"Are you new to money, much like Cristofano here?"

"I got lucky in trade."

"So, you see why these young girls want him. In a room of old rich men, here is a bachelor."

"They come with their own romantic ideas. They expect me to fall in love and propose. In general, I am against marriage," he said, then waved his hand in the air as if to erase what was just said. "Though not completely opposed."

"Too much focus is made on marriage," Bianca said. "I was married fifteen years to a fine enough man, yes, but I was young when I married. I see that now. Sixteen is no age to marry—it is an age to have fun. You see, I had it backwards. I had too much responsibility at that young age: to my husband, to my children, so now that he is dead and they are grown, I can be as I like."

"Surely marriage can be a beautiful event between those who love each other."

"Indeed. If two people love each other, why not marry? And if two cease to love, why not divorce? There, you see, there is the problem. It is no hardship to fall in love and marry, but what happens when that love ends?"

I thought again. It did happen that love could fade. When it did, why should the man or woman suffer through a loveless relationship? In my own religion, there was a dissolution of marriage. There was no doubt that love was fluid. I heard the other voice. What had Ephraim said about love? And did I still love him? I had died and yet that love remained, from us both.

"Love *should* not end," I surmised.

"Should, yes," said Cristofano. "But not everything happens as it should."

"True," I said.

"Reality is often different than we want. We cannot help but romanticize it because it is dull."

"You are a romantic?"

"One cannot help it when there is so much beauty." The Donna took Cristofano's arm in hers. "The trick is to live only in the present, to be happy with things as they are, now, in this moment. That is all that we are given."

The young girl in chartreuse stood up and walked past, making sure to lock eyes with Cristofano as she did, and then giggled as she walked away. He sighed as she left.

"Here is where we differ," Cristofano said. "Such liberal living is reserved for the wealthy who need not worry about money or standing."

I liked him more for this revelation.

"For most of us, we cannot help but worry about the past,

the future, because, for us, nothing is certain. That uncertainty prevents us from true happiness."

"What of commandments, of our duties to others?"

"Our duty is to ourselves, absolutely."

"That is the height of selfishness," I said.

"It is," she said. "Our minds exist to serve the self. Why are we here except to serve the self? Think about how you begin your life. A child is born to selfishness. Without it, how could they survive? When a child needs food, they will demand it regardless of the health of the mother; when they need comfort they will scream until it is given. So it is when you grow into adulthood. Name me a moment when you acted without selfishness, if you can. Think even of our Christ who, in the ultimate act of selflessness, sacrificed his life so that we might live without sin. And yet, what was the outcome of that? He rose from death and became one with God. You see?"

"Am I supposed to?" I asked.

"That act of sacrifice was selfishness. What did Christ receive from his death? He became God. It is not altruism if one gains something in return."

I tried to speak with confidence, but in truth I was no biblical scholar nor a student of the Torah. Still, I shared some insight. "It could be that it is the intent and the result that matter."

"Interesting," Cristofano said. "And what do *you* believe?"

"Good question," Azazel said.

It was impossible to answer them with the truth of my existence and how it showed the will of HaShem. I had to explain it another way.

"Life is sacred, but so is death. Without death, there can be no life. For our human souls to exist at all requires destruction: We must slaughter animals to eat, we must raze the earth to build, we must die so that others can live. If death were an abomination, then HaShem would have never created it in this world. He would have never given us the choice."

"Hm, you are full of contradictions," the Donna mused, turning her sights to the side. "That does give me something to think about."

Cristofano laughed.

"You're always so full of words. It's curious to see you silenced."

Bianca nudged him playfully. She then turned to him.

"Shall we invite her?" she asked. "She may prove enlightening."

Cristofano appraised me briefly.

"If she likes."

Donna Bianca called one of the attendants and asked for a pen and paper. When the attendant returned with a silver pen and a sheet of paper pressed with gold leaf Venezian lions at the head, Bianca took them and wrote down an address. She then gave the letter to me, held between her middle and forefinger.

"We are staying at this address." She handed me the piece of paper. "Come there tonight, and we can show you what it is to be a libertine. Whatever your desire, I guarantee we can provide it."

"I have work to do tonight," I said.

"Come now, Tziporah," said Azazel. "This may be fun."

I am not here for fun. I thought.

"Such a pity," Bianca said. "But before you must go ..." She then approached me and whispered in my ear, "Whisper the depths of your depravity."

I turned to her to shield my confession from those around me and heard the sound of Azazel's voice through mine.

I thought of saying nothing. Yet, the confession was on my lips before I could recall it.

"It is blood I need," I whispered. I reveled in admitting it aloud to an apathetic room.

To this answer, Bianca chuckled. A deep sound reverberated in her throat.

"Delightful," she said.

I took a long exhalation.

She pulled away so I could see her smiling face.

"I have heard of such fetishes before but have never experienced one myself. Come and show us what you can do. Now, you must excuse us," Bianca said, "as all this talk has made me want to take my young love here behind one of the curtains."

I watched them walk away, down one of the corridors. Azazel laughed, and I looked at him.

"What a fantastic woman," he said.

Never mind, I thought.

I continued around the party to find Zampieri and stopped in the middle of the corridor, even as all the other guests entered the ballroom, mesmerized by the gilded hallway, the frescos with images of the fickle Roman gods. It seemed that everywhere I gazed was gold. And then I saw the face I was looking for. There amongst the crowds, a man had lifted his mask to better drink from a glass. The man was Zampieri.

CHAPTER EIGHTEEN

I t was his mask that I recognized next. It was a colorful jester, a rainbow motley that covered the mask, extending to the five points that surrounded the crown. When he moved, the bells atop the points jingled. He was standing with two men in masks who were speaking to each other. One of the men had his Gato mask resting atop his head so that he could drink from his wine glass. The other wore a black Arlecchino mask. I craned to hear their conversation.

"He talks about the free market for businesses. He would be a fool to trample on the money that is made through our efforts," the Gato man said.

"That is what he has said in the past. As he has gained more followers and more power since his *Marcia su Roma*, who is to say he would not extend that reach? No. We must be careful," said Zampieri.

Arlecchino scoffed. "You are being paranoid. No matter who is in power, our class is always protected. They need us more than we need them."

"When it comes to money," said the voice belonging to Zampieri, "it is of interest to be cautious."

"Too much caution can result in missed opportunities."

"And too much risk can result in failure."

Zampieri turned to the man. "Are we still just talking about money?"

"*Basta!* Leave the man be," Arleccino said.

The Gato man shrugged and drank the remainder of his wine.

"I must say it is good to be at your party. Such a shame that it was not held last year. My condolences."

The man clapped Zampieri on the shoulder.

"It is good to have you here, although seeing you all again has made me realize that I much prefer to be in a house in mourning."

The men laughed, and Zampieri with them. I chuckled as well.

The man in the Gato mask tipped his glass but found it empty. He left to find a server to refill it. The other man was still with Zampieri, but I needed to speak to him alone. What I found that men responded to most was the suggestion of seduction, so I straightened my back and walked towards him.

"*Signore,*" I said and touched him gently on the shoulder. He turned. "I wondered if you would take a drink with me?"

"Oho!" exclaimed the other man. "Do not pass up the opportunity, Zampieri. They come less and less as time goes on."

Zampieri tipped his head down to find my eyes. He squinted and then opened them wide.

"Then I will take it," he said to his friends.

He took my hand in his, and I remembered all the times when he had done it before. Faustina's soul felt safe in his hands. I was not sure if I should.

"Such a firm hand," Zampieri said.

I had not realized how tightly I gripped his hand, and I let myself relax.

"Forgive me, *signore*," I said. "I am nervous to be in such a wealthy house."

"Ah, indeed. I remember my first time in the presence of richness." He led me away from the main rooms, where the partygoers danced and enjoyed their frivolity, and down a hallway. "I was a boy, and my mother was such a woman of faith that she had taken me to visit Roma, to the Vaticano. While there, we and a few others from the church were guided through the interior. All was gold and silver and richness. I decided then that I would bathe myself in such splendor. Now, to do it, I had either to join the clergy or find a less savory way to earn my wealth."

We turned a corner and found a closed door with a silver handle. He turned it, and it opened to a room that I recognized as his, though it had changed from what I remembered. I stepped into the dim room and Zampieri followed behind. He walked inside and turned up oil lamps which were set about the room. At each turn of the lamp, new spectacles of luxury glowed. There was more opulence than I had ever seen, as if he were shrouding himself in money to protect himself from sorrow. I noticed a photograph hung upon the wall in the room. It surprised me. Looking closer, I saw that it was a wedding portrait. The woman in the picture had a clean, simple gown with lacework accents on the collar and surrounding the edges of the veil. Such lacework might cost more than a half year's salary, I reasoned. Faustina was in many of the portraits and even frame photographs, spoiled with trinkets that merchants brought from the East, colorful silks to accent gowns, sweet perfumes, gold baubles; there was nothing that Zampieri did not give her.

Zampieri returned to where I stood and closed the door behind me. He then sat upon the bed, wrinkling the shiny silk sheets underneath. He pulled the jester mask off his face. He was as I imagined, yet with a few more wrinkles and more facial hair. He may have been a father, but he was also a man. There were certain things that men desired, no matter the age.

I removed my mask as well and held it at my side. We stared at each other for some time, and in that abyss between us was Azazel, who was like a wraith in the darkness.

"Shall you look on him with my eyes?" Azazel asked.

I shifted my sight to the demon. What I needed to know was in the old man's head. I nodded. I felt his finger on my forehead. In the room alone with the man, I could focus on his mind and on what I saw there. The visions that flashed behind my eyes were of unscrupulous actions that I suspected all men who desire wealth will take: lies, deceit, and yet also love and kindness. The love he had for his wife, and when she passed in childbirth, to his daughter. I saw Ephraim as well and the trust he had with the young man. I watched and felt his agony at Faustina's death.

"Now, then, *signorina*, you asked to take a drink. Was it a drink you wanted or something else?"

He gazed at me longingly. Though I knew of what it was he insinuated, I chose to speak directly.

"Something else," I said. "Your daughter's death."

Zampieri's face fell. He stood abruptly to walk towards the door and put his fingers on the handle.

"You may go. I will not think of death tonight."

"Nor does anyone wish to think of it," I said. "But I knew her."

Zampieri pulled his hand away. He came towards me.

"Were you a friend of hers?" the father asked. "She had so many friends." His eyes turned to some distant point. "The house was filled with chatter and parties." His eyes blushed red, his face contorting, fighting the sadness. "How I complained, then."

"She was a joy," I said.

"She was." He let out a shuddering breath. "Sometimes I am walking, and I can still hear her voice in the house, in her room, or in the garden, and I look, and she is not there."

"It is grief that makes life impossible," I said. "You do not want to live without them and still you continue in spite of it."

"How could she have died?" he said. "There was her body, lying on the floor, as if asleep. They said her heart stopped. How could it? She was healthy: never an illness, even as a child. How young she was. A heart failing is an old man's death, not one so young."

He could hold in the tears no longer and he sat, weeping, lifting his hand to rest on his forehead, hiding his tears.

Compassion compelled me to rise. Impulse coaxed me to embrace him, so I settled by placing a hand on his shoulder.

"All are called to Him in their time," I said, though my words sounded hollow, even to my own ears.

I wanted to tell him that it was an accident. That it was bad fortune, that Faustina should have been there, that curiosity made her lift the veil and gaze into the mirror. I wanted to tell him that it was me who had done it so that he could know the truth of her death. I wanted to tell him that were it not for Ephraim, both myself and his daughter would still be alive. If I had never been murdered, I would not have had to kill others. My death had been the catalyst for all the destruction that succeeded it. I had to find Ephraim to mend all the wrongs that had passed.

"What of her husband?"

He waved his hand dismissively. "Gone. Left after her body was found in some refuge in Salzburg. His guilt must have gotten the better of him. I cannot send the *polizia* to fetch him there. I even went myself to try to get him back, and all he did was keep his doors fastened tightly."

In his memories I watched as he pounded on a yellow door painted with red flowers. When the door remained closed, I felt Zampieri's powerlessness. He spoke to a priest in a confessional who advised him of acceptance and told him of "God's grace." His grace was the one who sent me.

"Perhaps an assassin?" I said with a smirk.

"I would not consider myself a vengeful man," he said. "I do not want him dead—I want to look into his eyes as he is shackled behind bars in the Ponte di Sospiri. But the coward will not return," he sighed. "I should have known better than to trust a Jew."

I bit the tip of my tongue. He was a murderer and untrustworthy, but it was not because of his Judaism. It was in spite of it.

"Where is he in Salzburg?"

"Why do you care?"

"I want him to see justice as well."

Zampieri remained where he sat, his expression unchanged from a solemn and tired demeanor. His frown lines and wrinkles and signs of age seemed more pronounced in the light illuminating from the oil lanterns.

"You said you were her friend?"

I nodded.

"Please," I said in an effort to convince him. "I know it may be impossible, but I want to try." I met his eyes with as sincere an expression as I could muster. "Faustina was my friend."

Zampieri scratched his chin.

"In those early days after she died, I never left the house. Every day I saw her, heard her speak. It was the same when her mother died, but this was different. How else could I feel when my child had been taken from me? I was filled with a—an insatiable fury. First God takes my wife, and then a man takes my daughter. And here I am, still living. How can I—how can anyone—keep living when there has been so much suffering?"

I did not have an answer to his question. I hoped that my guilt did not show on my face, so I shook my head meekly.

"We must trust in God. All suffering and all joy are by His hand."

He then kissed me on my cheek.

He stood up and went to a writing desk that sat before a window that overlooked the canal. He opened a drawer and then stood there a moment as if wrapped in thought. I paced near him, near the desk. In his eyes I saw the house where Ephraim lived. It was a house with a yellow door and a bronze address plaque with the number three, and under it, the name "Virgilgasse." In the sky were mountains, and there was a scent in the air of spring flowers and fried fish.

"If I could not compel him to return, perhaps you would have better luck. Much as I would like to believe that I would see him waste away in prison, I have little hope."

Zampieri held up a postcard of a cityscape, a river, and under the picture, a small script which read, "Salzburg von der Festung."

He handed it to me. When I took it, I flipped it over. There was the address for Zampieri's *palazzetto* and another address under the initial "E." On the blank space next to it were the words, *"Mi dispiace."* I nearly threw the postcard on the floor. After everything that had happened, all he had to say was that he was sorry. Had his hands never found their way around my throat, none of the subsequent deaths would have ever happened. I looked back at the man before me.

"Thank you," was all I could say.

"You can thank me by putting him in manacles."

CATORI SARMIENTO

I slid the postcard into my pocket and left the room, along with Zampieri, who slid his mask back over his face.

"I suggest you do the same," he said to me, "unless you do not care about scurrilous gossip."

I did not, but I followed his advice all the same. I thanked him again and made my way back through the house, intent on leaving and preparing my plans of how I would travel to Salzburg, to Ephraim. In my haste, I brushed against a shoulder and heard the crashing of glass and a shout. When I turned to the sound, there was a man who lifted his mask at once.

The man. I thought I recognized him. He looked like someone I once knew, but I was not sure. He seemed familiar. The set of his jaw, his cheek, how confidently he stood. I saw in his mind that he had contemptuous inklings, and I turned away.

"Interesting man," I heard from Azazel. He shifted from my side and before me, passing by the adoring women to view the man. "So many dizzying ideas in his head." Azazel looked at me and smiled, as if he knew a secret that he kept to himself. "He has plans for one of these women." Azazel clicked his tongue. "Who will the lucky one be?"

I peered at the man and found a memory. His beauty besotted a young woman, as it did to the young, vibrant woman speaking to him, her closed fan shielding her lips. She wanted to move to him, to wrap her arms around him and kiss his lips as she had once done.

Take me away from here, she would say, and he would gingerly take her hand, excuse himself, and retire to a quiet room where he would embrace her lovingly and tell her all the beautiful, comforting words that she wanted to hear. I tried to strangle the thoughts. They were lies. They were always lies. Even now, as he smiled and spoke to the woman, she was bashful, or feigned bashfulness, at the way he touched her hand, gently, as if in suggestion. When she drank from the cup he filled with sweet wine and a powder mixed in, I could feel his satisfaction. Then I saw her unconscious on the bed. My cheeks became hot. My muscles tensed. If I could get him somewhere alone, I could stab him through the neck.

I secured my mask.

He led me to an alcove. An open window overlooking the grand canal. A gondola passed below, the gondolier singing, his tune rising above the currents so that I could just hear the melody. The curtain furled closed behind me. I did nothing to attempt to hide my satisfied smile. There he was, standing, holding the glasses in his hand, one held out to me.

I could push him, I thought. He would fall into the canal and drown. I could make it look accidental. Kiss him and caress him and then suddenly he would find himself cascading through the air. I would scream and hurry inside to ask for help.

But what if he lived? I could not risk anything other than my own hand drawing his blood. Here, among so many eyes, I could not do it. I could. Who could stop me? A voice murmured doubt.

I have to hear him speak.

"Beautiful night," I said.

"Every night is beautiful in Venezia when you're sitting in a *palazzo* with a gorgeous woman," he said.

I smiled, a placation to his ego.

"I don't recognize you," he said.

"Should you? A masque should hide who we really are."

He laughed.

"How do you like *Italia*?" he asked.

I scoffed. I had lived in Venezia my whole life. When I was young and my eyes fresh and optimistic, I drank in every detail. I woke up every morning excited for the newness of the day, of fun to be had, of games to play. There was joy in the smallest things, a childish happiness of spotting a fish swimming in the canal and trying to catch it, of climbing a tree, of drinking the watered-down wine on Shabbat. I remember laughing and cheerfulness. All that was gone.

I shrugged.

"That's all you can do? You're in the most beautiful city, and all you can do is—" He mimicked my gesture. "You must embrace everything around you. Here," the man said, offering a glass.

I waved my hand in refusal.

"Come, it is *grappa*."

"Even more a reason not to drink," I answered.

The man laughed.

"Well, yes, of course it is strong. This is real alcohol."

"I do not usually drink."

"No? To drink is to live. You see, every chance we can, we drink. It is a real way to relax."

"You can have mine, then."

"*Salute*," he said, then drank from each glass and left the empty ones to sit on the balcony rail.

I thought I could stab him in the neck with my pin. With the noise from inside, I was confident no one would hear. I feigned smoothing out my hair to touch the pin. As I did, I felt my fingers quiver and my eyesight becoming blurry. The Demon Eyes were beginning to affect me. If I killed him and took his blood, I would feel healthy once more. My tiredness began affecting my resolve to kill him.

"Now, did you see all the women here?"

"What about them?" I could hear my own irritation as I said it.

"Romani, Italiana, all of them."

"And? What are you?"

He recoiled. "Me? I am Venezian." He drank. "True Venezian," he added.

I had no patience for the man, so I stood up to leave. He took my hand gently.

"So soon? You're too pretty to drink alone," I heard a voice say.

"Beauty has nothing to do with loneliness."

He waved his hand in a brushing motion.

I watched as he peeked through the curtain and gestured for another drink. As I watched him sully himself with drink, he became more unrecognizable. His hands struggled to hold the glass and then it slipped, and I saw an irregularity on his hands. Seeing his hands, I stepped closer to appraise them. This man's hands were different. On his right, his four fingers were stunted. They were short tips and small nails, the second knuckle missing on each.

As the man leaned against the balcony, he lost his footing and tumbled over. I ran to the edge to try and grab him, but all I caught was air. In a splash, he was in the canal, shouting. He flailed and tried to swim.

The server came and at once shouted to others to come and look. My head throbbed. I could not stay, so I left.

CHAPTER NINETEEN

I slinked from the party where all were looking over the balcony at the man now thrashing in the canal. They gasped and laughed at his drunkenness. As I passed the gilded hallways with the ornate decorations, I heard shouts and murmurings as I pushed past others. I could not dismiss the horrible feeling of being watched. It existed all around me; I felt their gaze on my back. It vexed me all the more, wanting to lash out at the next person I saw who looked at me unfavorably. I was sure that there was some delectable scent floating through the air that, despite my efforts, I could not detect.

Then there were calls for the *polizia*, and I moved faster. It was difficult to move very quickly, as I was becoming dizzy. My breath blew sharply against the inside of my mask. I stumbled once, and I heard voices directed at me. As soon as their voices emerged, they disappeared. I was focused on my immediate need. The Demon Eyes had drained me of some of my energy, and I needed to replenish it as soon as I could, but I could not do it until I was alone. I kept on until my feet sloshed in the flooded street. Some distance away, I stopped and hid in an alley. My fingers trembled as I retrieved the vial I had hidden away next to my skin. I slipped my mask off and let it fall with a splash onto the wet stones. Then, I opened the vial and shook the ash out into my palm, then spread it over my face. As soon as it touched my skin, I was relieved. The ailments that had been affecting me dissipated.

I soaked my hands in the water to wash the ash from my face, hoping that the water was clean enough, knowing that it was not. My mind cleared, and I knew where Ephraim was and that I would find him. That thought alone made me want to celebrate. With my mind sharper and my spirits renewed, I thought that I should indulge before the night was finished.

My feet led me to an unfamiliar street, and I found myself holding a piece of paper with Donna Bianca's address. Before me was a plain looking door and a coral painted wall. I knocked, and a strapping middle-aged man opened it. By his state of dress, I guessed he was a Gentleman's servant.

"Yes?" he asked.

I thought I must look disheveled and pushed the wayward strands of hair from my face, tucking them behind my ear and smoothing them back.

"Donna Bianca invited me," I said.

"Of course. She has been in high spirits tonight. You must be the 'intriguing girl' she mentioned."

"I suppose."

"And I assume you know the purpose for your being here? I'd hate to have to receive yet another reproach from one who misunderstood the Donna's intent."

"I know exactly why I'm here," I said. "The Donna and her young cuckold are libertines who wished me to join them."

The man chuckled.

"Then come in," he said.

The inside was much simpler than I had imagined. It was

not like the opulent house where we previously met. In contrast, this house was bare, with the most minimal of accents. Oil paintings were placed on blank walls. In the sitting room, detailed couch frames were padded with velvet or silk. I watched as the gentleman went upstairs. His soft inside shoes tapped on the marble steps.

I sat on the couch and melted into the comfort of the cushions. My heart still fluttered from the excitement of fleeing the scene, so I closed my eyes for a moment, trying to calm my heartbeat. I hoped that I would be safe in a wealthy home. The man fell over the balcony. No one could have seen me with him or where I had gone. I would have to repair it somehow. The freshest memories came when my soul was full, when I consumed the forbidden blood. When I opened my eyes, I saw movement through the lit room. It was a large rock that seemed to be wobbling over the tile. I thought I must be more tired than I imagined. When I got up to look closer, I saw that it was a rather large tortoise that was lumbering around the room.

"You have met Josephine," the Gentleman said.

"A . . . pet?"

"A gift." The man blinked slowly. "The Donna will see you."

The man led me out of the room and toward a flight of stairs. As we ascended the stairs, I glanced at the framed art on the walls, the porcelain statues set on side tables.

"I think you can find your own way from here. The Donna does not like me to interrupt unnecessarily."

As I moved out of the open entryway, there were the softest whimpers coming from behind a closed door in the hallway. I tiptoed towards it, unable to resist the temptation of eavesdropping. With long, carefully placed steps, I put my body flat against the door to turn the brass knob stealthily so that it made only the minutest click when it unlatched, opening it to a sliver so that I could peek through with one eye. Two bodies lay on a bed. Cristofano gasped for breath and Bianca, smiling, had a hand at his throat and then released him. When she did, the young man inhaled and then moaned. Azazel took my hand in his and used me to push the door open completely. I turned to chastise him but stopped when Bianca called out to me.

"What a surprise!" she said.

Cristofano turned. When he saw me, he raised his eyebrows.

"Will she join us?" he asked breathlessly, but then his attention returned to Bianca.

"Why else would she be here?"

Bianca gestured for me to go forward.

I stepped closer. A shout came from downstairs and stopped me. Soon, the door opened, and a uniformed Carabinieri emerged. I froze. The Donna followed my gaze to the men, and when she saw them, composed herself. She pushed me gently away from her and she stood.

"*Singore*," she said. "To what do I owe this intrusion?"

The Carabinieri took in the scene, with one whose eyebrows seemed pinned to his forehead, and the other who stared at Bianca's nakedness and then blinked to regain his composure.

"This woman must come with us," he said.

"And spoil our fun?" she asked. The Donna approached the men closer. "Or perhaps you'd like to join us and forget this trifling business?"

The younger officer was piqued at her invitation. He stepped forward, showing his arousal pressing against the inside of his trousers. How easy it was to change a man's mind. The other officer looked over, scoffed, and pushed the young man back.

"Ah, any other time, we may have, Donna. But this one's got to come with us."

"What do you want with her?" Cristofano asked.

"She was seen at the time and place of Console Endrizzi's death."

"Well, you must be mistaken," Donna said. "She had been with us all night."

"That's not what your man downstairs says."

Cristofano scoffed. "Are you going to trust the words of an old butler? He would mistake a cat running down the street for a bear."

The two officers were silent. The young one kept staring at the naked Donna.

"Even so," the old officer said, "I have to bring someone in."

The old officer stepped towards me. I thought of running at first but decided that running would make me look guilty. It would give them a reason to make me a scapegoat. I would get no fair justice from them. How easily had they dismissed my death the first time! They would absolve themselves of any oversight or mistake. My heart throbbed. I had to think straight and couldn't. I didn't want to go with them. Going with them meant prison. I would die there. It wasn't death that scared me but that I would leave my murderer free. What could I do?

"No need to worry, Donna," I said, changing my tone to mimic her natural confidence as best as I could. "I will cooperate."

I dressed, hoping that they didn't notice my hands shaking as I slipped my dress back on my shoulders.

"Gentlemen," I said.

The young man took me by the arm, but gently, as if in suggestion. As they led me away, the young man stole a last glance at the scene we were departing.

"We hope to see you again," I heard Bianca say as we left.

As the men led me down the stairs, I heard Cristofano curse loudly.

I walked with them slowly, trying to think of how I would escape their grasp. I could kill them, though I didn't want to. They may not be sinners. If I killed them, it would be a waste of life, particularly if they were the rare, good men who were the arm of law. I wanted to see if they could be, but I could not feel Azazel. I thought of him, mouthed his name to beckon him to come to me, and I felt nothing. Without him, I could not condemn these men.

I walked with them unaware of where I was, too focused inside my head. I could hear our footsteps, the water in the canal, and even as I tried to plan how I would walk away from these two officers, I was already behind the iron bars of the jail.

CHAPTER TWENTY

They took me by my hands. Hands that I had been strong enough to kill were weak against theirs. I would not fight against them. Fighting would give them reason to be brutal. Fighting would make it seem I was guilty.

My mind processed the moments in a broken sequence. I followed them as they led me across the stones, a heavy door, and the iron bars. I could not think. All I could feel were their hands, which removed my Bona Dea hat pin and the glass bottle. I had nothing else which proved dangerous. Soon, they guided me down a dank corridor, past wooden doors without windows, padlocked, though sounds came from behind. I knew then what they would do, but there was no fighting back. I could run, but they would likely catch me before I could make it out the door. They stopped before one of the wooden doors, unlocked it, opened it, pushed me in, then closed the door and locked it.

I wanted to scream. I was a moment away from pure blood. What I could have done with that! What memories could be extracted! I had two days. Two days and I would waste away. Two days.

I hoped there were rats.

It was then I noticed two others with me in the cell. One sat upon the floor braiding her hair in an elaborate fashion, and then when finished, ran her fingers through it and braided again. As she did, she would hum a low tune that murmured, easily lost in the other sounds that echoed through the bars and stones. The other was squatting against the wall with her pleated brown skirt gathered up to her waist; she looked at me and said, *"Buona sera."* When the smell wafted to my nose, I realized why she was squatting. I heard talking, banging, and at times screaming. If it came to it, I thought of sampling their blood, taking enough to survive another day. Not that I wanted to, but at times it was more important to do what was necessary.

I appraised my situation in the jail. The walls were all stone with one window no larger than my forearm, crossed with oxidized iron bars. Outside, the night sky blended into the emerging dawn that hid behind clouds heavy with rain. A dampness consumed the air inside the jail. The scent of the coming rains from outside, the sloshing canal waters beneath, the stain of urine and of unwashed bodies all combined in a smell that settled at the back of my throat. I swallowed to try to be rid of it. My heart began to beat faster. The confined space reminded me of how I was buried beneath the ground, dying as I was unable to free myself. I tried to calm my racing heart, so I took a deep breath, but with the stagnant, rotten air, my throat closed up. I shut my eyes and leaned against a wall. My legs were weak, so I sat.

I cannot be here, I thought.

Though the rest of my body was weak, my heart pounded as rapidly as if I were sprinting. My eyes darted around the room, searching for a way out. I looked back at the woman braiding her hair.

"How long have you been here?" I asked.

She continued as if she had not heard me.

I wanted to hit the stone walls and scream. Still, I had to keep my composure. Throwing a fit would solve nothing except make me look like a hysterical woman. I thought of the hands on my throat. I knew what men did to hysterical women.

My bladder ached from the wine I had hours before. In this small room there was no privy, only an open grate between the stones that led to the canal underneath. I squatted over it, pulled up my skirts and pulled my underthings to the side. The woman who braided her hair looked over at me, stared a moment, and laughed. She said something in a language I did not know and then turned away, still chuckling.

I stood up and rearranged my dress and slip, and I began pacing, for there was not much else to do inside these stone walls.

"Come along," the young man said.

They took me to a room without windows. In it was a single chair. The man prompted me to sit, so I did.

"You were at the scene, you fled, your mask was found with what looked like blood."

"You knew the Console Edrizzi," he said.

"No."

"But you were with him on the balcony just before he fell."

I wondered whether I should admit to that. If I did, would they designate me as his murderer due to happenstance? I wasn't sure.

"So," the other officer said, "the Console?"

I tried to think of a convincing lie. The longer I stayed silent, thinking, the more I worried that my silence would paint me as guilty. My mind was blank. I couldn't think. Where was

Azazel to whisper in my ear? I had to say something, so I decided on the truth. If the truth didn't work, I supposed that I could kill them.

"We were on the balcony," I said.

"Why?" one said abruptly.

"The Console invited me to drink with him," I said.

One nodded, and the other raised his eyebrows. I found it difficult to look at either of them. Where was Azazel now? If he gave me the Demon Eyes, could I use them to help me escape from the prison?

"Azazel," I whispered.

"What was that?" one of them asked.

I shook my head.

"The console invited me to have a drink," I repeated. "And he fell."

"Are you sure?"

"I am sure."

Though I said the words, I noticed that my hands were quivering.

"But there was quite a lot of alcohol. How can you be sure that is what happened?"

"The wine was not kosher," I said plainly.

One laughed. And in the distance, I heard Azazel laugh with him.

"Surely, you can tell that I am innocent."

After that, the Carabinieri officers said nothing at all. I was innocent of the cause of the man's fall, and yet I did at one moment intend to kill him. That it occurred by happenstance did not change what I had meant to do. And certainly, I was not innocent of murder. I had killed and intended to kill again. Did it matter to these men that those I killed were guilty? That they were absolved by humanity's justice by luck or error? These men could not see what I could. The facts were that I was near the Console before he fell over the balcony, and I had run. To them, I seemed guilty, and that was enough.

The one who laughed looked at me with what seemed to be sincerity.

"In truth," he said, "we can take your statement here, but it is likely you will be taken to the Carceri di Regina Coeli in any case."

The Carceri di Regina Coeli. The Queen of Heaven prison. I was motionless. I did not speak for some time as I tried to process what they were saying. I could not be in prison. I had a *mitzvah*, and I could not leave it unfulfilled. I had to find a way out. I could kill them and escape. No. There would be more. They would find me. Even if I killed these two *polizia*, there were others in the small jail who could come for me. And should I escape, where could I go? The only way out of the island was by train or boat, and they would surely patrol those avenues. And if I killed them, did they deserve death? These men were doing their duty. I would have to find another way. I tried to calm my nerves, though I was sure they could see through my facade. If I noticed my quivering hands, it was likely that they did too.

"If you confess," one began, "your time there may be shorter."

"I cannot confess to what I did not do."

"You must have done it."

I thought back to myself on that balcony, thinking of pushing him over the ledge, deciding against it. I saw him fall. I was sure it was an accident. He was drunk and fell. The surety the officers had of my guilt made my convictions waver. Still, I could not let them influence me.

"I did nothing to him."

They kept talking to me, saying the same thing with minor variations. I answered the same, and all the while I was thinking about how to get myself away from inside their walls. At times, their men changed. The original officers left and were replaced by two new men. Though their voices had slight variations, they began to look the same to me. They asked me questions, over and over, and no answer seemed to satisfy them. Always in the back of my mind were Azazel's murmurings. In between the spiraling voices, I saw the memories from the Console and what they had revealed to me.

At times I would stop answering, which made them shout at me. Then I would answer in the same way. It all became circular. I was not sure how much time passed. Eventually, they took me back to the cell with the other women and for once I was relieved to be there. I was so tired that I curled up on the hard floor and fell asleep. When I woke, it was to chapped lips and a dry throat. Azazel pushed my hair from my face.

"I do not want you to die, especially here," said Azazel.

"I will find a way out."

A wretched stench caused me to hold my breath. It was the woman with the braids who was squatting over the privy hole. I turned to the wall and traced the rough patterns in the stones to pass the time while I thought of ways to escape. I did not have many days before I would begin to waste away. There were two women near me who I could take blood from. Even if I did, I did not have my candle to perform the ritual properly. I could not make the ash. I would have to trust that fresh blood on my skin would perform in the same manner. With what device could I take blood? I had nothing to pierce skin; the *polizia* made sure of that. My teeth were the sharpest tools I had. I was forbidden from consuming blood, and I did not want to break that commandment, for what would become of me if I did? I only knew that I must not.

A sound came from one of the guards who brought a meager meal for each of us. The woman with the braids took hers first and had a scuffle with the other woman as she tried to steal her meal. This caused the guard to open the door and enter, removing both women and leaving my meal on the floor. I was happy for the silence. Though I did not eat the stale bread, I drank the tepid water. It was gritty and left a grimy taste at the back of my throat. Past the door, I heard shouts and screams from the women and the *polizia*.

"I could use the Demon Eyes," I whispered.

Azazel sat before me, crossed legged, with an elbow rested on a knee and a hand on his chin.

"And drain what little life you have left?"

I tapped my finger against the stones.

"If I do nothing, I will die here anyway. How else am I to leave?" I breathed in deeply and looked up at the narrow window.

If I were a bird, I would fly away with you.

I smiled at the memory of Ephraim whispering it in my ear only for that sweetness I felt to be replaced with hatred.

"When I ask," I said, "give me the eyes."

I looked at him and at his befuddled expression.

"Trust me."

I marked the time by the ringing of the bells from the Campanile di San Marco. The women had returned, more docile than before. Each time the bells sounded, one of the women would count the rings and then recite a Latin prayer.

When evening came, one of the guards opened the observation window, a horizontal slat that allowed him to pass objects through. The other women stood and made a line in front. There, the guard handed them a meal, or what constituted a meal in the holding cell: two rolls of bread and a wooden cup of water. The women did not complain. Far from it, they each took their share rabidly. The beginning effects of a lack of blood meant my appetite was beginning to wane. Nevertheless, I took the food and ate.

It was impossible to sleep in that cell with the women. The woman with the braids slept sitting up, propping her head in the corner, and snored so loudly that each time I thought I was drifting to sleep, her snuffling woke me. The other woman curled up on the stone floor and seemed to be sleeping soundly. I attempted to do the same. Halfway through the night, the *polizia* who passed by keeping watch had given three thin wool blankets through the opening in the wooden door. Because the woman with the braids slept, I was able to take one but was soon pushed out of the way by the other woman who snatched the other two, using them for herself. She eyed me, as if to challenge me, but I said nothing. I was tired from the lack of blood. All I wanted to do was sleep.

I listened for mice or small creatures from which I could take blood but had not heard nor seen any. My mind turned to the women in the cell. Their blood would be easy to acquire without killing them, as I had done to the fornicator at the cemetery. Yet, I had no weapon that I could use to incapacitate them. If I attacked one, surely the other would feel threatened and then lash out at me. I could assault them as they slept. That might create the bigger problem of the *polizia* finding me in a cell harming their prisoners and giving them more reason to suspect me. I would have to be subtle.

I thought of Ornias and how that demon had consumed the blood from babies by pricking their thumbs. That might be easy enough, and barely detectable, though, I wondered if I could pass that threshold; to drink blood was a great sin.

"Azazel," I whispered.

His form appeared next to me, lying on the floor facing the ceiling.

"What happens if I drink blood?" I asked quietly, so as to

not arouse the attention of the sleeping women. Feeling a chill, I wrapped the blanket around me.

"Ah, that is a thing you must not do," he said. "The candle purifies the blood. The ash rejuvenates the soul and protects from the ills present in the blood you take. To consume blood fully, to drink it, would cause the other souls to overtake your own. You would begin to kill without cause and seek out the innocent because theirs is the purest blood. You would have nothing of yourself." He paused to stretch about the floor. "I have seen it happen."

I traced the ridges on the stones with my finger, each one coarse against my skin. If I pressed hard enough, the peaks of the stones might cut my flesh. I did not deserve to die here while Ephraim lived. There was no innocence in a man who killed in such a way as he had. Neither was I innocent of all sin, but I did not kill the blameless, as he had.

I pressed my finger to the rough stone points. I deserved to die. I would die.

"I am sure you are telling me the truth," I said ruefully.

He chuckled. I was not sure if it was a lie or if it was true. What I did know was that Azazel wanted me to remain alive, and he would do what he could, say what he could, to make sure I kept living. I waited all day in the cell, tracing the stones with my finger, first on one wall and then around the entire room, careful to avoid the braided-hair woman as she was apt to scratch. I could not blame her.

If I spend much longer in here, I may start scratching, too.

CHAPTER TWENTY-ONE

Two days had already passed. I was beginning to have headaches which lasted for hours, and no amount of sleep relieved them. When the food came during breakfast, I gave it to the women to fight over but kept a scrap of bread. I placed the morsel on the floor and waited, watching, until a rodent would appear. One or two flies darted around the air with one landing on the bread I left. A hand snatched the crumb from the floor, spooking the fly. When I looked up, it was the woman with the braid who shoved the scrap into her mouth.

I had to get out. I would have one chance to get it right, so I watched the narrow window as the sunlight moved across the sky from morning to afternoon, and the bells from the *campanile* sang the hours. I peered out the crack in the door. The *polizia* who was there changed places with another guard. They exchanged the type of pleasantries that are said to keep an amicable relationship, then the other man left.

"Excuse me," I said.

The man did not respond. I said it again, louder this time, and the man looked over.

"I want to confess," I said.

"Are you mad?" asked Azazel.

The other woman in the cell murmured, "I knew she done it."

"What was that?" the guard asked.

"I have a confession," I said. "About the Console."

The man stood up quickly and removed me from the cell. He brought me to the single room where I had been questioned before and left me alone.

"The eyes," I whispered.

"What are you thinking?" Azazel asked. "What good are you to anyone in prison?"

I did not have time to explain myself to him, nor did I feel the need to. If I did, he might try to convince me towards a safer path. A safer path was not always the best one.

"Do it," I said.

The door opened, and I heard the *polizia* enter. Azazel groaned.

"This ought to be worth it," he said. "I'd hate to watch you die."

His fingertip on my forehead imbued me with his eyes. The brightness in the room at first made me squint. As soon as the *polizia* walked into my view, I saw the sins whirling around their minds. I saw what they knew. Of all the petty crimes they knew and ignored, one was revealed. They, not only these men who were already speaking to me and who I ignored, but also all of the Carabinieri within these walls knew about what the Console had done to so many women. The knowledge varied from one of the men before me, and he felt suspicion and guilt over taking a statement from a victim, so when told to destroy it, he did so. The other officer had responded to a scene where the woman was found barely breathing. He had done his best to find justice for her. He delved through files and statements, spoke with families, spoke with victims, and when he believed he would bring the Console to justice, he pleaded to his superiors. When nothing happened, and a new victim came to report the same disturbing details, he grew apathetic, and his apathy became his sin.

They were still speaking when I interrupted.

"I know what I want to say," I announced.

"You said you were here to confess," the other said. "So, confess."

The men waited. I shifted my sights from one to the other, my vision somewhat blurring as the effects of the Demon Eyes wore on me. Behind them was Azazel who was watching me with intense concern.

"The Console wanted to do to me what he has done to countless women before me," I said.

One officer raised his eyebrows.

"I do not see how that is different from what any man would do."

"It is different when a Console poisons a woman and does unspeakable acts to her," I said. "I imagine not all of them wake up."

The officers glanced at each other.

"That's why you killed him."

"I did not. With him now dead, what power is there to silence his victims? When they speak, who will they blame? What guilt have you in this?" My head began to throb.

"I warn you not to threaten the law."

I focused on them. My eyes bored into theirs, willing my influence over their conscience.

"It is not a threat, but a promise," I said. "Before you entered the Donna's home, I told her everything. You may put me in a prison, you may tell the gossipers and the newsmakers not to believe me, but who would disbelieve a woman of quality? Let me go, and I will tell her I was mistaken. And if you need a scapegoat for the Console's death, blame his own indulgence."

Azazel chuckled.

The two men were quiet for a time. I kept my eyes on them. This had to work. If not, I would be dead by the morning. The men said nothing as they left, closing the door behind them.

Azazel scoffed.

"Some good that did. Now you'll die in this place."

My mind pounded against the inside of my skull. My hearing was muffled. Black spots floated across my vision. When the guard came to take me, I barely heard him. The Demon Eyes receded, and all was dim and blurry. I staggered in my pace, dizzy, unsure of where I was. Then I realized I was sitting on a chair and before me were voices speaking, though I could not understand what they were saying. I could hear the words but could make no sense of them. What I did hear was Azazel's breath in my ear and Faustina's whispers. Was it he who took me up and guided me across the hallways and stones? Was it he who gave me my hat and pin, who put me back to the streets, who freed me from the jail?

I crawled at first, barely able to move, until I could stand, though hunched over. My vision still blurred, and black specks obscured my sights, but I followed an object.

It was an animal, soft and warm in my hands. I cradled it and took it with me to one of the alleys, hoping I would not be seen. I did not want to kill it. I tried not to, but it struggled so that when I pricked its front leg to drain the blood there, the pin went too far, and the animal yowled, spilling blood on me so that I could not hold it still enough to drip the blood into the vial. It wriggled and scratched me, then bit until I could no longer hold it, and it scampered away, leaving a trail of crimson spots.

There was not enough blood for the ritual, so I smeared what I had on my cheeks and waited. No memories returned, nor did I feel the relief that blood gave, but when I opened my eyes, the obstructions had disappeared. I blinked and rubbed my eyes to clear my vision. I could see. That was an improvement, but I would need more blood to fully recover. It would have to be more animal blood because I was too weak to fight against another human.

I stumbled towards the market where I saw the blurry figure of the fishmonger, and I waited until he was distracted and pilfered however many fish I could carry before I hurried away as quickly as I could. I heard him shout from behind me, but by then, I was already down an alley, hiding behind a potted olive tree. I went back to the abandoned home and performed the ritual there. After three fish, I approached a normal sense of being, and I was able to think more clearly. I went home and could do nothing more than sleep. At one point, I woke and felt Azazel lying next to me with his arm over my waist, embracing me tightly, and his head rested against my shoulder. For a fleeting moment, it felt comforting.

CHAPTER TWENTY-TWO

W hat would I say to Maria-Elena? I turned the thought over in my head as I walked to the orphanage. I would apologize and hope she would forgive me because I needed the work. She was a woman of faith; she would surely be prone to forgiveness. She also needed me to care for the children. I was fairly confident when I approached the door until I knocked, and I saw her on the other side.

Her expression was not what I expected. Her eyebrows were knitted together, and her mouth was pressed into a scowl. It was anger. It was the same expression she had given Irina when she misbehaved.

"Where have you been?" she asked.

I could not tell her the truth. If she knew, she might have told the *polizia,* and they would return me to jail. All I could do was apologize.

"Please," I began.

"No. Gone three days and not a word?"

Giorgio toddled towards her and pulled on her skirt. She picked him up.

"I give you a chance here and you take advantage of it. How can I trust you now? I need someone who is dependable, reliable, not someone who disappears for days without telling me. Think what position you left me in."

She acted as if I had a choice in the matter, and it stirred my annoyance. I bit my tongue to stop myself from blurting out the truth in defense. In the end, I could not say anything that would appease my position.

"I am sorry," I said.

Maria-Elena tilted her head to one side.

"An apology is not enough. You do it once and you may do it again." She repositioned Giorgio in her arms. "I thought this would work out, but I suppose I was wrong."

Please, no.

"Do not come here again," she said.

She closed the door.

I pounded on it. She could not let me go so easily, after all I did for her and for the children. One mistake and that was all it took to turn me out? I kept pounding until the door cracked open and Irina peered out.

"Irina," I said.

She passed me an unfolded roll of my clothes.

"Here," she said. "The other things are inside."

That was it. I had nowhere else to go. I needed money to go to Salzburg, unless I could beg my way there. How could she get rid of me without even listening to what I had to say? I thought the faithful were supposed to be forgiving. Since my rebirth I had found them as judgmental as the faithless, and more so, for the faithless did not shroud their judgment in piety.

For some time, I walked the alleys and streets, unsure where to go or what to do. Could I go to my family and convince them to take me in? Even if they did, would I want to be with them? I did not want them to see me with ash on my face. What about Donna Bianca? Would she help me? My thoughts went to de'Angelo. He had been turned out to the streets. How long before I started begging as he had? I thought of the Romani who relied on the charity of strangers to stave off hunger. There was no space for pride when one was destitute.

Where was Azazel now when I needed him? I thought of calling out to him. I wanted to tell him what had happened. He may not have sympathy, but he was the only being I could speak to honestly.

I stopped walking and sat on the edge of a pier looking out over the lagoon. It was evening and the sun was beginning to dip below the horizon, leaving the sky a dusky amber. I tapped my toe against the surface of the water, creating ripples. As I was peering into the water, I saw Azazel's reflection in it next to mine.

"I am happy to see you roused from your melancholy," he said.

"Am I?" I asked.

He sat next to me.

"Since you left the jail, you were barely responsive. You hardly woke. I thought the blood you took from that cat and those fish would not be enough to bring you back, yet here you are."

"Yes, here I am. Alive, but for what? I have no means to accomplish my *mitzvah*. I know where he is, but to get to him requires money that I do not have, unless I walk to Salzburg."

"Then let me help you," he said. "There's someone I have in mind."

As I followed him around the corner, I knew where he was taking me. It was the orphanage.

"Is this a joke?" I asked.

I looked over at Azazel, searching for an answer.

262

"What wrong has she done? She keeps a home for the children."

Azazel looked at me knowingly.

"Where do the children go when they are grown?"

"Well, they—" I started, and then realized that I did not know. I assumed they found families or apprenticeships, like the one Irina told me about. Suddenly, I needed to know the answer. Though the front door was locked, I knew that Maria-Elena kept the back window open so that Baci could go in and out as he pleased. I went to the window, opening it with a gentle push. Inside, the house was filled with night sounds: the deep breaths of sleeping babies and an exhausted adult.

I snuck around the cribs downstairs and ascended the steps to Maria-Elena's room. I would search her room to see first if what Azazel hinted at was true. If there was nothing, I would slink away as if I had never come. If so, I would wake the self-righteous nun.

I pulled open the drawers softly, rifled through her stockings and shirts, scanned the pictures on the walls. The last time I had been here was when we had helped Antonio. She had seemed a caring person, then. I looked over to where she slept. My eyes were drawn to her desk and to the safe beneath it. The safe needed a key, and I remembered Irina mentioning it. What had she said? The lamp. I stepped to it, reached a finger under the iron stand, and felt a small key. I took it and went straight to the safe. Once I opened it, I saw that within were mostly stacked pages, ledgers, and a wooden box. I looked through the pages first. In the dim light, I had to squint to focus on the writing, some of it typed and some of it handwritten. Most were adoption papers, custody papers, and other legal documents. Then I looked at the ledgers, some going as far back as twenty years.

The babies were sold. Some were sold young; others not

until they were old enough to work. A price for each one tallied. I noticed a pattern for the girl babies with money paid monthly for upkeep until they turned a certain age, and then there was a large cash payment. I looked up from the page, staring at the sleeping Maria-Elena.

"Some will pay highly for flesh," Azazel said.

My thoughts went to Irina. She would leave soon for what Maria-Elena told her was an apprenticeship. I gritted my teeth at the omission. An apprenticeship of a different kind. I thought of the babies, of what might become of them. I took a deep breath and put the ledgers back in their place. Then, I opened the box, knowing what would be stowed away inside, and found stacks of paper *lire*, some gold and silver coins, and even jewelry. I then closed the box and stared at the contents of the safe.

So, this is the truth, I thought. *All the pretense of protecting the children . . .*

That day that Crina came to take Antonio, Maria-Elena had refused, and relented when Crina had shown her legal rights. Maria-Elena had said that she was going to care for the baby since Crina could not. What a lie that was. She had kept him because she knew he might be of some worth to her. Warmth rose in my veins. It was anger stemming from the mother's soul, that her child could be used so carelessly–her child and the countless others who came through these doors.

I stood slowly. My mind fogged as I stepped forward, hunched over, and rose to the bed to sit next to her. I felt a fingertip on my forehead and sifted through her sins. I watched her send a boy away, the boy Irina loved, and watched as he begged to stay. I saw her give Giorgio some rum to calm him to sleep and give her time to herself. I saw that she met with the Console Edrizzi. There would be only one reason for her to meet with him. "What girls do you have?" he would ask. He would promise to take care of them, give them a better life than they could imagine. And she believed in some part that it was true, but a deeper place in her mind supplanted her with doubt and guilt.

I placed my forearm on the woman's neck, holding it steady with my left hand grasping her right wrist and pressing the entirety of her weight onto it. The woman's eyes flicked open as she strained to breathe. Her lips moved as if to form words. She flailed her legs and hit me with fisted hands, but the pain did not cease her motive. I pressed harder until her muscles quivered and she thought her arm might snap. As the woman fought, she gradually weakened. Her scratches and thrashes were feeble until they softened, surrendering.

To siphon what I needed, I had to be swift. I took my hair pin and pressed it into the woman's still-blue vein in her neck. Out spilled the blood that I gathered in a bottle. I stood up, my heart racing from the excitement. I would have to hurry before someone heard me. I was about to dispose of the body when a thought came to me, so I grabbed the money from the wooden box, stuffing it in my pockets, then replaced the documents carefully, as if undisturbed. Once finished, I cleaned the wound. I picked up the body and dragged it, pushing it down the steep steps. The body cracked and flopped as it tumbled down.

Dashing out the door, I walked down the empty alley with the warm blood in my pocket. Azazel was beside me, all the while showering me with congratulations.

"I did not think you would do it, you being so hopelessly clung to that human morality."

"It was morality that set death upon her head," I said.

He laughed.

"What fun we will have," he whispered.

I waved him away and went home, and when I covered my

face in the blood ash, the ensuing sensation was one of cascading euphoria that numbed my skin and eviscerated my mind.

A shadow moved across my vision, and I turned to see Azazel looking down at me. He spoke, and though I could hear his voice, I could not register the words. Thoughtlessly, I rubbed my fingers together and inhaled sharply at the sensitivity I felt in my fingertips.

I looked down at my hand to see my skin fuller, with more color, the veins underneath more present, my skin pink around the fingernails. My mind too, was sharper, more aware of the sights and smells around me. How desperate my room seemed to me now. Coal dust covered the hearth, spreading out to the marble stone floor. How had I not noticed it before? There was a scent to the room that was harsh and human, of musky skin and rancid bread, and the ash on my face.

I could feel my heart pumping and constricting as the beats resonated throughout my body. There was an invigoration in my blood that I had not felt since I was a young girl. Seeing the sunlight through the gap in the shutters, I reached out to it. How vibrant was the color! I wanted to grasp it, to feel it. I stood and opened the shutters, letting the light warm me. From the streets below I could smell the proclivities of life in the wafts of cooking coming from homes, the smoke puffing from chimneys, the brine from the sea, the rot from the canal, the sounds of footsteps walking on stone, a child's cry from the neighbor's house, and the bells ringing from San Marco's *campanile*. How beautiful the city seemed, even in its ugliness: a moment broken by the insatiable appetite that grasped my stomach. The meager bread on the table was enough for sustenance but not to enjoy.

I went to the wash basin and cleaned the blood with tepid water, leaving a bowl of saturated red. I dried my face and dumped the water out my window, letting it splash to the stones below. I closed the window, dressed in a set of clean, dry clothes, and with my money purse full, went out.

It was as if I were a child again, seeing the city in its wonder: the flowers growing from cracks in stone, the pigeons flying in the square that I chased momentarily in an impulse from a past life. I had the same joy that had been lost to me for so long. I was happy. What a relief to feel happy again. I had not realized it had been dampened in me until I felt it once more.

Looking up, the colors of the sky, though overcast, took on a new beauty to me. A day before I would have bemoaned it as dull weather. Yet, even with the sky a pastel gray, it seemed to me as if it were a light silver, the same as a clear pond shimmering in the dawn light.

Such invigoration pulsated through me, filling me with manic happiness. I had not a single worry that consumed my mind, nor a single doubt. I knew that I would find Ephraim. I had the knowledge of where he was and had the means to bring myself to him. And so I would enjoy myself and succumb to the jovialities which were so plentiful. With more money in my pocket than I had ever had before, I went to the shops as if I were a whirlwind of silver. I bought finery. For the first time in my remembered life, I wore silk and lace. Then I ate at the most luxurious restaurant I could find, and I drank wine.

And all the while there was Azazel with me, laughing, driving me to revel in my enjoyment.

Each taste, each sensation was at a peak. I ate until my belly was full, and when I could no longer. With evening arriving, I went to a bar, the joviality within calling me to enter. Inside there were men and women, even an older child, in happy conversation. I took a standing table and drank the sweetest wine.

And when an impromptu song arose, I sang with the others and found that the alcohol, which would subdue most, was barely felt when I consumed it. It came to a point when I was emboldened to drink some absinthe. The server prepared it with sugar and fire, and in his clumsiness, set the drink ablaze, causing inflamed drops to drip onto my arm. I was impervious to the weaknesses of humans.

Every tart, every slice of pizza, roll of sweetbread, cup of coffee, and gelato was an explosion of flavors. I walked the alleys, stopped to listen to a man playing a violin, hoping to gain favor from tourists.

It was as if the city was lit with heavenly sun. The shine on the dome of the Santa Maria Della Salute church made me squint. The gondolier sang as he guided the gondola along the green canal. I called the man. He turned the gondola towards me. I paid him, and I slid down, luxuriating on the seat, stretching my legs before me, crossing them at the ankles. I rested my arm on the side and laid my cheek on my shoulder and watched as people passed. Every stone seemed a marvel. Why had I never wondered how a city could stay atop water for so many centuries? It seemed like magic. A floating city, a spectacle of marble and sun that could at once be beckoned beneath the waves and forever lost.

The gondola passed under a bridge and turned an oblong corner, making the gondolier push against the sides of a house to guide us on our way, steering with the long rod to avoid damaging his possession.

A sparrow chirped from its place upon a tile roof. I looked up to spy it briefly before it jutted off into the sky. A street guitarist played a melody in the Spanish style, and it echoed as we drew farther away so that even as I strained to hear it, it faded.

I wished I could stay on the gondola. I was happy. It had

been too long since I felt it. I let the warmth of the sun fill me as I relaxed my body to a state of ease.

Then, I thanked the man as I stood, carefully, and lifted my skirts to extend my leg to the far step.

I had in my mind exactly where I wanted to go. In my new dress and my new confidence, I walked to the house where I would find the Donna Bianca and Cristofano. The doorman answered.

"You?" he asked.

"I expect you know why I am here."

"The Donna and her . . . associate are indisposed."

"They will want to see me. I can guarantee it."

He tilted his head to one side and squinted one eye, appraising me as he would a coin, to see if I were genuine silver or tin.

"How are you here?"

"Let me in, and I will tell you all about it."

The man laughed.

"Wait here," he said.

He closed the door on me, and I waited outside. In a moment, the door opened again, and he let me inside.

"They are upstairs. I trust you remember the way?"

"I do."

I went to ascend the stairs, and the butler stopped me by placing a hand on my shoulder. I turned.

"You said you'd tell me how you came here," he said. "When someone is taken by Carabinieri, they rarely walk the streets again."

"Even Carabinieri make mistakes."

"Not often."

The butler narrowed his eyes.

"You may call on them, if you like," I said.

His eyes relaxed.

"I think one visit from the Carabinieri is enough. I trust there will not be another incident."

"Not on my part," I said.

He removed his hand from me.

As I climbed the steps, I heard the unmistakable sounds of passion. The door was opened, and within, the room was illuminated in dim electrical lights and candelabras. I saw the two upon a bed with the Donna sitting atop Cristofano, her legs apart; she was half dressed, her blouse hanging from her shoulders, exposing her chest where eager hands caressed her naked breasts; her skirts were upon the floor along with Cristofano's trousers. I walked into the room, and at each step, I felt Azazel come nearer until his breath was on my neck. At a moment, I stopped, entranced by the urgency in Cristofano's movements as his hands gripped onto the Donna's thighs and his head tilted back, eyes squeezed closed. It was then she stopped her fluid movements, despite the young man's weak protest. She looked at me.

"Ah!" she said, breathing heavily, but in seeking to recover a steady airflow, took one short inhale and exhaled at once. "A ghost came back from the dead! I thought you lost. Come, no need to be shy here," she said.

I fixed on Cristofano, who appeared in a state of euphoric agony as the Donna reached beneath her skirts to play with what stood hidden there.

Rarely had I seen a man as such, and I was unprepared for what it aroused in me.

"Such a look of surprise," she said. "Surely you have seen a man on the edge of passion?"

I thought of the clandestine meetings I had in the alley corners. The urgency that came in the moments before, the necessity to reach a moment of satisfaction, the body's response to it.

"Yes," I said, almost in a whisper, as if the words could barely escape my lips.

Cristofano reached a hand beneath her skirt. She gasped and then let out a slow exhale, all the while with a smile spread across her face.

"You are trying to coax me," she said to him through a moan.

In answer, Cristofano sat up to kiss the soft skin at her neck and began removing her blouse. It was as if I felt it upon myself. I went closer, drawn in by their enjoyment. Cristofano bent his head to her breast, causing her to place a hand on the back of his head and thread her fingers through his hair.

As I watched them, I felt my arm stretch out so my hand could graze the length of his naked back, causing his skin to prickle.

The Donna's breathing hastened, and soon she cried out, and as she did, Cristofano chuckled at his success.

I placed my hand behind his neck and turned his face to mine. Then, I kissed him. When I did, he stifled a moan. I remained still as Donna had moved her body off him. When she moved, her skirts revealed Cristofano sitting naked beneath her with a curious contraption enclosing his most sensitive appendage. The Donna stood on the floor, removing her skirt. As she did, Cristofano reached to the back of my dress, unbuttoning it, and letting it fall.

My experiences had been limited to those hurried, lustful meetings in alleys and of the innocent conjugal meeting between newlyweds. Rarely had I the quiet opportunity presented to me and all it could offer. I relished it. I thought of this man and the one that came before and all that I had wanted to explore which had been restricted from me. I felt Azazel with me. I had become something other than a human, and with Azazel, had come to discover a satisfaction that I never knew was there, but in rebirth had revealed itself.

How different would it be with a man, now? I wondered.

Cristofano's hands were on me. In my reaction, I realized how I had missed physical touch. I stood frozen for a moment, to enjoy the sensation as I felt Azazel near me, his breath on my neck, his hand on my back, urging me forward. I placed my fingers over the back of his hands, feeling the veins, the knuckles, and the warmth that they brought to mine. I began to feel a comfort that had been missing. So long had it been that I had not realized that it was missing: to share a closeness with another–another who accepted me as I was, even for a moment's connection, had been a blessing.

"What do you want?" I whispered to him.

In answer he took my hand in his and placed it where his arousal stood constricted within a leather cage. I removed it, unclasping it at the base. As I felt him there, he let out a satisfied breath. I felt the bed shift as the Donna returned.

"It seems you are a selfless creature after all," she said. "Giving in to his desires as quickly as he asked for them. Have you always been so quick to please others?"

I turned to her even as my rigor increased. Young Cristofano began to breathe heavily beneath me and murmured blasphemes through his parted lips. I turned back to him. As I felt him reach the nearness of climax, I was transfixed upon his face. His eyes were closed, his head tilted back, exposing his neck, and I watched as the veins in his neck throbbed to the beat of his heart.

It was then that Bianca placed her hand on mine and squeezed. When she did, the man gasped.

"No," he said. "Not yet. Not yet."

I ceased for a moment. Those words were so close to what

the dead would say as they felt their life fading. There was the same desperation in his voice, the same need.

"You may not know this game," Bianca said, her tone lower than I remembered and with a hint of amusement. She then leaned over Cristofano, kissed him on his neck, and whispered, "You like to be teased, don't you?"

Cristofano smiled, opened his eyes, and said, "Yes." Then he kissed me. There was a full expression of acceptance between them that I could not quite decipher. Was this what love looked like? Or was it mere sexual freedom? I wanted to grasp it for myself. I did not love this young man, nor did I feel anything beyond curiosity for the Donna. But, for a moment perhaps, I could revel in their world.

I took my pin in hand and passed my hand over his face so that he could see what I was about to do. I touched the blade to his skin, and he quivered at the touch.

"Is this what you want?" I asked.

He gave the slightest nod. I placed the tip where I knew was safe and pierced his skin there and watched as the blood flowed. I pressed my fingertips to the warm blood and spread its freshness on my face. The thoughts of my murderer, of justice, were placated by joy.

There was something in me that drew him closer still. Was it my own desire for lust that made him look at me? His eyes betrayed his yearning, the very way he viewed me was that of wanting. I teased this rope, only sometimes letting it slack. I soon felt empowered by his lust as I held this man caged in my fingers; his inner turmoil pleased me. He hated and desired me at once. But his eyes still intruded inside me, his disastrous ideas infested my mind. If he knew that one breath against my neck would dismantle me, I would be untamed. I could feel his thoughts pass over me like fingers caressing my naked body. We were all locked in the moment that would break as soon as he opened his mouth to speak. But that moment, that was ours alone.

What must it be like to feel my heart in another's hands, I wondered. If I cut out my own heart, what would be its weight in another's hands?

Before me I saw Azazel, his eyes, and the shadow of his face. In his hands he held my human heart, the arteries still connected to the inside of my flayed chest. He smiled, an alabaster grin, and dipped his head to feast upon the heart. At each bite, blood spilled over his lips and fingers, dripping to the ground, and my body convulsed, as if the sensation of his teeth piercing the beating flesh permeated my entire body, forcing my breath to cease and my bones to tremble. Upon consumption, the remaining heartstrings settled between his lips, seeming as if he had bifurcated tongues slathered with my blood.

CHAPTER TWENTY-THREE

I walked along the canal and stopped where there were several boats floating, moored to the edge of the street. I had no desire to sleep in a boat again. I had a few hours until I needed to be at Maria-Elena's house. I would find a suitable place before then, so I walked through alleys and streets, peeked around corners to find the cleanest, sparsest spots, but it seemed that I was not alone in that pursuit. Many of the corners and crevices had been taken by others such as myself, some who were still asleep, nestled in their own small space, covered by a blanket or jacket.

I peered into empty homes, or homes which appeared empty at first, until I pushed through an unlatched window or door and the squatters living there shooed me out. I kept walking, knowing where I should go, and I let my feet guide me to the San Giorgio dei Greci, to the first place where I felt the blood upon my skin. I went to the *campanile* with my meager belongings in hand. There, I fashioned my clothes into a pillow and spread out my coat over my body. The flood water had submerged the floor below me and caused the inside to smell like a murky lagoon.

Though I was upset by the shrill Maria-Elena, I was also overcome with wonderful thoughts as I lay beneath the bell, staring up at its chamber. What had been in Maria-Elena's blood, in Cristofano's blood, that was so different from the others?

As I thought, I saw Azazel where he was, sitting on the edge of the *campanile*. Had he been here the entire time, waiting for me? I rose, head sloshy from the night before.

"I suppose she wasn't all bad," Azazel said. "You consume souls through their blood. What blackens their soul blackens yours; on the other hand, a golden soul will make yours glimmer."

I backed away from the demon.

"I . . ."

Had Maria-Elena been innocent? How could that be? Sickness bubbled in my belly, and I rushed to the empty chamber pot to expel the bile from my stomach, splattering sour pieces of vomit around the inside of the bowl. When I had expunged it, I lifted my head, gathering air, my heart beating so forcefully I could hear it throbbing in my ears.

"Are you saying she was sinless?"

Azazel clicked his tongue. "Maybe not sinless, for few are, but innocent enough."

I turned to see him where he sat at the table, hands resting on the edge, watching me with casual interest.

"You would have known," I said.

To this, he shrugged. The dismissive gesture riled me to stand, however unbalanced, and I rushed to grab him by the throat and pushed him down on the tabletop, spilling the wine and toppling the cup so it fell, shattering on the floor. I squeezed with one hand, feeling nothing of a pulse. Azazel laughed. His laughter pierced my ears, disarming my fury into resolve. I placed my other hand on his throat, pressing, leaning my weight into it, hoping to crush his windpipe, to cease his laughter. But I could not kill him. My muscles tired, and I relaxed, relinquishing him from my touch with an infuriated groan that seeped out of my clenched teeth.

"You lied."

"Not quite a lie. I see what they do, not whether it's a sin or not; that's up to interpretation. I am not God. You had the Demon Eyes. What did you see?"

I thought back to the sins I had seen from her and acted before I considered any others. The sins I saw I had felt were enough to warrant her death. Could I have been wrong?

"Did she deserve it?"

"Who can know for sure? It's done. Don't think on things you can't change. Her troubles are over."

"This is not who I want to be."

"It's who you are. Think how wonderful that soul felt. The vibrancy of life that came from consuming it."

Yet my killing of Maria-Elena had shocked me. I was sure I was doing the right thing by ridding the world of her. And when she was not as depraved as I suspected, when her blood filled me with jubilation, it disgusted me how I had enjoyed it. Perhaps that was the meaning of the lion and the beehive. That for one to flourish, another must die. I wondered if a demon could understand those spiritual insights.

"It was . . . relieving."

"Why stop?"

"Must I explain? Do you have no conscience?"

He spread his arms wide and tilted his head as if to bow. "I am that I am," he said.

I scoffed at the blasphemy.

"Do not think. The deed is done."

Perhaps he was right for the moment. With my mind sharpened by her blood, there was much I could accomplish. I took out all my notes and reports and opened my notebook to write down all I remembered, scouring my memories now that they were clear.

The chill in the air made resting in the *campanile* uncomfortable, so I took my belongings and sloshed through the floor waters to break my way into the main church. The doors were all locked, but after circling the grounds, I found a broken hole in a window that led inside one of the hallways. Since the window was already broken, I had no qualms about making the gap wider. I found a nearby stone and used it to break the glass. When I made a hole wide enough, I climbed through to the other side, inevitably cutting my palm and a few places on my legs as I did so. I stepped into some shallower flood water and made my way to a staircase that led to a storage room. Some vermin scuttled away as I entered. The room held nothing but old chairs and musky curtains, but it was warm and dry.

"The most innate religions force loyalty from the filial. He scoffed at the futility of humanity that, in the time that had elapsed from when the paint first touched the unmarked canvas until the point where his eyes turned to it, humanity was unchanged from the heretic bloodlust of his ancestors."

My breath was the only part of my body that I could recognize. The rest of my bodily sensations melted away into the bed, and only the thoughtful tap of my finger signaled that I was still alive. I laid my head down on the floor, gazing at the crusted ceiling. Sleep felt like a warm cotton blanket wrapped around my cold shoulders. I felt my mind descending into the abyss of dreams as my breathing disappeared.

In my moments of lucidity, I felt only the anguish that accompanied it. The restless night drew on into the dawn when

I saw the dull sunlight through the dank glass of the one window in the room.

A voice woke me. It was the echo of a young girl's call. I covered myself and picked up my Bona Dea pin, and I held my hand on the handle and looked out to spy a recognizable figure. It was Irina.

My heartbeat quickened. Had Irina seen me that night?

"I hope she didn't see you enact your justice on the baby-seller, or you might have to find a way to get rid of this one," Azazel said.

I ignored him. Irina had done nothing wrong, and I wanted to see her again, to make sure that she was well. I descended the steps and went outside through the gap I had made the night before.

Irina stopped at once and embraced me. When she released her embrace, I saw that she was holding her cat, Baci, in one arm and a basket of clothes in the other.

"Oh, I was afraid I wouldn't find you," she said. With Irina so close, I could smell her unwashed skin and a slight but pungent smell of the canal on her hair. "No one else would take me, and you were the only other person I could think of."

"Come," I said, and led her through the gap in the window. She complained in soft mumblings and had to pass the cat to me before coming through. Once we were both inside, I led her to the room where I had been sleeping.

"What are you doing here?" I asked.

Irina let Baci down on the floor. The cat walked around, sniffing at the floor and pawing at the furniture until it found a spot on a chair to sit on.

"You don't know," she said.

Irina walked in farther and flopped onto the lounge chair, letting her arms fall at her side.

"Giorgio woke up crying. He kept crying, crying, and I

thought Maria-Elena must have had too much wine to wake up, so I got out of bed to pick him up. That's when I saw her at the bottom of the stairs. It was . . ." Irina began to sob quietly. I stood, watching her for a moment. Deciding it would be best to comfort her, I sat next to her on the chair and put my hand on Irina's, who took my hand in hers, and felt that it was quivering. "I didn't know what to do. The babies were crying, and she was there, dead, on the floor, so I opened the upstairs window and screamed."

Irina started crying wholeheartedly. She slipped her hand away from mine to hide her face. When I had been a girl, Mama would stroke my forehead with her thumb to calm me when I was upset. I did the same to Irina. I wanted to say a prayer for her, but what prayer was there for a gentile? Perhaps saying it, too, was blasphemy. And yet, I wanted to ease Irina's grief.

"*Baruch dayan ha'emet,*" I said.

Irina softened her crying and lifted her head.

"What does that mean?" she asked.

"Blessed be the one true judge."

Irina sniffed and wiped her eyes.

Since she had calmed, I decided to question the aftermath of Maria-Elena's death.

"What happened after?"

Irina cleared her throat.

"The *polizia* came. They took me from the house, but I wouldn't go, not without Giorgio, but they took the babies, too, even though I screamed, and they carried me to their chambers. They asked me about what I saw, and I told them."

"Did they say anything about how she died?"

She shook her head.

"Just that she must have fallen and broken her neck. They said it was just as well. That the . . . the bastards should be raised in the church orphanage. After a little while, they let me go. It's been two days. The Ospedale gave me one meal and a night's rest and told me to go to the convent. I went there, and they were full. I barely slept last night on the street just outside. I didn't know whether to come to you or not, or if you would let me in."

I relaxed and slipped the pin into the chair seam. I considered telling Irina what her foster mother was doing, to ease the young girl's conscience. There was no reason to cry over the woman.

"Maria-Elena was kind to me," Irina said. "She was my mother. Not my real mother, but . . ."

"And that mother was going to sell her to the highest bidder," Azazel remarked.

"That was my family, my home. Where can I go now?"

I pressed my lips together and hugged Irina gently. Self-preservation told me to leave Irina to the streets. Surely a convent would take her. My memories of the streets stopped me, though. It was too easy for a young girl to succumb to prostitution. Maria-Elena had kept Irina naive of sin. A kind offer from a painted face and the promise of a home and a hot meal would entice the young girl. My stomach became queasy. Was Irina's situation better now than if she had been sold? I pushed the thought from my mind.

"You will stay here," I said, and I heard Azazel groan.

At the offer, Irina began to cry again, and I hugged her and kissed her cheek.

"Oh, thank you. I won't be a bother, I promise. I'll cook, I'll clean, I'll wash—"

"—That is not necessary."

"But it is. I'll find some work to do."

Irina gave a pitiful smile, showing the tiredness in her eyes and the exhaustion in her face. I turned away. Her face was too like my own.

"Take some rest," I said.

Irina nodded. She laid her head on the arm rest and closed her eyes. Meanwhile, I took the knife out of the cushion and hid it away, then went to the door to turn the lock. I went to my own bed and snuggled under the covers, pulling them over my shoulders, and then I relaxed in the small comfort I took in hearing Irina's breathing.

"I hope this isn't a mistake," Azazel said.

I woke briefly in the night to turn her body and felt another lying next to her. Through partially open eyes, I saw the outline of Irina's body curled up next to mine, and then fell back to sleep.

In the morning, I woke to find Irina still asleep. After a small breakfast of bread and cheese, I went to the dresser where I had hidden the stolen money and folded it neatly in half, slipping it safely over my breast in the confines of my corset. I needed to put the money somewhere safe if the *polizia* came looking. Irina could have mentioned to them that there was a Jewess working with Maria-Elena. Before leaving, I called Irina's name and rocked her body.

"I am going out," I told her. "Stay here."

Irina gave a sleepy nod.

I knew of the best place where the *polizia* were least likely to go looking, and that was in the Jewish quarter. Most Italian gentiles stayed out of the businesses there. Napoleon let the Italians know that the Jews had their own community to be left alone from mainland politics. Jews had their own banking and business rules that gentiles did not follow.

They greeted me with some suspicion. I did not live in the *ghetto* and was a single woman. An explanation that I was a widow and new to the city satisfied. The banker tested me by speaking in Hebrew, and I dutifully responded. I had remembered how resistant I had been to learn it in my youth and was now thankful for my parents' insistence.

It was a large sum of money. I had not counted it at the time, but seeing the banker do so before me astounded me with how much it was. I wondered what Maria-Elena had been doing with the money she was making. In my view, Maria-Elena lived frugally. Perhaps there were other vices that I did not know about. The stolen money was more than enough to live off for several years.

On my way home, I considered doing something nice for Irina. It was my fault that she was without a home, so I stopped at a pastry shop to buy a tarte. As I walked the road home, I began to feel dizzy, and wondered, when had I last had blood?

When I entered the house, I nearly collapsed on the floor. Irina was speaking. My head pounded as if my brain were to burst out of my skull and spill out my ears. My muscles ached so much that the thought of moving them was a monumental task. I managed to place the tarte on the table before I dropped it.

I felt my body placed into bed as an invisible hand drew the covers.

In the morning I woke with a dull headache and to the smell of bread and *caffè*. Without the strength to lift my head, I turned it to see Irina at the table reading a book and periodically sipping from a cup. At the sound of my stirring, Irina turned.

"Old Daniele hired me at the bakery in the mornings," she announced with a smile on her face.

"I went in there to get the day-olds. When I told him I was staying with you, he offered me a job. Isn't that wonderful?"

She kept talking, but I could barely understand what Irina was telling me as my head pounded. A weakness stole my coherent thoughts. She mentioned writing a letter and earning money that would go to her brother.

The candle flame weakened. In my rush the night before, I had not performed the ritual, and I wished Irina was gone just then to have a moment alone.

I sat up, and as I did, my head became so dizzy that I swayed.

"Oh, you look awful," Irina said.

I rubbed the back of my neck. The sound of another voice picked at my ear. I needed her gone, so I reached into my inner pocket and pulled out my money purse. Then, I took a few coins.

"I'm tired of bread. Go get something decent."

At the sight of the coins, Irina's face brightened, and she took them without complaint.

"Oh, there's a beautiful tarte I saw at the *patisseria* just as I was walking back. I'll buy the whole thing."

Before I could persuade her against it, Irina was out, the door closed behind her.

I sat, gathering the strength in my muscles to move. My entire body ached.

Pulling the stone from the wall and removing the vial of blood, I spread it on my face and sat back against the wall, absorbing the essence into my skin. Each passing moment, I felt my energy restoring. The aches receded. My pounding head settled. Once recovered, I stood and washed the blood from my face, then disposed of the water onto the street. I re-hid the vial and went to pour more to wash the night's sweat off.

"Feeling better?" asked Azazel.

Baci meowed, and I looked over to see him sauntering about my room before deciding to jump onto the fireplace mantel only to jump off again and leave.

"Just," I said.

"I have never seen you like that before."

"You have seen me weak from being without blood."

"No," he said. "With those two."

I thought of Cristofano and Bianca and my skin became warm. I felt him with me even as he had not touched me. It was his eyes that were like claws upon my back. I did not want to speak of it with him. I knew he had been watching me that night, but that moment had been mine. I wanted to cherish it, for it was the one moment of abandon I had since my rebirth. They had accepted me as I was and had shown me love for it. Love, of a kind.

"What of it?" I asked defensively.

Azazel was next to me and stroked my ear. His fingers were like cool lines of ice on my skin. My skin prickled, and I let out a breathy exhale. Azazel kissed the back of my neck. I wanted him and yet did not. He then began to sing, beginning as a hum and then a soft elucidation in the air. His song was in a language that I did not know, though the melody was deep and comforting. I closed my eyes and allowed myself to relax in his arms. We did not need to say anything to each other, and I was glad of that. I had no words for him.

The calamities of the past few days were settling. The only way forward was to go to Austria, to Salzburg, to kill Ephraim. I knew Azazel did not want me to go but neither could he stop me. He wanted to keep me alive, keep me for his own, and I wanted the freedom that came from knowing justice was done. Continuing a life as one of the *shedim* caused me grief. The constant ebb and flow of the changes in my soul, in my blood, made me weary. And there was the guilt that came from knowing I had killed at least two innocent people. Dying would give justice to them, too. How can I right the wrongs of the past? I knew my way forward, and I hoped that I could atone for Faustina's death and for Maria-Elena's. Yet what of Azazel?

Once I faded, he would be alone, or he too would fade with me. And my family? Should I stay alive for them? All I knew was that I wanted this to be finished.

I turned over in Azazel's arms, and we tumbled together with swift need. I did not care to linger on sensuality. I only wanted a release from myself and to feel him beneath me. When we finished, I took some money along with the key I had stolen from de'Angelo.

"Where are you going?" Azazel asked.

"Out."

My first stop was the train station. As was typical, there were some tourists around the steps to the station, one of whom had a camera and was taking pictures of the view from the topmost step. The cards on the train table clacked as they rotated to show the new times for arrivals and departures. I approached the ticket counter and waited in line behind a few others; a man ran past me, treading on my foot to reach the platform. When it was my turn, I stated my business directly to the man behind the counter who had a cigarette pressed between his teeth. When he exhaled the smoke, it escaped through the small dispatch hole under the window. He told me that the next train to Salzburg would be in three days and asked if I wanted a day or night train. I chose one for the night so that no time would be wasted in finding Ephraim.

On my way out, I nearly skipped with excitement. I was so close to being finished. Soon, there would be justice. There would be peace. I spent the remainder of the day sorting out what would happen to the money that I acquired from Maria-Elena. Then, I went to the bank and gave them certain instructions as well as exchanging a sum of *lire* for *krones*.

I realized that I had nothing to place my clothes in and went out to purchase an inexpensive luggage bag. I packed my meager belongings: a change of clothes, socks, all wrapped to protect some vials of blood. I would have to replenish these before I boarded the train. If I did not, I would have to subsist on animals. The train would take a day's ride, and I wondered how the streets of Salzburg were at night. In Venezian nights, there were few who looked above their drinks, but perhaps Austrians were different. I wanted to be of sharp mind when I met Ephraim, and to do that, I needed human blood. On the canal streets there were plenty of stray cats or wandering rats. I hoped Salzburg would be the same. I did not want to have to sneak onto a farm and slaughter a cow or goat. At least if I did, I could blame it on the wolves.

I removed the board on the wall where the candle hid, as I preferred to keep it on my person.

There was one more thing to do: I went to the alley where I knew de'Angelo stayed. Once I saw him, I stopped. He looked more desperate than when I saw him last. His facial hair had grown. Though his head was covered with a hat, his longer hair peeked out under the brim. His cheeks were thinner, his eyes tired, and he held himself differently than before. Before, he was still confident and boorish, but when I saw him, he was meeker. He did not stand or greet those who passed with anything more than a plea for money, for food, for a drink. It was my interference which had caused him to live on the streets, and I could alleviate it. As I walked towards him, the street smelled heavily of urine and of his unwashed body. When he saw me, his face brightened.

"*Signorina,*" he said. "I heard gossip on the streets about a woman who pushed the Console Edrizzi into the canal at a Carnevale party. You wouldn't know about that, would you?"

"I heard he fell."

De'Angelo eyed me for a moment, and then his lips spread into a smile.

"Good riddance to him, either way. He caused far too many

mishaps." De'Angelo shifted where he sat. "Come to take me to the Florian again?"

I sat next to him, knowing that the smell of the street would linger on my clothes.

"Not today," I said.

"Pity. That was one of my better memories since I've been on these stones. I still think about that cake."

As he spoke, his breath smelled sour.

"I came to tell you that I am leaving," I said.

"Leaving? To where?"

"Austria."

"Good food there," he said. "Good music, too. I once went to the Musikverein for a night with a lovely lady." He stared off down the alley. What a night that was."

"Somehow I cannot seem to imagine you with a lady."

"No? Well, it was a long time ago, and I was much younger." He breathed sharply from his nose.

"I came to give you this," I said. From my pocket I handed him a money envelope. He took it and opened the flap to count the contents.

"How did you come by this?"

"Luck," I said.

He folded the envelope and tucked it inside his coat, then buttoned it to the top and crossed his arms in front of his chest.

"Why give it to me?"

I breathed deeply. I then removed a key from my pocket and held it up in front of his face. His reaction was in the form of a ruffled brow and the tightening of his lips. He grabbed it at once. He held it, turned it over in his hands, and then turned to me.

"You?"

"I needed to know about the murder," I confessed. "So, I

took it from you. I did not think it would cause more than a minor annoyance from your superiors."

He scoffed. "It made them more than annoyed. They had been looking for a reason to get rid of me for years and finally found one. Normally, I would be angry, but, ah, I am too tired to be angry." He kept holding on to the key, turning it between his fingers. "How did you take it from me?"

"That evening at the bar. I waited until you were drunk and slipped it from your pocket."

He laughed.

"I must not have been a very good *polizia* if a stranger could steal from me so easily."

I was humbled by his acceptance of my transgression.

"No matter," I said. "Take the money and start anew."

He tapped the key with his forefinger.

"I had always thought of going to Nove to learn to make pottery and ceramics or to Murano to study how to make glass. Perhaps now . . ."

"Do what you must," I said. "Just do not let me find you on the streets again."

He laughed.

"*Grazie, signorina.*"

I smiled down at him, and I did not usually smile at men genuinely, but I felt safe in doing so with this man. Then, I walked away from him and towards home. Home. How strange it was to think of it that way. It was my home, broken and rotten as it was. It had been there when I most needed it and sheltered me from other eyes who may have seen the bloody tasks I did. In any other more respectable place, the sounds and smells would have aroused suspicion, but the home I had found was one where I could hide my desperation. It had served me, but I had no intention of returning to that abandoned place again once I was finished with my *mitzvah*.

When I returned home, Irina was there cleaning the main rooms. Her hair was kept from her face with a kerchief, and she had a rag in her hand as she was trying to wash the flood stains from the walls. Baci greeted me with a loud "meow" from his seat at the window.

"I would not bother," I told her.

She stood up from where she was bent over and inhaled.

"Might as well clean up in here," she answered.

"Hmmm."

As I went up to the single room, I felt a chill and so set about making a fire. First, I moved the soul candle from where I usually hid it and placed it on the mantel. The flame was burning but was fading. I would have to use animal blood. I had to consider when I should reap another human soul.

It seemed my body could never settle. There was a constant rise and fall in my blood and in my mind that so rarely calmed, so I fell asleep on the bed. When I woke, I went downstairs and found Irina sitting on the floor, Baci in her lap, with a book in her hand.

"Oh," she said, putting the book down. When I squinted, I saw that it was the *Tanakh*. "I worried you were getting sick from sleeping so long."

My heart sped.

"You have my book," I said.

"Oh, yes, I went in to check on you since you were asleep. I saw the book and thought about reading it."

I eyed her for a moment. If she had seen the candle or anything related to what I was planning, she was not prepared to share it. Had she the desire to, she would have already gone to the *polizia* while I was sleeping.

"Can you read that?" I asked, pointing at the *Tanakh*.

She flipped the open book towards me where I saw Hebrew on one side of the page and Italian on the other.

"I see," I said.

She turned the book back to her.

"It reads a little differently than the bibles I've read or what the priest says at Mass."

"It was bound to," I said.

"Irina–" I started. She did not look up from the pages. "I am going away for a few days."

At that, she looked up.

"Why?"

"Why?" I repeated. I looked at her then, a young woman with a cat in her lap reading the *Tanakh*. When I was gone, who would take care of her? It was by my hand that she came to me, that she was left without a home or family. After everything I had done, I hoped I could make that right. I felt Azazel whisper to me. The other soul pressed me forward, compelled to give this young girl the chances that neither of us had. As I watched Irina reading, I was overcome with the impulse to tell her the truth of who she was. I would go that evening to find the man who killed me. I would die. Should I leave Irina in ignorance and hope, or reveal her to the truth? I had been an innocent girl, once, and her heralding into adulthood had been swift and damning. Had I known the realities of the world at Irina's age, would I have received it, or was it better to enjoy the ephemeral joys of childhood? What gift would the truth give other than truth?

My belly fell into emptiness. Had that been what Maria-Elena decided? Shield them from the harshness of truth until a certain age?

What had my own parents done to teach me about the cruelties of life? My father and mother taught me the lessons from the Torah, and in my youth, I learned cruelty from those disgruntled few who preferred that a Jewish girl stay away from their gentile sons.

Emet, I thought. *Neither should a deceitful tongue be found in their mouth.*

I wondered if HaShem would hold me to that account.

I could start by telling her the truth. I walked forward and sat down next to her. As I moved, Azazel moved with me. His presence enshrouded me in warm comfort, settling me into ease, knowing that I was making the right choice. I let the words spill out of my mouth but did not hear them. I gave her portions of the truth. I told her how a man had hurt me and left me for dead and that I was going to find him. I told her about Maria-Elena and what I had seen in her safe, though I changed the details of when I saw them. It was as if I were sitting alone in an empty room, speaking to the air with only the echoes to answer me. She seemed to absorb what I said without reaction. Once I was finished speaking, we sat together.

"So," she said after a long while. "What is there to do now?"

"I suppose that would be your choice," I said. "There is money for you in the bank, in your name, to do with as you like. You could go to that boy you are fond of or stay here and find your own way."

"And you? You are going to find the person who did all that to you?"

"I will."

She looked away.

"Maria was doing that . . . with all of them? All the girls?"

"Yes. From what I saw."

"You said that she—" Irina's voice swelled as if she were going to cry. "—That she knew my mother, where she was."

"She showed me the house. If that is where you want to go—"

"I don't. I don't know." She turned back to me and held my hand. "You won't stay here?"

I wondered if Azazel whispered in her ear. In another time,

we could have been friends, good friends. But I would not burden her with my friendship when I would die so soon.

"I do not think I can." I could tell that she was upset and that she wanted me to stay to give her a sense of safety. I did not think I could give her what she wanted. "You are young," I said. "You have your whole life to become who you want. And you are free to be that person."

"I miss Giorgio," she said. "I never thought I'd miss him or any of the babies. Being away from them makes me want to find them and kiss them all. How can I be without them?" She began to cry and looked down at her lap. "How can I do anything alone?"

I put my hand on her back and rubbed there with my thumb.

"It is when we are alone that we can know ourselves," I said. "I know that may not be comforting to you, but as I see it, it is the truth."

CHAPTER TWENTY-FOUR

The first signs of the season touched the tips of my fingers: the beginnings of spring with the hidden whispers of winter. The trees began to change, sprouting green buds to issue the signals of a new repose. The air was warmer. The sun hid behind some thin clouds. Irina had fallen asleep next to me the night before. I brushed my hair briefly and placed a hat on my head, held in place with the Bona Dea pin.

When I rustled Irina from her sleep to tell her goodbye, she barely stirred. All she did was turn her head to me, then reach her arms up to pull her closer to me and kiss my cheek. I took one last look at her as she went back to sleep on the bed with Baci curled around her feet. Then, I kissed her on the forehead and walked away, knowing it would be the last time I would see her.

On the street, a young girl called out a name while she laid bits of cheese outside the door along with a saucer of cream. I glanced at her briefly and looked away. Her cat must be some-where. There were hundreds of them. It could not be the same as the one I killed, I decided, and quickened my pace.

I stopped when I saw a man sitting on the stoop of a house, overlooking the port and the Grand Canal. I watched as he took his hand onto the rough paper of the large sketchbook he was holding and felt it with his fingertips. Lying open in a wooden box beside him were a foray of pastels that were all mixed together in the bottom, all worn down in various forms where some had their paper ripped, and others had none.

I could smell the chalky scent of the pastels. The colors rubbed off on his fingers, forming an unending gray color that stemmed from the medley of hues rubbing together. He remained in the huddled position until he looked back, at the sand and the sea. Taking a deep breath, he blew the colored dust away from him into the air so that it disappeared into the earth. He held up the picture at eye level to compare it. As he eyed it, he brought the page back and, picking up a black pastel delicately from the box, darkened the currents in the water. When he finished, he blew the colored dust away once more and folded the flap of the notebook over to cover his sketch. He wiped his hands on the opposite side of the rag and tossed it into the box, shutting it closed and latching it. He tucked the sketchbook under her arm and turned to walk to another portion of the waterfront to capture a vision.

How different was his vision of the city than mine! He captured beauty; he captured a dream of the floating city, while all I could see were shadows and darkness or the blinding light from the Demon Eyes.

I was soon at the train station with my ticket punched and stepping through the train door. I wondered what he looked like now. Would he have the same youthful face as he once had when we were young, or had it chiseled into adulthood? I closed my eyes to remember his voice. How smooth and kind it had been, how tempered when he said my name, even in anger.

I felt excited. I had never been so far from Venezia.

Although the reasons were shrouded in the eventual murder of a man, it was exhilarating to travel somewhere new, outside the common canals and cobble streets. I did not watch the city fade into the distance. Instead, the world of Venezia became like a dream detached from reality. I looked forward, out the windows as the train passed over the water, past towns and hills, vineyards, and farms until there were higher hills and mountains. At a point near the base of the mountains, the train stopped to let off some passengers. One of the doors opened to let in the cool mountain air.

When I looked out the window, at the *centro,* there were sophisticated women with furs warming their necks. They all seemed to wear a uniform of black wool long coats buttoned up to their chin and stopping at their knees, or bubble coats with hoods pulled over their heads. Their feet were protected by heavy boots or galoshes, and their hands were covered with fashionable gloves; red, blue, purple, and black hands stood out in the monochrome world. The train lumbered up the mountain, the air within becoming cooler when it traveled through a tunnel. When it reached the other side, I rode past thick evergreens, green grasses, and wild mountain flowers. I stood up, struggling to keep my balance from the swaying train car, but I unlatched the window. With some effort, I pulled it down, letting in a rush of cool air and fresh scents so different from the muggy canals and dusty stones that I was used to. I wanted to jump from the train and lie in the lush grass in silence.

As I rested my head against the window, I wondered about myself, that girl who wanted to be a woman. My mother and the married women in my family wore a scarf. My father and brothers wore the *kippah.* I had not often covered my head, even when I should have. In the market, my mother would cover my hair, and I would pull it off. My willfulness deigned that I should not have followed their rules. Thinking back on it filled me with regret. I was too stubborn in my self-assurance that I did not consider her feelings. I had a clear path that I would take. If I wanted to do something, I would do it because I was sure that it was true. How she must have worried about me! How I had snuck around, lied, and shirked my religion! She had worried over my soul when I would not. Now all I did was worry about souls.

I wanted to apologize to her and lay my head in her lap as I did when I was young and have her stroke my hair, and all the while I would tell her how sorry I was. In my haste at loving Ephraim, I forswore my own family. I loved him with a fuller intensity than I had ever felt for anyone in my family. My life was with him. I knew it as a soulful truth. We were meant to be together. We should have been together.

When I stepped foot onto the platform in Salzburg, I first noticed the mountains in the distance and yellow and white houses nearby. It was early morning and the sun had not yet risen past the summit of the tallest mountain capped with snow. I breathed in the alpine air, fresh with spring flowers and moist grass. I walked out, following the other passengers who had just departed from the train. However, before I went out on my search for Ephraim and for the house with the yellow door, I needed to find a hotel and then blood.

Along the street were decorations to celebrate the coming Easter holiday. In storefront windows were painted or carved eggs, some hanging on ribbons and others in baskets or hung from bald tree branches. The paintings on some of them were of Christian symbols, of Christ, or of the Madonna.

"In faith, is there only one truth?" I asked, not expecting an answer.

"There must be," said Azazel.

"Perhaps it is only HaShem who can know it."

"How greedy of Him to keep it to Himself."

"Not greed," I concluded. I crossed my arms and looked over to where Azazel was scrutinizing a patch of violets. A honeybee landed on the stigma and crept to the center to gather pollen. "I saw the truth of the afterlife," I said, remembering the voice, the honeybees, and the lion. "The truth of death and of rebirth. It is like a view of the world from a spyglass. We can only see so much while so much more is hidden."

"Humans have such a small perception of the world," Azazel said.

"Yes," I answered. "And even as I am, with all I have seen, with all the truth I have seen, I wonder how much I understand the world. HaShem can show me the way–*has* shown me the way. Still . . ."

"Do you doubt?"

I let my arms relax.

"What is faith without doubt?"

I passed before a grand palace beset with vibrant gardens, the entrance to which was guarded by two muscular men who reached out towards each other with a fisted hand outstretched to the air. I stepped in, perusing the gardens by myself. In Venezia there were always so many people that a day did not pass that I did not bump into someone or have them bump into me. Here among the shrubs and budding blossoms, I spread out my arms and whirled around. I walked some more, touching each stone statue or stopping to look at the emerging flowers. I was not sure if it was the human blood I had absorbed which gave me a heightened sense of cheerfulness or if it was because I knew that the end would come soon. With my cause so close to nearing an end, I was at ease.

"What a happy mood you're in," said Azazel.

"And why not?" I asked. I motioned to the Grand Palace and the vibrant gardens. "I am in a beautiful place where I will finally find my murderer."

"Hm," he said. When I turned to him, I saw his face pulled into a grimace.

He did not need to tell me why he was in a sour mood. Once my murderer was dead, then I would die also. Much as I enjoyed Azazel, I was eager to fulfill my *mitzvah* and be at peace. I wondered how I would die. Once I killed Ephraim, I would take his blood and return to Venezia, to my family, and tell them that justice was given. I strolled through the gardens, past a grand fountain, and in the center of it, a statue of a Pegasus on its hind legs that teetered in such a way that it seemed that it would leap from its pedestal and into the air.

Up the stairs, I passed two gnomes that heralded my entrance. On the upper side was a wide clear space surrounded by green trees, and in front of them, in a circle, were statues of gnomes. In the morning, while the sun gently descended towards the earth, leaving a rusted glow, I sat among the stringy grass and wildflowers, letting the wind carry the alpine scent across my skin. I could only observe, in a way unable to feel myself attached to the moment at all. Azazel was with me. There was no need for either of us to utter a sound, instead allowing the shifting wind through the tree branches and rushing grasses to moan.

In the light, the sky burned around us, casting a shadow on forms.

When Azazel looked at me, I could not help but find him beautiful in the glowing light. In my eyes, I saw the remnants of myself. I found it difficult to look at me, as they instilled a piercing fear of a reminder of what we had become to each other. A cynical epiphany formed in my mind in which I understood the finite reality of life. There was nothing for me left to live for, but this final moment.

I took a path away from the streets and towards the riverside. There, the currents tumbled and rolled. If I were to fall, they would take me under, and I would not rise again to the surface.

"Azazel?" I asked.

He was staring up towards the trees, at a few birds who lingered there chirping at each other and said, "Hm?"

"Do you still feel . . ." I started and then stopped. I thought about abandoning the question for a moment, to dismiss it as a juvenile inquiry, but I pressed forward, curious as to the answer. "Do you feel envy?"

I looked over at him. He lowered his gaze, blinked, and stared up once more.

"Envy," he said, letting the word roll over his tongue, "is what brought me to you."

I searched his face to see if there was any humor in it, any hint that he might be jesting. On the contrary, he seemed serious. When he met my eyes again, his expression was one of frustration, and when he spoke, contempt was thick on his voice.

"What an ironic punishment of mine, that I can see the horrible transgressions of Man and do nothing to stop them. And you, there, who can do everything to stop them and choose to do nothing." He then laughed without humor, placing his hand to his forehead to shield his eyes from mine, and shook his head once. "Yes, I feel envy. I feel everything a human can, and more, because I can see to the depths of their depravity and to the height of their joys, and I have to watch as they continue to destroy their own paradise. After Genesis, you would think they all would learn and abandon this cursed cycle." He rolled his fingers into a fist. "Had I the opportunity you were given, I would not hesitate to slit the throats of all who wronged me or who wronged the innocent. I would not have your mortal scruples."

"Perhaps because you have not been entrusted by Him."

"Have I not?" he asked, raising his hands up as if proclaiming to the heavens. "For who else placed these horns upon my head?" He let his arms fall. "I may never have seen, nor felt, what you call the Merkavah, but how else can I or you be here but for the *grace* of God?"

The way he emphasized the word "grace" in his sardonic tone made me clench my teeth.

"Never mind," I said. I found a stone upon the path and kicked it into the river. With the rolling currents, I did not see where the stone touched the surface. It disappeared into the water, consumed by it.

I decided to walk about the town and look for the house. There was no sense in ignoring the opportunity of taking in the sights of the city as I did so. I went again to the Schloss Mirabell to walk through the gardens, and as I ventured out again, I saw a white castle on a hill overlooking the city. On a whim, I took the funicular to the Festung Hohensalzburg where I viewed the city from high atop the white tower of the castle. Looking down from the tall hill instilled me with fear. I had never thought myself afraid of heights before. Yet, here, the imposing stones and the steep hill made me cling near the interior walls.

As I walked, there was a family taking in the sights with a young boy playing and jumping along the cracks in the stones. At once he called out, "Watch me!" and when the parents turned, he ran towards the wall. The mother screamed at him to stop as he rushed to the edge and reached out her arms to catch him. The boy stopped as suddenly as he started and laughed at his jest. She shouted at him in reprimand. The father, too, scorned him, then took him by the hand, and despite the boy's wriggling, would not let go.

What is it that makes children endeavor to terrify their mothers? I wondered.

When I took the funicular down, Azazel rode with me,

though he did not say much beyond his quips about the memories of those riding within. I began to feel tired, weak. I needed blood. When we came to the square, there were already crowds in two lines, leaving the center empty for a procession. Those who were there waiting were dressed in as much extravagance as they could afford. One of the clergy passed out palm leaves folded into crosses. These they handed to the prospective viewers.

Vibrant palm fronds paraded in the air, held by clergymen in white and red silk robes. One elder in the lead had robes adorned with golden brocade, heralding the memory of Christ's entry to the Holy Land. They celebrated with palm leaves, and three days later, my kin would remember with lamb's blood.

At the thought of lamb, I searched for a place which sold live animals, but I found none. While I had a vial of ash should the need arise, fresher was best. How I wished Cristofano or Bianca were here to give their blood to me freely! I would need to be focused when I found Ephraim. I would do it tonight, I decided. I would find his home when it was dark, when I was rested and rejuvenated so that I would not falter. I had some blood which I brought with me but would need more. In the end, I found a pet shop which sold live birds. There, I bought one of the finches, along with a cage to keep it in.

When I returned to the hotel, I hurried to my room and took the blood from the bird.

After disposing of the body and the cage, I went past the front desk, where the clerk had a radio playing. He greeted me when he turned his head from the ledger. Nearby, I noticed a bookcase adjacent to the desk, filled with books. Azazel went to the shelf.

"All German, it looks like," he said. "Though, why wouldn't they be?"

He pointed at one of the bindings.

"Take this one," he said.

I walked over to the bookcase and followed where he was pointing. The title of the book was *Die Verwandlung*.

"I cannot read German," I said.

"Then it's fortunate that I can. It is called *The Meta-morphosis*."

Curious as to what interested Azazel in the book, I slipped it from the shelf. Before leaving, I made eye-contact with the desk clerk to show him that I was borrowing the book, and he gave me a smile and a nod.

As soon as we returned to my room, Azazel nagged me to open the book. I did not until I had used some of the bloody ash I had stowed away and washed myself. Only then did we sit together on the bed with me turning each page as soon as he told me he had finished reading and would summarize each point in the story. At times he would pause, trying to decide how one word would translate to another. The story was of a man who transformed into some kind of vermin. Azazel said he became an *"ungeheuren ungeziefer"* and went to great lengths to explain the details of the meaning of the linguistics of each word that I found somewhat interesting. His talk reminded me of how Mother and Father would discuss specific Hebrew words and how they portrayed meaning and feeling.

It was a comfort to sit alongside Azazel in a clean room and act as though we belonged together in that moment. By the time we had gone through the entire book, it was approaching evening. Thoughts of the story and the man who changed into a beast flew out of my mind.

I needed to find Ephraim's door, so I stood up and dressed.

"Stay," Azazel said.

Stay with him and share my warm bed? I considered it for the briefest moment. It was a notion that I had to push aside. He had persuaded me against my better instincts before, so I could not, no matter how tempting it was to see him luxuriate on the blanket.

When I walked away, I followed street signs, trying to match my memory of the house with the streets. I did not know how much time had passed, how many circles I had made until, finally, I saw it. My heart fluttered. I could do it now. Finish it. Let it all be over and have some peace.

I knocked. There was no answer. I knocked again, then pounded. Still nothing. I let out a small scream and sat before the door. Then, I saw a light behind the curtain. He was there. I stood still, unable to move against the gravity of the moment. I breathed and adjusted the Bona Dea pin in my hat. Then, I stepped forward and knocked on the door.

CHAPTER TWENTY-FIVE

At the turn of a key, my heart leapt. Footsteps on marble. I thought of running. Of hiding. Then I thought of the brooch, of his hands on my neck, of the others that I had killed. What had I to fear from him?

"Who—" he started the moment he saw me, and then silenced.

At first, I thought I would be afraid to see him once more. He had killed me. I had died already and was prepared to die again. I lifted my head stubbornly to meet his eyes. Seeing Ephraim, I wanted to embrace him at once, to whisper in his ear, to feel my hand in his. It made me want to kill him all the more.

Contrary to my expectations, he broke into a laugh.

"I didn't expect a woman. Did someone send you here to mock me?" he asked, chuckling to himself.

Someone had. I walked inside, not waiting for him to invite me in.

"HaShem," I said.

As Ephraim closed the door, I felt Azazel walk beside me.

As the words evaporated in the air, the man's face contorted into an expression of silent terror.

"You are a murderer," I said. "You killed a girl. You killed her unborn child. HaShem sent me to give them justice."

"What do you mean?" he said.

I took the pin from my hat and brandished it at Ephraim, and he raised his hands forward as if to plead.

"You took it from her," I accused.

"No, you don't understand. It wasn't me."

"So say all murderers."

All the intense love I felt for the man seeped into my body. I remembered his kindness when we first met. How I had been trying to pick a few olives from the tree near the water well and how he offered to pick the ones I could not reach.

"Of course, I can reach them," I had said and promptly climbed the tree to prove it.

He laughed. We did not exchange names until the third time we met, and thereafter we found excuses to see each other. My sister Miriam became suspicious of my sudden helpfulness in the chore of gathering water from the center well, but as that meant she did not have to, said nothing to Mother. I then began to sneak away when the house was sleeping, meeting outside the *ghetto* in the alley behind a shop and other times in the abandoned orthodox church where no one but vagabonds and the stone saint's eyes might see us. The thought of what we did there made my cheeks flush. I thought of Faustina. Did he kiss her the same as he did me? Did he kiss the soft skin beneath her ear in the seconds after a euphoric reprieve? Did they hold each other and watch the sun rise?

My heart settled into resolve. All I could see in the room was the tip of the blade and the man's naked neck. Finally, it would happen. All that I had done, all that I had killed to get to this point. Finally, justice.

I tried to will Azazel into my presence, to give me the Demon Eyes. He would not come. He did not want me to die, and once I killed Ephraim, I intended to die. I needed the eyes.

What had Azazel said about me before? That I was like the *shedim*. If I was a demon, then surely I could give *myself* the perception bestowed upon others of that ilk. I closed my eyes to concentrate on how it felt before when Azazel would press his fingertip to my forehead and bestow his vision onto me.

How painful would it be to see his memories of who I had been, to see his memories of Faustina? If I could use them for a moment, just to see if he was telling me the truth. That could be enough.

I felt a warmth on my forehead. When I opened my eyes, at once the room was ablaze in light, and I fixated on Ephraim.

What I saw was my life through his eyes. How the memories of us were dimmed in shadows. All the joy that had once emerged when lingering on them had been replaced with guilt, shame, and sadness. With Faustina there was joy once more, if only a sliver. There had always been guilt, and he felt the shame and sin of leaving his faith. I did not want to see more, and yet, I had to look at him, to keep my sight focused so that the truth would fall from his lips.

His expression was that of a stunned sparrow caught in the mouth of a cat. I stepped forward, and his words stilled me.

"It was Agostino Vianello."

My hands stalled. It could not be another man. Agostino? Such a gentleman could not have been the one. I had come all this way, certain that it was Ephraim. Everything I saw pointed to him. It was what made the most sense. It had to be him. And yet, doubt crept up my spine. How would Ephraim have known the *farmacisti* by name and his relationship to my death if it were not true?

"That is a lie," I said. All men who were about to die tended to lie to save their lives. But how would he know the name? How would he know the man? Doubt stayed my hand.

I had been so sure it was him. He looked like the man in my memory. If it weren't for me noticing his hand, I would have pushed him over the side with little qualm. I was humbled by my thirst for justice. Was it really justice if I took out my past transgressions on a man who was innocent without ensuring that it was true? My memory was still so fragmented, I was not sure that I could trust it as I was. Yet I had the Demon Eyes. My eyes would persuade him to confess. In that, I could trust.

"I'm many things, but I'm not a liar. Tziporah and I . . ."

Hearing my old name made me tighten my grip.

"He knew what we . . ." Ephraim started but stopped and sighed. "He knew." His lips tightened, and he looked away. "I don't know how. Maybe it was the pregnancy or just suspicion. Maybe she told him." He exhaled, and then a stilted smile drew across his lips. "She was always forthright in truth."

He turned to me. Though he was smiling, his face was sad, and his shoulders slumped. I wanted to go to him, to tell him that I was here before him. That I still loved him, or a strong part of me still did. That portion of my soul relaxed my fingers until the knife teetered on the tips, ready to fall to the ground.

"I am here," I said in a whisper so discreetly that I barely heard it myself. Azazel. I needed him to tell me if this man was honest. I needed his Demon Eyes to see the truth where I saw only doubt. I was so close to reaping justice, so close to peace and death. I had envisioned my dying. I was almost there, and it was slipping away from me with each word he said.

"If you loved . . . Tziporah." I said the name weakly. "How could you marry so soon after her death?"

His smile faded.

"I had to flee from there. Everything in the *ghetto* reminded me of what we had together. I couldn't walk past the water well or the synagogue without grief. I couldn't bear to see her sister fetch the water again. Every time I did, I imagined it was Tziporah. I just couldn't be there anymore. I found work elsewhere, and that work put me towards Faustina." He paused and walked to one of the satin chairs that stood before the open window. He sat and rested his arms on it. "With Faustina ..." He stopped and turned his hands so his palms faced upwards. "It was a different love. I was lonely, grieving . . . she made me feel like I could be a whole man again. And when she died. I—I ran away like I did before. Now I think I must be cursed. Death seems to follow me and those women I love. First my mother, then Tziporah, then Faustina." He relaxed his hands and leaned forward in the chair. I knew that look of despair. It was the same look I'd seen on myself when I faced doubt; it was the same as de'Angelo's face when I found him a beggar on the street. It made me believe in his innocence.

"Sometimes I wonder if there was some wrong we did, some sin, that marked us."

"Love is no sin," I said.

"I hope that is true." Ephraim became silent, and I saw that he was crying. Then, he wiped the tears from his eyes.

"The last time I saw her—we liked to sneak out to where we knew we would not be caught. The best nights were on the Shabbat, before Sunday, when most were out at night looking for fun. That was when she told me."

I saw the memory. I was nervous to see him. I had not bled for two months and had been hiding the terror of what that meant. I had to share it with him. There was no one else I could share it with. Such a secret could not be kept for long, and I had to make a choice. We were young. I had barely turned seventeen. Ephraim was nineteen and beginning his work in trade. It was surely possible for us to marry. I would be expected to carry the child. Though Ephraim had used some precautions, with our young minds, we had acted and had not thought about the consequences. I had expected our lives to continue as they were without interruption. Knowing that a life would be growing inside me and the gravity of what that meant made me unsure when I had been so sure before. All the confidence I had in my youth disappeared with that under-standing.

"She was pregnant," I said.

Ephraim nodded.

I had told him what I could do. There were *farmicisi* who helped girls like me. One drink of a purgative and it would be as it was. Or, we could marry and keep the pregnancy. With enough coaxing, our parents would agree, I was certain. Still, I had witnessed my mother and her pregnancies, one after the other, and the deaths that inevitably came with them. How her body had changed each time, ravaged and healed, created and destroyed, and how she had to give all of herself to growing and nurturing life. I did not think I was entirely ready for that kind of sacrifice.

"I was a—a coward," Ephraim said. "I could have been kind to her. I *should* have been kind. If I could go back . . . hold her and tell her everything would be fine." He lowered his head and cried again.

The words he told me whispered in my memory.

"I do not want to be a father," he said. And there, he left me, a young girl in an alley.

What else could I do then but rid myself of the pregnancy? Single girls did not raise babies. I could not tell my parents. The shame I would place on myself and on them was tremen-dous. Where else could I go but to a *farmacisi* who always showed me kindness? A man I could trust. I could not move against the realization. It was a lie to distract me. And yet the name stopped me. My sister told me of him, of the man who tried to propose, of one I barely recollected. A young man to whom I had once given my affections . . .

"It was Agostino," I said.

He walked closer to me and picked up the knife that had dropped on the floor. He grabbed my hand, which made me inhale sharply at his touch. I hadn't realized until then how I missed his touch, his smell. He turned my hand over and placed the knife in it.

"You want to find justice for Tziporah, go kill him. God knows I won't stop you." I scoffed at how unceremoniously he spoke HaShem's name. "If I could do it myself, I would. As it is, my actions are followed too closely by my widow's family. As soon as I set foot in Italia, they will arrest me. They are already suspicious that I poisoned Faustina."

I relaxed my hand, letting it fall to my side.

"You are sure it was him?"

"As heaven and earth are my witness."

Give ear, o heavens and I will speak, and hear, o earth, the words of my mouth.

"Why not tell that to the *polizia*?"

"I did. But by that time, they had decided it was a suicide and left it at that. Why would they arrest a *farmacisi* who does so much good for the community over the death of a Jewish girl?"

I nodded. Having spent enough time with de'Angelo, I could surmise that the *polizia* would want less work for themselves.

"Who are you to her?"

"A friend."

I returned the knife to where it had been hidden, and Ephraim slowly put his arms down and straightened his back. He appraised me carefully, all the while tapping his finger against his thigh.

"Then do what you must. I have no pity for the man."

I looked down at my closed fist and felt the ache as my nails pricked my skin. Then, I put my hand on the dresser's cool surface.

Feeling Ephraim's hand on mine filled me with an ache that tightened my stomach, including his fingertips that I remembered so well. I remembered his hands as gentle and yet with a coarseness that came from hard work. His hands were similarly coarse, hard at the fingertips, with his writing hand having a thick callus where the pen rested. When I looked at his face, I saw aged lines that had not been there before. I wanted to hold him. I wanted to feel his naked skin against mine. I wanted to take us back to what we were. Anger flushed through my cheeks.

Feeling weakness from the effects of the eyes, I said, "I need some of your blood."

He raised his eyebrows and scratched his temple in the same manner as he always had done when I suggested something daring.

"Blood?" he asked.

"Yes."

"First you say you came to kill me, and now you ask for blood. Why?"

I thought of a lie. I remembered Ludovico Zampieri.

"Faustina's father," I said. "I know him. I know that he wants you dead. If you gave me your blood, I could make him think that you are."

"Clever," said Azazel. "I don't know if I should be impressed or concerned."

"You think that would make him leave me alone? Some blood?"

"I met with him before I came here."

"Did he send you to kill me?"

"Not exactly."

He looked out the window and shook his head.

"That man will never leave me be." He shrugged one shoulder. "Although, if I were in his position, I might not either." He looked back at me. "It would be a blessing to be alone for once."

Ephraim considered my proposal, but I knew that he would agree. The Demon Eyes were persuasive. When he nodded and sat on one of the chairs, I removed the vial from my pocket. It had some ash but would have to do.

"You won't need much, I expect?"

I shook my head and held my pin, but upon seeing it, he protested.

"I think I will do the cutting," he said. "Convincing as you are, I don't know if I trust you not to kill me."

He chuckled, and I did as well. How I had missed that laughter. How we had laughed together in the dark.

He stood up and left the room. When he returned, it was with a kitchen knife. He sat again, and I knelt before him. He rolled up his sleeve on his left arm and pierced his forearm with the tip of the blade. He winced and removed it when blood began to purge from his skin. I held the vial near the cut. My hand shook even as I tried to steady it. When the blood stopped, I pressed on the wound, pinching it to encourage more to flow. To be this close to him after so long, I wanted to take him in my arms and lie with him once more. I could feel that Faustina wanted that as well.

"You look . . . ," he began.

I pulled the vial away and stopped it up. Ephraim pushed a lock of hair from the side of my face and kept his hand there. A force aside from my own made me embrace Ephraim, a quick hug as I dared not linger.

"Be well," I said.

I departed the house, not looking back. If I looked into his eyes again, I would never leave him. I held the warm vial in my hand and cried quietly as I walked back to the room. My lips quivered as I tried to calm myself and felt a weakness, a lethargy that came from the Demon Eyes. I stopped abruptly. The vial was cooling but warm as I sat on the street where there were no people and, hidden in the night, I opened the vial and poured some of the blood in my palm. I stopped the vial and put it in my pocket. A pool the size of a fingertip sat in my palm. I played with it, feeling the substance beneath my finger. I held the finger to my nose, smelling his blood. It was metallic and sweet, like the scent of spring rain on an iron cage. I could go back to him one last time.

No.

Just once, to say goodbye. To apologize. To feel him in my arms and hear him speak.

No. There is no return. It cannot ever be as it was.

There was a haze of memories that belonged to Ephraim. I saw my face, I saw Faustina. How beautiful she was. She was joyous and kind. I could see how he would love her. She had a sense of honesty that was similar to my own, though expressed differently. Whereas I was honest in my unkempt wildness of mind, her honesty was in her compassion and her kindness and her happiness.

When she kissed Ephraim, he felt at peace, that the death of his sweetheart had been a bad dream that could be purged by her love. It had been a mistake to think she could cure him, for my death and my life remained forever in his memory until it became so overwhelming that he had to reconcile his shame. Ephraim did not speak of me to Faustina in any more than suggestions. He told her that there was a girl before but that she died from an accident. His omission of how deep our love was made me put my head in my hands and cry a little more. I had died because I loved freely. The memories changed to seeing myself as a girl riding on a boat in the lagoon with my father and mother as we fished. Then Mother waded in shallow pools catching little Moeche crabs.

My own memories interceded. A *farmacisti*. I knew one. My thoughts took me to the *farmacia* where I went with Maria-Elena and my intense reaction to stepping foot in that place. He was always so helpful, so kind, even when I did not deserve it. I had been there before in the evening just before it would close. I wore my *tichel* to better shroud my appearance. I had seen the man and his reaction to me.

"I need a remedy," I had asked.

At first, he was kind, even flirtatious, until I uttered the name of the purgative. Then his eyes changed, his face fell, and before I could scream, his hands were on me. I fought him. I scratched and kicked and bit. Then his hands were on my neck, and though I fought, I could not breathe.

Azazel had been beside me. He would have seen the man. Could he have known, even then? Could he have known and never told me? My heart raced and my skin became hot.

"You knew," I said to Azazel.

He straightened and looked at me. His obsidian eyes revealed nothing. I stood there waiting for an answer. Finally, his lips spread into a smile.

"I told you before," he said. "I have no interest in watching you die."

If I could kill him, I would not hesitate to plunge a sharp object into his beautiful face.

"I promised to help you, and in return, you said you would do the same."

His smile faded, and he turned his eyes upwards as if thinking, and then focused on my face.

"I have."

"You knew," I said.

"Rid him of his misery."

It took a moment to discern his meaning.

"A most foul thing. You'll do him a favor," Azazel said.

"I saw his mind. He did nothing—is doing nothing—that deserves death."

Azazel placed his fingers at the nape of my neck.

"His memory, his life, is a shadow on yours. You cannot move forward until he is gone."

I shirked away from his touch.

"You need me," he said.

"I do not want your help. Not like this."

I began walking away, but he followed as I sped up, returned to the hotel, and packed up my things. I would return to Venezia as soon as I could.

"You can't do this," he said.

"I can. I will. That is not justice. What wrongs has Ephraim done?"

"Plenty."

I stood still, considering. I had seen some. He had wronged my memory, he had concealed truths from Faustina, from my own family, but despite my anger towards him, he was not deserving of death. Not by my hand.

"This is not the same as the others. I saw those ones in their sin. If I kill this man . . ." I shook my head and walked away, out of the church, and to the dark streets. I felt the dizziness beginning to corrupt my balance and searched for an alley creature to fit my needs. I made my way to the patisserie where I suspected there would be mice or rats and hoped that would be enough to satiate. A shadow turned the corner.

"You think you are above them?" Azazel asked. "That you are somehow better?" He laughed mockingly. "Tell me what makes you different from your murderer?"

My face grew hot.

"It was you who offered this to me," I said. "You who showed me the sins of Humankind and who amongst them deserved death."

"Did I put the knife in your hand?"

"You may as well have. You showed me their sins."

"Ah," he said. "And I am the scapegoat again? What is it that the Torah says about the *shedim*? That they are servants of HaShem who give Man the choice of good or ill."

"Was it not us who saw that it was He who gave us this chance? Why else do I live but to enact His will? What other reason is there?"

"I will never know Him," he said and turned his eyes briefly to the ceiling, then closed them as if annoyed by a trifling thought. "Much as I feebly try."

"It is not for us to know," I said, mirroring the words I heard from the rabbi, from the Priest, from somewhere in my subconscious that remembered the divine sylvanian forest. There had to be some meaning for why I came back, and it had to be to make things right. Surely it was better that the sinners I killed were gone and my murder would be reconciled. Or was it? Were the wrongs that had been done made right by death?

"I am close," I said, thinking of Ephraim and the truth of his words. "One more and it is done."

Azazel pushed his hair back between his horns and held his hand there a moment, tapping his thumb against the base of his horn. He looked to the side, away from me to a dusty spot on the floor where a cat paced. "Sin does not end with one man's death."

An intrusive image of the crucified Yeshua came to me, his face drawn down in agony, eyes pulled towards the heavens, the blood streaming upon his brow from the thorny crown, his thin skin draped over protruding ribs; the curled fingers and limp wrists hanging, propped against a wooden cross by thick nails driven into the wrists and ankles.

"No," I said. "But death can temper it."

I spoke with an effort that felt like there was a peach pit in my throat.

"There are terrible things we do to those we love *because* we love."

The brightness stained my eyes. I could fall asleep on the withered grass and dissolve in the dry earth. A sudden sadness welled inside me that was brought on by nothing, void of consciousness. The flowers were eyes judging me as I walked the streets. Yellows, red, blues, all shouting at me to be happy. I was as invisible as dust. I was sure this was real, but I could not feel my face or my hands, and my body had dissolved into the air. It was enough to make me scream into a storm, for the sky to cry with me. I cried, and none would look at me, purposefully turning their heads to leave me. There would be no comfort. I shrank into myself, trembling. There were voices, but I could not understand them. There was a sense of voices, muffled, reverberating through the air and towards my skin.

"Please," he said.

He turned to leave, and as I saw him dissipate, I said, "Wait," without knowing why or what I was going to say next.

To my delight, he remained, a half specter looking down at me.

"I do want you," I said. "But this is my *mitzvah*. You must understand. You carry one, too."

He nodded once.

"I do."

He laughed, and so did I. I walked to him and settled one kiss upon his lips before he disappeared beneath them.

"Perhaps we will meet again, in *Olam Ha-Ba*, in the world to come."

CHAPTER TWENTY-SIX

A gray shade hung over the city when I returned to Venezia. High waters from the canal sloshed over the plateau to a height that rose to just below my ankle. It wetted my socks as I looked for a place to shelter from the rain for a moment.

I was unsure what brought me there. Some internal force propelled my feet over the cobblestone streets and bridges. Though I stood in the shadow of the Santa Maria della Salute church, I could see with clarity the statues guarding the enclaves of the building, protecting the holy innards against the villainous outside realm of humanity. As I stepped ever closer, I saw the bowed heads of beggar women, their heads so close to the ground that they could kiss it. They wore dark shawls on their heads to cover their faces in either shame or disguise, I could not tell. With their outstretched arms, they held a cup, or with their palms outward, to gather the coins tossed to them by the generous. Some stretched their bodies out upon the steps in a plea to the religious to pass their generosity onto the poor, the destitute, the unlucky. They shook their hands as if to imitate old age and pleaded with cracked voices, as if their throats were parched since they were born, and their thirst not once quenched. One even stood at the entrance to the church itself, for no one was able to escape their presence.

The statues of angels overlooked the church, staring down at the people below, their immortal eyes judging and pleading to all those who upturned their gaze to the heavens to see the twisted bodies of the eternal creatures.

Still lingering was the purpose of my life. Justice. And when I fulfilled it, would I split in half, the dead returning to the dirt and the woman in the mirror resurrecting?

There was an immense beauty in the manner in which the afternoon light shone down onto the cobblestone and reflected off of the leaves. I felt taken back to a scene stolen from a time where the lives of Humankind were governed by a renaissance where art was the center of the world. I allowed the music to seep into my pores, down my hands, and into my fingertips.

I ought to have felt forgiveness. That is the testament of life: to forgive those who have wronged. And yet a stronger urge pulled towards retribution. Could I not be as vengeful as Him? He who extinguished the Canaanites, who set the world to flood, who sent the plagues to bring men to their knees?

I sloshed through the rising flood waters that spread out over the stones as if the city were sinking into the lagoon. Bits of trash floated in the water. I did not care to linger on the thought that I was wading in the same water that held the contents of people's chamber pots, soiled laundry water, and discarded food. Rain continued falling and, having no umbrella, I could only continue to soak as I made my way to the abandoned home that I called my own.

It was *Pesach*. The Passover rituals were not likely to come to my door. My feet took me through the alleys, down familiar paths, through the stone walls of the *ghetto*. The roaring of the ram's horn beckoned me there.

The rabbi held a *chalaf* blade strong against the ram's throat even as it struggled, eyes wide and terrified, knowing what must come next as the blade severed the throat, esophagus, trachea, arteries and veins in one strong stroke, and then held the head to let the blood spill upon the cobblestones in exsanguination.

I went to my father's house, hoping he would tell me what he knew of Agostino. I touched the *mezuzah* and murmured the prayer. When I knocked, Fiona answered. She asked who I was, not remembering the last time I visited. When I explained, she sought out mother.

"Ah, Aviva, come, come," she said. She motioned for me to enter.

"What brings you here?"

"I went to pray and thought I might see you," I said.

"Of course," she said as she walked back into the house, letting me follow her to the drawing room where I saw a woman sitting on the floor, little Moshe, and another child in front of her. When she looked at me, her face brightened.

"So good to see you again!" she said.

I was puzzled at her response. Clearly, she knew me, but where had I seen her?

One day there will be as many Jews as there are stars in the sky.

Gia Piexoto. She gave me a copy of the *Tanakh*.

I thanked her for it again. The door opened, and my father entered. The puppy, Romeo scampered down steps to greet him with an excited yip. He bent to pick up the puppy, who licked his face eagerly.

"Oh," Father said when he saw me. "Happy to see you here. There is always room for more in this house."

I approached him in the hall.

"I will be plain," I said, knowing well my father respected honesty above all else. "I am trying to find who killed your daughter."

"A killer? Why? When the *polizia* called it suicide."

"Who is that?" It was my mother's voice, and she came through the main door, holding a bowl in hand and mixing the contents therein. When she saw me, she smiled. "Ah, so good to see you! What are you talking about?"

"Nothing, nothing," said my father.

"Your daughter was murdered," I said. "I want to find who did it."

Mama stopped mixing and stared at us both for some time. She walked in and placed the bowl carefully on the table. She wiped her hands on her skirt and sat down. She did not speak for some time but merely kept her hands on her skirt and looked at the door. Finally, she took a deep breath, closed her eyes, and then turned to me.

"If there were a killer," she began, "what could be done about it?"

"Justice," I said.

"Do you even know who the killer might be?" my father asked.

"I think so."

"Then go to the *polizia* and tell them. Do not risk your life for a supposition." He scratched his cheek.

I left, defeated. As I walked, I heard the door open, and footsteps come out. When I turned, I saw my mother, with my little brother following closely behind.

"You know who it is?" she asked.

"I think it was Agostino," I said.

"You know him?"

"I know only that he asked to marry Tziporah."

"Yes, but," she lowered her voice. "There was more. Come," she said.

She took my little brother up in her arms and walked to the quiet spot by the synagogue where the walls were thick and shaded. "For my husband, it is easier that she has been mourned and remembered, but for myself, I still can feel her here. I can hear her in the house. Sometimes I call for her when I am not thinking and then find myself in a deep despair." Tears began to fall from her eyes. Little Moshe said, "Mama," and touched the tears on her cheek, wiping them with a finger. She took his hand in hers. "It is not enough to remember her in prayers. If there is a man who killed her, and you know it is him, bring him to us. I want to look in his face and know why he took my daughter from me. You say it was Agostino?"

"I do, but I need to be sure. What can you tell me about him? How did he know Tziporah?"

I heard the rain begin to fall in a strong downpour.

"To that, I know only what he told us. He came one evening and sat with my husband and me. At first, he insisted only on talking to my husband, but I would not leave. We had always agreed on proposals together, the same as with my eldest son. So, the man spoke and said that he had often seen Tziporah near the *farmacia* and sometimes spoke with her. He said he found her interesting and that he would make her a good husband.

True, he was not Jewish, but a good husband need not be. I was unsure of this man as was my husband. Who was he, but a stranger? How could we know what type of man he was for our daughter? And I knew how fond Tziporah and Ephraim were of one another. I had expected that he would propose marriage soon. How could I accept this man when I knew already that there was one who loved her and who she loved in return? We refused, but we offered that if he was interested, he could speak with Tziporah and see if they could court for some time." She sighed. "He was not pleased with this answer. He said then that–" She paused and looked at Moshe. "–He said some words that are best not repeated here. But that anger he showed always made me wonder. He was so nice as we sat together, and in a moment's turn, showed nothing but wrath."

I nodded. The world was filled with nice men who went to much trouble to appear nice when it suited them and shed the veneer when any trifling matter scratched upon it. Their fragility was a danger to all who passed by. For who knew what benign comment or inopportune glance would send them into rage?

"What if he could be killed?" I ventured carefully.

My mother closed her eyes.

"There is a story from the Sanhedrin that says: 'It is preferable that he should kill you and you should not kill. Who is to say that your blood is redder than his, that your life is worth more than the one he wants you to kill? Perhaps that man's blood is redder.'"

She opened her eyes. Mother had often answered me in the same manner, not with a direct act of guidance but with a story or a parable. It was left to me to discern wisdom from it.

My thoughts were interrupted by the tapping of rain that came on our heads. We rushed inside the house and looked out at the rain that poured in heavy waterfalls down the glass and on the stones.

"Stay here for the night," she offered. "Go tomorrow when the rain has passed."

I agreed. That evening, I sat to dinner with them and allowed myself to enjoy their company. Father showed me the Nuremberg Egg, and I did not feign fascination. I played with my siblings in a way I had not done for years.

Miriam had prepared a place for me in my old bed once night came.

I thought of letting this revenge go. I could live as I was, even be part of my family again in some small part, and I thought of being with them, of seeing my sister, my mother, father, my other brothers and sisters, my old friends. It could be a semblance of a normal life, even if it was less. It was a bittersweet fantasy filled with those I loved, but it would not be my life, not in the way I desired. I wanted what I had, what was taken from me. I wanted to be who I was before: a girl who could love and be loved with a full heart. And I was not that girl anymore. That loss drove the need for justice. I could never return to the way things were, but I could extract the reparations for what was lost.

I slept heavily, undisturbed by malicious thoughts or nightmares. It was a beautiful, dreamless sleep. When I woke, I spent great lengths telling each of my family that I would miss them. I gave a final farewell, heartfelt, sincere, truthful, in a way that I had not before I died. To say goodbye to my mother, to my sister, was the most difficult. I hid my sadness as best I could, for to them I was little more than a stranger. And when I left, I turned the corner and let myself weep.

Sitting by the door of the *farmacia* was a familiar black dog, his hair a silken sheen in the light. He sat steadfast against the stones, watching those who passed with alert eyes. He seemed to me a formidable statue, no different from the stones around him, except for the eyes and the twitching ears that followed every movement. I walked near him cautiously, expecting him to stand rigidly and bare his teeth at my approach. As I stepped to the threshold, the dog barely moved, except to turn his head to follow my path with inquisitive eyes, and when I brushed closely, he sniffed at my fingers and wagged his tail slightly as if to brush away a fly at his hip.

There was the sound of a hissing cat outside and the scratch of claws on stone. I peeked out the window to see a spotted orange and white calico with its back arched and the black dog prostrate before it, his rear in the air, tail wagging, and head bobbing as if to coax it into play.

"Ah," said the man, who came to the window. "Leave her be. She doesn't want to play." He then returned to his spot behind the counter. "Every other day they do this. You think one of them would learn." He sighed. "I don't trust cats, as you know."

I looked at the man. Studied his face. The set of his jaw, his lips, recently wet from the drink, his clean trimmed beard, his hair kept combed and parted at the side, just over the edge of his left eyebrow. He was entirely unremarkable. Were he in a crowd, sitting in Synagogue, or in a church pew, I would never have recognized him; he would blend in with all the others. But this was the man who killed me. He had looked into my eyes as I fought him to live, even as I scratched and bit. I looked at the scar on his wrist, the one he claimed was from a cat bite, the one that looked so much like human teeth. He had strangled me until my last breath and threw my corpse into the canal. He was the very man I had been searching for, longing for, so that I could enact retribution. So plain a man was he that I could scarcely believe it could be him.

"Are you Agostino? Could you help me?" I asked.

"Indeed," he said. "And what ails you today?"

"Oh," I started, trying to think of what I should say. "It is only," I started to think, tapping on my cheek.

"Yes, a sickly pallor," he said.

I stopped tapping and furrowed my eyebrows.

"Poor diet is often the cause." He turned to the row of bottles on the shelves behind him and began perusing the contents. "It's often too common among certain areas—the

Romani, for example—who frequently forgo the better halves of meat, for those are too expensive. I've heard that to remedy the affliction, some take to ingesting the algae that lines the canal walls."

That seemed like an exaggeration to me. As often as I walked the streets and perused the canals, I had never seen anyone dare press their lips to the rancid waters. Perhaps I was not looking, or perhaps it was a fabrication, the little stories and rumors people share to feel a connection, to feel important. The truth of the story did not matter. Once spoken, it became true in someone's mind. I thought of what Azazel said about Descartes. If we create truth in our minds, and that truth, whether observed or not, defines our perception, does it matter if the thought was true or false if my mind believed it was true?

Agostino presented a bottle containing a powdered substance.

"You must add this to a draught of *clean* water." I did not like how he emphasized the word "clean" as if I was filthy and offended him by my presence. "And take it twice daily."

He placed the vial on the countertop gently so that it clinked against the marble. I stared at it, touching the tip of my knife handle in my pocket.

Stab him in the eye, I thought. *Do it now that you have a chance. Do it and be done.*

I could not. There was doubt. I was wrong with Ephraim. I was sure it had been him before, and it was not. And what about Maria-Elena? I had thought her guilty of taking and selling children when the truth was opaque.

"Do not worry about money," Agostino said.

When I looked up, his eyes were soft and kind.

"No—I . . ." I looked into his eyes to scry meaning from them. Where were his sins? Surely, they were there, just behind the veneer. I wanted to see them, and even so, I was not sure.

"Excuse me," I said, ducking out.

Outside the door, I exhaled. My mind was dizzy and unfocused. I saw the black dog walking toward me. He licked my fingers with his warm tongue and tapped his forehead on my palm, begging for attention. I scratched behind his warm ear, then he sat in the spot by the door. I stepped away, and when I did, I heard the black dog whine.

Being wrong about Maria-Elena and Ephraim made me doubt my certainty that it was Agostino. In the face of death, I found that most people suddenly found honesty. Ephraim had. All I may need to do is hold the Bona Dea pin to his throat, and a confession would no doubt flow from his lips. It could also make him lie.

CHAPTER TWENTY-SEVEN

I waited until the *farmacia* was nearing to close. The black dog lay sleeping, his body sprawled out on the warm stones, his paws wobbling as he whined, no doubt chasing rabbits in his sleep. I watched as Agostino shuttered the windows and then rushed to the door. As I watched, the black dog raised his head to me, half-opened his eyes, twitched his nose, and relaxed his head back on the stones, returning to a restful sleep. I kept a hand in my pocket where I held the head of the pin. Then, I grabbed the handle, opened it, and entered.

"We are closing," he said with his back turned to me, replacing a bottle on the shelf.

I turned behind me and, seeing the key in the lock, twisted it closed. He must have heard it click, for he looked at me.

"I'm taking no more customers tonight. You'll have to come back on Monday."

I had not realized that it was Shabbat. How fortunate that he had not yet been to confession. He could confess to me.

"Did you know Tziporah Curiel?"

His face did not change. He merely walked forward.

"Who asks?"

"I want to know what happened to her."

At this, he exhaled and smiled.

"Drowned. Do you read *il giornale*? Not to worry, I'm sure you can go to the *polizia* and ask them."

"I need not. I know it was you who killed her."

He scoffed. "That's a serious accusation." He stepped forward and went to the door, passing by me to grip the handle with one hand and gently pressing my shoulder with the other to turn me out. "Now, if you'll please leave."

His touch made me recoil with a thrash, causing my hand with the knife to swing upwards. When he saw it, he backed away. I wanted to kill him. Shove that pretty little knife through his eye. I could not. I had to know why. Justice was not enough. I needed a confession.

"I should have expected you to be a thief."

"Not a thief." I straightened my stature. "You knew Tziporah. You killed her. Why?"

He laughed. "You're mistaken. What would I want with a Jewess?"

He moved to unlock the door, and I grabbed his hand so forcefully I felt my fingernails dig into his skin. When he tried to wriggle free, I held tighter.

"Get off," he said.

"Confess," I answered.

"You're insane."

"Murder makes it so," I said as I stepped forward and held the knife to his throat.

He pushed against me, and I found my adrenaline strong enough to meet him. In doing so, the tip of the blade nicked his skin, and he began to bleed. He tried to push me away, but I was stronger. Fueled by contempt, I felt the warmth of the Demon Eyes.

"Confess," I shouted.

The man turned from my face and struggled against my resolve. He wriggled his body, kicking me, trying to resist. The longer he fought me, the weaker he became, until he softened and had to stop to catch his breath. He groaned in defeat.

"You don't know what it was like," he said breathlessly. "Seeing them—seeing *her*—every other night just outside the window, hearing them mewling and moaning the same as the alley cats in heat. And why should a man like that get such a gift? What kind of whore was she to rough in the streets? Every time I heard them down there, I knew it should have been me there, with her. I could treat her better. You would be horrified to know the lustful, depraved, acts they had done. I would have been good. I would have shown her how to be better."

What ego this man had, to think he knew what I had wanted. I was tempted to kill him for those words alone, but I tempered my rage. I wanted to know why this man would take my life. I wanted his death to be as agonizing as mine was. Killing him quickly would be a grace that I was not prepared to give.

"And when you heard them, why did you not shutter the window?"

"What would that matter? I would know they were there."

"Could it be that you delighted in their passion, all the while wishing it were your own?" I mocked as I pressed the tip closer. "Did you wallow in your own depravity as you watched?"

How common for a man to deflect his shame onto a woman.

He spat on my face. In response, I did the same. A sharp pinch touched my ribs, and I inhaled at the sensation, stagnating my movements. In short retaliation, I stabbed the man's collar bone with the hairpin. He screamed, the kind of scream that rose from the deep recesses of the belly, escaping in a full breath from the throat and through the lips like the painful howl of a wounded bear. He opened the door and left. I followed.

When I caught up to him, I tightened my fingers around his arm, and he thrashed. In his thrashing, he pushed me away, and I fell against the cobblestone. At this, he lunged, intending to push me into the water, but slipped, and pushed us both into the black canal. Without time to hold my breath, I found the threat of drowning immediate.

We struggled to push each other down so one of us could climb back onto the stones. Once, I tried to swim away, and he caught me, fingers gripping desperately, pushing me so that he could rise to the surface. I grasped his neck and kept him down even as my muscles weakened in a constant tumbling of our wills splashing and grappling at each other in the putrid water. My breath was fast disappearing. I would die again. I was certain. But so long as he would die with me, I would be satisfied. My eyes opened to the dark and putrid waters, seeing little but his shadow, hearing the air escape his mouth in bubbles. He would die in darkness as I had.

Middah k'neged Middah, I thought. *Measure for measure.*

In the *Pirkei Avot*, the *Chapter of the Fathers*, there was a story about the sage Hillel. When he came upon a skull in the water, he said to it: "Because you drowned others, you were drowned." What the dead man had done was done to him. What death came to me was done to others.

I felt the demon near me. Azazel was there, his face before mine, and on his horns were buzzing bees crawling to and fro.

"It is you who are Azazel, truly," he whispered.

I settled into a calm as I felt my *nefesh* fading. Tumbling, cool water flushed through my nose. Convulsions came. I stopped fighting and let the canal take me.

My face was cold, body upturned, and breathing. In the distance was a floating black mass. The bleeding was unrelenting, and I saw the stains on my shirt, my skirt, down my leg. Tiredness overtook me. When I opened my eyes, the lethargy had gone, replaced with a sense of vertigo. The blood had tempered. The pain had subsided into a dull ache.

All I saw were the sins of Humankind like strands in a skein of pale wool. Hearing them sent my mind aflutter with intrusive fancies. How many had passed with darkness in their minds, with stains already marking their souls? I thought of the innocent babies born into this world who were living at the whims of those around them. It seemed cruel luck that some should be born into kindness and others into cruelty. In those desperate moments, I thought how kinder it would be if those pregnant in the midst of cruelty should never be born, and thus saved from all manners of sin and injustice.

Consumed by the thought, I stretched out a hand and felt a stone wall. I bowed my head and closed my eyes. The air warmed, and the wall seemed softer to my fingers. Soon my thoughts dissipated, leaving doubts and fears empty. I had wondered before if I was still Jewish after being reborn since I had not been born from a Jewish mother. Neither had I been before a *Beit Din*, a rabbinical court which would oversee a formal conversion, nor immersed in a *mikveh* to cleanse myself in the pure ritual water. What mattered most to HaShem? Was it how I was born, how I lived, how I died, or was it intention? I committed my reborn life to HaShem's will. I believed in the shining light of the Torah. That was the truth I knew. As I stood, I murmured the *Shema Yisrael*.

About me were stone walls and the rush of water. There were voices, mumbles, screams, and a dampness that penetrated my bones. It felt as if my muscles were dissolving. My mind was numb, empty. In the distance, the blurry shadow of a young woman mouthed my name. She looked so much like Irina. The only voice that I heard said, *"Yashen."* It was an old word of many meanings, one of which was "sleep." It was the voice of my mother. I could feel a warm hand on my back as she sang to me:

"Durme, durme, sin ansia ni dolor,
Cierra tus luzyos ojitos,
Durme, durme, con savor."

There was no light that I saw, only a warmth that emanated outwards from my heart. That Merkavah, that chariot of light that ascends souls to heaven did not come for me. In that divine trance, which consumed the devout, it was silence that welcomed me, and the immediate release of the burdens of living.

What is sweeter than honey and stronger than a lion?

In my mind I held a still-beating heart. It dripped over my palm and fingers with a thickness like oil. I stuck out the tip of my tongue to its fleshy core and licked and let the warmth permeate in my hand until the gentle throb gradually ceased and the muscle cooled. I let it drop from my fingers. With the blood still on my hands, I drew it over my face and breathed in the iron fragrance. At once the pain receded. My weary skin grew plump with life. The demon before me dissipated until all I saw was a heart in my hands grown cold in the star-filled night.

ACKNOWLEDGMENTS

A special acknowledgement goes to Rivka Begun, who gave me valuable feedback on the story. I want to also thank Rabbi Mendel Adelman at chabad.org for patiently answering my many questions about the intricacies of Jewish practices.

I would be remiss if I did not give a special thanks to my editor, Cecilia Kennedy, who gave thoughtful and decisive feedback on this novel.

ABOUT RUNNING WILD PRESS

Running Wild Press publishes stories that cross genres with great stories and writing. RIZE publishes great genre stories written by people of color and by authors who identify with other marginalized groups. Our team consists of:

Lisa Diane Kastner, Founder and Executive Editor
Cody Sisco, Acquisitions Editor, RIZE
Benjamin White, Acquisition Editor, Running Wild
Peter A. Wright, Acquisition Editor, Running Wild
Resa Alboher, Editor
Angela Andrews, Editor
Sandra Bush, Editor
Ashley Crantas, Editor
Rebecca Dimyan, Editor
Abigail Efird, Editor
Aimee Hardy, Editor
Henry L. Herz, Editor
Cecilia Kennedy, Editor
Barbara Lockwood, Editor

Scott Schultz, Editor
Rod Gilley, Editor

Evangeline Estropia, Product Manager
Kimberly Ligutan, Product Manager
Lara Macaione, Marketing Director
Joelle Mitchell, Licensing and Strategy Lead
Pulp Art Studios, Cover Design
Standout Books, Interior Design
Polgarus Studios, Interior Design

Learn more about us and our stories at www.runningwild-press.com

Loved these stories and want more? Follow us at runningwildpublishing.com, www.facebook.com/runningwild-press, on Twitter @lisadkastner @RunWildBooks

RUNNING WILD
RUNNING WILD PRESS

www.ingramcontent.com/pod-product-compliance
Lightning Source LLC
Chambersburg PA
CBHW070309040726
47501CB00018B/550